To Katharin

with best wishes,

The Faraway

Franzeska G Ewart

Franzeska

Wilde & Grey

Franzeska G Ewart has written over thirty books for children. *There's a Hamster in my Pocket* (2011 Frances Lincoln) was short-listed for a Scottish Children's Book Award, and chosen for Richard and Judy's Summer Book Club.

The Pen-pal from Outer Space (1998 Mammoth) and *Shadowflight* (2001 Egmont) were both Guardian 'Books of the Week'.

After years of teaching English as an Additional Language in a Primary school, she developed the use of shadow theatre to promote language development in all ages. Her methods are described in *Let the Shadows Speak* (1998 Trentham Books).

In 2009 she was chosen by the Royal Literary Fund to be a Fellow, working for two years in the University of the West of Scotland in Ayr.

She has mounted a small exhibition of her artworks, inspired by *The Faraway.* The cover design is reproduced from one of these paintings, *Pedro Barba Sky.*

The Faraway is her debut adult novel.

Franzeska G Ewart

In memory of my parents
Matt and Kate Ewart

.

CONTENTS

1   Part One   1

    Chapters 1-19

2   Part Two   167

    Chapters 20 -37

3   Epilogue   311

4   Acknowledgments   315

Nobody realises that some people expend tremendous energy merely to be normal.

Albert Camus

PART 1

I've been absolutely terrified every moment of my life – and I've never let it keep me from doing a single thing I wanted to do

Georgia O'Keeffe

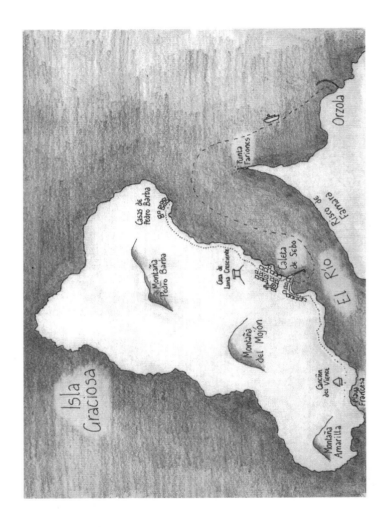

CHAPTER ONE

Celina Wilde takes a pencil from the tub on her desk and draws a row of twelve ovals on the paper attached to her easel. Underneath, she draws another row – thirteen this time – then sits back in her chair and wonders whether she has done enough to merit a cup of coffee and a cigarette.

Above the two lines of ovals is the outlined shape of a dragon and it is upwards, towards this shape, that the ovals, wide-eyed and awestruck, must appear to look. So far, however, there are no eyes to open wide, nor features to express awe. Despite a week of sketchings-in and rubbings-out, the illustration has hardly advanced at all.

Leaning over to the bookshelf, Celina drags out a copy of *Lost in the Snotgrass Swamp* – the fifth book in the *Beeboo* series – and opens it. A small rotund creature, with antennae protruding from its metallic head and a collection of multicoloured lights shining from its pot belly, stares back at her. There is a banana at the end of each antenna, and these bananas identify this feisty little

Alien as Beeboo himself, distinguishing him from RaaRaa and GooGoo whose antennae sport, respectively, cherries and grapes. When she did the last illustration, Celina got RaaRaa and GooGoo's antennae-fruit mixed up and had to redraw, and this simply cannot happen again. She must keep her mind on it. The deadline looms.

But keeping her mind on it has become impossible. For weeks – months – every pencil-stroke has had to be hauled up from a well of exhaustion, and now the illustration on the easel, destined to be the centre-spread of *Beeboo and the Swamp Creatures*, is threatening to be her nemesis. Even if she were to manage a night of decent sleep, the thought of dreaming up suitably awed expressions for twenty five Alien faces makes her want to weep.

Looking round furtively, as if Melanie, her editor, might be watching from a corner, Celina erases four ovals from the top row and five from the bottom. Then she adds two half-hearted banana antennae to the top left oval before throwing the pencil down and picking up a packet of Benson & Hedges. Ramming a cigarette in her mouth, she leans her elbows on the desk and rocks herself back and forth. A low moan escapes from her lips, as of an animal in pain.

Round about the easel is an array of fluorescent-pink heart-shaped Post-Its from Melanie. Week after week these Post-Its arrive, stuck to corrected proofs of the last BeeBoo book and inscribed with tiny, neat messages like 'Hope B.S.C.'s coming on well?' and 'Simply dying to see B.S.C.!!!' and each time one appears it makes Celina nauseous with anxiety; though not nauseous enough to provoke any real action.

Even the last one, which arrived yesterday and read 'Let's have coffee Monday and look at B.S.C. together!' did not force a pencil-stroke out of her; but today, she knows, she has come to the end of the road. That last little pink Post-It was a note of finality.

If only she can appease Melanie on Monday with a couple of semi-decent drawings and a reasonable centrespread, the rest of the illustrations can wait till next week, or the next. And by next week, or the next, she will have faced her demon and then – surely – she will feel marginally less dreadful?

Cigarette clamped unlit between her lips, she leafs through *Lost in the Snotgrass Swamp* till she finds a picture of Lord Dragoo, and begins to copy his fiercely benevolent face. But though she takes care to tip the angle of the dragon's head down a fraction and adjust the line of its neck and wings to accommodate the perspective of the new drawing, it does not work. The lines which should express sinuous muscles are rigid and unnatural, and the face looks more like that of a village idiot than the keenest brain in all of Planet Zargon.

Giving up on Lord Dragoo, Celina adds a pot-body to the Beeboo oval, then stops. Heavy footsteps are ascending the stairs and heading for the shower room. Water hisses, and one half of the duet from Bizet's *Pearl Fishers* booms out badly.

Celina replaces the pencil in the tub, but does not move out of her chair. She should, she knows, go upstairs right now and have a bath and change, because otherwise she will get into a rush and not be there to welcome the dinner guests. By the time she gets downstairs all four, having been sucked neatly into settees, will be sipping gin and tonics, and chatting charmingly with Max who will, as usual, be playing the perfect host.

Pauline and Felicity will look as though they have just stepped out of a beauty parlour rather than an operating theatre and, when she, Celina, makes her breathless entrance, will turn with that amused, slightly patronising, look scientific people reserve for artists, and then one of them – Felicity, probably – will stand up and peck the air on either side of her cheeks and say, 'Celina, darling! How lovely to see you again! And how are all those cute little dinosaurs?' and Celina will – just and no more – stop herself from saying, 'They're fine, thank you. And they're not dinosaurs. They're bleeding Aliens.'

She runs upstairs to the bathroom, but the door is shut. Surely Luca has not decided to take his monthly bath? She sits down to wait on the bottom step of the next flight when the bedside phone rings.

It is almost certainly Kalinda, and she is sorely tempted not to answer. Then she hears Max, from the shower, shouting "Phone, Celina!" and then, "*Phone*, Celina!" and she drags herself through to the bedroom and picks it up.

"Hi!" She tries to sound enthusiastic, but she is never enthusiastic about speaking to Kalinda. And today she is even less enthusiastic than usual, because she knows why Kalinda is phoning.

"Hello." Kalinda's voice is dry as a husk. "Have you done it?"

There is a pause while Celina pretends to consider the question, but Kalinda sees through her. "You haven't, have you? Celina, it's been four months ..."

"Three. Three months."

"Three months then. Have you found the key?"

Celina cheers up. "Yes – found it. It was in that little suede-covered chest with the brass studs, you know the one we used to ..."

"Good. So why haven't you used it? You promised."

There is another pause during which Celina rehearses her possible excuses: Monday's *BeeBoo* deadline, the endless dinner parties Max's medical friends seem to require, Luca's Eggs Escapade (she had forgotten about that till now), but in her heart she knows why she has not used the key, and it has nothing to do with Aliens, surgeons, or sons.

"I've been terribly busy," she tells Kalinda. "And tired. Really tired. I think I might be anaemic."

Kalinda's breath sounds like a small but furious gale. "When then? When are you likely to regain the energy required to climb a flight of stairs and turn a key in a lock? We have to get started, Celina. Henderson needs those papers."

Celina stares down at the phone's dark grey mouthpiece. There is stuff that looks like compacted biscuit crumbs stuck in its holes, and she can see her breath sitting in droplets on top.

"You don't understand," she says, and immediately wishes she had not.

"What is there to understand, for heavens' sake?" Kalinda spits back. "You *always* over-dramatise," and then, "*When,* Celina?"

More water gushes into the bath, followed by a series of man-splashes. An insistent pounding begins in Celina's right temple, like a small, dangerous heart. Kalinda's visit is due, and if the papers are not there when she arrives, she is sure to make a great show of finding them herself.

"Now," Celina says, surprising herself. "I'll go now. Right this minute."

She shouts the last three words and, before Kalinda can tell her not to be so ridiculously theatrical, bangs the phone back onto its cradle and runs downstairs. She picks up the key labelled 'Mother's studio' and heads back up, her feet thudding on the stairs.

To hell with the meal. She'll show Kalinda.

The last flight of stairs is steep. It is a modern addition, built when the loft was converted to a studio flat, to house the increasingly feeble-minded, but by no means finished, Imogen Wilde. The door to this room has been locked for nearly a year, ever since Imogen's cheeks, after almost eighty gloriously ruddy years, turned the colour of pale Yellow Ochre and sank inwards to coat her bones.

The ghastly change seemed to happen overnight, and the fatal nature of whatever grim disease process it presaged must somehow have doused a light in Imogen's spirit because calmly, and with great dignity, she had allowed herself to be carried gently down to an ambulance which took her to the private Nursing Home in which everyone knew she would soon die.

Celina climbs this last flight of stairs very slowly, but when she reaches the studio door she still has to stand for a while, regaining her breath. Forcing her back straight, she pushes in the key, turns it, and enters.

For a while she stands in the shadowy entranceway, frozen. Then, shocked by her own frailty, she gropes for the light switch and, walking in with small hesitant steps, gazes round at her mother's life, the view of which is blurred by sudden angry tears.

CHAPTER TWO

If she were to listen hard enough, Celina could swear she would still hear her mother breathing the way she breathed in the last weeks she spent here. Low and crackling, that breath was, like wind through dry leaves.

Wishing it were possible to close her nose against the faint but still-discernable smell of oil paint, she walks into the centre of the big room and wonders again at the glory of its light. For even now, with evening falling, the studio is as perfect a room as any artist could wish for.

The last of the day's sun, flooding through its big windows, is reflected softly back from eggshell-white walls. Its drawers and cupboards and plan chests glow with the warmth of good wood, as do its fine-grained English Oak floorboards. No expense, of course, was spared when the studio was planned, for Imogen was paying and Imogen, as everyone who knew her could testify, always got the best.

'It has to be a north light,' she had insisted. 'A studio must have north light. And the window must be enormous – floor to ceiling. I need as heavenly a view as London can provide.'

And so it had been. In a matter of months the plans were drawn up and approved and the work completed; but sadly, as the new studio went from strength to strength, Imogen did not. In those last months of independence her mind deteriorated markedly, and by the time she and her goods and chattels were settled in, even the abundance of north light was not sufficient to pierce the darkness of her dementia and illuminate those tiny gold-veins of inspiration the disease had spared.

Resolute as ever in the face of adversity, however, Imogen had given it her very best shot. Every morning she struggled to rise and dress herself, although usually when Celina popped in to check on her she was still clothed in one of her shiny robes – robes bright with birds and flowers that told of gayer lives and times – and was gazing out of the window, sipping coffee. Eventually, around mid-day, she would don her paint-stiff smock, mix her colours, choose the brushes she had carefully washed in turps the night before and stand, palette poised, in front of her easel, like a great gaunt statue.

Sometimes, when Celina was working in her own studio, she would imagine her mother standing like that, hour after hour, staring at a blank white square, making no mark, and she remembered how, in her hey-day, Imogen was renowned for the boldness of her strokes. 'When Imogen paints,' an aunt had told her once, 'she moves as though she were the wild conductor of an orchestra, playing a concerto for canvas and colour.'

The wild conductor had most definitely put down her baton in those last days, but there were the odd, terrible, times when Imogen did manage to put paint to canvas, and Celina had witnessed two of these. Coming into the studio with fresh sheets, she had watched in horror as, face contorted with confusion and fury, her mother examined the meaningless mess on the easel before her.

For a long silent time she stood like that and then, with an explosive grunt, she slammed down her palette, threw herself into her chair, and stared out over the roofs of Highgate, as though hoping to catch sight of the Muse that had deserted her.

The first time it happened, Celina had gone over to the window and placed what she hoped was an empathetic hand on one bone-sharp shoulder, but it had not been the right thing to do. Shrugging the hand away and raising her chin high, Imogen had told Celina haughtily to '*Pon las sábanas en la cama, y déjame en paz!*' at which Celina withdrew, obediently placed the sheets on her mother's bed, and fled.

The second time had been worse, for this time the canvas was well and truly caked with bright Titanium White and brash Cerulean Blue – the makings, presumably, of a sky – and when Celina meekly entered her mother swung round, pointed the loaded paintbrush straight at her and, advancing unsteadily, aimed it at her chest, like a small sky-blue rapier. '*Niña mala ...*' she growled as she approached. '*Enriqueta diabólica ... niña mala ...*'

In these last days, Imogen often reverted to the Spanish of her youth, for her father had been a diplomat and the family had lived in a variety of Hispanic countries. She would give everyone Spanish names with which she berated them mercilessly, and Celina was never sure how best to deal with this. Should she collude and be the frequently-errant, often downright diabolical, Enriqueta, trying to do her best and always falling short? Or was it better to try to bring her mother back to reality by gently reasoning with her?

Mostly, she decided, it was kinder to collude; for if Imogen believed she was a teenager in Madrid, visiting the Prada and trying to paint like Goya, or a young woman in New Mexico, mesmerised by the clarity of desert light and never-ending skies that inspired her beloved Georgia O'Keeffe, why bring her back to the reality of grim, grey Highgate?

Reasoning was a waste of time anyway, because her mother always refused adamantly to be brought back, brushing aside Celina's reasonings with such a patronising air that sometimes Celina actually began to doubt her own version of reality. That 'My *daughter*? Really, Enriqueta, don't be so ridiculous. *No tengo ninguna hija*! I do not have a daughter!', combined with the proud raising of the chin and stern black gleam in the eyes, made Celina feel like the little girl again; the bad little girl, the bad twin, telling lies, inventing stories, getting it all terribly wrong as usual.

There is a painting, of sorts, on the easel now. It must have been sitting there for at least a year, proclaiming to the empty room the extinction of Imogen Wilde's brilliance. Guiltily, Celina takes it down and pushes it into the space between two plan chests. The plan chests, she knows, are full of work – charcoal sketches smudged with energy, pastel studies whose simplicity speaks volumes, and fabulously loose water-colour life-drawings, where skin glows translucently because Imogen knew just how little paint to apply.

She should take them out, frame them, mount a retrospective: 'The Unseen Work of Imogen Wilde'. People would pay a lot for them, dead artists always being more sought-after than living ones, and for a while she stands there, imagining it. It would be held in some West End gallery like Gallery Cinq or Jakoby, who always loved her mother's stuff and, when first she died, were never off the phone. If Celina were to suggest a retrospective now, they would jump at the idea.

There would be a big opening night, with canapés and wine and Kalinda and herself in long skirts, accepting their mother's praise as though her brilliance had anything to do with them, and gleefully counting the red spots on the canvases and working out how much they would have to split between the two of them. It might be enough to pay Luca's University fees, if he ever woke up long enough to go to University; or for a holiday, for her and Max to loaf about on a beach somewhere, loathing one another. More realistically, it would perhaps keep the Beeboos at bay for a while ...

"Celina! Are you ready?" It is Max, and of course she is not. Furthermore, the question is rhetorical because he knows from experience she never appears till the guests are there and, if he is honest, he prefers it that way. Celina is convinced he actually enjoys showing people to their seats and pouring their drinks with his eyebrows raised the way she imagines he raises them when he tells someone their disease is terminal. 'It's inevitable,' those eyebrows say. 'One tries to rise above it, but what can one do?'

She walks to the door, shouts down at him. "I'm looking for mother's house papers. The ones Henderson needs. The food's being delivered," she adds. "Just carry on without me."

It is a relief to come back into the studio. Despite the initial anger – the initial red blinding rage – it is comforting to stand here now, in the last of the light, in her mother's realm with her mother gone. And the smell, the dreaded paint smell which all these months she imagined lingering in every nook and cranny, waiting to waft out as soon as the door was opened, is hardly noticeable. Going over to the window, she sits in the wicker chair with the back like a peacock's outspread tail, and admires the view anew.

There are no two ways about it, it is a stunningly good view, and an unusual one for London in that there is so much sky. Once, Imogen told her, a swan had flown by, just at her level, heading for the Heath. As she spoke, her face had shone and she was the artist again, seeing everything in terms of form and colour, light and shade. The clarity had lasted only a few moments, however, before clouds of confusion rolled in again.

Now Celina stares out, almost expecting to see her mother's swan, but of course none flies by. She gazes over the housetops, at the roof gardens with their tubs and trellises and neat little metal tables, which in a few months will be set again with glasses and candles for sunset suppers; and then further, to where Highgate Cemetery sprawls. Then she looks down on the trees that surround the house, liking the novelty of being able to see into the criss-cross mesh of bare branches. This is the view birds get, and she wonders vaguely if birds see in colour, and if so does the small swell of green buds stir something inside them, and make them think of nesting and mating and laying eggs?

The peacock-tail chair creaks as Celina pulls herself out of it, and the sound is such an echo of Imogen's last days it stops her short. Holding herself still and tall, she takes deep breaths and tells herself that this is now, not then. That there are no demons any more. That Kalinda, as ever, was right. She had indeed blown this thing out of all proportion.

Not yet ready to face the downstairs, she walks over to the picture hanging above her mother's bed. Careful not to make a dent in the white counterpane, she leans over and examines it, surprised by the force of its familiarity. It is like seeing a friend after a long time and wondering what accounts for the subtle changes in their face, for this evening the stark brilliance of the picture – a picture she must have seen thousands of times – strikes her as if for the first time.

The picture is not one of her mother's, though its influence can be seen all round the room in Imogen's own bleached deserts and striated red-ochre mountains. It is not even an original, but a print, and it has hung above Imogen's bed, in its simple wooden frame, wherever that bed has been. It should, Celina thinks with a stab of guilt, have been in the Nursing Home with her.

Hills – Lavender, Ghost Ranch, it is called, and the caption below tells Celina it was painted, in New Mexico in 1935, by Georgia O'Keeffe. No longer caring about the sanctity of the sheets, she kneels up on the bed and, leaning across its lace-edged pillows, reads the picture's title and date aloud, liking the eerie power of the words. Then she does a little sum and works out that her mother would have been twenty-five when it was painted.

Lately, she has been doing these sums a lot. Out of the blue, for no reason, she will find herself suddenly thinking, 'How old was Mother when Raine was born?' or 'How old were Kalinda and I when Daddy left?' or – and this is the one which now occupies her, 'When was Mother my age?' Laboriously, because she never could do numbers, and eternally grateful that Imogen was born in 1910 because it is an easy date, she works it out.

'Mother was my age in 1959,' she tells herself, and then, 'And in 1959, when Mother was forty-nine like me, I was nineteen,' and then, 'Which is three years older than Raine is now.'

She has no earthly idea why Imogen's death should have prompted all these sums. Perhaps it is a way of charting her own progress; of seeing how her life is shaping up compared to that of her mother. Or perhaps it is linked to her lifelong, and hitherto impossible, task of understanding her feelings for her mother. For when

Imogen was alive, no sooner had Celina formed a theory to explain these feelings than Imogen would say or do something to explode it. With Imogen gone, however, the task is finite. Doable, perhaps. The only person left to argue with the theories is Kalinda.

Banishing her sister from her thoughts, Celina lets her eyes drift up through the cinnabar striations of *Hills – Lavender* to its velvet fawn summit, and imagines her mother in 1935. Tall and beautiful, hugely talented, free as a bird. And as that last thought hits home, Celina realises her fists are clenched tight and she is longing – *longing* – for a cigarette.

The doorbell rings, but though she jumps as if caught in some underhand act, she does not move from the bed. Then she hears Max open the front door to receive the evening's meal, and she can almost feel the cigarette packet in her hand, imagine her fingers pulling back the golden lid, scrabbling about inside, extracting a cigarette then breathing in the wonderful, bitter-dry tobacco smell.

"Celina!" She can smell the Turkey Parmesan, and she knows Max has come half-way up the stairs with it so that he can swear. "Will you come down and serve this ruddy food," he yells, "before we all die of starvation!"

Celina dismounts the bed and, crossing over to Imogen's old desk, lifts the carved wooden box that has always sat on top. Pushing it under her arm she leaves the room, re-locks the door, and descends, the box digging at her ribs. At least, she tells herself, this represents some kind of progress. Now she can tell Kalinda she has started looking.

Depositing the box on the hall table, she makes for the kitchen where she spoons the contents of the polystyrene containers onto the best dinner service. Armed with two platefuls of Turkey Parmesan, she makes her entrance, pecks the cheeks of Pauline and Lionel and Felicity and

Brad, then returns to the kitchen for more food and it is then that, quite out of the blue, a thought occurs to her. It is a wild thought, heady with illicitness, and it brings a surge of energy hotter and stronger than any she has felt for years.

The thought is that, now she has finally dared to enter Imogen's studio, she can go there whenever she feels like a smoke. Sitting on the peacock-tailed chair, with a glass of red wine and a pack of twenty, she can savour the fabulous roof-top view, without the worry of anyone smelling what she has been up to. It will certainly beat skulking in the back porch, or leaning halfway out of her studio window then desperately fanning the air lest her secret wafts out, which it does anyway because, like their mother, both Raine and Luca possess quite remarkable olfactory organs.

The idea of a smoking haven is wonderfully cheering, and throughout the evening Celina returns to it again and again. Then, during the cheese course another, much more illicit, thought occurs.

It is a dizzyingly dangerous idea, and although she doubts she has the courage to carry it out, the very thought of it makes the hairs in her neck rise. Compared to this idea, the Smoking Haven idea pales into insignificance.

CHAPTER THREE

On the Monday after the dinner party, on the Northern Line somewhere between Highgate and Euston, Celina watches her deconstructed reflection flit along on its sooty backdrop and wonders how someone whose exterior is as neat and trim as hers can possibly be in such a state of mental turmoil.

Because 'mental turmoil' is what Celina is in, and has been since the small hours of Sunday morning. Her dark hair may be cut in a smart bob to emphasise her high cheekbones and slender neck, and she may be wearing her smartest black suit and her cleanest white silk shirt, but inwardly she is in complete disarray.

And the disarray does not end there. The black leather case on her lap whose contents, over the years, have had hard-nosed picture-book editors clutching their flushed faces and purring with delight, now contains three mediocre single-page illustrations and a centrespread that is not even moderately acceptable. Finished in haste yesterday evening, it is probably the worst illustration Celina has ever done; but such was her state of mind yesterday that the fact it exists at all is nothing short of miraculous.

For in the small hours of yesterday morning, shortly after the birth of the Smoking Haven idea, her rosy glow was extinguished by a shocking revelation. And that revelation, which happened in the twinkling of an eye just as the dinner party was grinding to a close, has forced her finally to admit that at least one of her mother's gloomy predictions was correct.

The revelation happened at around 1 am, long after the profiteroles had been scoffed and the cheese board reduced to crumbs and, if you had the kind of imagination that dreams up such things, you might think it was engineered by Imogen Wilde herself, reaching out from beyond the grave to smile grimly and say, '*Mira*! What did I tell you?'

The way it happened certainly seemed like some darkly ironic divine intervention. The guests, replete at last, had risen from the table to sip liqueurs, and Max had excused himself and left the room – presumably to go to the toilet – and as soon as he had gone Felicity stood up too and said, 'Oh, silly me! I have a box of chocolates for you in the car,' and rushed out. Shortly afterwards Celina, bored beyond measure by the Pauline/Brad/Lionel trio and their interminable medical chit-chat, had stood up and excused herself as well.

Her mother's box had been occupying her thoughts since well before the profiteroles. Even if the house papers were not inside, she was increasingly curious to find out what was. If nothing else, there might be some tidy little sum sandwiched inside, for Imogen had always insisted on keeping wads of cash hidden around the place. But there was another rather satisfying thought which had come to Celina as she bridged the gap between two profiteroles with a bank of foamy cream, and that thought had deepened her already rosy glow to a rich Carmine Red.

The thought was, that if she took even the most cursory of rifles through the box, she could phone Kalinda first thing in the morning and tell her that the search for the house papers was well and truly under way. And even if she found nothing (and if she found money, that could be her little secret) at least Kalinda would see she was seriously trying.

The cursory rifle, however, did not happen, because as Celina walked into the hall she saw, standing right in front of the wooden box with their backs towards her and their hands around one another's waists, Max and Felicity. Whether the door made a small noise, or she herself gave a gasp, she does not know, but whatever happened they dropped hands and turned to face her. And it was in that moment, as they faced her with the unmistakably naked expressions of the guilty, that Celina realised that Imogen Wilde, all those years ago, had been right.

'You make a handsome couple,' she had said, grudgingly, on Celina and Max's wedding day. 'But,' she had gone on, with an arching of the eyebrows and a shake of the forefinger, 'he has wandering eyes, and those eyes will lure other women into his bed. You mark my words, Celina, you won't keep him.' She had given her the worldly, pitying look of a woman well-versed in the luring of other women's men to bed and Celina, despite her absolute, hormone-led conviction that things would always be fine, that Max could never desire anyone but her, still heard in them a small, chill echo of doom.

And that doom-ridden echo was never really quieted. Like some dark, insistent dog, it followed Celina all her married life, fawning against her, twisting itself in between her legs, whimpering at her door at nights.

Lately, particularly in times of stress, the whimpering had crescendoed into a mighty howl and now, as she battles her way out through the crowds at Euston, it bellows over their noise, giving her no choice but to listen and recall, as she has recalled a million times before, just how it all went wrong.

Because it had started well. Imogen was right when she said they made a handsome couple, and Celina can see their wedding photos in her mind's eye now – tall, slim, and black-haired the pair of them, and brown as berries. In the early days, showing the photos, she would say, 'Don't we look like twins? More like twins than Kalinda and me, and we came from the same egg!'

As for the come-to-bed eyes well, yes – Max did have those – but then, in those days, so did she, and very happy she was to come to bed with him, as often as their busy lives allowed, until … Well – until what, exactly? Until when?

A fragment of memory, excruciating in the pain it evokes, flashes before her. It is a memory that often pops up, often out of nowhere and especially when she is tired or depressed, as though appearing bang on cue to drag her even further down. And today, of course, because she is both tired and depressed, it is brighter and clearer than ever.

There it is, as ever: their third Christmas table, set with red plates and golden crackers and heaving with food, and Max's face opposite her, eyes bright between the flames of crimson, holly-decked candles. She can still smell the tang of pine needles as she listens to his voice, low and confident and a little slurred, and see those bright brown eyes sweep from guest to guest, excluding no one.

She can see his face too, shiny and flushed with wine and success. Max, life and soul of the party, centre-stage, keeping everyone entertained with his wit and wisdom, on the evening when everything changed. When, all of a sudden, she saw him differently.

The realisation had happened in just one small moment of time, yet even now she can recall every tiny detail of that moment, and the moments before it, and the time after.

Before it, and serving as an accompaniment to the prawns in Marie Rose sauce on a bed of avocado, there had been a debate about the successes and limitations of current cancer treatments. With the arrival of the turkey, sage stuffing, and roasted rosemary potatoes, this had opened out into a more general discussion of the aging process. By the time the sherry trifle was produced, this had segued into the management of elderly, bewildered patients. And it was then, as Max waxed ever more eloquent, that the moment itself arrived.

Spoon laden with quivering jelly, Max had made several reasonable points around the general 'quality of life' theme, with which everyone concurred. Then he had widened the topic out to include voluntary euthanasia.

There was nothing inherently cold or heartless about what Max said. It was the way he said it that had upset Celina. She had never seen him this animated, underlining his points with sharp little darts of the trifle spoon, making jokes that surely only a doctor could laugh at, angrily shouting down anyone who made a point that weakened his case. And the more animated he became, the more he seemed to change into someone quite unlike the Max she had married.

She had watched him, and his spoonful of uneaten jelly, as if through a pane of glass. Then, quietly, she had risen from the table and gone to the bathroom where, her forehead pressed against the wall, she had wished she were dead. It was as though, in those short candlelit moments, her whole recent life had been exposed as a sham; the man she had idolised exposed as an angry, bombastic charlatan. It was as though the thin veil of her being had been forever torn.

In the mornings that followed she woke with a feeling of sickening dread at the day ahead. Like some pale ghost of herself, she went through the motions of life as though not quite a part of it. Eventually, imperceptibly, the hurt faded, or became so engrained she did not notice it, but her feelings for Max were never the same. A smear of Paynes Gray had sullied the Titanium White of their marriage. Its brilliance would ever after be dulled.

Years later, one particularly boozy evening, she had attempted to explain it to her friend Anna. 'I always wonder if it was a kind of post-natal depression,' she had said, 'because surely I'd seen Max being overbearing before. I actually think, she remembers adding, 'I had a nervous breakdown, but no one noticed.'

At the time, it had indeed seemed curious to Celina that no one had seen the change in her. In particular, it seemed incredible that Max had not. Surely, she would think as they lay side by side and Max, cupping her breast, raised his eyebrows in that charming way of his, he must see the change in me? Surely, as she arched her back obligingly and cried out, he must know?

Ever since then, year after year, she has asked herself: was Imogen right? Was he like that all along – arrogant, superior, opinionated, self-centred? And were her eyes so full of fairy dust she could not see what was blindingly obvious to everyone else?

She has always suspected the answer to be 'yes' but now, at last, she knows it for sure. That far-off Christmas evening, with their tiny daughter asleep upstairs, she saw the reality of Max. That evening, she fell out of love with him forever, and really, despite clinging to the marriage for over fifteen years, has she not always known that, in the end, Saturday night was written in the stars?

It is mid-afternoon, and although traffic roars on Euston Road, the pavement is mercifully free of crowds. With an almighty effort Celina pushes away the crimson candles and Max's jelly-laden spoon and marches in the direction of the Bluebird Café. The nearer she gets to the café, however, the more her stomach twists and turns and, to make matters even worse, as she walks in she realises she has no idea what Melanie looks like.

They have arranged to meet 'as usual' in the Bluebird Café and this 'as usual' of Melanie's means they must have met there before, but if they have Celina has no recollection of it. Now she is here, though, she vaguely remembers the potted plants, and the tables with their blue tablecloths, nestling between shelves of second-hand books. She wanders around in the semi-darkness, in search of a familiar face but failing to find one.

But then, she tells herself, she is bound to fail, because picture-book editors are all of a type. They are all young and female, and they are inevitably long-haired and pretty, and more often than not they have names like Melissa or Amanda or Melanie. They always seem to be on the move too, having babies or shifting jobs, so that sometimes you meet one who looks familiar and it turns out she was your editor years ago, when you worked for some other publishing house, and if she still remembers you and the book you worked on together, you are darned if you do. In the end, when you have been in the business as long as Celina has, all editors blend together into one rather lovely, homogeneous, mass.

Thankfully, as she reaches the last table, someone stands and waves and calls her name and there she is: young, long-haired, pretty Melanie.

"Lovely to see you at last," Melanie says, breathlessly, as they embrace and now Celina remembers breathless

Melanie, who has, despite her youth, some kind of chronic chest problem and – it is all coming back – has to watch what she eats because 'dairy' brings it on. "I'm simply dying to see Lord Dragoo again." The breathlessness continues as she leads Celina to the darkest corner table. "He's always been my favourite Planet Zargon character, you know!"

Celina, feeling like a mother who has broken a beloved toy, smiles as enthusiastically as she can, and while Melanie bounds off to get her a coffee she slips off her jacket, checks the lining for sweat stains – another habit she has acquired of late – before hanging it over the back of her chair. Then she takes out the folder containing Lord Dragoo and company, and places it on the table in front of her.

Melanie deposits the coffee, asks anxiously whether Celina requires a muffin and when she declines, flops back into her seat with a wheeze. "So," she says, "how are you?"

It is the wrong question, and no matter how Celina cups her coffee and breathes in its comforting aroma, it takes her a few moments to say the required, 'Fine, thank you'. And the trouble is, now she is sitting opposite Melanie, she remembers that Melanie is an unusually sensitive and kind young woman, which is exactly the kind of person Celina would prefer not to be doing business with today.

The hesitation before the 'Fine, thank you' is imperceptible, but Melanie notices it. Her alabaster forehead crinkles and she leans forward till she is just too close for comfort. "Are you sure, Celina?" she says and then, before Celina has the chance to insist, shakes her head and withdraws again. "Sorry," she says. "Mustn't project …" Eyes bright with incipient tears, she picks up her coffee mug and buries her beautiful young face in it.

Celina opens the *Beeboo and the Swamp Creatures* file.

She is near to tears herself now and today's meeting, which was always going to be bad has, with Melanie's own little existential crisis, taken on an extra layer of awfulness. She slides out the least disastrous of the illustrations, and holds it for Melanie to see.

Here, even in the café's dim light, it looks worse than it did at home. If someone else had done that illustration, and Celina had been asked what she thought of it, she would say it was 'competently mediocre'. But 'competently mediocre' is not enough for arguably the best children's publisher in London. More importantly, 'competently mediocre' is not enough for her.

"Oh," Melanie says – and now Celina is the mother who gave the wrong birthday present – "Yes. Yes. It's lovely." She smiles bravely, but Celina knows she is searching the drawing for something specifically good to say about it, and finding nothing.

"It's not good," Celina says. "I know it's not. I'll re-do it. It's just that I've had a few problems lately. Mother died, things to sort out, and then there's Luca ..." A wave of exhaustion threatens to engulf her as she remembers those eggs, and she finishes with a lame, and very probably untrue, "You know how it is ..."

Melanie blows her nose into her paper napkin, then pushes the napkin stoically up her sleeve. She gives Celina an intense look. "Of course we understand," she says, and Celina imagines the entire staff of Apricot Books giving her a corporate hug. "Of course we do. In fact, you know, I was saying only yesterday to Philip, 'Celina's been under a lot of strain lately. Perhaps we need to give her a bit of a 'sabbatical'?" She draws little quotation marks in the air round the spectre of the word, to show she is not entirely serious. "Bit of a break, I mean," she clarifies. "Extension of deadlines ..."

But Celina clings to the word 'sabbatical' like a

drowning man to a log. It may have been dismissed by the editorial quotation marks but its echo still lingers. For a split second, she lets go of her back muscles. At Melanie's next sentence, however, her spine is ramrod-straight again. "Actually, a break might be a good thing because just wait till you hear this" – she takes a deep, crackling breath – "we've been hatching some amazing plans for Beeboo! There've been meetings at international level, and it's going to be so big." She leans further into Celina's comfort zone, and Celina moves her hands away lest she is suddenly impelled to grasp them.

"There's going to be a television series!" Melanie's face lights up so happily she does not even wheeze. "Probably stop-frame animation, though we're also thinking of having actors dressed up in Beeboo costumes, and there'll be a Beeboo Songbook – that's just being written – and videos of course, and then there's the spin-offs – merchandise, dolls and suchlike, and activity books too – basic numeracy, literacy, all done through Beeboo and his friends' little world. Phonics, word puzzles, word searches …"

Celina feels herself tip very slightly forward. When she looks up, small pricks of light are blotting out part of Melanie's face, and at the same time Melanie's voice, '… join-the-dots, colouring-in, board games …' sounds increasingly hollow and distant, as if she is slowly being beamed up to Planet Zargon.

Gripping onto the edge of the table, Celina waits for her to run out of breath. She half-closes her eyes and peers through the dazzle, which now occupies most of her field of vision, and tries to calm herself sufficiently to wonder where the toilets are. A roaring heat is travelling up from her legs, and she has to be alone when it hits her face.

"So," Melanie concludes triumphantly, "what do you think? Isn't it awesome?"

"Very" – Celina pushes back her chair and stands unsteadily – "but you'll have to excuse me. I'm going to be sick."

CHAPTER FOUR

Alone at last in the Bluebird Café toilet, Celina leans against the cubicle wall and checks the progress of her migraine by attempting to read the 'Stress Incontinence' notice on the door.

The left side of her field of vision is almost completely absent, blotted out by a pulsating crescent of grey dazzle, and it is a dazzle she knows of yore. She has always called it the 'birds in flight', because that was how the doctor described it to her when she was nine; and she knows she was nine, because after the consultation she and Kalinda were taken to choose their tenth birthday presents.

She remembers the day well. Their mother – and, surprisingly, Celina is sure it really was their mother, and not, as was more usual, one of her mother's many child-minding minions – took them to Oxford Street, and Celina got a pair of black stretch-nylon ski-pants and a big cardigan with metal buttons and a pattern of greenish-brown stags flanked by bright green fir trees. Kalinda, dismissing the ski pants as baggy at the knees and the stags on the cardigan as the colour of baby poo, had chosen a watch with a red strap and a black dial that told the time in different countries, and all the way home Celina had wondered why.

The watch was enormous – far too big for Kalinda's tiny wrist – but even so it was quite difficult to make out the time in England because of the mass of dials showing the time in all the other places. It had worried Celina hugely – even more than the 'birds in flight' actually, because now that the doctor had given that a name it did not seem so much of a problem any more – and as the weeks went by it continued to worry her.

The doctor had, in fact, given Celina's affliction two names. Its proper name, the name she would tell the teacher when she could no longer do her sums because the numbers kept disappearing, was 'migraine'. And 'migraines', he had gone on to tell her, were nothing to worry about. They were just 'hormonal', which meant Celina was not, as she had imagined, going to go blind or die tragically young of a brain tumour, but was simply growing up; and her mother's friend Barbara had already explained what else 'hormonal' would happen quite soon, in the light of which the 'birds in flight' were small fry.

But the watch, and Kalinda's reasons for choosing it, continued to worry Celina. Why on earth would you want to know the time in Rome, or Paris, or Buenos Aires? Why would you want to know the time in anywhere else but London?

Although she was dying to know, in the weeks before the birthday she had held back from asking, because somehow she felt the answer would eventually reveal itself to her. But as the days passed no such revelation was forthcoming and on their birthday, when they officially received their presents, she had finally given in and asked Kalinda why she had chosen it. And Kalinda had replied haughtily that it was patently obvious; that of course it was because she wanted to know what time Daddy was having, wherever in the whole wide world Daddy was.

Immediately, Celina bitterly regretted the baggy-kneed ski-pants and the poo-coloured stags, now exposed as the immature birthday presents they had always been. A watch that let you know when your daddy would be getting up, or coming home from work, or eating his dinner, was *patently obviously* much more mature. The fact that no one actually knew where in the world Daddy lived was perhaps a bit of a fly in the ointment, but presumably Kalinda had taken that into consideration and would keep her geographical options open. The point was that the thought was there, and all through the second decade of the twins' lives, that thought had rankled. Come to think of it, it still rankled with Celina that it was her twin who, at such a tender age, was capable of such a highly superior thought. It had marked Kalinda out forever as the superior twin.

There is a soft tap on the cubicle door and Melanie asks if she is OK. "I'm fine," Celina assures her, opening the door a crack and smiling her best smile. "It'll soon pass. Please don't worry.

"I'm best to sit quietly," she adds, with a sudden flash of inspiration, "somewhere not too bright, and it's good if I can eat something, so if you don't mind I'll just tidy myself up then pop back to the table and maybe even have that muffin. And I'll give you a ring tomorrow and we can meet when I've had a chance to re-draw?"

As she speaks she gradually pulls the cubicle door as far as she can without shutting it in Melanie's face, and when Melanie says, "Yes, of course, that's exactly what you should do, you poor thing," and, handing in her jacket and briefcase, backs off discreetly, Celina leans her forehead against the Stress Incontinence notice and takes long breaths in. Then, putting on the jacket, because all of a sudden she is ice-cold, she emerges from the cubicle and prepares to find her way back to the table.

Melanie is still there, with a new mug of coffee and what looks like a blueberry muffin. Wishing beyond anything that she could summon Lord Dragoo – preferably with a packet of twenty Benson & Hedges in his handy cigarette-lighter mouth – to whisk her home to bed, Celina sits down.

"What would help most," she tells Melanie, "would be if I could have a cigarette. Apparently the nicotine constricts your arteries, but of course I know you can't do with smoke, so maybe once I've had the coffee I'll go and walk about outside." She fingers the muffin and feels her throat fill with acid. "And this looks heavenly, thank you." She wraps it in a napkin and pops it into her briefcase. "I'll save it for later."

She begins to stand, but Melanie has moved in for the kill. "Celina," she says gently, "do you mind if I ask you something?" She puts a hand over Celina's. "Have you ever thought of talking to someone?"

In answer, Celina takes a packet of cigarettes and a lighter out of her briefcase and places both firmly on the table. She withdraws a cigarette, lights it, and inhales.

"No," she says, blowing the smoke as close to Melanie's left ear as she dares. "No, actually I haven't."

Melanie opens her mouth again, but Celina takes another drag on the cigarette, sending her ducking down into her lime-green satchel. For a while she delves about in the satchel, then takes out a small pink-coloured card which she slides across the table towards Celina.

"We all go through periods when things get on top of us," Celina says, ignoring the pink card, "and the death of a parent is never easy. I'll be absolutely fine." She exhales again, and this time Melanie coughs. "I like the 'sabbatical' idea, though. Could that be arranged, do you think?"

Melanie does not answer. Instead, she points to the name printed on the pink card and Celina, suspecting suddenly that it and the sabbatical could somehow be linked, deigns to peer closer.

"Inge van Deth," Melanie says reverentially. "She's a therapist and she's frightfully good. German, I think. Or maybe Dutch. Probably Dutch, because she really is amazing. Helped me ever so much, to see my life differently."

She gives Celina a long, intense look during which Celina wonders what being Dutch has to do with being an amazing therapist and why, if you were a therapist and your name was 'van Deth', you would not adopt a more life-affirming pseudonym. More importantly, though, she wonders whether Melanie is a particularly good advert for a therapist of any name or nationality. "Perhaps" – Melanie squeezes her hand – "you'd take Inge's card and have a think about it?"

Celina stands up and grinds out her cigarette in the ashtray. "I'll think about it, but I have to say it's probably not for me. Thanks so much for the coffee and everything," she says, picking up the card and making a show of putting it carefully in her pocket, "and I'll phone you …" She is aware she is panicking now, for her vision has almost cleared and she knows of old that the mother of all headaches will soon follow. As she and Melanie walk out of the café door, she decides that whichever way Melanie turns, she will turn the other.

"Take care." Melanie gives her a warm 'goodbye' hug. "And remember, Inge's there if you change your mind." Then she turns right and, mercifully, is gone.

Celina leans back against the Bluebird Café's window

and wonders again where to go. The Underground is out of the question, and for a moment she toys with the idea of visiting Pippa, who works in a solicitors' office in one of the nearby squares and would doubtless ply her with cups of coffee and let her pour out her troubles.

It is a tempting idea, for Melanie was right in saying she needed to talk. But then, when she thinks about it, Pippa, whose marriage to the aptly-named Gabriel is as perfect a marriage as it is possible to have, and whose relationship with her mother borders on the divine, would only get upset and not really understand.

She would, of course, be hugely sympathetic, but Celina knows if she were to say something like, 'I don't think I ever really loved Max,' Pippa would give her that bewildered, almost frightened look of someone entirely out of their depth. How can anyone, that look would say, not love their *husband*?

Celina has seen that look of Pippa's often. In the early days, before she stopped blowing off steam to her about Imogen, she would see it regularly. 'How is it humanly possible,' the look had said then, 'not to love your *mother*?'.

One particularly gruelling day, in exasperation, Celina had broken down and admitted to Pippa that not only did she not love Imogen, she hated – actually hated – her. She had gone on to say that, moreover, she truly believed that Imogen hated her too; and ever after has regretted both admissions. Her relationship with Pippa has never been the same because secretly, she is sure, Pippa thinks of her as an irreparably flawed character, whose problems all stem from this one awful, unnatural, hatred.

Today, as she walks away from the café, Celina wonders if Pippa is right. Is that it, then? Is she doomed to a future of failed relationships because the one vital one was so seriously flawed? Come to think of it, both vital parental relationships were wanting, because Daddy was never there to have a relationship at all. What earthly hope has she of being even remotely well-balanced?

Crossing Euston Road, she finds a dingy Greek restaurant with deep red velour seats and a smell of yesterday's menu and, seeking out its darkest corner, orders a glass of Diet Coke with which to swallow three painkillers. Closing her eyes, she leans back and concentrates on the pain.

These days, Celina's migraine headaches are not as bad as when she was a child, when she was afraid to move her head because it felt as though a small throbbing stone was in there which, if rolled around, could rip her brain to pieces. Perhaps age has diminished their ferocity, or perhaps they are every bit as bad as they ever were, but now she has known worse pain. Whatever the truth of the matter, the taking of painkillers is merely a matter of form because nothing, except time, dulls the merciless wing beats of those birds in flight.

Cupping her head in her hands, she leans over the table and imagines the painkillers reaching her stomach, and the stomach acid eating into them, and then a gland, or a muscle, or something, sending the tiny active ingredients up into her pounding head, and at last she notices a small but definite easing.

She picks up her briefcase, clicks it open and, ignoring the Lord Dragoo fiasco, withdraws a clear plastic folder in which, back to back, she has put two things from her mother's wooden box. She examines each in turn.

The first, which is mainly handwritten and in Spanish, would appear to be the house papers Henderson needs, and she hopes he will be able to make more of their ancient spiky writing than she can. All she has been able to decipher with confidence is a name, but it is a name that is familiar, in a story-book kind of way: Casa de la

Luna Cresciente, House of the Crescent Moon.

Turning the folder over, she looks at the other object of interest, which is a sepia photograph of a woman who must surely be Georgia O'Keeffe, standing in front of an easel on which sits a painting of pale, striated hills under a coffee-coloured sky. She is wearing a long dark dress and her hair is drawn back into a chignon from which dark stray wisps have escaped. Hanging on her back by a cord, as though it has been slipped off for the photograph, is a wide-brimmed black hat.

Celina pulls the photograph out and, turning it over, rereads the writing on the back. 'Ghost Ranch,' it says, in faint brown writing. '1940'. She looks again at the photograph, at O'Keeffe and the far-off mountains and, very slowly, like wax dribbling from a candle, the idea that came to her on the night of the Turkey Parmesan dinner spills out again in all its bright, dizzying splendour.

There had actually, she remembers now, been two ideas that fateful night. First, there was the fairly mundane one of using her mother's studio to smoke in; but later, that idea had given birth to the bright dizzying one. Now, she revisits the second idea.

Had it only seemed a wonderful idea because she had drunk the best part of a bottle of red wine? Or could it actually be that, stone-cold sober in her rosy velour corner, with a photograph of O'Keeffe and the deeds to the House of the Crescent Moon before her, it still is?

An unexpected surge of energy propels her out of her seat, and when she has paid for the Coke, she heads for the Underground and, by dint of staring stolidly at the floor, makes it back to Highgate without disgracing herself. As she walks up the slope to the street, she almost collides with a large woman with a mass of wild grey curls striped with green. The woman is wearing a rainbow-coloured pashmina and carrying a bulging backpack.

"Oh, I'm so sorry," she says, and she reins in the backpack. Her accent is American, and for a few moments she walks alongside Celina, snatching little glances at her, as though she feels she knows her and wants to engage her in conversation.

Come to think of it, she might well know her. What with the pashmina and the green-striped hair, she looks definitely arty, so perhaps they met at some gallery opening or publishers' party; but the Underground journey has taken its toll and the headache has returned with renewed vigour. With a polite, 'Not at all,' Celina marches on up the slope, and she does not slow down until she can no longer hear the woman's laboured breathing behind her.

When she gets home, Luca is sitting at the kitchen table watching television. Beside him, propped up on a vase of tired daffodils, is an envelope on which, in Max's writing, her name is written.

"How come you're home so early?" she asks as, with a feeling of utter wretchedness, she rips open the envelope and tears out the letter.

"Suspended." Luca flips the television channel. "The thing with the eggs."

Celina holds the letter, still folded, to her chest. Her heartbeat makes it vibrate. "So, *did* you throw them at the Head's car?"

"Sort of."

"You can't 'sort of' throw eggs." She opens the letter, scans it. Max is leaving her 'for both their sanities.' She takes the remote out of Luca's hand and turns the television off. "You either throw an egg," she hears herself say, "or you don't throw an egg."

Luca stands up and lopes towards the door, pausing to

turn and give her a withering look.

"If you're going to be pedantic," he says, "then yes, I threw an egg." And he is gone.

CHAPTER FIVE

The evening, up in Imogen Wilde's rooftop studio, is uncannily quiet.

Celina sets a wine glass and a half-full bottle of Australian Red on the coffee-table beside the cane chair and, sinking back into its cushions, fills the glass. In the background her headache still rumbles on, and she knows she should not be drinking wine, but she takes a large gulp anyway, for she knows she will not endure tonight sober. The day has left her bruised and dazed, and tonight is the first time she can remember being in the house alone since her mother's death.

Both children are out. Five minutes ago, when she was in the kitchen opening the wine, Luca popped his head round the door to inform her he was off on a sleepover. "Biology field trip in the morning," he explained. "Darren's dad's running us to the station so it's better if I'm there."

"But you said ..." Celina had started to say, but then the problem of how Luca could be suspended but still be allowed to go on a field trip became too hard for her pounding brain and she gave up. In much the same moment she also thought of, then abandoned, the idea of grounding him.

Max would have grounded Luca. Any responsible parent would. But then Max, who would doubtless have known the intricate logic of why you could go on a field trip when you were suspended from school, could also have offered to ferry his son to Darren's house in the morning. With the family car gone that logistical problem is, at the moment, beyond Celina and as the door slams behind Luca, she is overwhelmed by a heady mix of guilt and relief.

Raine is also sleeping over, at her friend Emily's house. They are baking cakes to sell in order to raise money to go to Nepal to build a bridge, and again the logic of it all eludes Celina. What can the Nepalese possibly want with a team of middle-class English schoolchildren who do not know one end of a hammer from the other? The whole venture will no doubt be invaluable in building said middle-class English schoolchildren's characters, but who in their right mind would want to walk on a bridge built be Raine and Emily? Come to that, who in their right mind would want to eat a cake baked by Raine and Emily?

Now, as sunset reddens the sky and the wine works its magic, Celina gazes over the pink-tinged rooftops and reflects once more on the day's events. All in all, it has not been the best of days. She has had, and still has, a thumping migraine headache. The Beeboo project, which she had hoped might eventually run out of steam, seems set to run and run. To cap it all, she has bumped into, and deliberately ignored, Mercedes Glass. And Mercedes Glass, whose name came to her, in a flash, as she poured out the first of the wine could, possibly, have been worth stopping and talking to.

Mercedes Glass. Celina says the name out loud and lets her mind conjure up the wild-haired American whose backpack nearly felled her at the station. Mentally she replaces the unruly grey-and-green hair with a similarly unruly blue-black bush and sees, with a clarity that surprises her, the big wacky American artist who appeared – how many years ago? – at one of the first Beeboo book launches. She gulps down more wine and, bit by bit, memories start to flicker. Mercedes Glass had been at the launch because she had painted a mural on the publisher's wall – that was it. And had she not even given Celina her a business card, and urged her to contact, and go for a coffee?

The business card, bright and modern, with graffiti-style letters on a red brick background describing Mercedes as an 'environmental artist' had remained stuck to the fridge door for so long it had become part of the landscape, but Celina had never dialled the number on it. Despite a definite fellow-feeling – because there had been a fellow-feeling, hadn't there? – there had never been any coffees with Mercedes Glass, but when Celina tries to figure out why not, she draws a blank.

Abandoning the struggle to remember, and telling herself that, in any case, a reunion this afternoon would have been a complete disaster, Celina fast-forwards her thoughts to her present predicament and realises, to her surprise that, despite everything, part of her feels almost festive.

It is a feeling not dissimilar to the one she remembers on the last day of school, when she and Kalinda waited to be driven home for the holidays; a feeling of ordinary, tedious things ending and other, better, things beginning. For is there not to be the 'sabbatical'? And are sabbaticals not usually a year long? And a year, surely, would be long enough. To start with, anyway.

She heaves herself up and, rather unsteadily, makes her way over to her mother's easel where a blank canvas now sits in place of the badly-painted sky. Beside the easel is a paint-encrusted palette and some of Imogen's oil paints. Celina lifts one small, fat tube of Ultramarine and another, larger, one of Mixing White and, savouring the feel of their buckled metal, looks around the walls at her mother's skies, and mountains, and vast, desert spaces. Her head buzzes with a chaotic mix of pain and wine and simmering excitement.

From Imogen's vast array, she chooses a palette knife with a long flat blade and a bulbous little wooden handle. She squeezes two fat worms of paint, one white and one blue, onto the palette, fits her thumb through its oval hole and, with the knife's blunt blade, mixes one into the other till she has a mound of pale sky blue. Then she squeezes out another, larger, turd of the Ultramarine and, spooning the pure colour up onto the largest brush she can find, paints a series of bold horizontal lines across the top edge of the canvas. The colour is darkly magnificent and, not bothering to wipe the brush, she scoops up the pale blue and paints a block of colour lower down the canvas, so that now she has two large blue areas, dark above and pale below.

Her whole body is quivering now, and the remains of the headache forgotten. Choosing a stiff-bristled little brush, she begins to stipple the two blues together, gradually mixing and blending so that soon there is every shade of Ultramarine in her sky. Then she stands back, narrows her eyes, searches for flaws, for this sky of hers must fade imperceptibly to a white horizon line.

Slamming down the palette, she reaches over to the big earthenware jar and feels the bristles of each paintbrush in turn, squeezing them, splaying their hairs, imagining the effect they will have on the paint. Finally, she decides on the biggest, softest fan brush and, whispering it across the wet canvas, moves the colour back and forth, up and down, till very gradually it fades from dark to light without the slightest jarring line. With a clean brush, she adds pure white to her pale horizon then blends upwards, lightening the whole area save for the very top, which she leaves in all its darkly wonderful blueness. She fetches her glass, returns to the canvas and, drinking the wine down to its last dregs, appraises her first oil-painted sky. Downstairs, the phone rings.

The next stage for this painting – because it is not simply a wine-fuelled flight of fancy, but has been planned, off and on, these past few days – is to put in some animal bones as a foreground. It is not, of course, a very original idea. The walls of Imogen's studio are littered with prints of O'Keeffe's skulls and femurs, gleaming white against their badlands backdrop. Here in oh-so-civilised Highgate, however, in a studio packed with sun-whitened bones, it is the nearest she is going to get to emulating O'Keeffe and, by proxy, Imogen Wilde.

The pelvic bone of a sheep (cow? deer?), high on top of a bookshelf, catches her eye, and as it does the phone stops then immediately starts again. This time her conscience cuts in, for it could be Raine, or Luca and, sloshing some more wine into her glass, she negotiates the stairs to the bedroom.

"I've been trying to get you all day." Kalinda's voice is icy. "Where have you been? And have you ..."

Breezily, Celina interrupts. "Got them! Got the house papers! It's called Casa de la Luna Cresciente. The papers are all in Spanish of course, but definitely what Henderson wants. Definitely authentic."

There is a muted 'Good' from Kalinda, then a silence during which Celina takes as quiet a sip of wine as she can. "They're covered in official stamps and seals, and there's a map, and a plan of the house, which seems to have four rooms." She pauses, waits for some response from Kalinda, but Kalinda simply says, "Right ...?" and Celina grips the phone more tightly and, closing her eyes, feels the room spin.

"Did you know the house was called Casa de la Luna Cresciente? House of the Crescent Moon? Isn't that such a beautiful name? Reminds me of the House of the Rising Sun ..." She gives a kind of hiccup and tastes wine welling up.

"Are you drinking?" Kalinda says. "You sound drunk."

"No. Not at all. But I've had a terrible migraine." As Celina speaks she is aware that her legs are tingling and the contents of her stomach feel curdled. It must be the smell of the oil paints.

"Had an awful day, actually," she adds. "Really quite awful."

All of a sudden the awfulness of the day, made real by being spoken, brings her perilously close to tears. "Bad meeting with my editor," she goes on. "Abysmal meeting with my editor. Nearly threw up in the toilets. *I* nearly threw up in the toilets, I mean. Not the editor."

Kalinda is clearly unimpressed. "So, you'll take the papers to Henderson tomorrow then? Take them. Don't post them."

Celina listens to the silent house. Outside, near the window, a bird is singing, audaciously shrill and tuneful.

"Celina?"

"Yes, yes, of course. I'll take them. Next time I'm in town."

"Not the next time you're in town. Tomorrow."

"I'm not going in tomorrow. I can't do the Tube again tomorrow. Can't I just send them?"

There is an intake of breath from Kalinda's end of the line, but Celina cuts in. "Do you ever remember Mother telling us she met O'Keeffe? Because I found a photo of her, with 'Santa Fe, 1940' on the back. Do you suppose Mother took it?"

There is a long sigh from Kalinda. "You need to *see* Henderson. You need to discuss things with him."

"Do you remember? Mother saying she had met O'Keeffe?"

"Of course I remember her saying she met O'Keeffe. But 1940? I doubt you could travel to the States in wartime." Her tone ices up. "*See* him, Celina," she says. "*Ask* him things!"

"Daddy's name was Francisco Jesús, wasn't it?" The names slur together alarmingly.

"Francisco Jesús Quesada," Kalinda barks back. "*Are* you drunk?"

"I'd hoped, perhaps, there would be a photo of Daddy in Mother's studio, but there wasn't. It seems funny, not to even know what he looked like. Do you have any photos of him?"

Kalinda sighs a terminally deep sigh. "Look, Celina – I need to go. I don't have any photos of our father, and I doubt very much if Mother would have kept any, given the circumstances, but we can talk about it when I see you. We're still on for next week, aren't we? I'm going to phone Henderson in the morning" – she continues before Celina can protest – "and tell him you're coming in with the papers at 11.30. OK?"

"OK," Celina hears herself say. Then, "What do you mean by 'given the circumstances'? What 'circumstances'?"

"I'll come on Friday," Kalinda says wearily. "Go and drink some coffee."

Celina replaces the phone and tries to call to mind what she was doing before it rang. It had been something important, but what?. Draining her glass, she retraces her steps and then remembers. The bones. She was going to get the bones.

Climbing back up to the studio, she drags Imogen's footstool from its place by her chair and reaches up for the pelvis. After several attempts she manages to grab it, but as she pulls it down a whole array of tiny toe-bones and vertebrae rain onto her head. Sitting on the footstool, she holds the bone up to the window and, through one of its holes, examines the darkening sky.

This is what she will paint. On top of the blue sky whose horizon fades to white, she will superimpose the bony landscape of hills and valleys and tiny fissures, and inside it she will paint the view from the window. And, what is more, she will sleep up here too. She will paint and eat and drink wine and smoke and sleep here, in her mother's room, in her mother's clean white bed underneath *Hills – Lavender* and then, somehow, it will all be all right.

She looks over at the bed with its lace-trimmed counterpane and plump white pillows, and the thought occurs to her that there, in her mother's most intimate place, she might dream her mother's dreams, but she brushes it aside and pulls down the heavy blinds. Then she feels her way in the darkness, hands outstretched, to the crisp clean cotton, the antique Spanish lace.

Leaving her shirt and trousers in a crumpled pile on the floor, she lifts the counterpane and sniffs the interior, but there is only the faint soap smell from the very last laundry and she clambers in, stretches her legs down into the smooth cotton coolness, and watches darkness spin.

So alarmingly does it spin that for a moment or two she wonders whether she might be sick, and the thought of defiling the pure white bed makes her sit up and throw the covers back off. But the comfort of the bed draws her back, and she rolls onto her side, draws her legs up, and shuts her eyes once more.

What, after all, does it matter if she messes the bed? If she does, she can simply strip it and put on fresh sheets. There will be no more temper tantrums, no more fuss, no more guilt trips, nothing. For now there is no mother to infect her with her own frustrations and fears; no mother to look down her lofty nose at her. There is no mother any more to stop her from doing anything she wants to do.

CHAPTER SIX

The morning Underground ride to give Henderson the house papers is, if anything, worse than the previous afternoon's and, pulling on a cigarette, Celina recuperates on a bench in the shadow of St Paul's.

Letting the exhaled smoke waft over her face, she wonders whether passers-by, peering through the smoke-screen, can see the tell-tale signs of a woman who, last night, passed out in a drunken stupor in her dead mother's bed, and decides they probably can not. The chances are that not one person even sees she is there, for the days when men and woman alike craned their necks to admire her flawless skin and dark eyes and sleek blue-black hair are gone. Nowadays, despite religiously-applied moisturisers, and carefully-shampooed-in colourants, and meticulously shaped and lacquered fingernails, she is invisible, hidden behind the grey smoke-screen of middle-age.

The previous night had been utterly dreadful. When she had first crawled into her mother's bed she had fallen asleep almost immediately, but it had been more of a passing-out than a proper sleep, and it had taken her into the old familiar dream she always feared. At first, when she woke to perfect darkness, she did not know where she was, and then the smell of the oil paints told her and she lay, unable to move, realising the enormity of what she had done when she dared to pick up her mother's paints. For the dream had never been so vivid; its blues had never glowed with such intensity and its reds had never seemed so dangerous. And that smell – the smell of Imogen's paints – had overlaid it all.

Eventually, nausea compelled her to wrench herself out from beneath the sheets, but the bedding clung, tight and damp, and when she managed to emerge, like some hideous insect from its pupa, she had to sit for a while, head on hands, letting the room rotate around her.

Then, all of a sudden, her stomach spasmed and she knew she must vomit. Feeling her way in the darkness, she reached the studio's bathroom as the stuff rose into her mouth and then, unable to face the bed again, had dragged herself downstairs.

It was still quite early – just after eleven – and she badly needed to talk to someone, for if she could talk, the nightmare colours might fade and the feelings of disembodiment go. But she could think of no one to whom, at nearly midnight, she could confide, nor any words to describe feelings so bizarre as hers. In the end, she had made herself a milky drink and, curled up in the chair by the fire, had let the television soothe her as best it could.

Despite all her efforts, however, the dream-images remained bright, and the familiarity of the room, rather than being a comfort, added to her distress, because she could feel no connection with anything there. She was as insubstantial as a ghost, haunting her own house.

Now, as St Paul's strikes the quarter, she stubs out her

cigarette. Shading her eyes against the sunlight, she looks around at the benches and shrubs and pathways, trying to feel the reality of the day; but the nameless fear the dream always evokes clings, like oil. Straightening her back, she takes a deep breath and heads off in the direction of Henderson's office.

With any luck, the handing-over of the house papers will take less than five minutes, leaving her free to do whatever she wants, and panic is already building at the thought. For, once her duty for the day is done, what *does* she want to do? Where on earth does Celina Wilde want to go?

Not back to the north-lit studio to paint bones on the great blue canvas, of that she is sure. The old fear has well and truly washed that grand scheme away. And as she pushes her way through the revolving door into Henderson and Fox's gleaming white premises, the thought comes to Celina that all she can do is return to the safe, tedious little world of Beeboo and Lord Dragoo and the Swamplice. Her stomach rolls and she tastes stale wine in her mouth, and wonders if she smells of it.

"These are the papers for Mr Henderson," she tells the receptionist, half-turning away to underline the fact she does not intend to stay. "I'll phone him later in the week." She begins to walk towards the door.

"Mrs Sinclair!" the receptionist calls. "Could I have a word please?"

Celina cups her mouth with a surreptitious hand and breathes out. There is definitely a smell of stale smoke and bad wine. She turns back and attempts a smile at the receptionist who, echoing the smile, reveals a perfect set of squeaky-clean teeth.

"I wonder if you could just take a seat, Mrs Sinclair?" The receptionist indicates a rich brown waiting-area equipped with settees, a drinks machine, and a magazine-strewn glass table devoid of ashtrays. "Help yourself to a coffee. Mr Henderson's with a client, but he won't be long and he would really like to speak to you."

Defeated, Celina fills a mug with black coffee, takes a magazine and sits on the settee. If the receptionist was not there, she would consider closing her eyes, but as it is, she sips the coffee and, despite herself, allows her thoughts to return to last night.

The milky drink had soothed her stomach enough that eventually, at around midnight, she had actually felt hungry and had gone into the kitchen where, ignoring Max's letter, she made herself a peanut butter sandwich. Accompanied by a mercifully muted Mrs Thatcher celebrating ten glorious years in office, she ate the sandwich and tried to think of other things, but the dream's clawing anxiety remained. She was like a small child, after an unspeakable nightmare, with no warm parental bed into which to crawl.

Eventually, Margaret Thatcher having been replaced by the black-and-white image of a man with a waxed moustache, with the words 'Salvador Dali 1904 – 1989' printed underneath, she turned the set off. Then she found her address book and curled up with it on her knee.

It was, of course, ridiculously late to call anyone now, but the need to hear her own voice and thus prove her own reality had become a desperate need. There must, surely, be someone, somewhere, she could talk to. Not, obviously, about the dream and the weird feelings of dissolution it had triggered, but about Max. If your husband left you, you were allowed to phone someone late at night, weren't you? And perhaps, if she talked about that, and about Luca and Raine, and about all the down-to-earth, practical problems Max's leaving was going to cause them all, perhaps then the wordless fear would dissipate and she would get things into perspective.

Finding someone to talk to, however, had proved impossible. Despite her earlier reservations, she had rung the saintly Pippa first. The lunacy of the idea had, however, kicked in after the first dialling tone, for of course Pippa would insist on coming over, and would talk in kindly platitudes all night. She might even, if the worst came to the worst, invoke the name of Jesus. At the third tone, Celina hung up.

Then she had toyed with the idea of ringing Anna, but had decided against that too because Anna, like Pippa, would be with her in a flash, and would be bound to bring a bottle of wine, which she would proceed to drink herself. She would then spend the rest of the night talking about all the bastard men she had ever known, and in the morning Celina would have to listen to a reprise of the 'bastard men' over breakfast; and when Anna finally left she would feel more washed-out and wretched than before.

Zareen, likewise, was quickly dismissed because Zareen, though remaining reasonably sober, would be sure to segue neatly into a lengthy account of her own divorce, and the signs she had missed and everyone else had suspected but had not liked to say; and it would turn out that she, Zareen, had had her suspicions about Max and Felicity for simply yonks and was dumbfounded, simply dumbfounded, that Celina had not …

Eventually, when it really was far too late to phone anyone, Celina had found a Diazepam tablet left over from God-knows-what crisis, crawled into the marital bed and, horribly aware of Max's lurking smell, had curled up as near the edge as possible and lay, more or less awake, all night.

The sharp eau-de-cologne scent which always precedes Henderson brings her back to the present, and its familiarity is vaguely reassuring. "Celina," he says as she struggles up, "how are you?" Then, taking her elbow as though she were an invalid, he eases her back down and squeezes her hand in both of his.

"I'm fine," Celina says, defensively. "I just came to give you the papers. I gave them to your receptionist. To Carol," she adds, recalling the name badge pinned to Carol's pert bosom. "They're in Spanish and of course I don't really ..."

"Celina, Celina ..." Henderson is shaking his big head and smiling at her. "Max phoned me. I'm so sorry."

She stares down at a magazine on the table, from whose front cover an unnaturally beautiful couple smile out. They are lying on an enormous four-poster bed that appears to be made of gold. A flaxen-haired baby sits between them, a beatific smile on its doll-like face and one porcelain hand stretching towards the camera. 'After all the agony', the caption reads, 'Amelie has found true love at last.' Celina reads the caption, over and over again. 'Agony' she thinks, is a good word.

"Celina?" Henderson's hand is on her shoulder now, and he is kneading it with one big thumb. "You know if there is anything at all I can do ..."

"I'm fine," she assures him again. "It wasn't a surprise." She squirms free and moves along the settee into her own space where she straightens her back to stop everything giving way; because actually, Max's leaving *was* a surprise. It was a relief and an insult too, but mainly it was a surprise, and no way on God's earth is she sobbing into Henderson's eau-de-cologned shoulder over it.

"When do you think you'll be able to deal with the house papers?" she says, re-reading the magazine caption rather than look at him.

"He wants a divorce, Celina," she hears him say.

"Perhaps we could go into my office?"

She knows, of course, that she should. She should let him lead her into his neon-white space, and she should ask him if it is all right to smoke, and he will say 'Of course' and give her an ashtray, and then she should sit very still and let him tell her the ins and outs of divorces. Then, armed with a plan, she should go home and phone Kalinda and tell her all about it, and when Luca and Raine get home she should tell them too although, somehow, she has a sneaking suspicion Luca may already know.

But she cannot talk with Henderson now. It is as much as she can do to stand up and brush out the creases in her jacket and fold it over her arm, then press her briefcase to her chest and, muttering something about making an appointment later in the week, sidle round the table and march towards the door with her head held as high as she can possibly hold it.

As she walks she is aware of Henderson shadowing her, telling her he will let her know as soon as possible what must be done about the Casa de la Luna Cresciente, but all she is really thinking about is being somewhere, alone, with a cigarette and – finally, finally – phoning someone.

Emerging from the revolving door, she heads back to St Paul's and finds a relatively clean telephone box. Setting her handbag on its ledge she takes a packet of cigarettes, and a small address book, out of the handbag and flicks over all the names she rejected last night. To her surprise, she finds Rhianna's and wonders why on earth she did not think of her right away, because Rhianna, unlike all her other friends, managed never to meet Max, which makes her the perfect choice.

After a few rings an answering machine cuts in, and she hangs up. St Paul's twelve o' clock bells begin to chime as she pushes herself out and, putting on her jacket again, walks in the direction of Ludgate Hill. Perhaps the shaky legs and the disembodied feeling is partly because she needs to eat, so she goes into a coffee shop and orders coffee and a sandwich.

The atmosphere in the coffee shop is warm and damp and, slipping her jacket off and feeling inside its pocket for a tissue, Celina finds the pink business card of Inge van Deth, the German – or Dutch? – therapist who enabled poor wheezy Melanie to see her life differently. She lays the card on the table, and as she pecks at her sandwich and drinks her coffee she keeps looking at it and reading it. When she has finished, she walks back to the phone box, dials the number, and listens to a recording of Inge van Deth urging her to leave a message to which she will reply as soon as possible.

The voice, with its low, steady timbre and gentle burr of an accent, is reassuring, and as Celina pushes her way back out into the street, the sun is almost warm on her face.

CHAPTER SEVEN

Two days later, on a cold but sunny morning, Celina stands on the threshold of Inge van Deth's practice.

The practice is in an affluent area, and there is an array of eight buzzers at the side of its door, each with its own smart brass nameplate, and as she pushes the one labelled 'Inge van Deth, Psychotherapist' she pictures a wizened old lady with snow-white plaits wound round each ear, like braided headphones. There is, however, nothing remotely moribund about the woman who opens the door and, with a reserved smile and a jaunty swing of her flowery skirts, ushers her into a wide tiled hall, then downstairs to a low-ceilinged basement room.

The room is instantly comforting. Painted in whites and creams, it smells herbal – of rosemary perhaps – and Celina is reassured by this subtle promise of healing. The lighting is comforting too, with fat white candles giving it a sacred quality, and in one corner there is a low table made of pale pine, on which sits a scattering of jade animals and a box of paper tissues. On either side of the table is an armchair made of fine-grained white leather, and the armchairs are round and plump. They remind Celina of white marshmallows.

Taking Celina's jacket, Inge gestures towards the chairs. "Sit wherever you like," she tells her, as she hangs the jacket on the back of the door. When Celina is seated, she lowers herself into the chair opposite, pushes her hair behind her ears, and smiles the reserved smile once again.

Celina has chosen to sit in the first chair, with her back to the door, partly because it feels more sheltered, and partly because there is a painting on the facing wall which draws her. White-framed, it shows a pale duck-egg blue sky above a sea whose low grey waves move to and fro, like salty heartbeats. It, and the rosemary smell, and the candles, make the room feel like a place apart, in which secrets can be divulged and forgiveness granted.

Not only that, now that she has the time to look she sees that Inge, despite her strong young voice on the phone, has traces of grey in the brown of her hair and the tiniest of age-lines around her mouth.

"So," Inge says, "why don't you tell me first what has happened, why you have come?"

This is, of course, the very question Celina has been dreading ever since, two days ago, Inge returned her message, and in those two ghastly days she has rehearsed her answer well.

"My mother died three months ago, and my husband left me four days ago," she says, aware that she is speaking haltingly, like an actor not entirely sure of their lines. Then, abandoning her script, she lets the words flow out by themselves, punctuated by tiny intakes of breath, as though each phrase takes so much effort it makes her gasp for air.

"I'm very confused and upset and, although I have lots of friends, and a sister – a twin sister actually – I seem to have absolutely no one to talk to. Almost all my friends –

the friends I could speak to – know me as Max's wife and somehow, for a variety of reasons, that makes me uncomfortable."

She looks at Inge, hoping for comment and, when none is made and a little questioning frown given instead, she continues. "I can't work. Or, I should say my work is suffering; and I can't sleep, and I've been having migraines and nightmares and weird feelings, as though I'm separated off from reality. I seem to have no control over anything and the feelings – the detached feelings – scare me. I think, perhaps, I know why I get them ..."

Her voice tails away then and tears roll down her cheeks faster than she can wipe them away. Inge pushes the box of tissues towards her and half-withdraws the top one.

"I never cry," Celina says. "I'm good at coping, usually. It's just that it's been so much, all at once. Too many life-changing things coming all together, and it's kind of floored me. And I haven't been able to talk to anyone about it and now, when I do, it feels odd. Like taking your clothes off in public. I've never had psychiatric help before, you know. When I have problems I just get on with it, but this time I can't seem to."

She gives what she hopes is a bravely cynical laugh and then, in case Inge should think her flippant, adds, "I'm actually a bit of a wreck at the moment, and I'm dying for a cigarette, but I don't suppose ..."

She searches for signs of disapproval in Inge's healthy, freckled face, but if Inge disapproves, she does not show it. "Perhaps," she says, with a small, apologetic shake of the head, "we start with your mother? Tell me how your mother's death makes you feel?"

Celina blows her nose, takes a deep breath and, staring at the painted sea, tries to quieten her mind sufficiently to explain exactly how her mother's death makes her feel;

but although she tries very hard to give a clear account of herself, as soon as she begins to talk she finds she has lost her grasp of time sequence, syntax, and normal grammatical sentence structure.

"The night – the morning – the early morning – when they phoned me, the people from the Nursing Home – to tell me she had died – because I was not with her when she died, you see; I had been with her that day, twice, and she seemed stable and they had told me it would be all right to go home, but then it was, in the end, quite sudden and without warning, at three in the morning or thereabouts ..." The tears are flowing copiously and it occurs to Celina that perhaps these tears, and all her subsequent unshed tears, have been building up for months and months, and now that the dam has been breached they will never, ever stop. Despite the tears, or perhaps because of them, she allows her words, relieved of their need to be in tidy sentences, to continue to tumble and trip over one another, jumping and jostling to be out.

"I listened to them telling me she had died, and how she had died, and who had been with her and so on, and I was only half-listening, and that was when I first noticed that I was afraid. Just afraid, nothing else. There was no grief. I don't remember any grief. There was only the initial shock, even though it shouldn't have been a shock really because I knew it was going to happen, and then the fear.

"I remember I lay there, in the bed, for a while after the call, not waking my husband, and I was looking over at the dressing table which I could just make out in the darkness, and I was wondering, Why am I scared? and I didn't understand why I was, but I was. I was scared witless, and ever since then, whenever I lie in bed in the half-light and look over at the dressing table, I remember that fear, and I still wonder why I felt it."

She takes her eyes off the sea to look at Inge, but Inge's

face is as expressionless as ever. "Yes, I wonder what you were afraid of?" she says. "Are perhaps still afraid of?"

There is a long silence during which Celina considers this. She has often considered it before, of course; mainly at night while Max snored beside her and lately, increasingly, when she has been cooking or walking or attempting to draw. Always, though, she has considered it alone but now, in Inge's underground world, under Inge's watchful eyes, it is different. Safer, and yet at the same time more dangerous.

"I've thought of all kinds of reasons why my mother's death should have frightened me," she begins slowly. "But I don't think any of them accounts for how badly I felt when I was told she was dead. I mean, I certainly wasn't afraid of missing her, because there was never affection between us, even when I was a child. My mother lived for her work, you see. For her art."

There is a sharpness in her voice now that makes her stop, and as she listens to the echo of her own words, heat flushes her cheeks. "We were made very aware of the fact that Mother was a famous artist," she goes on, aware her voice is rising. "We were never allowed into her studio, my sister and I, when she was working. It was expressly forbidden, and we never ever broke the rule ..."

A choking sensation, as though something has closed over her windpipe, forces her to stop, and she looks over at Inge to check whether she has spotted the lie. Nothing in Inge's face shows disapproval or condemnation however and, covering her mouth with a new paper tissue, Celina waits till her throat is relaxed enough to allow her to swallow.

"And then there was the fear that with my mother gone I'd be forced to be closer to my sister," she continues, moving into safer territory, "and that has been rather difficult, but on the other hand it hasn't been that bad. I mean" – she gives a little laugh – "we haven't killed one another yet."

A wave of exhaustion hits her and she sinks back into the chair. "I honestly don't know why I was afraid," she says, and though she speaks in a tired, helpless way, nevertheless a small note of defiance creeps into her voice. "I thought perhaps you might be able to help me with that?"

She stares at Inge. Candle wax sizzles in the silence.

"So you were not at all close," Inge says, "your mother and you?"

Celina shakes her head. "We were very distant. All my life, I held my mother at arms' length and she did the same to me. But even so" – a jolt of surprise makes her sit up – "my life revolved around hers. At the end particularly, but in a sense always."

"And it is hard to have lost that centre? You are perhaps no longer sure which way to go?"

An image of Imogen floating in the sky with a fifty-year old foetus orbiting around her like a small pink moon pops into Celina's mind. She holds onto the image, seeing the cord that joins them stretching further and further, becoming thinner and thinner, till it shears right through. Sleepily, she sees herself floating away, the cut end dangling uselessly in space; and as she watches she wonders vaguely where Kalinda is, because surely she should have been joined too. Then, in the silence Inge allows her, she steers her thoughts back to the morning she heard about her mother's death.

It was a grey, cold light, that November moonlight, and it drained light and life from everything it touched. On the dressing table the perfume bottles, the hairbrush, the photo of Raine at three, wearing a yellow sun hat, all were reduced to monotone, and as the voice on the phone rumbled on she had only heard disjointed words and phrases ... no pain ... was not alone ... no distress ... peaceful ... too quick for us to call you but then that's such a blessing ... and all the while she had stared and stared at Raine's beaming, dimpled face, and the ice cream she held out to the camera, and the grey sun hat that was really yellow, and it was when, at last, the voice stopped and she rolled over to wake Max, that the fear hit her like a wall of water.

"Perhaps that's what it was," she tells Inge at last. "Perhaps I was afraid because I realised that without my mother to worry about, I would have to think about my own life, and there were things about it that I didn't – that I don't – like. Yes – I think that's partly it. But there's something else. There's another reason, a much worse reason."

She is holding the paper tissue, soaked with her tears, and now she twists and pulls at it, drawing it out as far as it can go without breaking, then forming it into a circle round her forefinger.

"It's somewhere, inside my head, but like a shadow, or something you see in the periphery of your vision and when you turn to look at it, it disappears." She bends her finger, further and further, till the tissue ring tears in two. "Do you know what I mean?"

There is the tiniest movement of Inge's head; the hint of a nod. "It frightens you to look directly at it, perhaps?" she says, and then she smiles – more openly this time – and it is such a wise, empathetic smile that Celina feels tears welling up again. Because of course that is exactly, precisely it.

"This awful way I'm feeling can't possibly be bereavement, because really my mother's death was a blessing, a relief," she says, wondering at the words, which surely come from some other, wiser, Celina. "It's a terrible thing to say, but I wanted it to happen. I wanted –

so desperately wanted – my mother to go. Sometimes, before she was ill, I would catch myself thinking that she would never, ever die; that she was actually immortal. And I would tell myself not to be stupid, that it was a nonsensical thing to think, till one day I realised that of course it wasn't. It wasn't the least bit nonsensical, because if I died young, and my mother outlived me, she *would* never die. As far as I was concerned, I mean. And then I would never ..."

In the marshmallow chair it is impossible to sit up straight, and Celina kicks off her shoes, draws her feet up under her, covers her face with both her hands and then, all of a sudden, she begins to howl.

The howls are not loud. They are long and low, as though coming from some dark unknown place deep inside her, but they rumble on and on, orgasmic in the way they feed on themselves and gain momentum. And though she is doubled in on herself, howling and weeping into the privacy of her own hands, Celina still feels the nearness of Inge, and at last it is this knowledge that makes her stop as suddenly as she began.

Horrified beyond measure, she jumps to her feet and shuffles into her shoes. Grabbing a handful of tissues, she dries her eyes and then, standing, looks at the floor, the table, the jade animals.

"I'm sorry," she says. "I can't do this. I knew I couldn't ..." She dares a glance at Inge, but Inge is completely still and calm, as though nothing whatsoever has happened.

"And then you would never ...?" she says, but Celina is looking round for her jacket, then walking towards it, saying, "I can't. I have to go. I'll send you a cheque." Still Inge does not move, and it is only when Celina has pulled the jacket on and hoisted her bag onto her shoulder that she speaks again.

"Perhaps, if you would like to go outside and have a

cigarette?" she says very gently. "We still have a lot of our hour left. You can take your time. Think, perhaps, of what you did not allow yourself to say just then? Of what you would 'never' do …?"

Without committing herself to returning, Celina slips out and up the stairs, and as she runs towards the front door her hands claw at the fastening of her bag and stir about inside. By the time she pulls the door open she has a cigarette in her mouth, and she hunches her shoulders against the rain that has begun to fall, and lights it. Leaning against the wall, she stares out at the shiny pavements and re-runs what has just been said in the basement room. In particular, she re-runs the sentence she did not allow herself to complete; the sentence that led to those appalling howls.

They had not reached their climax, those howls, for she had not allowed them to. But if they had, and that climax had words, what would those words have been?

She finishes the cigarette, lights another, and forces her thoughts back to the thing that always lurks, hazy and out of focus, at the periphery of her vision. With each of those terrible howls of hers, had it not begun to come into focus?

She stubs the cigarette out on the wall and throws the butt away. For a moment longer she stands on the step, balanced between staying and leaving. Then she turns and walks back into the hall, the clip of her heels marking time on the tiled floor.

CHAPTER EIGHT

When Celina pushes the door of Inge's consulting-room open and breathes the rosemary smell again, she could swear that Inge has not moved a single muscle but has sat, quite still, at Celina's service, in Celina's absence.

Then she sees that, actually, Inge must have moved, because a glass of water now sits on the table, between the tissues and the jade animals. With an apologetic smile, she hangs up her jacket and sits back down.

"Sorry about that," she says, and she sips some of the water. "I know I shouldn't need to …"

In answer, Inge inclines her head slightly. 'Go on,' her body language tells Celina. 'You have made your dramatic exit, and now you have made another entrance. The stage, once more, is yours.'

Celina withdraws a bundle of paper hankies from the box and moulds them into a loose ball. "There's something I need to talk about," she says. "I know I need to tell someone about it, because I'm sure it's somehow at the root of everything, but up till now I've never been able to …"

She pummels the ball of paper. "It's difficult, because it's so deeply personal, and so difficult to put into words, and so frightening."

Inge observes her for a few moments. "It might help your current anxiety if you were able to bring it to the surface," she says quietly.

Celina breathes in. "It's something that happened in my early childhood," she says. "It scared me to death and it changed me, I think, for ever. Limited me, always. The trouble is, I don't remember it properly. Bits of it are missed out, as though I know they're there but I can't quite see them. I often dream it, too, so that sometimes I wonder if perhaps it is only a dream, or a story. Like when you think you remember doing something, but it's because someone told you about it so often that it's the story you remember rather than the actual thing."

"Try," Inge says. "Try to verbalise it."

"It's not just a story, or a dream. I'm sure it's not. It is an actual memory, because parts of it are so real, so vivid, they can't just have been a dream or something somebody told me. I've dreamt it several times since my mother's death, and woken in such a terrible state of unease, as though I'm fragmented ..."

As she says the word 'fragmented', Celina shivers at its brutality. Wrapping her arms round her chest she hugs herself, holds the atoms of her body together. "As though I'm separated from reality," she continues. "As though I don't properly exist."

Releasing herself, she takes a drink of water and concentrates on its coldness. "Sometimes, after I have the dream, I can't shake off its aftertaste for days, and often, when I'm feeling like that, I'll have a migraine. I'm having them quite often," she adds. "I'm told they're hormonal, and of course I'm at that time of life ..."

"So, what do you think causes the dream?"

Celina clutches the ball of tissues to her mouth. Heat waves are rolling up from her legs to her groin, and the water seems to have closed her gullet. "I'm sorry," she says. "I feel a bit sick."

Sitting back in her chair, she forces herself to take deep breaths. "It's the smell of oil paint," she says. "That's what brings on the dream, and the migraines, and the feelings of being cut off from everything. It's as though the smell draws me back to a memory, and that draw is so hard, it takes my whole being with it. It separates me off from reality."

"You become," Inge says, "dissociated."

The moment she hears Inge's word, Celina feels calmer. If Inge has a name for it, someone else must have had it.

"It's always been there, just under the surface, that thing with the oil paint smell," she continues. "When I was a child, I hated going near Mother's studio because of it, and anyway Mother expressly forbade us to go into her studio, and half the time I was away at school, or she was away, painting or exhibiting, and someone else looked after us …"

She kneads the tissue ball angrily. "But when I grew up, I wanted to be an artist too, so I went to Art School and that was when the smell thing hit me. It knocked me sideways, actually, because I'd almost forgotten about it by then. All the same" – she clenches and unclenches the hand with the tissue – "I never completely forgot about it, because it was why I chose Illustration and Design rather than Painting, which I would have preferred …"

She feels her throat close again, as though a band is tightening round her neck.

"It must have been hard," Inge says, "to be constantly in such an anxiety-provoking environment?"

Celina looks wildly round the room, panic building, and

then her eyes focus on the pattern of flowers in Inge's flowing skirt, and she imagines herself drawing the flowers, distorting their shapes to make the material fall in ripples and folds, then filling the folds with shadow to give them form. She swallows, and continues.

"I suppose I must have got used to it. I remember, sometimes, I'd have panic attacks and have to leave lectures, and I assume the panic would be triggered by sitting beside someone who had that smell about them. But I survived" – she sits up as straight as the chair allows – "because I am a survivor, you know. I get what I want, sooner or later. And Art was – is – what I want. Painting," she corrects herself, "is what I want."

She can feel tears again, burning to flow. Briskly, she wipes them away.

"I have a name for the dream, and the feeling the dream gives me," she says. "It's a very silly name, and I've never told it to anyone, ever. I've never spoken it aloud." She glances up at Inge, who inclines her head invitingly.

"I call it the 'Schism'." The word barks its way out, and when it has gone Celina covers her mouth in shame. It feels like shouting the most vulgar, the most forbidden, word. "It's such a silly name, 'Schism', isn't it?" she says. "I discovered it when I was about nine. Heaven knows where, for I was never a particularly bookish child …

"I think perhaps it made me think of 'chasms' and 'schizo', and gaping rifts, and so it became my secret way of referring to the feelings I couldn't really handle." She stops, her face still hot with shame. "Does that make any sense? Do you understand?"

A slight furrow appears in Inge's forehead but she gives a nod and now, because 'Schism' is out in the open and Inge is still there, and the candles still flicker and the sea in the picture continues to breathe in and out, Celina feels a little of Inge's calmness settle around her.

"So," Inge says, "can you, perhaps, tell what you remember of the incident which gave rise to the Schism?"

As the private word comes from someone else's lips, Celina relaxes back in the chair. "I was very, very small when it happened," she says, "because in my memory everything is very big. I remember I went up to my mother's studio, and pushed the door open. I didn't knock, or make a noise. I just pushed the door open without a word. I must have needed something, or been upset or ill I think, because, as I told you, we were never, ever allowed to disturb Mother in her studio. It was drummed into us."

She stretches out her fingers and looks down at the naked ring finger of her left hand, and the unaccustomed chips in the bright red of her nail varnish. Her fingers, she finds herself thinking, are beautifully shaped. They are quite unlike Imogen's. For all her elegance, Imogen had lumpy hands.

"And when I pushed the door open," she goes on, "I had a most terrible sense of foreboding, and I'm sure it wasn't simply because I knew there would be a dreadful row if I disturbed Mother at her work. It was something else; something entirely else. It was as though, as soon as the door swung open, something awful drew me in."

Her throat closes again. "Go on," she hears Inge urge. "You are fine."

"My mother was standing, with her back to me, facing her easel. She was wearing a cornflower blue dress, covered in bright red poppies. I remember it so clearly, the dress. I can still see it, in my mind's eye, as clear as day. I know I didn't dream the dress."

She takes a sip of water and holds the glass against her chin. "My mother must have heard me, because she turned and looked down at me, and I always remember her being so tall, so high above me. And it was then, when she turned, that I knew I had committed a dreadful, unforgivable, crime."

Once more, as Celina's throat constricts, Inge gives her that same nod, that same calmly questioning smile. Patiently, she waits till she is ready to speak again.

"I can't explain why it was a crime" – Celina bangs the glass down on the table with such force that the jade animals jump – "or why it was unforgivable, and I don't know what happened next, other than a confusion of angry noise and movement. It is as though I ceased to exist. As though" – her voice falters now, because there are no words on earth for this – "as though the wrong I did, coming into my mother's studio that day, was the end of everything."

There is a low buzzing in her head. She looks up at the sea picture, at the deep brown colour at the base of the waves that gives them both solidity and translucency, and tries to summon words to express the ineffable.

"And it was," she says at last. "It was the end of everything. Because after it my father left, and we never saw him again, and my mother was always angry."

She sobs into what is left of the damp ball of paper and sees, out of the corner of her eye, that Inge has withdrawn a whole new, dry, bundle for her. Taking the bundle, she holds it to her face. The tissues, she notices for the first time, are perfumed. They smell of roses.

CHAPTER NINE

"And you know that it was you – a tiny little girl – who caused your father to leave and never return?" Though Inge's voice is gentle, there is just the ghost of a smile on her face

Celina glares at her. "I've never doubted it, ever."

She is leaning forward now and her back, separated from the chair, feels damply cold. In some other, everyday, part of her brain, she hopes she has not marked the marshmallow.

"So why are you so very sure that your father's leaving was your fault, Celina?"

It is the first time Inge has used her name, and though comforting, that use of her name is also challenging, for it implies collusion. Whatever happens now, they are in it together. Aware, now, that time must be running out because there is something in Inge's energy – a subtle change of expression and a shift in her position in the chair – which suggests that the hour must be almost over, Celina frowns with the effort of concentrating for the last minutes.

"I just do," she says, aware that the earlier confidence has left her voice, and now it sounds weak and childlike. "In fact, I remember that for a while I thought he had died, but then Mother must have explained to us that he had just gone away, so then I knew I hadn't killed him. Although I often used to wonder whether Mother was telling the truth, and I still wonder. I wouldn't put it past her to have hidden his death from us. But whatever it was, going away or dying" – she gives Inge what she hopes is a look of steely determination – "it was my fault."

Inge leans a little nearer. "You know, Celina," she says, "you were only a baby."

There is a strange clicking sound in Celina's throat as she breathes in, and for the tiniest of moments a feeling of elation washes over her and she wonders if there might be a bubble of laughter trapped down there, trying to escape.

"Kalinda, my twin, thinks it was my fault too. She said it, once, when we were about ten. 'Daddy left because of you,' she said."

She glares once more at Inge, daring her to argue, but Inge merely raises an eyebrow, and Celina hears the leather of her chair creak.

"At any rate," she concludes, "ever since I opened up my mother's studio last week, and began to use her paints, that sense of wrongdoing has got much, much worse and the feelings of dissociation have scared me more than I ever remember. Which is why I came." Not taking her eyes off Inge, she reaches down for her bag. "It's time to stop, isn't it?"

Inge nods. "Perhaps, before we do," she says, "you might complete the sentence you left hanging in the air? 'And then I would never …?'"

Celina searches in her bag for her cheque book. The answer to Inge's question is so easy, now. "If my mother had not died, then I would never have looked for my father. With her alive, I wouldn't have dared. How much do I owe you?"

Inge stands. "£25. And shall we make an appointment for the same time next week?"

Celina pictures an entire week stretching before her. "Perhaps I could come sooner? Could I?"

Inge goes to her desk and leafs through a diary. "I'm afraid I am fully booked till then. But I write you in for next Thursday? At two o' clock?" and she indicates that Celina is now free to thank her and go.

Outside, rain is still falling. Standing on the top step, breathing in the smell of the soaked streets, Celina wonders what to do next. Her mind is numb, as though she has been robbed of all thought and yet, strangely, her senses are more acute than usual. There is a dreamlike clarity to the shiny pavements and the bare trees with their tight, tiny green buds; a sense of expectancy, of things waiting to burst out. For a few minutes, she continues to stand on Inge's threshold, watching it all. Then, all at once, the need for coffee propels her out into the rain, and she walks smartly along tree-lined streets till she finds a café.

Once inside, she sees that the café is actually a small arts centre, its foyer filled with tables strewn with booklets and flyers, and its notice boards crammed with exhibition notices and cinema posters. Several open doors lead into galleries, each with a young person sitting on a chair beside it, holding a sheaf of leaflets.

Ignoring the inviting smiles of the seated young people, Celina walks over to one of the tables, rifles among the booklets, and picks out a directory of London artists and their studios. Then, following the scent of coffee, she walks into a café area and buys a coffee and a cereal bar from the emaciated young woman at the counter. Seated at a table covered in red oilskin, she flicks through the

'G' section of the directory. As she checks each name, she runs through her memories of Mercedes Glass which, over the past two days, have become less and less hazy. Their meeting has, in fact, come back to her in some detail.

It was in 1976, the launch at which they met. She knows that for sure, because 1974 was the year the very first book in the Beeboo series came out, and in 1975 it won a big award and she and Bryony Garden, the author, were given contracts for a series. They had both worked like dervishes to have the second book ready for publication in time and, as soon as it was poised to hit the shelves, the publishers pulled out every available stop to provide as impressive a splash as possible.

Mercedes was commissioned to do the mural of Lord Dragoo and the Aliens, and a huge number of influential people – educationalists and TV people, and some teachers and librarians – were invited; and, to provide a suitable audience for Bryony's reading, there were also a couple of classes of pre-fives from the local nursery school.

The launch had been billed, on dragon-shaped, silvered invitations, as an 'Alien Party' and the children kitted out in little padded satin costumes, with silver plastic hats with cherries and bananas dangling from them. The combination of the costumes, and the cameras, and the lashings of green lemonade soon pushed them into a welter of over-excitement, and before long they were screaming and running around in circles like small fat brightly-coloured maniacs. In the middle of the screaming circle the two of them, Mercedes and she, had stood clutching their glasses of awful green liquid, miserably far from their comfort zones.

In contrast, the flaxen-haired author was in her element. She, too, had come prepared for the party, having found (or knitted?) a Beeboo jumper in bright fluffy wool, and sporting cherry earrings with flashing lights inside. She had brought along a guitar and a passable singing voice with which she roundly entertained the few children who could be coerced into sitting down for more than ten seconds.

There had been songs about the Aliens and their fruits of choice, and a very long and complex Lord Dragoo song, whose dizzying selection of actions and sound effects had proved way beyond Mercedes and Celina, but which was, evidently, tremendous fun for Bryony and the children. To begin with, Celina had done her best to keep up her enthusiasm, because she was painfully aware that her agent – who, incidentally, had not deigned to perform one tiny Alien action, nor drink one tiny sip of green lemonade, and had, in fact, managed to persuade someone to provide her with a cup of black coffee – was watching her like a hawk, making sure she was behaving herself.

At the third verse of the Lord Dragoo song, however, as Celina was attempting to 'swoop and dive and *whoosh* through the skies' without spilling lemonade on her red silk dress, Mercedes had caught her eye and given her the most deliciously anarchic wink. Celina had winked back and then, very surreptitiously, they both hid their glasses behind some potted palms and sloped off to the Ladies, where they fell into one another's arms and laughed and laughed at the utter, unadulterated, awfulness of it all.

They had talked for as long as they dared, and Celina had said how tense all the noise made her, and Mercedes told her she should go to Relaxation classes, and study Reiki, and Aromatherapy, and a whole host of other wonderful things, none of which Celina had done. Then she had given her the red-brick business card and issued the invitation to coffee that was never accepted.

Celina flicks over to the next 'G' page in the directory,

but there is still no 'Glass' entry. Disappointed, she dips her rock-hard cereal bar into the coffee, manages to salvage one wet dollop before the rest vanishes into the depths of the mug, and looks on down the list and there, perhaps, it is: Mercie Grey, *Imago* Studios, with an address in Smithfield, and a phone number.

To be on the safe side, she searches the rest of the list, but there are no more entries of interest and she goes back to Mercie Grey and reads the name and address again. Could this be Mercedes Glass? Could she have remarried or, more likely, divorced Mr Glass and reverted to her maiden name? And – of course – hadn't she introduced herself as 'Mercie' and said she had a Spanish mother? Or was it a grandmother? Yes, it was a Spanish grandmother, because she had used the word *abuela*.

And – Celina's heart sinks a little as it all comes flooding back – there was a Georgia O' Keeffe connection too. Mercedes had mentioned how much she loved her work, and they had ended up talking about the Ghost Ranch landscapes, and how sad it was that O'Keeffe's eyesight had gone, and that had led, of course, to Imogen, and Mercedes had shrieked in delight at the revelation of who Celina's mother was, and had said that of course she knew and *adored* her work, with its wonderful 'homage' to O'Keeffe ...

Come to think of it, perhaps that was the reason she never got back in touch with Mercedes Glass. For in those days the world was filled to overflowing with people who adored Imogen Wilde and lost no time in telling Celina how much they adored her. Perhaps, even in those early days, she was too vulnerable to the eclipsing effect of Imogen's bright talents to seek out the company of yet another fervent fan?

Pushing the directory into her bag, Celina finishes her oat-enriched coffee and realises, with surprise, that for the past half-hour she has neither had, nor wanted, a cigarette. She walks out into weak sunshine, inhales the musty, heavenly, rain smell rising from the pavement, and sets off in the general direction of the Underground station.

It is still quite early and, pleasantly aimless, she finds herself dipping in and out of the rather superior charity shops with which this area abounds. In the window of one, a red hat with a broad brim and satin band catches her eye, and she goes in and tries it on, pulling it this way and that till she finds the best angle.

It reminds her of the gaucho hat hanging on O'Keeffe's back in Imogen's photo, and it makes her think of hot Spanish nights, of flamenco, of bullfighting, of cigar smoke and rich brown wine. Its style and colour perfectly complement her features, making her look strong and confident and altogether rather daring, and as she pays for it, she tells the shop assistant to cut off the price tag so that she can wear it right now.

"If you don't mind my saying, madam," the shop assistant says, "that hat was made for you," and Celina smiles graciously and thanks her. Then she puts it on, tips it to the crucial angle, and makes her exit.

Too right, she thinks, that hat was made for her. It has been waiting in that shop for her to buy, on just such a day as this. For this is the day the fear was faced, and the red hat is her reward. It is like a medal, she reflects as, raising her chin, she gazes down at the passers-by. It is solid proof that she can, despite her inner turmoil, be brave. Moreover, it is just the hat to wear when she goes to see Mercie Grey, in her studio in Smithfield.

And what is more, she decides as, turning, she heads off smartly to the Underground, she will not let Mercie Gray's address languish in her pocket as the business card languished on her fridge. She will go to Smithfield and see her, right now.

CHAPTER TEN

The Smithfield street that houses *Imago* turns out, when Celina finally tracks it down, to be a rather dismal alleyway lined with dreary tenements, the *Imago* one being the dreariest.

There is a huge array of labelled buzzers on the right-hand wall of its doorway and, increasingly nervous, she reads each name in turn. Three of them are embossed in white on strips of coloured plastic, and others are scrawled on bits of card in biro. Finally, in between *Senga's Tattoo Parlour* and *Terry's Tanning*, she finds a relatively clear and bold little label with *Imago* printed in red capitals. She is about to ring the buzzer beside it when the front door opens and a woman with a cigarette in her mouth, carrying a tray of small bottles and what looks like a travelling torture chamber, comes out. She gives her a not-unpleasant look and, with a jerk of the head, indicates that she should go in.

"I'm looking for *Imago*." Celina takes the weight of the door from the woman who, she assumes, is Senga the tattooist, and carefully sidles past her terrible tray. "Do you know which floor it's on?"

"Third floor, door on the right." Senga looks down at Celina's smart black leather shoes. "And I'd mind my feet if I was you." And she clips away, on unsteady high heels, towards the meat market.

Wending her way between discarded carry-out boxes and crusted pools of what might well be vomit, Celina climbs till she reaches the third floor and the door marked – this time in triumphant black on emerald green – *Imago*. The door is not locked, and she pushes her way into a small hall, through a pair of swing doors, and into a narrow dark corridor at the end of which she can see the white-painted walls of what has to be a gallery. The rank smell of the stairs has been gradually replaced by the cocktail of paints and oils, solvents and varnish, with which she is so familiar. Despite herself, she feels excitement tingle through her nervousness.

Making as little sound as possible, she edges her way up the corridor and, standing on the threshold of the gallery, slips off her hat and peeps in.

The gallery is not overly large and, compared to the subtly-illuminated spaces of Jakoby or Gallery Cinq, is shabby and poorly-lit. In its centre, dominating the space, stands the massive figure of a woman sculpted out of chicken-wire. The figure, which must be well over six feet tall, is firmly planted on great wire feet and its head, neck and shoulders have been swathed in papier mâché, patches of which gleam under the light. Its arms, legs and large pendulous breasts, however, are still devoid of the paper covering, and as Celina continues to gaze at the sculpture she realises that it is not a single figure at all, but a mother with a small bundle clamped to her left breast. Although the figure is roughly sculpted and has no facial expression, there is a monumental tenderness in the stretch of its neck and the incline of its head, and for a while Celina cannot tear herself away from the big shoulders, the sinewy neck, the flow of hair cascading down towards the suckling child.

She is somehow certain that this is Mercedes' work,

and equally certain it is a self-portrait, so when, at last, she allows her eyes to move downwards and make sense of what is below the baby, the shock she feels is so visceral it makes her pelvic muscles contract. Covering her mouth, for she cannot stop herself from gasping out loud, she takes a small step back and tucks herself away behind the door.

Angry voices are approaching now, and she can hear at least two sets of footsteps echoing through the gallery. Telling herself that no one can have heard the gasp, nor the wild thumpings of her heart, she lurks behind the door. The conflict between flight and fright is similar to the one she had earlier this afternoon when she smoked on Inge's doorstep, but now, as then, she forces herself to stay in the moment. In particular, she forces herself to keep looking at the gaping chasm where the wire woman's belly should be.

The voices are right in front of her now, and there are two. The louder by far belongs to Mercedes who, with the sleeves of her kaftan rolled up to her elbows and her hair bristling with wallpaper paste and indignation, has come to stand on one side of the belly. Facing her is a tall, angular man with a beard and long dark hair.

"For fuck's sake, Matt!" Mercedes screams across at the man. "You can not be serious!"

"You bet your sweet life I'm serious, Mercie." The man's voice is gravely with determination, but so quiet Celina has to strain to hear what he is saying. "I'm tellin' you," he continues, "you cannae hae Selestino's poems cascadin' oot o' her fanny. It's no' right, an' you can scream as much as you like, but you're no' doin' it. It's no' in good taste."

Mercedes rakes her hands through her hair, the movement dislodging a pair of red-framed half-moon spectacles on a beaded chain. The spectacles tumble down to rest on her bosom.

"Good taste?" she screams. "*Good taste?* They will be coming down through her *birth canal* and cascading out through her *vulva*. They will be being re-born, from the same source as Selestino himself was born. It's deeply symbolic, and it's *art*. Good taste has bugger all to do with it."

"It bloody has," the man says. "It's bloody pornographic."

A small woman with bright orange hair, clutching a bundle of multicoloured wool, steps out from behind the figure. "All men are threatened by the potency of the female reproductive system," she says, in a soft but authoritative Irish voice, "so they idolise their own external genitalia while deriding, even denying, their female counterparts." She gives Matt a withering look. "There's nothing pornographic about Mercie's idea. It's actually very beautiful."

Matt turns his anger onto the Irish woman. "I wasnae deridin' anyone's external genitalia, Ivy," he protests. "I'm quite the thing wi' external genitalia, as it happens. I mean tae say" – his voice rises and his arms begin to flail – "have I ever said anythin' against your wee knitted tits an' clitorises? No! Because they arenae a' that realistic. They arenae in your face like this is. Crivens – whit aboot folk comin' in wi' weans? You'll scar them for life, so you will!"

Celina takes a tentative step backwards. She glances behind her, but the swing doors now seem an enormous distance away.

Mercedes steps so close to Matt their noses almost touch. "If you have a problem with the Madonna, Matt," she says, "I'll find another space for the whole *Songs of Selestino* exhibition. I'm sure there are places with less anally-retentive attitudes. Now, if you'll excuse me, I need some air ..."

Turning her back on them both, she strides towards the door. Horrified, Celina presses herself against the wall, briefly considers her options, and realises she only has one. As Mercedes draws level, she steps forward.

"Mercedes?" she asks, and as Mercedes stops, puts on her spectacles, and looks her up and down, she adds, "I'm terribly sorry. This isn't a good time. I should have phoned."

To her relief Mercedes grins widely. "You're Celina Wilde, aren't you? I saw you the other day, at the station!"

"Sorry, yes. I wasn't quite sure it was you, and" – aware she is drenched in sweat, Celina takes a step back – "I'm afraid I had the mother of all migraines ..."

But Mercedes brushes away Celina's apologies with a shake of her shaggy grey-and-green head. "Oh, migraines!" she says. "I used to get them all the time. They're hormonal, you know. Have you tried Evening Primrose?"

Without waiting for a response, she takes Celina by the arm and pulls her into the studio. "I was going to go out, but it's nearly dark. Come into my studio and I'll make us coffee."

She leads the way across the communal space, past Matt and Ivy and the wire figure and, without bothering to introduce any of them, ushers Celina through a purple, star-spangled door bearing the notice 'Mercie Grey'. The first thing Celina notices, as she enters the narrow, high-celinged room, is that there is no hint of the dreaded oil paint smell.

"Sorry about the mess. I'm living here at the moment." Mercedes lifts a heap of clothes and a wicker basket off what turns out to be a small bed, and motions to Celina to sit down. Then she goes over to a low table and lights a joss stick protruding from the groin of a small wooden Buddha. Celina sits down on the bed, places the red hat carefully beside her, and looks around.

Every surface of Mercedes' studio is covered. There are three wooden chairs, each of which is piled high with bras and pants and hairbrushes and scarves and tampon boxes, and there is hardly an inch of clear space on the floor; but whereas the bed and floor and chairs are strewn haphazardly with objects, the rest of the studio, although crowded, shows evidence of meticulous order.

Underneath the one small, high window is a long desk whose surface is dotted with neat little piles of notepads, and jars of well-sharpened pencils, and pots of paintbrushes, all scrupulously clean. Above the desk, shelves reach right up past the window to the ceiling, and these shelves heave with materials, each of which is ordered in its own particular space. There are cans of spray paint sitting in neat rows, with their colours clearly displayed, and bottles of clear liquid, and canisters of brightly-coloured paint powder. There are tins of paint too, and an army of plastic glue containers with pointed nozzles, and boxes of wallpaper paste. In between all of these hang the tools of Mercedes' trade: hammers, pliers, fretsaws, hacksaws, wire cutters, scissors and big broad brushes.

A double sink takes up the rest of the window wall, and the other three walls are patchworked with paintings and collages, weavings and sketches, and as Mercedes fills the kettle and spoons coffee powder into two tin mugs, Celina gazes around, comparing this room with Inge's clean bright sanctuary. The two spaces she has inhabited for the first time today could not be more different, but they share one vital property. They feel exciting, as though important things could happen in them, and yet they feel safe.

"So" – Mercedes hands her a mug round whose handle she has wrapped a piece of paper towel, then flops down on the bed beside her – "what's up? I see you're still illustrating Bryony Garden's books. Gawd – don't those Aliens run and run!"

Celina arches her eyebrows. "Don't they just," she agrees. "And, just between you and me, I often wish they'd run themselves into the Snotgrass Swamp and drown there."

Mercedes laughs. "I know what you mean. I can't stand doing the same thing over and over again. I'm always looking for new challenges."

"Exactly. And that's what I intend to do. I'm negotiating a sabbatical …" She attempts a sip of the coffee, but the tin mug is searingly hot and, with difficulty, she deposits it on an empty piece of floor. Then she looks around the walls again. "Your work's so strong and loose and vibrant," she says. "And I love your use of colour. The pinks and oranges and turquoises just leap out at you. What's the wire figure all about?"

Mercedes, whose generous lips seem impervious to the heat of her tin mug, takes a large gulp of coffee. "Oh yeah – the Madonna. I presume you heard Matt's diatribe?"

Celina nods. "I take it he isn't too keen on some of her more" – she glances down at the floor, then up again – "intimate aspects?"

"The trouble is the thing is so bloody big I've had to work on it out there" – Mercedes cocks her head towards the door – "and you would not believe how many times a day one or other of them seem to have to pass comment. It freaks me out, bigtime!"

"It would freak me out too." Celina pauses, thinks about it. "Just imagine being on show while you're working. Imagine people seeing all the bits that aren't right yet, but might be if you did them differently …"

"Exactly. Only yesterday, Matt got a bee in his bonnet about the whole papier mâché thing. Said she was better just being wire. Said he thought papier mâché painted pink was going to be tacky ...." She bangs her mug down on the chair beside her. "Well to hell with him! I have my vision, and maybe it *is* tacky. But shit, it's my vision, and I'm sticking to it."

She gives Celina a triumphant smile, and Celina feels the earlier bubble of laughter rise a little higher. "So what exactly is the problem with the ... with the poems cascading out?"

Mercedes looks suddenly solemn. "OK," she says. "Let me explain the whole thing. I'm putting together an exhibition called *Songs of Selestino*. It's a kind of memorial to my son, who died in September. The whole thing's going to be set out like a church on the Mexican Day of the Dead – low light, music, incense – and round the walls there'll be stained glass panels, lit from inside, and candles and icons. The Madonna's right in the centre, and she'll be painted in bright colours and holding the shrouded corpse of a newborn child. Selestino's songs will flow out from her womb space and coil around her body. "

She stops, as though waiting for a reaction, but Celina has hardly heard the details of the exhibition.

"Your son?" she manages to say. "He died?"

"Oh, yeah. Selestino died last September. He burned to death," Mercedes tells her matter-of-factly. "You might have seen it in the papers – the 'Paedophile Poet' case? My son's alleged love affair with an underage girl he supposedly lured into drugs and suicide?"

She leans down and, scraping around among the debris on the floor, unearths a jar of biscuits. She takes two biscuits out and dips one in her coffee. "Ginger snaps." She offers Celina the jar. "Want one?"

Celina shakes her head and dredges back in her memory to last September and yes, of course, she knows the story inside-out. In between Max's dinner parties and Luca's suspensions and Imogen's last garbled insults, she had watched it on television and read it in the papers day by day as it unfolded. She and Raine had both watched and read it, in fact and, now she comes to think of it, it was the one subject they had talked about together. But to think that Selestino Glass – and surely that surname should have rung a bell – was actually Mercedes' son …

She looks round the studio walls, seeking out the pictures, the collages, the prints that, now she knows, must all be of Selestino, and she pictures the Madonna's great mournful head and the gaping chasm in her belly, and wishes she could think of something to say. More than anything, though, she wishes she had the courage simply to reach out and touch Mercedes, as she herself longs to be touched.

CHAPTER ELEVEN

"Did you notice the Madonna's belly's hollowed out? I'm going to make a kind of cabinet of curiosities in it, with illuminated shelves, to display little things that belonged to Selestino."

Mercedes' words, punctuated by crunchings of biscuits and slurps of coffee, continue to flow as Celina, deep in her own memories, half-listens.

"I have a box filled with things I've gathered," Mercedes is saying. "His first tooth, some of his toys, a reed from his clarinet, shells, that kind of thing. I want the whole *Songs of Selestino* to be a huge celebration of the goodness of his life because, you know what, honey – my son maybe wasn't perfect, but he wasn't a sexual predator. He fucking *wasn't* ." She glares into her coffee as though it contains all the evils of the world. "Hence the run-in with Matt," she adds. "He's such a Puritan."

She heaves herself off the bed and, picking her way over to one of the shelves above the desk, takes down a shoe box. Sitting beside Celina again, she opens it. This time she sits marginally closer, and as she delves in among the treasures in the box, Celina thinks about Raine and herself, and the Paedophile Poet scandal. These times together, in front of the television, are the last times she remembers communicating with her daughter.

She had even, now she comes to think of it, deigned to listen to one of Selestino Glass's songs on Raine's CD player, and had had to concede that, in contrast to the cacophony of sound that usually blared out from it, it sounded almost tuneful.

Perhaps – the thought is infinitely sobering – these were the last times she truly communicated with anyone; because after Imogen died, it was as though a glass dome descended around her, and that glass dome has been there, separating her off from reality, ever since.

"I have this seal he liked" – Mercedes tips up a brass seal to show its carving – "and his favourite pen, and this key-ring he got in Florida – look – in the shape of a flamingo …" she breaks off and looks at Celina with sudden concern. "Is that coffee still too hot for you, honey? Shall I add some cold water?"

"It's fine now." Celina takes a sip. The coffee is far too strong, and tastes metallic. "The girl who died at the same time – Kat? – what was she like?"

Mercedes is silent, thinking. "She was like her mother," she says at last. "Quite sweet, but with a massively over-fertile imagination, and hugely immature." She darts Celina an angry look. "She and Selestino had known each other since Kat was four, which is why the story of them being lovers is such bollocks. Selestino would never have been attracted to a fifteen-year old girl. The idea's crazy." She shakes her head, as though shaking away the mere idea of it. "Why do you ask?"

Celina takes the seal out of the shoe box and, closing one eye, examines it closely with the other. What she thought was a circle is actually a coiled snake.

"My daughter, Raine, didn't believe the papers either." She turns the seal round and round, chasing the serpent's tail. "The more they reported the story, the less she believed that Kat had been lured by Selestino into sex and drugs and suicide. She used to say she was sorry for Selestino Glass. That he was the one who'd been manipulated." She smiles at Mercedes. "She's a great fan of your son's music. She listens to his songs all the time."

She turns the seal towards Mercedes. "This snake, eating its tail – does it have a meaning?"

"Apparently it's a symbol of eternity, from Ancient Egypt. Selestino found it in a car boot sale years ago, and it became a kind of lucky mascot."

She leans across, clasps her hand over the seal. "Your Raine was right. Both Kat and her mother were arch-manipulators, but the media were the worst. I often wondered if it was because of the scandal in Cleveland last year. All those children being taken away by the social services. People in authority got obsessed by sex, if you ask me …"

"Raine said some of Selestino's lyrics could be interpreted as advocating sex with children," Celina says. "But she never believed they were."

Mercedes nods. "The press fastened on things, like his songs, and the strange nature of the fire, which was all concentrated round the bodies and the fireplace, and they basically manufactured the 'suicide' story. Then later they said maybe it was a drug-induced accident, not 'suicide'"

"An accident?"

Mercedes takes the seal. She holds it out, small in the centre of her big hand, and her breathing is laboured, as though she is struggling for air. "They decided maybe it was faulty wiring on the electric fire, which of course was my fault. Anyway" – with a sudden impatient gesture she lays everything back inside the box – "I don't really like talking about it. It brings on my asthma."

She takes an inhaler out of her pocket and sucks three times. "I'll sort Matt out," she says, between breaths. "And I'll finish the Madonna and mount the *Songs of Selestino* exhibition the way I want it. I owe it to the memory of my son to show what kind of man he really was."

She walks back to the desk and replaces the box. Then she sits back down, flings an arm round Celina's neck and holds her head against hers.

"Thanks for sharing what Raine said, honey," she says. "You have no idea how I appreciate it. You know, you tell yourself you're right, and they're wrong, and you know in your heart you are" – she nuzzles her face into Celina's shoulder, and Celina is acutely aware of the brittle-dry curls brushing against her cheeks – "but when the papers are full of pictures of your son with 'tragic songster lured young lover into sex 'n drugs lifestyle' printed below, and the mother of the 'young lover' keeps telling you she's lost her daughter because of him, you do begin to doubt yourself. You wonder if you got it wrong all along and he *was* a drug addict, and he *did* have suicidal tendencies and a proclivity for young girls, and he just talked a good game to his mom. Worst of all, you wonder if he said something you would have noticed if only you'd listened better ..."

She is crying now, her tears trickling down the side of Celina's face, and there is something immensely moving about feeling another's tears. Then, as suddenly as they began, the tears stop and Mercedes pulls herself away, picks up a cloth from the floor, wipes her face with it, then proceeds to dry Celina's.

"Jeez, honey, what a friggin' mess I've made of you." She wraps the cloth round her index finger and runs the pointed finger down each of Celina's cheeks in turn, then along her jawlines. With her other hand she supports her chin, like a mother with a child. "You have such a sympathetic face, you know," she says, "and such a sympathetic voice, and up till now there really hasn't been anyone I could open up to, not properly. Matt tries, but he's ... I mean, he's not ..." She shakes her head, gives up on trying to verbalise what Matt is or is not, and goes on dabbing at Celina's face even though it is completely dry.

"How is the girl's mother now?" Celina asks when Mercedes has gone back to her coffee. Her face still tingles from the unexpectedness of Mercedes' caresses, and there is a strange weakness in her body as though, were she to stand, her legs might give way. "The papers were quite critical of her too, I remember. Said she gave her daughter too much freedom. Didn't she have a complete breakdown?"

Mercedes drains the last of the coffee. "Oh Christ, yes. Dawn's been in a psychiatric ward ever since, and I'm not saying the press coverage caused her breakdown, but it sure didn't help. I mean, when you're a mother in the depths of grief and guilt and despair, and you read in the dailies that the whole thing was your fault for not bringing up your kid properly, it's pretty much the last straw. The perennial problem of being a mother is that you're damned if you interfere, and you're damned if you don't."

She beams at Celina. "I'm going to get some more coffee? Would you like another?"

Celina shakes her head and watches Mercedes stomp back over to the kettle. "You had a son as well, didn't you?" Mercedes asks.

"Luca," Celina nods. "He came after Raine. He's fourteen now, so he would have been about three when we met." She closes her eyes for a moment, remembers Luca clinging to her legs, looking up into her eyes, ferociously needing her. "I think I was closer to Luca when he was small than I ever was to Raine. Raine was always so confident, somehow. Luca had more of a vulnerability."

She looks over at Mercedes, silhouetted against the window, her mass of hair backlit to form a halo. Her face is all but hidden by clouds of steam from the antiquated kettle, and she is unaware she is being watched. Celina, however, peering through the steam, sees the expression of infinite sadness in that big strong unguarded face, and is reminded of a host of Italian paintings of the Madonna of the Seven Sorrows.

"I can't imagine how it feels to lose a child," she says.

Mercedes does not turn. "Don't even try," she says, and then, "Fuck this." She pulls the kettle plug out as though extracting a tooth, throws as much boiling water onto the floor as into her mug, and carries the coffee back to the bed. "So, are you still married? And what are your kids doing now?"

Celina looks back at the pictures of Selestino. She longs to bring the conversation back to him but, sensing Mercedes' need to be taken away from her problems, searches instead for something positive to say about her own family.

"I suppose they're doing well enough at school." She is aware of the flatness of her voice, and a weariness in her body. "But we pretty much keep ourselves to ourselves these days. They're difficult," she adds. "Moody. And as for being 'still married'" – she forces out a laugh and instantly feels somewhat better – "I've just been left for another woman. 'Just been left' as in, at the weekend!"

Mercedes stares, open-mouthed. "Oh-my-gawd," she breathes. "I feel awful now, going on and on about

myself, when you've got heavy-duty stuff going on too."
She touches Celina's arm. "Have you time to tell me
about it?"

Celina glances down to her watch. It is almost five, and
tonight is Parents' Night at Raine's school, and Kalinda is
due in the morning. Irritating though both these calls to
duty are, she also finds them oddly comforting.

She stands. "I'd love to stay longer," she says, "and I'd
love to tell you all about Max, but I really have to go, and
now I'm going to hit the rush hour." She picks up her hat,
begins to head for the door. "I'd like to meet up with you
again soon, though," she adds, because Mercedes, sitting
on the cluttered little bed with her mug of boiling coffee,
looks suddenly quite distraught. "And I'd like to know
more about the *Songs of Selestino* exhibition, and your
plans for the Madonna. It's been so stimulating to hear
about it!"

Together they pick their way across the floor, and
Mercedes holds the door wide. "Adore that, by the way,"
she says, as Celina positions the hat. "I'd love to paint
you in it. Naked" – she winks – "except for the hat!"

Unable to think of a suitable response, Celina follows
Mercedes across the open area outside, and as they pass
the Madonna she imagines the dark chasm back-lit, and
the array of tiny illuminated treasures glowing out. In the
corner of her eye she sees Mercedes rummaging around
in her pocket, and she waits while she finds, then hands
her, a business card.

"How about next week?" Mercedes says. "There's a
place near here where they do great nachos!"

"I'd love that, Mercedes," Celina puts the card carefully
away in her bag. "I adore nachos."

At the outer door, Mercedes hugs her as close as the
brim of her hat allows. Her embrace is soft and warm and
she smells of rose-sweet musk. As their bodies part,

Celina is struck by the thought that, if you discounted Max, it is years since she inhaled another's air or smelt another's skin. Certainly, it is years since she wanted to go on inhaling it.

"Call me 'Mercie'!" Mercedes' call echoes down the corridor. "And ring me! *Hasta pronto*!"

CHAPTER TWELVE

"So" – Kalinda squirms around in her chair, positioning and repositioning the cushion behind her back until it is in exactly the right place – "Max has gone. Well, well, well."

Finally comfortable, she settles back and stretches her black Lycra-clad legs luxuriously out in front of her. Since Imogen's funeral she has, Celina notices, put on quite a bit of weight, and the rounding-out of her face, combined with her new wavy hairstyle, gives her a distinctly middle-aged appearance. Her tan jumper, with its big, unflattering cowl neck, and the Lycra bell-bottom trousers with which it is teamed, add to the matronly effect. If – heaven forbid – you wanted to be hyper-critical, you could describe the once-elegant Kalinda as decidedly frumpy.

"Well, well, well?" Celina tops up Kalinda's glass with sparkling white wine. "Is that all you can say?"

Kalinda gulps down a couple of mouthfuls, then raises her eyebrows. "Oh honestly, Celina" – she smiles serenely – "you don't really expect me to be hugely sympathetic, do you? I mean to say, you and Max's relationship has been shaky for years. When you're together, you do nothing but growl at one another, and when you're alone, all you ever do is complain about him. We've all known for ages that your marriage is on the rocks.

"I hate to say it," she adds, scooping a generous portion of salted peanuts from the bowl on the coffee table and hurling them into her mouth, "but Mother did always say it wouldn't last, and Mother had an uncanny eye for that sort of thing."

"Wouldn't last?" Celina screams across the table. "It lasted nearly twenty years, which is a damned sight longer than any of her liaisons did!"

"It is for the best, Celina," Kalinda continues calmly. "Now you can make a clean break while you're still young enough to find someone else. I'm sure that's what I'd do." She licks the salt from her lips, then sucks every last crystal from her tongue. "Not, of course, that I'm ever likely to be in that position," she adds, self-satisfaction oozing out of every pore. "How are the children?"

Celina watches Kalinda scrape the last of the peanuts into her mouth. She is dizzy with exhaustion. This morning she has not only tidied the house from top to bottom and prepared the lunch, she has also braved the morning rush hour to collect the house papers from Henderson so that Kalinda will have absolutely nothing to complain about. Not only that, before leaving the house she intercepted and forcibly removed Luca's 'Living Dead' sweatshirt, then watched while he replaced it with a freshly-ironed school shirt. That accomplished, she had a similar row with Raine over the length of her skirt, sending her back to her bedroom to change into something less like a curtain pelmet.

The previous night, moreover, she hardly slept because

the events of her quite exceptional day were buzzing around her head so much and now, nauseous with fatigue and dying for a cigarette, she closes her eyes and imagines one of the peanuts lodging in her twin sister's airways and choking her, slowly and painfully, to death.

"How can you be so blasé about Max leaving?" she says, thrusting the folder with the house papers at Kalinda as violently as she dares. "How can you say it's 'for the best'? We have two children, for goodness' sake. Who seem to be fine, since you ask …"

Kalinda peers at the papers over her spectacles. "My Spanish is terribly rusty," she says, "but I rang Henderson yesterday morning, and he's filled me in on the place. Apparently it's on a tiny island off one of the Canaries. Isla Graciosa, it's called. I've done a bit of research …"

She opens her bag and takes out a guide book from which protrude a number of luminous yellow markers. Opening it at one of the marked pages, she hands the book over to Celina. "Pretty drab little place, by the look of it. All there seems to be is scrubland and extinct volcanoes and a couple of villages. And they don't have any asphalt roads, apparently. Just sand tracks."

Celina takes the guide book. There is only one blurred black-and-white photograph on the marked page, and the landscape it shows looks rather like the surface of the moon. Its foreground is a great broad plain stretching far into the distance, to end in a series of low black hills. The plain is dotted with low dark mounds and Celina wonders whether these are boulders or some kind of inhospitable desert plant.

"I can see why Mother would have liked it," she says. "It must have reminded her of the desert in New Mexico."

She looks over at Kalinda. "Henderson told me the house was bought in 1935. Why did we never hear about it? Why did Mother never take us there?"

Kalinda makes the noise she always makes when the answer to a question is too blindingly obvious for words. The noise is made by blowing air explosively through the lips, and sounds a bit like a donkey's bray. Kalinda has, Celina reflects, been making that donkey-bray noise for the past fifty years. It is probably the same noise as she made when asked why she wanted a tenth birthday watch that showed the time all over the world, and its annoying effect has not diminished one whit since then.

"Did Mother ever take us anywhere?" Kalinda retorts. "And anyway, she'd have bought the house so that she could paint, and she never wanted us around when she was working. I bet she thought of the Casa as her secret hideaway. You know how Mother loved her secrets."

Kalinda smiles and nods, and the sisters are momentarily united. "It was her 'Faraway'," Celina murmurs. "Mother's 'Faraway'." And when Kalinda gives her a quizzical look, she explains. "That's what Georgia O'Keeffe called the countryside around Ghost Ranch, where she went to paint. It was so isolated, and so stripped of detail, that she could concentrate on the few simple forms that were there."

She flicks through the guide book till she finds a map. "Graciosa's just off the coast of Lanzarote. Isn't that one of those awful, touristy, places, full of English pubs and 'Kiss Me Quick' hats?"

Kalinda wrinkles her nose and nods. "Dreadful place, I imagine. Though it wouldn't have been touristy in the thirties. The house probably cost next to nothing." She picks up the house papers again. "It seems to be a reasonable size. Four rooms, kitchen and bathroom, and standing in its own space. The trouble is, we've no way of knowing what sort of condition it's in. It's probably in ruins."

She rests the papers on what has, with mysterious

rapidity, become a more than ample bosom, and sighs. "What it needs, of course, is for someone to go and see what it's like. If it's half-decent, maybe we could do it up and rent it out. Could be a nice little earner."

Celina turns back to the lunar landscape. It is as uninspiring as before but, she tells herself, the photograph does it no justice. The sky, doubtless, would be azure blue, and the volcanic peaks might not be black. Perhaps they are red, like O'Keeffe's incongruously-named *Hills – Lavender*. Or if they are black, perhaps they are not uniformly black. Perhaps they are striated in a hundred different, merging, tones of grey.

"I've got a sabbatical coming up," she says. "I'm going to paint."

Kalinda raises her eyebrows. "I didn't know illustrators got sabbaticals. So, the publisher's actually paying you not to illustrate?"

Celina feels her face redden. "Kind of. There's a bit of a hiatus in the Beeboo series, and I haven't been all that well. I might be anaemic."

Kalinda looks her up and down. "Everyone our age's anaemic." She leans towards her, as though sniffing out her deceit. "So, are you suggesting you go out there and take a look?" she says and, before Celina has a chance to respond, answers her own question. "Oh no, of course you can't, can you. The children ..."

Celina is about to hand the guide book back to Kalinda and go and lay out lunch when, somewhere deep in her mind, in roughly the same memory-bank as that which houses the plan to use Imogen's studio, something stirs.

"Can I hold onto this?" she says and slides the guide-book into the house papers folder. Then she picks up her empty glass and goes to the kitchen, where she uncorks another bottle of wine and sets it on the table alongside a platter of salmon and a bowl of potato salad.

"Would you like to come through?" she calls as, feeling suddenly rather celebratory, she re-charges her glass.

CHAPTER THIRTEEN

A few hours after the singularly successful lunch Celina and Kalinda, replete and relaxed, are strolling companionably towards Highgate Cemetery. After its shaky beginning, Kalinda's visit is being marginally less awful than Celina had feared.

During the lunch she had made sure the wine flowed, and that controversial subjects like divorces and sabbaticals and Spanish houses were avoided, the conversation centring instead around Kalinda's new car, and Kalinda's new mushroom-brown calf-leather three-piece suite, and Kalinda's possible promotion to Head of Mathematics. Tedious though the resultant conversation was, the tactic has paid dividends, and now that the afternoon is reddening into evening, and there is only tonight and next morning's breakfast to get through, Celina is altogether calmer. As they catch their first glimpse of Highgate Cemetery and, pointing, shout out in unison, 'There it is!' her mood, for a moment, borders on the euphoric.

Highgate Cemetery is a favourite childhood haunt, and

as they near its gates the silence that has settled between them, far from being awkward, is as comfortable as an old glove. Celina's earlier exhaustion has become a pleasant drowsiness, and she is content to walk beside Kalinda, breathing in the leaf-mould smells and hearing the blackbirds' rustles and cries, and thinking about what she will do with the week end, and then the week ahead.

She is not wearing the red hat. Earlier, as they were putting on their coats in the hall, she took it from the hat stand and stood in front of the mirror, positioning it, while behind, her reflection vying for position, Kalinda tucked stray strands of hair under something that looked like a small dead animal, and all of a sudden the red hat seemed wrong. It was, Celina realised, too much of a contrast to her sister's shapeless fur and, as she donned a bland navy-blue beret, it occurred to her again that the red hat is, actually, not merely a hat; it is a signal, a statement of intent that marks her out as still youthful, still vibrant and, most importantly, still capable of change. And when she ushered Kalinda out of the house and they began to walk down the hill towards the cemetery she found herself wondering whether, these days, a stranger seeing the two of them would even take them for sisters, let alone identical twins.

"Do you remember," Kalinda says as they meander along paths lined with tombstones so ivy-covered that the stone appears to have been turned to living green, "how we used to race to find Marx's tomb?" and Celina, laughing, replies, "Yes – and you always won because you had a sense of direction and I never did. You've no idea," she decides to add, "how much it annoyed me. Every time we came I'd think, this time I'll beat her. This time I'll be first. But I don't think I ever was."

Kalinda shakes her furry head. "No," she agrees. "You never were," and, to her credit, she laughs any hint of complacency away.

For just a moment, Celina wonders whether Kalinda might break into a run right there and then, and give her one final chance to break her duck, but her sister's middle-aged plod continues, and Celina falls into step with her. Absorbed in their own thoughts, they continue to walk side by side.

Dreamily, Celina makes her plans. Some time over the week end, she will phone Mercedes and suggest lunch next week. She will also suggest that after lunch they go back to *Imago* and that Mercedes gives her a proper guided tour; and the thought of that lunch, and the conversation afterwards, makes a ribbon of intense pleasure unfurl down her back. She is, she realises, positively aching to be sitting on the cluttered little bed again, surrounded by Mercedes' vibrant art works and with Mercedes beside her, talking endlessly about ideas and colour and form.

She also wants to ask Mercedes more about her son's death, the details of which, interspersed with half-formed memories of her conversations about it with Raine, continue to trickle back to her. She particularly wants to ask Mercedes more about Kat's mother Dawn who, she remembers, was described in the papers as a 'wannabe novelist', too engrossed in her work, allegedly, to care for her wayward daughter.

The night before, as she tossed and turned and waited for morning, she had found herself re-running those far-off discussions with Raine, and wondering which ones were real and which fantasies – or realities so warped by time as to have become fantasies. Had Raine, for example, actually said, 'I reckon that girl Kat's mum was too wrapped up in her career to care for her properly'? And then, had she added, 'Like you are'?

Or was the 'Like you are' merely an embellishment,

courtesy of Celina's guilty conscience?

When this nocturnal sifting-through of memories became too upsetting, she had comforted herself by mentally pushing open Mercedes' star-spangled studio door and standing in the middle of the little studio, with its superficial clutter masking neatness and order and its walls shimmering with creative energy. It had been such a wonderful contrast to Inge's sacred space, and it occurs to her now that, while Inge's room had calmed her when she needed calming, and enabled her to begin to clear her mind of fear, Mercedes' had gone on to fill a little of the space that fear had left behind. It had been a blessed exchange.

Not that Mercedes' studio is anything like as grand as Imogen's, of course, she reflects now, as the last rose of evening light slips into greyness. For one thing, it has virtually no natural light and for another, its space is quite pathetically inadequate for the kind of work Mercedes is doing. In fact – and the thought suddenly quickens Celina's steps so that she rushes on ahead of Kalinda's funereal pace – if Mercedes had a proper studio, like Imogen's, she would not have to work on her Madonna in the open public space, under her colleagues' perpetual scrutiny, would she? Nor would she have to sleep on a bed so tiny and cluttered that she surely cannot turn over without being harpooned by a hairbrush.

Slowing down to let Kalinda catch up, Celina suddenly pictures Mercedes and herself dragging the Madonna's swathed figure up four flights of stairs, manoeuvring it through Imogen's door, and planting its great wire feet solidly on Imogen's oak floorboards. 'I've had an idea!' she imagines herself telling Mercedes on Monday. 'Let's swap studios! I can't work in mine, you see. I can't stand the smell of oils, and you ...'

She files the thought away in the mental folder marked

'Totally Impractical' and, as Kalinda joins her, they begin to chat about what they have seen on television, and how amazing it is that Margaret Thatcher has been in charge for ten whole years, and where on earth has the time gone and, to Celina's surprise, the realisation that the 'studio-swap' thought is totally impractical does not dampen her spirits in the least. And as she and Kalinda peer between ancient gravestones to see the first tight snowdrops piercing through last year's old leaves, she recalls Mercedes' throaty laugh and in that moment knows that, all these years, this is what has been missing from her life. Just this. Someone to share creative thoughts with, to be interested in her and the art – the adult art – she might be capable of producing. Someone to take that art seriously, even drive her on to greater things.

But there is yet another dimension to Celina's imaginings about Mercedes and her studio. In between all today's anxieties and frustrations, she has found herself recalling Mercedes' final comment, which at the time had robbed her of the power of speech while causing her cheeks to heat up alarmingly. She has even caught herself imagining, in detail, what it would be like to be painted naked by Mercedes and, more often than she feels she probably should, has pictured herself peeling off her clothes in preparation.

Sometimes she does this demurely behind a screen, but sometimes – which is much the more exciting – she does it in full view of Mercedes, blatantly, like a stripper. Each time she has the 'stripper' fantasy, she wears different clothes, which she peels off in an endless variety of ways, and so far the most exciting fantasy of all has been the one in which she is wearing her favourite dress, which is a silky green one with buttons down the front.

Very slowly she undoes the buttons, letting the material slip to one side, and the more buttons she undoes the more obvious it is that she is not wearing a bra. Looking boldly out at Mercedes, she continues to undo, until at last the dress slithers off to reveal red lacy, insanely skimpy, underpants – underpants the like of which Celina neither possesses, has ever possessed, nor is ever likely to possess. Even more slowly, and still holding Mercedes' gaze, she peels them off, and drops them at her feet.

When she is completely naked she dons the red hat and stands, or sits, or lies in front of Mercedes and sometimes, when she lies, she has her legs primly crossed and sometimes not. Then Mercedes walks towards her and, leaning so close that Celina is engulfed in her rose-musk scent, gently repositions a hand, a foot, an arm.

As if this were not titillating enough – for these fantasies, once started, assume a momentum all their own – there have been, once or twice, occasions when, bending over to adjust the angle at which Celina's arm meets the slight swell of her stomach, Mercedes has actually bridged the space between the small firm breasts with her own hand.

'Hold it like this, honey,' she whispers huskily, moving her big strong fingers a fraction upwards, to cradle a breast. 'Like it's a pomegranate, the fruit of love ...' She presses very gently down, and Celina, relishing the roughness of her fingertips, hesitates as long as she dares before doing as she is told.

At last, however, Mercedes, satisfied that the pose is just right, goes to her easel and begins to work. Keeping her eyes fixed on the middle distance, Celina listens to the sharp scrape of charcoal, or the soft fluid swishing of brushstrokes, as each subtle flesh tone is laid down, and every intimate detail recorded. And all the while, as Mercedes' lines caress her, her body tingles with longing, its deepest pleasure zones awakened after long sleep.

The combination of stomach-curdling fear and intense

pleasure that these imaginings evoke reminds Celina of childhood fairground rides, and is none the less pleasurable for being tinged with guilt; and as she and Kalinda round a bend and stand at last before Marx's tomb, she wonders if she might pluck up the courage to re-live some of them with Inge Van Deth on Thursday. It would – and here she has to wipe a little smile off her face before Kalinda notices – be interesting to observe how impassive Inge's face is really capable of remaining.

The tomb, here in its own special place apart from all the others, surprises Celina and Kalinda, as it never fails to surprise them, with its size and solidity. Standing side by side in front of it, every bit as small as they ever were, they gaze in awe at the massive hair-framed face, the deep-set thoughtful eyes. Someone has laid a single red silk rose on the slabbed area below the inscription, and its colour gleams in the dusk, an oriflamme in a desert of grey.

"How old were we when Daddy left?"

Kalinda frowns. "About two, I think. Maybe three. Why the sudden interest in Daddy?"

Celina shrugs. "I suppose I'm just interested because Mother is gone and I keep wondering if he's gone too, or whether perhaps he's still alive." She laughs. "I keep wondering whether we're orphans now, you and me!"

Kalinda makes a sound that, though veering in the direction of the donkey-bray, stops just short of it. "Oh honestly," she says in a gently chiding voice, "what on earth does it matter if we're orphans or not, when we're on the brink of our fifties and we never knew our father anyway!"

"But is he?" Celina persists. "Is he alive? Did Mother ever tell you? And why he left?"

Kalinda takes a long breath in. "It's nearly dark, Celina, and it's getting cold," she says, and she turns. "We should get going, in case they lock us in for the night." She shudders. "Imagine, two little orphan girls among all those ghosts!"

She marches briskly off, and Celina runs to catch up with her. "Did she, though? Did she ever talk to you about what happened? Because I remember, when we were about ten, you said ..." She stops, looks up through the web of bare black branches, into a grey sky slashed with greyer clouds. Kalinda was right – it is cold.

"What then?" Kalinda says sharply. "What did I say?"

"You said he left because of me. Because of something I did."

"Of course I didn't," Kalinda retorts. "You were a baby, Celina. People don't leave because of something a baby did. You're imagining things. You always did imagine things."

"I'm not. I know I'm not." Celina has a sudden urge to link arms with her sister, to pull at her so that she has to stop, to make her turn and face her, eye to eye; but of course she does not, because they never touch. It is an unwritten rule, an understood. Even at Imogen's funeral, after the brief obligatory embrace, they did not touch.

"I remember it as though it were yesterday," she insists. "'Daddy left because of something you did.' That's what you said, or something like it."

"Well, if I did, I certainly don't remember. Why on earth would I say that? It doesn't make sense."

Celina sinks her hands deeper into her coat pockets. Her bones feel as though they have frozen, and all the heart-warming thoughts of Mercedes and Mercedes' studio have gone. Every bit of joy has left the day, and all the wretched tiredness and insecurity has returned.

"Surely, at some stage, you asked Mother why he left?" she asks wearily. "Surely you wanted to know? Surely there's a bit of you that wants to know now?"

A flock of crows flaps raucously out of the trees and rises up into the sky like pieces of charred paper. In the distance the gates are just visible against the shadows, and as they head towards them they see a squat figure drawing them closed. Waving and shouting, they break into a run, and when they have safely made their escape from the cemetery they keep on running until they reach the main road and their way is lit once more by streetlights. Then, in silence, they continue on home and it is only after they have taken off their coats, and ascertained from two badly-written notes that both children have been home, eaten, and gone out again, that they move into the kitchen and, comforted by mugs of hot chocolate, begin to talk again.

"I did once ask Mother about Daddy, actually," Kalinda says, slowly. She leans over towards Celina, and when she speaks again the chocolate has sweetened her voice. "I'd quite forgotten, because it seemed so insignificant, but yes – I asked her. And she said something odd."

"How do you mean, 'odd'?" Celina's face burns. "And why didn't you tell me?"

Kalinda smiles and shakes her head. "You know how Mother was, Celina. She said things for effect. She loved to shock. That's why I didn't bother to tell you. It was so stupid and illogical I just forgot about it. But anyway, if you like, I'll tell you now."

A worm of anxiety turns in Celina's stomach. She nods.

"You remember the hard winter, about seven years ago, when she had that fall? She was still perfectly lucid, and she asked me to help her set up a new health insurance. I must have needed to know what her status was, so I asked her, 'Is Daddy still alive?'"

There is a pool of spilled chocolate on the white melamine table, and Kalinda dips her finger into it and, absentmindedly, pulls it into the shape of a star. Her brows furrow with the effort of remembering, and Celina bites her lip and forces herself to wait in silence.

"She gave me one of her looks," Kalinda says at last. "You know? When she half-closed her eyes and drew her eyebrows down and stared at you through those dark hoods of eyelids, and her eyes looked like two black shiny lines?"

Celina nods. She knows that look all right. It was malice personified. "And then what did she say?"

"She gave a kind of grunt, and then she said, 'Yes. Francisco is, as far as I know, still alive.'"

Kalinda sits back in her chair, takes a crumpled tissue from her sleeve, and wipes the corners of her lips with exquisite care.

"So, Daddy was alive seven years ago. But that's not odd ...?"

"She said something else. Something silly."

Kalinda raises her eyebrows, as though savouring her final moment of power, and Celina, transported back to a hundred such childhood moments, briefly imagines how it would feel to hurl hot chocolate at her sister's head.

"Stop being so annoying, Kalinda!" she shouts. "You're being just like Mother!"

Kalinda raises a defensive hand. "All right. She said: 'Francisco is alive, but he is dead. Quite dead.'"

"Alive?" Celina repeats. "But dead?"

Kalinda sighs and nods. "Those were her exact words – 'Francisco is alive, but he is dead, quite dead'. Of course I did ask her to explain, but you know Mother. She gave me that superior look and clammed right up and that was that. I filled in the form, and forgot about it until now. I don't think I even bothered to tell Roy, it was so insignificant."

Celina glances up at the clock on the wall. It is only eight-thirty, but she is light-headed with exhaustion and her thoughts are edged with panic. Ridiculous though her mother's words clearly are, there is something immensely sinister about them. "Didn't she just mean it in an ironic way?" she says. "Like, 'he's still alive, but he's dead to me'?"

Kalinda shrugs. "Maybe. Probably. Yes, that's probably what she meant." She yawns and stretches. "Are we going to have something to eat, Celina? I'm starving."

Celina stands and pushes her chair back. She opens the fridge, looks in, and closes it again. Then she takes bread from the bin and four eggs from the rack, and fetches what is left of this afternoon's wine. As an afterthought, she goes back to the fridge and grabs another bottle. "Scrambled eggs with cheese and tomatoes be OK? And some more plonk?"

"That'll be fine," Kalinda says. "And by the way, Celina, I'd just like to say that if I thought for one minute I was like Mother, I'd shoot myself."

Celina places two wine glasses on the table and as she fills them she looks anxiously at her sister, but Kalinda is smiling. "I shouldn't have said that," Celina says, smiling too. "No one could possibly be like Mother. But surely that's the point about wanting to know about Daddy? Maybe we're like him. Bits of us, anyway. Wouldn't you like to know what he was like?"

Kalinda takes the glass and, clamping it firmly between her lips, takes a swig. "I honestly can't see the point at our age," she says. "Our personalities are fully-formed. We're immutable. What does it matter any more who we take after?"

Celina carries her glass over to the work surface. She pops two slices of bread into the toaster and concentrates on cracking eggs and adding milk and whisking. When all is ready she fills each plate and presents one to Kalinda.

"Do you think Daddy ever went to the Casa de la Luna

Cresciente?"

Kalinda shrugs. "Possibly. No reason why not."

"So, there might still be stuff of his in the house?"

"Seems a bit unlikely. Who knows how long it's been standing empty. Thirty years? Forty?"

Celina considers this and is forced to concede that Kalinda, as ever, is right. She pictures the two of them as they were this afternoon, walking through the cemetery, Kalinda with the dead animal on her head and she with the dull beret.

She should have worn the red hat. She should not have been afraid to underline the difference between herself and Kalinda. For Kalinda is not always right. Sometimes she, Celina, is the one who is right.

But there is a more profound way in which they differ, and surely it is at the heart of everything. Kalinda is, and probably always was, immutable. Celina is damned if she ever will be.

CHAPTER FOURTEEN

Though the pavement sparkles with frost, the Monday morning sun is shining as Celina walks briskly down the slope to Highgate Station and, spotting Mercedes' rainbow form, hurries to embrace her.

"Great to see you, honey!" Mercedes hugs her warmly. Still keeping hold of both Celina's shoulders, she steps back to examine her from head to toe, approvingly taking in the black cape, the grey silk scarf, the black leather boots, the trim black bag. "You are so bloody elegant," she says. "And can you believe the day?" She slips a hand under Celina's arm and they leave the station and wait together, arms linked, to cross the busy road.

The phone call to Mercedes, made late on Saturday night after Kalinda had retired to bed for her 'beauty sleep' – and Celina had congratulated herself on concealing any amusement at *that* – has not, as hoped, resulted in a visit to *Imago*. Instead, it is Mercedes who has travelled to Highgate to meet Celina, and now they are on their way to the house of the tragic Dawn. There is, of course, a certain tinge of disappointment at not seeing the studio today, but on the other hand Celina is intrigued by what she has already gleaned of the reason for their meeting, and is dying to hear more.

"Oh honey, I'd adore you to come to the studio," Mercedes had said when Celina suggested the visit. "It's just that something kinda major's cropped up with Dawn, and I've promised I'll go to her house in Highgate on Monday. I should go tomorrow but …"

She had sighed then and Celina, not wanting to appear pushy or desperate but, after two solid days of Kalinda's company, feeling a bit of both, had said carefully, "Don't worry, Mercie. I quite understand. We can make it later in the week. Or next week …"

There had been an awkward silence then, and she imagined Mercedes flicking through her diary, wondering when, if ever, she could fit her in, so she added, as hesitantly as possible, "… of course, you know I live in Highgate too …"

Immediately there had been a whoop of joy from Mercedes' end of the line followed by, "Oh yeah of course! Of course you do," and then another, smaller, whoop which segued into a breathless cascade of speech. "So maybe we could meet up before I go, and have coffee and a cake somewhere. Or maybe" – and this time it was Mercedes choosing her words with care – "I mean, I know you're busy but I'd love your input on this, if you could maybe spare the time to come with me ..?"

Mercedes had paused after the audible question mark but Celina, rather than jump right in with, "Yes, of course I have time – when are you going?" had allowed herself the luxury of a moment's silence. There was, after all, something rather pathetic about someone with so much disposable time.

"It's such a delicate situation, you see, this thing with Dawn," Mercedes went on, "and I'm in it up to my frigging neck, which is why I'd so love to discuss it with someone who's not involved. I've been leaning far too heavily on Matt since the fire, you know – confiding in him and crying on his shoulder – and most of the time he's been great. Lately, though, things have changed. The cracks in our friendship are definitely showing ..."

The cascade, hijacked by a bout of painful coughing, stopped then restarted rather more hoarsely. "He hardly knows Dawn, but recently when I've complained about her he'll tell me I'm being unsympathetic. I ask you, honey – it's not him who has to trail up to the hospital every day and listen to a stream of negativity and hopelessness, is it? And it's not him who's lost his son and who's being told the whole thing was his son's fault. And then there's all this stuff about the Madonna, and that's pissed me off bigtime ..."

Her breath had failed entirely at this point, and after a silence during which Celina made as wide a variety of sympathetic noises as she could muster, Mercedes had cut to the chase with, "Would you come to Dawn's house with me? I'd love if you would," and Celina, overjoyed, had replied with a muted, 'I'd be more than happy to. I'll meet you at the Underground.'

"So, where's Dawn's house?" Celina asks now as the mid-morning traffic rumbles by and the crossing signal stolidly refuses to turn green.

Mercedes waves over in the general direction of the cemetery. "It isn't far, and I know a short cut. Dawn and I swapped houses last summer," she explains. "Dawn wanted to be in the city, in my flat, to write her book. It's a historical novel, set during the Great Fire. Apparently my flat survived the Fire because it's a basement, so it's the perfect setting."

"Your flat's seventeenth century?" Celina gives the crossing button a series of jabs. A scene replays in her mind of police climbing up a spiral staircase onto a pavement, and reporters jostling their microphones forward, and then the fleeting back view of a slight, sobbing woman sandwiched between two policewomen, but she does not mention any of it. Instead, she says brightly, "I imagine that must have been inspirational for Dawn. To be in the exact location she was writing about."

Mercedes gives an irreverent guffaw. "Too right it was! The first time she saw it, she kept pressing her ear against the walls, and saying this was where she simply *had* to write, that she could hear the stones talking to her. Crazy, I know, but that's Dawn all over – and it suited me down to the ground to do a swap. The flat's tiny and pretty awful, and when Selestino said he was coming over from the States on business, I knew I couldn't inflict it on him again." Her voice drops. "It was perfect, being here in Highgate with Selestino. We loved the garden, and the light, and the space."

The cars finally grind to a halt and they cross. For a while they walk in silence, and Celina notices Mercedes' grip become tighter, and her hold closer.

"So, you said something major had cropped up with Dawn? Do you mind talking about it?"

Mercedes looks at her in some surprise. "I'll talk about it till the cows come home, honey," she says. "But, you know, we've only just met and I don't want to go on too much." She laughs. "Matt says I go on too much!"

"I'm not Matt. And I really am interested."

Mercedes steers them into a quiet avenue. "The main reason I have to go to the house is to get Dawn clean jeans and tee shirts. But there's something else I'm to pick up. Something she's only just told me about, that could be important." She glances at Celina. "That could potentially be upsetting …"

"Something to do with Selestino?"

"Something to do with Selestino and Kat, yes. Kat's camera – the one she was using just before she and Selestino died. I've been asking Dawn for weeks if there might be anything among Kat's things that would give a clue to what happened, and every time I ask she puts on the Sarah Bernhard expression, and says she can't possibly think about it because it's too painful." She gives a snort. "You know, honey, I hope you don't think I'm unsympathetic too. I mean, Dawn's a dear, dear friend, but her constant passivity is driving me up the wall. It's gone on way too long and it's not helping anyone, least of all Dawn."

"So admitting to the camera is progress," Celina points out. "Do you think there are photos in it that might give a clue to why they died?"

"That's what I'm hoping." Mercedes turns, her eyebrows knotted with anger. "You know what? I can't stand it when people can't, or won't, change. I mean, Dawn's decided that my son seduced her daughter and persuaded her to kill herself, and she's not interested in hearing any other explanation. She's got her version of the truth, and she's sticking to it."

Celina smiles. "My twin sister Kalinda won't change either. And that's because she can't see any need to. She never has seen a need, either. Perhaps it's the same with Dawn? She's assumed the role of victim, and changing would be too uncomfortable?"

"Changing might just expose her own guilt, you mean? Because – you know what? – she didn't care for Kat the way she should have. She let her do whatever the hell she wanted, as long as she was out of her hair and she could get on with listening to walls."

Celina pauses before responding. Once again, she recalls that conversation with Raine about Kat's mother and her career. She has run and re-run it a hundred times in the past days, and is surer than ever that Raine did add, 'Like you are.' She can see her, as clear as day, leaning against the fridge with a Pepsi can, her face hidden between two dark brown curtains of hair, saying it.

"Teenagers are hard work," she says. "Perhaps sometimes we do have to give up on them a bit and get on with our own lives. But I can see how hard it must be for you."

Mercedes is silent as they enter a narrow bin-lined lane. "This is the short cut," she explains, and leads them out and into an avenue of smart detached houses. They crunch up a gravel driveway, and at the yellow front door Mercedes rifles through her backpack and withdraws a set of keys.

"The thing is, Selestino never ever was." She ushers Celina into a big shadowy hall. "Hard work, I mean."

Celina follows her through the hall into Dawn's sunny kitchen, where Mercedes dumps the backpack on the table and pulls out a bulging bakery bag.

"I'm going upstairs to get the clothes and the camera," she says. "Maybe you could fill the kettle, and I'll make us coffees and we'll have Chelsea Buns and Danish Pastries and Custard Doughnuts. And then," she adds with an apologetic look, "you tell me all about what *you*'re doing!" And with a wink and a '*hasta pronto*', she is gone.

Alone in the kitchen, Celina fills the kettle and then, sitting at the red gingham-covered table, she looks around at Dawn's warm pine cupboards, her pale lemon walls hung with bright red-framed prints, and her Welsh dresser laden with blue-and-white china and cards and pine cones and shells. As she compares it with her own clinical black granite teamed with oh-so-hygienic melamine and stainless steel – Max's choice, of course, though Max never cooked – a glorious feeling of possibility begins to glow inside her head.

There is going to be a change in her life. She is certain of it. She may be terrified out of her wits by the prospect of it, and highly uncertain about its nature, but that is irrelevant. There is going to be one.

Closing her eyes, she pictures another, faraway, Spanish kitchen at whose big scrubbed table, young, slim and hopeful, sit her mother and father. They are offering huge platters of freshly-caught lobsters and big-bellied jugs of rich red wine to their coterie of artistic friends; and as she watches the wine flow, excitement quivers through her body like a nervous shoal of small silver fish.

CHAPTER FIFTEEN

When Mercedes arrives back in the kitchen with a pile of clothes and a plastic camera bag, her face is flushed with excitement, and that excitement adds – if that were possible – to Celina's own.

In Mercedes' absence, she has fetched three plates from the dresser and arranged the cakes from the bakery bag on one. On the other two she has, after some deliberation – buns and pastries and doughnuts not being things she would ever choose to eat – placed a knife and fork and a piece of kitchen roll. She has also found some ground coffee, a coffee-jug, and two blue-and-white striped mugs, and while Mercedes, having laid the camera bag carefully on the table, pushes Dawn's clothes into her backpack, she busies herself making the coffee.

As she carries the coffee-jug to the table, she notices her hands are trembling.

"There's no milk," she says. "Can you take it black?"

Mercedes looks approvingly at the table arrangement. "Sure," she nods. "Black's best!" She fills her mug brimful, blows on its surface, and drinks. Eschewing the knife and fork, she picks up one of the Custard Doughnuts and, oblivious to the globs of yellow fondant exuding from its many orifices, munches happily. Then she wipes her fingers on the tablecloth, picks up the camera bag, and opens it.

"It's just a cheap thing," she says. "If there are photos in it, they won't be good.

She peers at the back of the camera. "There's a film in it. Can you see if it's finished?"

Celina squints at the tiny window. "It looks finished, but we should take it to the chemist and let them open it, just in case."

Taking both Celina's hands, and the camera, in hers, Mercedes gives all three a sticky squeeze. "That would be great, honey. You're sure you have time?"

Celina nods. "I should buy sun cream, actually. In case I go to Lanzarote." She laughs at Mercedes' surprise.

"I've just found out I have a house on a small island off its north coast, courtesy of my mother," she explains. "Isla Graciosa, it's called. And the house is the Casa de la Luna Cresciente."

"Casa de la Luna Cresciente?" Mercedes makes the name sound particularly mysterious and exciting. "So, you've never seen it?"

"No one has. It was my blessed mother's secret hideaway. I'd like to, though. But, practically speaking, I don't see how I can ..."

Mercedes gives her a quizzical look. "Why in hell's name wouldn't you go? Escape to the sunshine, find your Casa by the sea, do some painting? I tell you something, honey – if it was me, I'd be off like a shot!"

She leans closer, and Celina breathes in her rosy muskiness. Her hands have been released, but some of Mercedes' warmth still tingles on their skin.

"I don't feel able to make big decisions yet," she says,

more abruptly than she means to. Then she buries her face in the coffee mug. "I've just started seeing a therapist, actually …"

There is a sharp intake of breath. "A *therapist*?" Mercedes gasps. "But you're so … together." She moves just a few inches away and scrutinises Celina, as though seeing her in a different light. "Is it the husband thing?"

Celina shakes her head, laughing. "The husband thing, the mother thing, the sister thing, the children thing …" She is on the brink of adding 'the Schism thing' but Mercedes' look of growing concern stops her short. The Schism, for now, will remain her secret. She will not sully this clean new relationship with it. That is what Inge is for.

"You know what?" she says brightly. "I've got half a bottle of Chardonnay in the fridge, left over from my demon twin's visit. When we've handed in the film, why don't we go on down to my house, and I'll make lunch?"

Without a word, Mercedes pushes back her chair, sweeps the coffee mugs and plates off the table, and dumps them unceremoniously in the sink. Then she gives the tablecloth crumbs a cursory swipe with her sleeve, gathers up her things, and leads the way out.

The sun has disappeared, and there is a smell of snow in the air, and by the time they reach Celina's front door her black cape and Mercedes' rainbow colours are dappled with white. In the hall, Celina helps Mercedes out of the pashmina, and drapes it over the radiator. Then she shows her into the kitchen.

"Have a seat at the table. Would tuna pasta be all right?" and she fetches the Chardonnay from the fridge and fills two glasses.

"*A nuestra salud*!" she says, giving Mercedes the fuller of the two glasses and holding out her own to be clinked.

"*A nuestra salud*!" Mercedes repeats, gulping down

almost all the wine. "You have a fabulous Spanish accent!"

With a modest '*Gracias*', Celina hurries to refill Mercedes' glass and then, her head buzzing pleasantly, she throws a large dollop of butter into a pan, puts water on to boil, and begins to chop an onion.

Mercedes leans back in her chair, as though putting as much space as possible between herself and the wipe-clean melamine. She looks round at the black granite worktops, the smoked-glass cupboard doors, the stainless-steel accessories, and Celina, aware of the impression of utter sterility this kitchen of hers must give, longs to point out it had never been her idea, but does not.

For what kind of message would it give Mercedes if she were to say, 'None of this is my taste, you know. My taste is gingham and scrubbed pine like Dawn's'? What would Mercedes think of a woman too spineless to make her needs known on the relatively small matter of a kitchen?

After a while, Mercedes takes her spectacles out of her backpack and walks over to examine the photographs on the door of the monstrous silver fridge. She points to a smiling Max, champagne glass raised to the camera and free hand resting affectionately on the shoulder of a very beautiful, beaming young girl. "That's the husband, is it?"

"Last year" – Celina nods – "on Raine's sixteenth birthday. And the one below – the cool dude in the 'Living Dead' tee shirt – is Luca. He's fifteen and currently lives on Planet Zargon."

Mercedes scrutinises Max, Raine, and Luca in turn. Then she returns to the Max-and-Raine photo.

"She's stunning," she says, and Celina, turning to check whether her glass needs a top-up, sees that the vase of daffodils, more withered than ever, is still sitting there with Max's note propped up against it. Slamming down the onion knife, she hurls vase and flowers into the sink, and the note into the bin. Then she throws the onion pieces into the pan and stirs them around furiously.

"Tell me about *your* husband?" she shouts above the sizzling. You did have one, didn't you?"

Mercedes rolls her eyes heavenwards. "Orlando Glass," she says. "Mad as a fucking hatter. When he finally left, I burned every photo of him, and I cut him off all the photos we were in together too."

"In what way was Orlando 'mad'?"

Mercedes snorts. "He was into Scientology. You know? Auditing? Engrams?"

Celina tips a load of pasta into boiling water. "I saw a TV programme about Scientology once. Isn't it a form of brainwashing?"

"And bloody expensive brainwashing. Basically, they believe you've got these bad memories, called 'engrams', that stop you being mentally healthy, and the aim of Scientology is to get rid of them, which is the 'auditing' bit. The more engrams they audit out, though, the more they find lurking underneath, so as long as you keep paying up, the process is pretty well infinite."

"So Orlando never got rid of his engrams?" Celina collects a cucumber from the fridge and begins to slice it.

"Orlando got completely obsessed with his engrams. Then he decided to shack up with his auditor, and that was the best day of my life. Are these your books?" She reaches up to the shelf above the table, where a pile of Beeboo books lies stacked, and begins to look at each in turn.

Celina holds the cucumber as firmly as the smoked-glass chopping board will allow, making a mental note that tomorrow she will buy herself a decent wooden one. Then she looks along the row of stainless-steel containers, and the sober white tea-towels, boil-washed into submission, and for one heady moment she has to forcibly stop herself from giving them the same fate as the farewell note. She heaps tomato sauce on top of the onions and stirs till the mixture smells reasonably appetising. Above it, however, she could swear she can still make out the musk of Mercedes' perfume, with its undertones of rose.

Perhaps it is not a smell as such, but more of a smell-memory, which has become imprinted onto her brain cells, like Orlando's engrams. Or perhaps little atoms of it are stuck inside her nose, so that she can smell it all the time. Max's after-shave used to do that, in the early days of their marriage. It was called 'Bolt' and it had a spicy smell, like cinnamon and nutmeg mixed with lavender, and it came in a manly black bottle with an embossed pattern of nuts and bolts.

In the morning he would splash it all over himself, and before he left for the hospital she would bury her face in the jagged skin of his jawline and surround herself in a cloud of 'Bolt', euphoric as a cat in catnip. All day, as she did her drawings, that 'Bolt' smell would waft around her, and every time she moved and released a fresh cloud of it, she would feel a rush of longing so strong she could hardly wait for Max to be home again, holding her in his arms.

The heady scent of 'Bolt' faded with the years, though; and by the time those fateful Christmas candles were lit, Celina was no longer remotely moved by its charms. Max may still have doused himself in it for the benefit of the nurses and theatre staff, but as far as Celina was concerned, its raw sweetness was overshadowed by the sweat-smell it no longer masked; the acrid smell of disappointment that still, despite washings and ironings, clings to the sheets.

She looks over at Mercedes, who is staring so intently

at the centre-fold of *Beeboo is Missing!* that for a moment she wonders whether she has actually fallen asleep. She takes cutlery over to the table, and as she sets it down, puts a hand on Mercedes' shoulder.

"Oh honey" – Mercedes jumps at her touch, then flings exuberant arms round her waist and hugs her close – "I'd forgotten how brilliant your drawings are!" She points to the thundery sky with its red-glitter lightning-flash from which, very small and pale and with his antennae-bananas alarmingly bruised, a terrified Beeboo is running. "I love the way you get your colours to glow with light. It's as though the whole page is vibrating. And look at the action in that figure, and its expression … Oh-my-gawd, honey –if this is what you do for children, I can't wait to see what you deal up to adults!"

She jumps up and pulls Celina into a bear-hug, and Celina, muttering thanks, allows herself to revel in the unfamiliar softness of her embrace. She has never been enfolded in softness, ever. Even if Imogen cuddled her babies – and the idea of Imogen cuddling anything other than a man is a strange notion – surely her elegant body, even when young, was all hardness and angles from which no child could derive comfort? And surely – the intensity of the thought shocks her – Imogen would have baulked at the very idea of her tiny daughters' mouths coming anywhere near her shapely breasts?

Resting a grateful head on Mercedes' shoulder, she looks down at the table, and as she does a memory overwhelms her.

It is a memory of her and Max, in this very place in the kitchen, one early spring evening, long, long before it was sanitised. The table, in those days, was indeed scrubbed pine, and it already bore the comforting marks of married life – wine-glass rings, gashes where the meat-cleaver slipped, greasy spots from over-enthusiastic fondue parties. The walls had not yet had the bright green whitewashed out of them either, and were dotted with photos of lobsters and fishes and underwater plants, and hung with bits of dried seaweed, and charcoal sketches, for it was here that Celina worked.

The scent in her nostrils was not the same either. It was, of course, 'Bolt', but the feeling the scent evoked – that liquid looseness and longing to be engulfed and entered by another – was identical. That evening, Max had lifted her bodily onto the table, and she had let herself be lain back on the hard, warm wood, like a sacrificial lamb. As he slid inside her, she had arched her back against the unyielding wood and, like never before, felt every inch of him throb and grow. Raising her legs high and linking ankles around his back, she had pulled him closer and closer, screaming aloud at the utter joy of it.

The screaming had taken Max by surprise, had made him swell inside her, and the little sobbing sounds he made as he rocked her back and forth had been so touching, so unexpected, that she had not held back as she usually did. Instead, she clawed his back and sighed and screamed till waves of desire burst into a crescendo of sound that came from both of them at once.

When it was over, she released her hold on him, buried her head in the furrow of his neck, sobbed her gratitude into his skin. And afterwards, lying by his side in bed, she whispered into his ear. 'I think I've conceived, Max.'

She had, too. That evening, they made Raine. And somehow – though Max told her it was impossible and she was just being over-imaginative – she was sure she felt the new hormones that very night, laying down soft layers of baby-bedding in her womb. So full of happiness did she feel, and certainty that everything was exactly as it should be, it was inconceivable she would ever be empty again.

"If you're not too hungry" – she uncoils herself from Mercedes' arms and stands unsteadily apart from her – "I could show you my mother's studio before we eat?"

Mercedes assures her she is still full of Custard Doughnut, and so she drains the pasta, pours it and the sauce into a casserole dish, flings in a canful of tuna, and pushes the dish into the oven. Then, without looking directly into Mercedes' face, for to do so would show an expression she prefers to hide, she leads the way to the stairs.

CHAPTER SIXTEEN

"I'm not sure why I locked this," Celina says as she pushes Imogen's door open for Mercedes to step inside. "I used to keep it locked so the paint smell wouldn't get out, because I'm allergic to it, but it seems to have lost whatever smell it had."

Mercedes steps into the studio. She looks around, clutching her cheeks. "Look at the light!" she says, as Celina knew she would. "Look at the space!" She turns to the wall opposite the great wide window. "And look at those paintings! Oh – my – gawd ..."

"Having Imogen move in was all Max's idea, you know. It was the last thing in the world I wanted. But now I have this amazing studio ..."

"So Max was OK with your mother?" Mercedes runs her hand over the paintbrushes and jars on Imogen's work-table, her touch as gentle and reverential as if they were saintly relics.

Celina tosses her head impatiently. "Max wasn't one bit 'OK' with Imogen, but then it wasn't going to be Max who cooked her meals and washed her sheets and put up with her tempers, was it? And it was Max who was going to benefit from the huge extension Imogen paid through the nose for. At least, he thought he was."

She looks over at Mercedes' astonished expression. "What's wrong?"

"Nothing, honey," Mercedes assures her. "It's just that I've never seen you angry before." Arms outstretched, she takes a step towards Celina, but Celina sidesteps out of her way. A gentle touch, she knows, will turn the anger to tears and, right now, anger feels better. Going over to Imogen's bed, she sits awkwardly on its edge and Mercedes, keeping her distance, goes over to lean on the back of the peacock-tail chair and drink in the view.

"When they phoned me to tell me my mother had died," Celina says, "I was, all of a sudden, terribly frightened, and I've never been able to work out why. I wonder" – she lets her eyes drift down to the solidity of Mercedes' legs, and the scuffed toes of her purple leather boots – "if it could have been a fear of the anger I was at liberty to unleash at last. I was never any good at expressing anger, you know."

"Or maybe you were afraid you *wouldn't* unleash the anger." Mercedes lets go of the chair and walks away, not to Celina's side, but back to the wall opposite the window. "Maybe you were afraid you'd turn all those years of rage, with your mother and with Max, onto yourself." She makes a sweeping gesture that takes in the whole room. "This work is awesome," she breathes. "Utterly frigging awesome."

To her embarrassment, Celina realises that the sweeping gesture has included the easel with her own work on it and, as Mercedes begins a slow, careful tour of Imogen's walls, she hurries to remove it. Taking care not to touch the surface, because the bones she painted in the foreground the day before are still wet, she lifts the painting off the easel and leans it against one of the plan chests. Then she turns to check that Mercedes has not noticed, and is relieved to see that, oblivious to everything else in the room, she is viewing a row of four square mountain views which have always hung together, on this brightest of walls. She is pleased to see that, of all Imogen's paintings, Mercedes has chosen these for close examination.

For Celina has always loved these four paintings. Each represents a greyish-brown mountain seen from a low viewpoint, its summit hazy against a piercingly blue sky and its elephantine feet protruding out into the desert.

The surface of the mountain is whorled with curves, like rainbows whose every colour is a different shade of brown. Any irregularity, any jagged angle, has long been eroded by desert winds, and as Celina moves to stand behind Mercedes she realises for the first time that not only is the summit flat, it actually dips down slightly in the centre, like a saucer seen from the side.

"These are better than anything of your mother's I've ever seen," Mercedes whispers. "They have O'Keeffe's simplicity and strength but they've got a luminosity and a movement that O'Keeffe's lack." She wheels round to face Celina, her eyes wide and bright.

"Look at the way the foothills roll towards you, as though they're molten. Your mother may have been a cantankerous old witch, but she was a bloody visionary." She puts on her spectacles, peers closely at each of the bottom corners in turn, then knits her brows. "There's no date. There's not even a signature. Where did she paint them?"

Celina shrugs. "Mother never dated her work, never signed it unless it was going to be exhibited, which I always found odd, given how ego-driven she was. I did once look at the backs to see if there were any details, but there was nothing. Just some writing in Spanish, now I come to think of it, but nothing of any importance."

"They look like the mesa of New Mexico." Mercedes walks slowly past the paintings, pausing at each in turn. "But in another way, they don't. Somehow, even though there's no sense of scale, they look less gigantic."

"I always thought they were painted in New Mexico," Celina says. "I even believed – till very recently – that my mother had gone there and met O'Keeffe. Just in the last few days, though, I've been wondering ..."

Mercedes looks nonplussed. "But surely, at some point in your mother's life, you must have asked her where she painted? And whether she'd actually met O'Keeffe?"

Celina laughs, and the sound is brittle in the air. "I believe Mother really thought if she told you something, that made it true. She was a very complex woman, Mercie. Bitterly cruel to herself, and bitterly cruel to others."

Mercedes holds her arms invitingly wide but again, though a part of her aches for the comfort of the warm fragrant body there is, something – the need, perhaps, to follow through this line of thought unbroken – which stops Celina from succumbing to the embrace. Instead, she pulls herself ramrod-straight.

"She used to tell people she knew O'Keeffe, and she hinted she'd painted with her, out in the desert at Ghost Ranch."

"Her 'Faraway'," Mercedes says dreamily. "Wasn't that what she called it? And I reckon she meant it as a state of mind too, don't you? That clear space you have to have in your mind to do decent work?"

Celina nods. "That space I can't seem to find any more." She shakes the thought away. "But whether Mother actually went to the States and met O'Keeffe," she says briskly, "is another story."

Turning away from the paintings, Celina walks over to the window and, sitting on the peacock-tail chair, gazes out at the cold grey sky and the large, loose snowflakes that have begun to fall.

"Mother never went to New Mexico," she says, suddenly decisive. "She couldn't have. There was a world war looming."

Mercedes puts a tentative hand on Celina's shoulder, just as Celina, in this very place, once laid hers on Imogen's sharp, unwelcoming bones. Celina does not shrug it off.

"Maybe she told you she'd gone, because she herself wanted to believe she had?"

Celina feels the tingle of tears at the back of her eyes. "I think the truth of the matter" – she glances over to the four striated mountains, and suddenly everything makes perfect sense – "is that those four paintings were done in another 'Faraway' entirely."

She smiles up at Mercedes, and Mercedes slips both arms down over her shoulders and leans against her. Together they watch the last of the flakes slither down the glass and turn to tiny rivulets of water.

"Look," Celina says, pointing up. "The sun's trying to come out."

Mercedes follows her finger. There is brightness in the edge of one of the clouds, and a small but distinct patch of blue has broken through the leaden-grey sky. "So you think that other 'Faraway' might be Isla Graciosa?"

A faint tomato smell is announcing the readiness of the meal, but Celina holds Mercedes' wrists and feels her lean a little more heavily against her. She slides her hands slowly down and searches out the spaces between Mercedes' fingers. Slipping into them, she feels the big hands close round hers.

A shaft of sunlight, almost warm, lights up their

interlaced hands, and Celina watches the snowflake shadows slip from skin to skin. It is the nicest feeling in the world, being here, in her mother's chair, cradled by Mercedes. She never wants it to end.

"I'm sure it is Graciosa," she breaks the silence at last. "Just then, when you talked about the foothills looking as though they were molten, I realised. Those mountains are volcanoes, and Graciosa's got at least three. That's where those pictures were painted."

Mercedes' body is rocking now, moving them both back and forth, as though they are bobbing on small waves, and Celina wishes she could fall asleep like this, like a small child in its mother's arms.

"Do you think," Mercedes whispers, "we should rescue our lunch before it burst into flames?" and, reluctantly, Celina releases her fingers, pulls herself out of the chair and hurries to the door.

"Is this yours?" she hears Mercedes say and, looking back, sees she has spotted the bones painting by the plan chest.

"Don't look at it," she says. "It's awful. I'm just getting a feel for how different oils are from gouache or watercolour."

But Mercedes is crouched down, examining the painting. "It's not awful," she says. "I love the colours, and the vibrant way the edges collide. And the glow in the sky."

She straightens up. "You have to go to this Isla Graciosa, honey," she says firmly. "No excuses, right? You have to see these skies and these volcanoes for yourself."

CHAPTER SEVENTEEN

"I'd sell my soul for a 'Faraway'," Mercedes says, as she demolishes the well-browned pasta. "I'd love somewhere to work that's private, away from Matt and Ivy."

"And somewhere with better light," Celina adds. "Your studio's very dark."

"It's the darkest frigging studio in *Imago*. It's just about as dark as the Hell-Hole."

"The Hell-Hole?"

Mercedes makes a face. "That's what Kat called my pathetic basement flat, and boy was she right." She shudders. "Actually, I never thought of it before, but 'Hell-Hole' ... it's almost as though she had a premonition."

She is silent then, moving her fork over the sticky remains on her plate, and Celina leans over and gives her arm a little squeeze.

"Sometimes I really do think of moving back in, you know, and using it as a studio," Mercedes goes on. "But it's way too small, and anyway, I'm not up to it. I know it's crazy, but part of me imagines Selestino's still there, and if I go back I'll see he's not. Crazy, huh?"

She puts down the fork, pushes the plate away, and places both hands on the table, palms up, as though she is about to have them read. The palms are dry and hacked and criss-crossed with scars, and Celina, picturing the great towering Madonna, wonders how long Mercedes must have spent, cutting the chicken wire with pliers, bending it out of its own insistent curves, forcing it into the contours she needed.

It must have taken weeks – months – and all the time those sharp ends pierced her skin and left marks like stigmata whose pain, perhaps, drowned out a little of the pain of Selestino's death. The urge to grasp those hands and say, 'Come and work in mother's studio. Come and live here' is so strong Celina has to swallow it back.

"You're far braver than me," she says instead. "You cope with your problems positively, whereas I stop myself from doing things; even things I really want to do. Like going to Graciosa," she adds, before Mercedes can. "I do long to be there, in the sun, in that sparse landscape, painting, where the smell of the paint doesn't bother me …"

"So what's stopping you?" The edge in Mercedes' voice cuts through the pathetic longing in Celina's. "Not the children? Oh Christ, Celina!" Her tone sharpens. "You're not telling me you can't go because of the children?"

Celina pulls herself upright again. "Actually, I am," she says. "I feel terribly guilty about having been so self-absorbed and letting them become so distant. Now it's just the three of us, I need to try harder with them. And I can't leave now. I'd feel like another rat, deserting the sinking ship."

She looks earnestly at Mercedes, willing her to understand, but Mercedes simply stands and gathers up the plates.

"There are other reasons too." Celina stares miserably down at the melamine. "I keep having migraine headaches, and sometimes they make me feel really quite ill. But mainly, it's because I can't leave the children."

There is a crash, and pieces of burnt pasta and a spray of sauce splatter over the table as Mercedes clatters the plates back down onto the table. "They've got a father, haven't they?" She spits the words out like sharp-edged stones. "Leave them with him. Let *him* explain why he's screwing somebody else and buggering up their lives. For fuck's sake, honey – get *angry*!"

Without waiting for a response, she sweeps up the plates again and heads off to dump them on top of the daffodils. Head swimming, Celina goes to the fridge to fetch another bottle of wine. She stirs around among the mess on the work surface till she finds a corkscrew.

The cork is hard, and she has to lean all her weight on it to break through its outer crust. When the screw finally engages, she holds the neck of the bottle tight with one hand, as though throttling it. Pressing down with all her weight, she forces the corkscrew further and further down, groaning with the effort of it.

The cork makes little squeaking noises as it spirals ever deeper, and then, quite suddenly, the resistance lessens. Jamming the bottle between her knees, Celina pulls. The cork moves ever faster, then emerges with a triumphant pop and a small spray of foam.

"You're right," she says, banging the bottle down on the work surface with a force that makes both of them jump. "The whole thing's Max's doing, and there he is, happily ensconced in his love-nest Brighton, with no responsibilities to his family."

"Exactly. So give him some!" Mercedes stands up and holds her glass out to be filled.

Celina listens to the laughing sound the first glass of wine always makes, and all of a sudden everything is so obvious, and so easy. She fills her own glass, then moves a little closer to Mercedes, marveling at the breadth, the openness, of her smile.

"Thanks." She clinks her glass against Mercedes'. "I'll definitely think about it."

"Do more than think about it, honey." Mercedes takes a step forward and, placing her hand on the side of Celina's neck, rubs her thumb very, very lightly over her Adam's apple. "*Do* it," and she moves nearer so that the sides of their heads touch. She brings her other hand up to stroke Celina's sleek hair and, not daring to move, Celina revels in the moist warmth of breath on her ear, the electric charge as the big hand moves down to embrace the nape of her neck. It is as though every part of her has come alive, every inch of skin is fired with desire. Then the kitchen door flies open, and Raine rockets in.

Celina stiffens and pulls away. She leans against the table and watches the kitchen fill with the crackling of nylon, the shaking of long dark hair, the fine spray of water droplets from Raine's parka. She has not felt like this since the day Kalinda caught her trying on one of their mother's bras, and she dare not think how red her face must be.

"This is Mercedes," she says, too cheerfully.

Mercedes steps forward. "Call me Mercie," she says. "And I guess you must be Raine? What amazing hair! And what incredible bone structure! Christ, I'd love to paint you."

"Your hair's pretty cool too," Raine says absently as, edging Celina aside, she reaches over the table and takes down a sheet of paper from the shelf. She gives it a cursory look then flings it onto the table, then throws herself into a chair.

"You didn't fill in the form for Nepal." Her tone is one of resignation. "I told you last week it was due in tomorrow. You said you would."

The blood drains from Celina's face. "Oh Raine, I'm so sorry. I meant to but ..."

Raine takes a pen out of her pocket and begins to write her name on the top of the form. "Don't bother," she says. "I'll do it myself. I knew I'd have to."

Mercedes picks up her backpack and, taking Celina's arm, motions towards the hall. "I'll go," she mouths, and when Celina protests she adds, loudly, "I must paper the Madonna's breasts tonight."

"Paper the Madonna's breasts?" Raine looks up. "What with?"

"Papier mâché." Mercedes gives Raine a wink. "By this time next week, so help me God, she will be well and truly swathed. From tits" – she indicates her own chest – "to ass," and she gives herself a resounding slap on the bottom. "Nice to meet you, Raine!"

In the hall, Celina holds out Mercedes' pashmina. "Thanks for making me see sense about Max," she says, wrapping the warmth around her. "By the way, shall I pick up the photos for you? Bring them to *Imago*?"

"That would be great, honey." Freeing her arms from her woollen cocoon, Mercedes gives Celina a hug. "I'll phone you tonight. Now go and sort out your beautiful daughter!" She plants a kiss on Celina's cheek, so close to her lips that Celina tastes Chardonnay. Then, in a rainbow-coloured flurry, she sweeps out into the night.

Mentally girding whatever loins she has left, Celina goes back into the kitchen and sits down beside Raine. Taking care not to breathe into her daughter's face, she tries to ease the form out from under her arm, but Raine holds it fast.

"I really am sorry, Raine," she says. "I'll do it now.

OK?"

Raine grimly continues to write, and Celina tops up her glass.

"And after school tomorrow, if you like, we'll go into town and I'll buy you something to wear in Nepal. I imagine you'll need to be demure."

Raine graces her with the smallest spark of interest. "Can I get a tattoo?"

Celina gives the form another tug. "No," she says. "You may not get a tattoo. The offer is a demure dress."

Raine eyes her, sensing a trap. "From Marks and Spencers?"

"From a shop of your choice." And she tugs again.

With a long-suffering sigh, Raine relinquishes the form. Draping herself across the table, she watches Celina write the word 'asthma', score it out, replace it with 'athsma', and then examine both words dubiously.

"So," Raine says, "is Mercie an artist?"

Still looking at 'athsma', Celina nods.

"A real artist, I mean. With a studio?"

Celina nods again. Leaving 'athsma' she tackles the next question. "She's a real artist," she says, "with a real studio. Called *Imago*."

"And she paints pictures?" Raine persists. "And sells them?"

"*I've* got a studio," Celina points out, somewhat petulantly. "*I* paint pictures and sell them. *I'm* a real artist."

Raine frowns at the form. "I've never had asthma," she says. "And that's not the way you spell it, and it's not the way you spell 'rubella' either."

"You had an asthma attack when you were three, and it's as well to err on the side of caution. So, how do you spell 'asthma'?"

"That way." Raine points. "The way you scored out.

And why is Mercie making a Madonna? Is she religious? She doesn't sound religious." There is a thoughtful silence, then Raine adds, grudgingly, "She's quite cool."

Celina puts down the pen and sits back in her chair. She takes a long, deep breath in. "Mercie's preparing an exhibition called *Songs of Selestino* and the Madonna is its centrepiece. She's going to incorporate Selestino's poems into it, and she's hoping it will somehow clear his name."

She looks carefully at Raine. Her perfect brow is shadowed by tiny creases. "Mercie is Selestino Glass's mother," she says quietly.

"You're kidding?" Two bright spots of pink flush Raine's face. She looks as beautiful, and as fragile, as a china doll.

"No," Celina says. "I'm not. I only just found out. I was dreadfully shocked."

"But why didn't you tell me before? Why didn't you tell me before he died?" Raine jumps up and stands facing Celina with her hands on her hips. The brown of her eyes is skimmed with furious tears. "Shit, Mum! You could have got me to meet him!"

Celina rises from her seat and puts an arm round Raine's shoulders. Unexpectedly, Raine does not shake it away. "I didn't know," she says. "I only just met Mercie. I don't know her all that well."

Raine's frown deepens. "You *seem* to know her well …"

"We met years ago, but then we lost touch. At the time, we talked briefly about our children, but I didn't know her son's name. When the Paedophile Poet story hit the papers, I didn't make the connection. And anyway, Mercie's name's 'Grey' now," she adds unnecessarily.

"In a sense," she steers the conversation into safer waters, "the *Songs of Selestino* exhibition is Mercie's way of working through her grief. And you're right, she isn't religious, but she's interested in religious iconography." She sits back down, looks at the form again. "When did you have your BCG? Year Six or Year Seven?"

Raine sits back down too. She looks exhausted. "Year Seven," she says. "Why did Mercie say she'd love to paint me?"

Celina does a careful calculation and fills in the appropriate date. "She said she'd love to paint you because she admires your hair and your skin and your bone structure. All of which" – she gives Raine what she hopes is a Mercedes-style wink– "you got from me."

Reinstating the 'asthma', she ticks the remaining boxes and signs the bottom of the form. "There." She slips it into its envelope. "Done." She takes another mouthful of wine and, when Raine does not immediately flounce out, asks, "How are you feeling about Nepal? Are you excited?"

Raine wrinkles her perfect nose. "I suppose so." She gets up, but does not move away. "It's not for ages, you know."

"Has the school told you who you'll be staying with?" Celina persists. She pictures Raine, all alone in a Nepalese house, with new, Nepalese, parents and new, Nepalese, brothers and sisters. She is, she realizes, more than a little vague as to where Nepal actually is. Is it in India?

"Not yet. But you'll be getting an Information Pack." She looks at Celina. "You don't have to worry, Mum," she says. "It's all very well organised."

Celina hastens to assure her she is not in the least worried and then, bracing herself with another long breath in, she says, "How would you feel if I were to go away? Just for a week or so. Would you be happy to stay with Daddy?"

Raine's eyes open wide in alarm. "With Daddy and Felicity, you mean? In Brighton?"

Celina nods. "Brighton's nice," she says. "We went there once, do you remember? And Luca would be there too of course. And it would only be for a couple of weeks. It's just that your Aunt Kalinda and I ..."

Picking up her satchel and hoisting it onto her shoulder, Raine makes for the door. "You mean, miss school?" she says, stopping but not deigning to turn round.

"Maybe at the Easter break then?" Celina tries. She watches Raine pulls her back straight and stand with her hand on the doorknob, glaring at the floor. Then, in one angry movement, the door is pulled open and Raine swings round.

"Luca and I," she informs Celina, "can't stand Felicity. Also, Felicity has three children who sound perfectly revolting. I can't speak for Luca," she concludes haughtily, "but I personally would sooner eat my own vomit." And she closes the door with a terminally loud slam.

For a while Celina sits very still at the table. Heat is creeping up her body, and there is a feeling of pressure in her head, as though every tiny blood vessel is expanding at once and filling her brain with too much blood. She wonders if something might be about to explode.

She looks over at the sink, at the mountain of dishes on the drying-rack. Propelled by an urgent need to bring something, however small and insignificant, to a conclusion, she swipes the tea-towel off its peg, and begins to dry and put away.

The repetitive action is calming, and as the pile of dishes slowly diminishes she lets her thoughts drift back to Inge's room, to that moment when she dared to expose and name the unlanced boil that was the Schism; and it occurs to her that all she has actually done *is* expose and name. The boil itself is still very much intact.

It is like those memory-things Orlando paid the Scientologists to get rid of, and she tries to remember the word. She has a feeling it began with 'n', but the more she tries to bring it to mind, the more it slips away. Whatever the n-thing was, though, it had reminded her of her Schism, for surely that was what the Schism was? A persistent bad memory which refused to be cleared? A malignant thing, hidden deep inside like a cluster of insect eggs, from which one day a host of tiny gnawing worms will hatch?

Flinging down the tea-towel, she hurls herself out of the kitchen and upstairs to Imogen's studio, where she throws a blank canvas onto the easel. She fetches a palette and a fistful of brushes and squeezes worm after worm of paint onto the palette, till its surface gleams like a small rainbow.

She selects the largest brush and smothers it in Vandyke Brown with a tinge of Mixing White. Slightly to the right of centre, and with its perspective steep as a small child would see it, she sketches the rough outline of a woman with one arm outstretched, holding a paintbrush out in front of her, like a rapier. In the woman's other hand, she scribbles the shape of a palette, and then she adds four black lines to form a rectangular canvas with the tip of the rapier in its centre. Below the rectangle, she paints three thick brown lines to represent the splayed legs of an easel.

Taking two broad-bristled paintbrushes, she fills in the shape of her mother's dress – the cornflower blue, the poppy red – and she works quickly and confidently, for she has always, in the dream, seen that dress as clear as day. Now, in blazing clarity, she reproduces its colours, its length, the slight sheen of its texture, and the way it gathers round her mother's slim waist before dropping in folds that cling, here and there, to her bare brown legs.

The neckline of the dress, and her mother's face are, however, less clear. Did the neckline plunge, revealing a tantalising glimpse of Imogen's breasts? Or was it sedately collared? Certainly, as photographs show, Imogen was never averse to revealing her flesh, and surely the scene took place in summer, for Celina remembers the heat of the studio, and the heady oil-paint smell, and her mother's bare feet, large and firmly-planted, like those of Mercedes' Madonna.

But no matter how hard she looks inward, the more that part of the memory smudges and blurs, as though her mother was too tall for her to see her face and hair. In the end, giving up, she rounds off the neckline and mixes a little Burnt Sienna with white till she has a flesh tone like her own. With a long-haired, finer, brush, she begins to paint.

For surely, if she begins, she will be able to picture that face of her mother's clearly enough to bring it to life on the canvas? After all, she has seen countless photos of Imogen in her thirties, with her head held high and her velvet skin glowing brown. She has seen the proudly-arched eyebrows, the deep-set dark eyes, the finely-chiselled nose that she and Raine share. She knows too that it was Imogen who gave both her and Raine their manes of flowing black waves, for those old photographs show them cascading down onto her shoulders, or swept elegantly up from the nape of her neck to lie in elegant coils.

And as for Imogen's expression, she has no doubts at all that on that fateful day it was one of utter fury; and 'utter fury' is an expression she has seen, on an older Imogen, countless times. All she has to do, surely, is to call that expression to mind and then airbrush its wrinkles, intensify its eyes, flesh out its lips, resurrect its sunken cheeks and add the bloom of youth to its faded skin?

But, try as she will, the face she, the child, saw that day remains resolutely hidden, and when she brings the brush to the canvas, she can summon up no mental image to copy. At last, frustrated beyond measure, she paints a long slim neck and tops it with an oval shape, the features of which she all but obscures with long blue-black hair. Then she steps as far back as she can before Imogen's bed blocks her way and, sitting on the white counterpane, drinks in the scene.

Now that she has stopped painting, she is aware of the strong paint smell and she breathes deeply, trying to rid her lungs of it, but no amount of exhalation can flush it away. It is as though it has impregnated her nasal tissues and is clinging to them, like embalming fluid. And now, in the far corner of her vision, a small grey light has begun to flicker. The birds are preparing to fly.

She sinks back onto the bed, closes her eyes, and watches the pulsing light-shape float, amoeba-like, in her imperfect darkness. Her tablets are downstairs, and she knows she should go and take one; but her exhaustion presses her down onto the bed and, defeated, she rolls onto her side, draws her knees up to her belly, and thinks about the scene she has just painted.

The tall slim body, in its vibrant blues and reds, is as true to life as it can be and the face, anonymously blank and hidden by hair, is as good as she is ever going to manage. She has painted her memory as faithfully as she can. Now, for the first time, however, it occurs to her that this memory – the memory of the figure – is not the whole story. All these years, in all her dreams and waking visions, the figure has dominated. Today, she realises for the first time that there is more than Imogen in that memory.

Ignoring the dazzling mass, she forces herself to concentrate on the scene. Panning away from Imogen herself, she focuses on Imogen's canvas. For there is something else she remembers. There is.

There is the beginning of a picture on that easel. Its exact details are hazy and seem to exist slightly out of the frame, like the 'birds in flight' that always flicker in the periphery of the visual field but never come truly into view. But there is, for sure, a shape. There is a shape and, what is more, that shape has a colour. And as she continues to stare into the farthest reaches her memory, she sees that the colour is red.

CHAPTER EIGHTEEN

Two days later, with Mercedes' wallet of photos in her bag and the remains of Monday's migraine still nagging away inside her skull, Celina makes her way to *Imago.*

Although she is eager to see Mercedes and her work again, this second visit is not quite the longed-for event it once was, for events of the past two days have washed the joy from everything. It is as though she has swept a grey wash over the bright canvas that was Monday, smearing its colours, blurring the fine detail, dulling the sparkle.

It began, of course, with the Schism painting, which is still sitting on the easel, behind the firmly locked door, with the abandoned palette on the floor and the brushes, bristles set hard, scattered around it.

What on earth possessed her to try such a dangerous experiment? Why, when she knows she is in a delicate state, did she not at least wait till later in the week? Why did she not wait till tomorrow, so that the next day Inge could put her back together again?

For the fiasco that is the Schism painting has answered no questions at all and, far from elucidating and comforting, has left Celina with a new fear. And whereas the fear she had before was awful because its meaning was unknown, this new fear is worse, for its meaning has such far-reaching implications.

Most of Monday evening she lay on her bed, in the darkness, running and rerunning the red image through her exhausted brain, telling herself it could not possibly be what she imagines. That it could not possibly be that bad. For if it *is* that bad, then her plans – the trip to Isla Graciosa, the search for her father – are pointless. Anything she learned about him would be so utterly grim she would rather not know.

And it goes beyond her father. If that red shape is what she thinks it is, she might as well forget the sabbatical, forget painting, for if she really witnessed what she believes she witnessed, no amount of hours in Inge's fragrant room could ever wash away the stain of that scene. She will never be free of it; she will never be an artist, a painter. All that will be left for her to do is to pick up her pencil, crawl back into Beeboo's safe, little world, and draw herself into twee oblivion.

Yes, Monday evening had been bad. Of all the lonely times she has spent recently, it was the loneliest; and the knowledge that Luca and Raine were in the house had accentuated rather than diminished that loneliness. For after a heated conversation together, the two of them had shut themselves inside their separate rooms to smoulder to the beat of whatever music was currently numbing their brains. They said not a word to her all night, but their joint outrage seeped through the walls till morning when, without a word, they left.

Sometime during that endless evening – eleven, or even later – the phone had rung. Celina was in the kitchen by then, drinking strong coffee on top of a double dose of painkillers, and had not even considered answering it. It would be for Raine and Luca, she told herself. No one with adult sensibilities would ring at eleven.

The ringing had stopped then, and immediately started again, and suddenly she remembered that in this very kitchen, just a few hours before, Mercedes' hand had caressed her neck and her breath tingled her ears. Had she not said she would phone tonight? As quickly as the stone inside her head will allow, Celina ran into the hall.

The conversation that followed – or rather, the stream of consciousness that followed, for Mercedes hardly breathed long enough for Celina to say anything – reminded Celina of the phone call from the hospital the night Imogen died. To begin with, it had been a flow of words and phrases she heard but could not process. And while the nurse who had told her of Imogen's passing had spoken very softly, as if to an invalid, Mercedes' voice was so strident it assaulted her eardrum.

With an enormous effort, however, she had forced herself to concentrate, and eventually had got the drift of the call, which was that dry rot, or rising damp, or something, had been found in *Imago* and, there being no money to fix it, Matt had decided to apply for Arts Council funding to mount a joint exhibition. His work, and Ivy's, would be shown alongside a significantly censored Madonna, and the emphasis would be on having plenty of merchandise to sell. There would be no incense, no candles, no icons, no stained glass. In essence, the *Songs of Selestino* exhibition had been dropped.

'He's going to call it *A Womb with a View*,' Mercedes had hollered into Celina's ear. 'What kind of damn fool title is that? The Madonna'll be surrounded by Matt's giant sperm balloons, and Ivy's mammary face-flannels and vulva oven gloves and – get this – she'll just be *holding* Selestino's poems. *Holding* them, in her hand, so the whole fucking point's lost. I can't bear it" – her words disappeared into a volley of coughs – "I simply ... can not ... bear it.'

There had been a merciful silence then, as Mercedes, presumably, covered the mouthpiece to cough some more. During the silence, Celina shuffled over to the counter, took a packet of cigarettes out of her bag and – to hell with Raine and Luca – lit up. She moved the phone to the other ear in time to hear Mercedes say, 'So that's it. I'm through with *Imago*. I'm moving back to the Hell-Hole.'

Another silence followed, this one definitely requiring a reaction from Celina.

'I'm so sorry,' she said, dragging on the cigarette and playing for time. For a while she said nothing more, and that was partly because finding the right words was such an effort, and partly because she was aware of not saying anything she might later regret. Mainly, though, she said nothing because – amazingly, now the barrage of words had ceased – she wanted to savour this moment.

For with Mercedes' last sentences, a kind of uneasy calm settled over Celina. Confused, frightened, and brain-addled she might be, but as she listened to Mercedes it dawned on her that she was not, after all, alone. Max had gone, her children had ganged up against her, but there *was* someone who needed her. Her life did not consist solely of the awful riddle of the Schism.

Carefully, she murmured platitudes. She was, she told Mercedes, right behind her, whatever she decided to do. Nothing, she assured her, was more important than artistic integrity. Mercedes was right to leave *Imago*, but perhaps the Hell-Hole was a bit extreme? If they put their minds to it, could they not come up with a better solution? Dawn's house, for example? Or somewhere?

Then, as Mercedes agreed that it all needed further thought, and had sobbed out her gratitude, Celina reminded her that the photos would be ready on Wednesday morning, and suggested she deliver them on Wednesday afternoon. She apologised for not coming sooner, but told Mercedes to call her any time at all. She also suggested strongly that Mercedes do nothing too precipitous; and all the while, as this miraculously cool, calm, collected Celina spoke, she had the bizarre feeling that she was outside herself, looking at herself, listening in awe to her own wise words.

Then, very gently, she said 'goodnight', hung up and lit another cigarette. And as she smoked, she reflected that, for just a few minutes, her theory about the red shape on the canvas had seemed the most ridiculous thing in the entire world.

Now, as the *Imago* building appears through the cold misty rain that swathes London, she is not sure what she thinks about anything. Her thoughts are in chaos, there is a low buzzing in her head, and she feels as though she has been on a long sea voyage.

Yesterday, pussy-footing around her flouncing daughter and sullen son, she actually found herself wishing there was some kind of therapeutic Casualty Department to which she could go, so frighteningly acute was her confusion and sense of detachment. With the aid of alcohol and nicotine, however, she had survived, and now it is a relief to be here, on Mercedes' solid threshold. As she climbs the filthy stairs, she tells herself that things could be worse. Today she has Mercedes to take her out of her own head. Tomorrow she will have Inge.

Mercedes' face is sombre as she ushers her in, and she squeezes her tight.

"*So* happy to see you, honey," she says, as she leads her over to her studio door. "Matt and Ivy are out, meeting some Arts Council arse, so we've got the place to ourselves."

Celina slips inside and, taking off her sensibly grey hat, finds a space to sit on the bed. If anything, the little studio is more cluttered than before.

"Coffee?" Mercedes asks.

Celina takes the wallet of photographs out of her bag and places it on the bed. "Just a half mug, and plenty of milk, please," she says, and she waits for Mercedes to fill the kettle.

"Christ" – Mercedes picks up the wallet and sits down – "I can't tell you how fucking scared I am."

She begins to open the envelope, and Celina watches the big strong fingers, clumsily tearing at the paper. Mercedes' hands are so different from hers, with their leathery skin and their scars and callouses, and their nails cut right down to the quick. Each nail has a dark half-moon at its base, and pink paint caked to its sides, as though no amount of turpentine could clean all the stains away. They have toiled, these hands, while hers, with their elegant shape and carefully-applied nail varnish, have been cosseted.

Not wanting to intrude when Mercedes sees the photos for the first time, she turns away and looks at a row of seascapes to her left. They are done in acrylic, their colours bold and wild and vibrant, like movement captured. Could she ever be capable of such looseness, such spontaneity? Or is she condemned to a life of controlled neatness?

Probably she is, now.

She hears a gasp, and turns to see Mercedes hold up the first photo for her to see. It is a blurred image of, probably, the Thames.

"Oh-my-gawd," Mercedes breathes. "I remember this. It was the day Dawn and Kat and Selestino and I climbed to the top of the London Monument. You know – the memorial to the Great Fire? It was a god-awful day," she adds, shaking her head at the thought of it. "Dawn and Kat were high as kites, talking on and on about Dawn's book, and the Great Fire, and they kept asking me if they could light a fire in Kat's bedroom."

She turns suddenly to Celina, brows furrowing. "You know, I'd completely forgotten about Dawn and Kat wanting a fire. Of course I told her she couldn't, that in any case the fireplace was boarded up. But I should have told the police, shouldn't I?"

Celina puts her hand over Mercedes'. It is surprisingly cold. "It was probably the shock," she says. "At the time, it would have blocked everything out."

"But it was crazy, to want a fire in August," Mercedes insists. "I've probably withheld vital evidence. Do you think I should go back to the police?" She looks pleadingly at Celina. "Do you?"

Celina sits quietly, not knowing what to say, and she wonders if this is how Inge feels, when her clients wail at her from their white marshmallow chair, wanting her to tell them what to do. Wanting her to make their decisions for them.

"Would you like the case to be re-opened in the light of new evidence?" she decides to ask. The question, which she assumes she got from the television, sounds great, and she hopes it makes sense.

Mercedes looks startled. "Is that what they'd do?" she asks, and Celina shrugs.

"And then they might finally find out if it was suicide?" Mercedes flips the photo over and picks up the next. She gasps again, and for a while is silent, looking at its every detail. From time to time, little noises escape, like tiny whimpers.

Her lower lip is quivering, and Celina wonders whether, somewhere in the chaos of the studio, there might be a bottle of brandy. At last Mercedes turns the photo round.

This photo is an interior scene. In the foreground, in profile, is the furred grey profile of a young man. Long-haired, bearded, his dark eyes are like two small pits in the pallor of a flash-lit face. It is barely recognisable, but she knows who it is.

"It's Selestino," Mercedes breathes, and she runs the tip of her finger over the blurred features. "The last photo. Oh God ..." She covers her face with her hands and sobs into them.

Gently, Celina takes the photograph and looks at the spectral form of Selestino Glass. If you used a bit of artistic imagination, you could see how focused those washed-out eyes were, how intently he gazed over to the back of the room, as though something there had arrested all his attention.

What was he looking at? What was in the background? For it is clear to Celina that this is not a photograph of Selestino at all. It is a photograph of the mantelpiece in front of which Selestino is sitting.

Celina waits while Mercedes finds a tissue and wipes the tears from her cheeks. Then, pulling her close, she rubs her back, round and round, in small circles. When she feels a little calmness settle over her, she holds up the photograph again.

"Do you see, Mercie?" She points to the mantelpiece. "It's an old fireplace. Where do you think it might be?"

Mercedes peers through her spectacles. With a little cry, she points to a bright pink and turquoise shape, on the top right of the photo. "It's the spare bedroom in the Hell-Hole," she says. "Kat's bedroom, and Selestino's before that. I recognise the mirror. I made the frame." She shakes her head in disbelief. "But there wasn't a fireplace. There was a white plywood thing, with an electric fire in it."

Celina peers closer. The dark old wood of the mantelpiece has a carving in it, and it is surely at this carving that Selestino Glass is looking. Although his features have been blotted out by the light, the carving is quite clear. It shows a snake biting its tail and, below, the date '1666'.

"They must have taken the plywood off," Mercedes is saying, "and found this underneath. And then they must have lit a fire. So the fire that killed them wasn't started by faulty electrics at all … But why didn't they tell me they'd found the original fireplace? Why didn't Selestino tell me?"

Once again she looks at Celina, begging her to supply the answer and Celina, searching for words of explanation or comfort but finding none, makes do with cradling her in her arms and rocking her to and fro.

"That day at the Monument, I felt so alone, you know," Mercedes whispers into Celina's shoulder. "As if the three of them had a secret they weren't sharing with me." She looks up at Celina, her eyes glassy with tears. "If Selestino kept this secret from me, how many other secrets did he keep?"

She sinks back into Celina's shoulder, and Celina rests her chin on the wiry curls. She thinks about Luca and Raine last night, hermetically sealed away from her. "Don't children always keep secrets from their parents?" she says.

Mercedes looks back at the photograph. "Sure," she agrees. "But this is just a fireplace, for Christ's sake. And it was in *my* flat. Why on earth didn't they tell me about it?"

Celina thinks back to the seal, with its tiny amber snake. "Selestino liked that image, didn't he? The symbol of eternity? So he must have been amazed to find it on the fireplace. Perhaps it had a secret significance for him?"

She dips her head to see Mercedes' expression, but Mercedes is spreading the rest of the photos out on the bed and looking at each one in turn; and suddenly the utter desolation of the scene hits Celina. Excluded from Mercedes' grief, with no words of encouragement left to say, she feels exhaustion engulf her. Her own problems, she knows, will soon flood back, sucked in by the grim vacuum exhaustion creates.

Desperate to keep those problems at bay for a little longer, she looks along Mercedes' row of photographs. There are several more views of a blurred Thames, and another two photos of the fireplace – one with a flashlit Selestino and one without – and she picks up the latter and concentrates all her attention on the snake.

For is there not a connection between Selestino Glass and that eternal snake, other than the brass seal? The more she looks at the photo, the more sure she is that there is, but try as she will, her brain will no longer focus. Her headache has worsened, and all she wants is to be home, with a cigarette, and a coffee that does not taste of tin.

"May I take this?" she asks Mercedes, and Mercedes, looking up at her as though she has forgotten she is there, nods vaguely.

Celina slips the photo carefully into her bag. Then she picks up her hat, and stands looking down at Mercedes. The image of those rats leaving the sinking ship springs once more to mind, but she tells herself that, for now, she has nothing left to give.

"Are you all right?" she says, and though she half-expects Mercedes to smile, and leap up, and fling her arms round her with a 'Sure, honey, I'm just fine!' she is not surprised when all she does is haul herself up and, leaning an arm heavily on her shoulder, accompany her in silence to the door.

"I'm sorry, honey," she says, as they embrace. "I wanted to talk to you about the Hell-Hole and *her*" – she indicates the Madonna, her upper half now painted flamboyantly pink – "but I'm completely done in. I need space to think things out. Could we meet later in the week? Maybe have an Indian?"

"I'd like that," Celina says. And with a chaste kiss, they part.

Outside, Celina knots her scarf and pulls her hat as far down her forehead as it will go. The rain is like a cold grey shroud, and her bones have turned to ice. Her head still pounds and there is a dull ache above her heart. In some indefinable way, she feels she has failed Mercedes; and again she thinks of Inge.

Does she ever tire of listening and encouraging? Does she ever, even for a moment, long to scream out her own anger, or her own grief?

Summoning up her last dregs of energy, Celina heads for St Paul's. As she walks, she tries to picture the benign little snake in the photograph, and as the crowds close dizzily in around her, she forces the red shape out and the snake in, and somehow makes it home.

Tomorrow, she tells herself as – relief beyond measure – she sits in the downstairs toilet and clandestinely inhales, she will perhaps find some solace. Today she has listened as best she can. Tomorrow she will be allowed to talk.

CHAPTER NINETEEN

When Inge Van Deth leads Celina into her consulting-room and smiles her familiar empathetic smile, it is as much as Celina can do to stop herself from bursting into tears. And as she eases herself down into the marshmallow, she feels quite alarmingly old and brittle.

She watches Inge sit down opposite and smooth the folds of her creamy-yellow skirt. Her own charcoal-grey jumper and black trousers feel like a blot on the landscape of this pale room, and she is acutely aware of the smell they must be carrying, for she has lost count of the number of cigarettes she has smoked in the past twenty-four hours. Her whole body is trembling. Even her lips tremble, as though afraid of what they are about to say.

"I've had a bad few days," she begins. "A perfectly dreadful few days." Then, overwhelmed by the impossibility of finding words for the nightmare she has been living since Monday, she gives way and lets her tears do the talking.

As Celina sobs, Inge sits very still, only moving to steer the box of paper tissues in her direction. After a while, when the sobs show no sign of abating, she fetches a glass and a bottle of water, and pours some out for her. Moved to more tears by this simple act of kindness, Celina takes the glass and drinks.

"So, you have had a challenging time since last we met?"

Celina puts the empty glass on the table, and though she tries to do so quietly, her hand is shaking so much it makes a small clatter. She would kill for a cigarette.

"At first it was fine," she says. "In fact, at first, after talking to you about the Schism, I felt such a relief and release. The depression I'd had, and the dreadful anxiety, just lifted and I could see things clearly. In fact, I could see and understand things I'd never seen or understood before, and the whole world seemed full of possibilities. I wouldn't have believed it could happen, such a change. But it didn't last." She reaches for a tissue and wipes away a new tear. "I thought it would."

She looks over at Inge's broad face and sees the sad, all-knowing smile. "You thought your feelings of well-being would last forever?"

Celina considers the question. "I did. Which is stupid, I know. But I thought I had made such a breakthrough, getting the Schism out into the open, that everything would be easier." Feeling like a customer returning a piece of damaged merchandise, she adds, "I really thought it had gone for good."

Whether from anxiety, or cigarettes, or last night's wine, or a combination of all three, her mouth is still so parched that her tongue has difficulty articulating words. She refills the glass.

"I even did a little painting with oils," she continues, between sips, "and I felt all right. I didn't get a migraine, didn't get any feelings of dissociation, and so I began to think that perhaps I really could start to paint the way I want to. Even go away, to my mother's house, and paint there.

"But on Monday I decided to do an experiment. I decided to paint the scene I saw as a child. I thought that, if I did, I would remember exactly what happened. What my mother said. Even why my father left." She holds the water glass tight against her lips, but still they tremble. "I had the most dreadful reaction. I've never had such a severe migraine. In fact, I can still feel it.

"I know this sounds melodramatic, but the night after I did the painting, I felt as though I had lost my mind. That I had literally taken leave of my senses. I couldn't think straight. I still can't think straight."

She looks hard into Inge's eyes and, concentrating all her attention on them, sees that their brown is not uniform. There are small flecks of amber, like tiny petals, around the pupils, and along the pink lower rim of each eye is the tiniest sliver of white, where the light hits.

"Look. Look at my hands, even now." She holds them out for Inge to see, and the glass falls and rolls under the table. "I'm so anxious, every bit of me's shaking. In fact, it's only anxiety that's holding me together. Without it, I don't think I'd exist at all."

Together they watch Celina's trembling hands and then, disappointed but also rather reassured by the lack of reaction from Inge, Celina covers her face and presses the fingertips hard against her head. "I feel so ill," she says. "Physically ill. Do you think I might be ill?" Parting her fingers, she peeks out between them, like a small child playing Hide and Seek.

"What do you think is causing your anxiety?" Inge asks. "Is it, do you think, a result of the smell of the paint, or was there something else. Something you painted, perhaps?"

Celina reaches with her foot for the glass and, without bothering to wipe it because surely even Inge's floor is pure, fills it again. She takes another mouthful of water, but no matter how much she drinks her mouth remains dry, and now she feels sick. Gritting her teeth, she recalls the image she had watched grow on the canvas. The scarlet pool, the red pointed shape rising from it.

"It was what I saw my mother paint that terrified me. I'd never been able to see the picture on her easel before, you see, though somehow I knew it was there. But since my last visit the mists have cleared a little."

She takes a long, shuddering, breath in. "It looked like a knife in a pool of blood, and I had a terrible feeling that perhaps she ..." She feels her throat tighten, and she begins to retch. Twisting round and half-rising, she covers her mouth and looks over at the door.

"Would you like to go upstairs and have a cigarette?" Inge asks gently, but Celina shakes her head. She sits back into the chair and focuses on the seascape, breathing in and out with its waves.

"I need to tell you," she says firmly. "Because, to be perfectly honest, in my heart of hearts I think it's a load of nonsense, but for some bizarre reason I seem to have to torture myself with it." She forces a smile. "I thought," she goes on, still smiling, "that perhaps my mother killed my father. That she painted her crime and then committed it, or the other way around – she committed it and then painted it. Only, whichever way round it was, I came into her studio and disturbed her, and that's why everything went wrong ..."

There is silence while Inge digests the information. "You think your mother" – she speaks slowly and carefully – "plunged a knife into your father and left him lying in a pool of blood to die."

Inge's face is completely expressionless as she speaks, but there is something in her voice – the gentlest of mocking tones – that suddenly makes Celina laugh out loud. The sound is strange to her ears, as though she has never laughed quite so vehemently before.

"No," she says. "No, of course I don't. Or perhaps" – she laughs again at the sudden, joyful, realisation – "she did paint him with a dagger through his heart. Perhaps she did. Because that's the kind of thing my mother was always doing – portraying things as the truth because she wanted them to be true. And if the marriage had gone wrong, she'd want rid of my father, because she always needed everything to be perfect. So she wouldn't actually kill him, but she'd feel like it."

Gripping the arms of the chair she leans forward and, squeezing its white leather into folds, laughs out the words. "And if I saw my mother painting a picture of my father's mutilated body when I was just two, is it any wonder it upset me? Is it any wonder it did me permanent damage?"

She gazes over at Inge triumphantly, but her triumph is not reflected back. "That would certainly be a most traumatic experience," Inge agrees cautiously, "for a young child."

Unable to sit still any longer, Celina pushes hard against the softness of the chair and stands up. The trembling has lessened, and now surges of energy are coursing through her limbs, and she wants to be out of the safe little room and into the afternoon sunshine and away to St Paul's, to Mercedes' studio. Because Mercedes would believe what Inge seems so sceptical about. Mercedes would believe her without question, and the two of them would rejoice together in the life-changing revelation.

"Why are you so cynical?" she shouts at Inge. "Don't

you believe that's what I saw, and that's what has become ingrained in my brain" – she stops, suddenly remembering – "like an engram? And that engram, that Schism, has ruined my life up until today?"

As soon as she has said her piece, the flat rudeness of her tone – rudeness hitherto reserved solely for her nearest and dearest – shocks Celina to the core, and for a moment she wonders if she has gone too far and will be ordered to leave. Inge, however, merely raises her eyebrows slightly, and Celina flops back into her chair and glares at her with a malice that would have done Imogen Wilde proud.

Several silent minutes pass, and the chastening thought comes to Celina that this – this struggle to make sense of the strength of one's emotions in the face of utter incomprehension from those who are supposed to understand – is the same struggle Raine and Luca are probably engaged in half their waking lives. No wonder they sometimes refuse to speak.

"I'm sorry," she says, her voice calm and her tones measured. "That was very juvenile of me. I want it to be the solution, so that I can be rid of the fear once and for all. And I want you to agree that it is."

There is a short pause. "And perhaps I do agree, Celina." Inge leans forward. "I did not say I did not agree, did I? It may well be the solution, and finding that solution may diminish the fear the memory evokes. But as to whether you can rid yourself of it once and for all …" She holds her hands out, palms upwards, and Celina imagines the Schism perched lightly on one of them, like a bird preparing to fly.

"I'm thinking of going away" – she uses the new, calm voice, the new measured tones – "to a volcanic island, to paint and to find out who my father was. Who my father is."

Inge inclines her head, as though listening out for Celina's unspoken next word. "But …?"

"But I don't know what to do with the children. And I'm worried that if I paint in oils, the Schism will come again."

Inge moves back in her chair, crosses her legs, assumes a more casual pose. "Finding someone to look after the children," she says, "is probably not an insurmountable problem. And the Schism has not killed you yet." She tilts her head sideways. "Will you go alone?"

Mercedes' face flashes into Celina's mind. "Alone," she says. "There are so many things I need to do. I couldn't ask anyone else to come."

She looks at Inge for signs of approval or disapproval but sees neither. For a while, as they sit in silence, she wonders whether she is waiting for Inge to grant her permission, but, unsurprisingly, Inge's face remains neutral. And as the silence drags on, Celina knows there is something else she should bring up. Despite her earlier bravado, the very thought now appals her. For a while she toys with the idea of taking a cigarette-break.

"I've met someone," she says at last. "I met them just after our last session, actually. I'd known them in the past, but not well …"

Inge raises her eyebrows.

"A woman." Celina, eyes firmly directed downwards, dredges the word up and out and listens for a reaction. When there is none, she dares a look at Inge and sees a very small, but none the less encouraging, smile. It is, however, only when Celina manages to articulate the words, "Who I'm attracted to," that Inge's face becomes animated.

"And how do you feel about that?" she asks.

Celina looks back down into her lap. She pictures Mercedes' artwork clamouring out from every wall of her studio, and her deep-throated laugh, and the utter joy of her soft scented closeness, awakening every pore. She also remembers how, yesterday, sitting on the tiny bed with Selestino pressed to her breasts, she had wept so hard no words could comfort her.

"I don't know," she says, but when she looks across at Inge it is evident from the frown that this answer will not suffice. Reluctantly, she searches among the mass of conflicting feeling for words that could possibly describe what she feels.

"I've never thought of being attracted to women," she says at last. "I mean, I suppose, in the past, there have been crushes, but never anything serious." She takes a sip of water, watches Inge over the rim of the glass, alert to the slightest change in her expression. "I've always regarded myself as heterosexual," she goes on, aware of an iota of outrage in her voice. "I've always regarded myself as normal."

Inge's lips twitch into a smile and out again. "And now you are attracted to a woman, that makes you abnormal?"

Deep in Celina's throat, the laughter-bubble begins to rise again. "Of course not," she says. "But I *am* confused. I'm having so many feelings I can't remember ever having before, and some are atrociously bad and some are unbelievably wonderful. It's like being a teenager again!"

"You are open to new ideas," Inge says simply. "And some are good ideas, and some are not."

Celina laughs. "And I suppose the only way to find out if something is a good idea is to try it. But my emotions are so raw, that I'm afraid I might get carried away. As though, now Max has gone, there's a vacuum waiting to be filled ..."

"And you should be careful how you fill it?"

Celina nods.

"This woman – her name's Mercie – has terrible

problems," she says. "She's lost a son, and there are rumours about him being involved in drugs, and underage sex, and perhaps even a suicide pact. She's desperate to clear his name, and I'd love to help her, but I need to be a lot surer of my feelings before I get into anything deeper. The last thing Mercie needs is another problem ..."

Inge changes her position in her chair, and for a moment Celina wonders if the hour is already up. Suddenly, quite out of the blue, she feels an urgency to be planning, arranging, packing, flying into action.

"If you don't mind," she says, "I think I'd like to go now." She reaches for her bag, takes out the cheque she has already written and hands it to Inge. "The longer I think about going away," she says as they move towards the door, "the more reasons I'm going to find not to."

Inge watches Celina slip her cape over her shoulders. "At least," she says, "you will be warm."

Celina fastens the cape. "I'll go for two weeks," she says. "That should be long enough to sort things out. And maybe sort myself out too." She unhooks the hat but does not put it on.

"Can I do this?" she asks suddenly. "You saw how fragile I can be. Can I do this alone?"

Not waiting for Inge's answer, she opens the door, returns Inge's smile, and leaves.

PART 2

The difference between false memories and true ones is the same as for jewels: it is always the false ones that look the most real, the most brilliant.

Salvador Dali

CHAPTER TWENTY

The bus to Orzola, the little port from which the ferry sails to Isla Graciosa, spends the first half of its journey meandering through cobbled village streets, sun-dried farmland, and fields filled with dishevelled cacti.

When it reaches the last lap of its journey, however, it fairly gallops along the coast, as though drawn homeward by the scent of the sea and the sight of distant blue islands.

Kicking off her sandals, Celina draws her feet up onto the velvety roughness of the seat, wraps the skirt of her green summer dress tight around her legs, and stares out of the window. The bus is going far too fast for her, and as she watches the coastline race past, the knot of excitement that has tingled in the pit of her stomach since early morning turns more and more to one of anxiety. For though the sun shines in a cloudless sky, and the sea is picture-postcard blue, near the waterline that blue is stretched and thinned into glaucous veils veined with webs of foam, over which bright white waves furl. Were it not for the *Prohibido Fumar* notice, she would have lit up ages ago.

According to the elderly couple from Grimsby in the seat opposite, who every now and then look up from their thermos flask and egg sandwiches to gaze fearfully at the sea, there are thirty-five miles per hour winds today and the distinct possibility the ferry will not sail. If it does sail, the couple from Grimsby do not intend to be on it, and Celina is not at all sure she can bear to be either.

To take her mind off the possible horrors to come, she gazes out at the tundra-like landscape and imagines her mother and father driving along this same sea-licked track, in a bright red, roofless, sports car.

One hand on the wheel and hair blown in the wind, Imogen watches the breakers on the black rocks which, after centuries of being dashed by waves still remain resolutely ragged. Every now and then, she turns to point something out to Francisco, whose left hand holds his white straw hat while his right rests easily on his wife's shoulders. When she turns, Imogen's words are whipped away by the wind, and he moves closer to catch them. Then he smiles and nods and, pulling her close, whispers through her hair.

Bizarre though Celina finds this idea of a young-and-in-love Imogen and Francisco, she begins to imagine what they talked about as they drove. Did Imogen, seeing the distant volcanoes, talk excitedly about what she would paint? And did Francisco talk about what he might paint too? Because, for all Celina knows, he too might have been an artist. Or was he a writer? A poet? Are there, somewhere, notebooks full of his watercolour sea-studies, or his pirate stories, or his poems, all inspired by the same wild rugged desolation that inspired Imogen?

He must have done something to pass his days while Imogen painted. Come to that, he must surely, in order to have attracted Imogen in the first place, have had some kind of creative side, even though all traces of him, and his work, have disappeared. Perhaps the Casa de la Luna Cresciente will reveal something of him?

She checks her watch. It is 11.45 and they are due to arrive in Orzola at noon to catch the 12.15 ferry. In the seat behind, two young women are discussing, in German, the forthcoming crossing, and Celina notices they keep using the word *schrecklich*, which she recognises as 'dreadful'. Turning her back on the window, she takes the envelope containing Mercedes' photograph out of her bag. It is odd, and hugely comforting, to see the little carved snake in such a different setting. She holds it up close and examines its details.

The carving is so crisp and fresh it is hard to believe it dates from the seventeenth century, but then who knows how long it was boarded up? The wood is shiny, as though it has been newly polished, but as Celina holds the photo a little closer she sees a certain dullness around the carved area. Closing one eye, she focuses in on the surface of the snake and sees that its surface is covered in minute scales, surely carved by the tiniest of chisels.

The bus gives another, bigger, lurch and she hears an anxious voice above the squealing of brakes. She also smells, near at hand, the distinct odour of hardboiled egg. "Sorry to disturb you, love," the man from Grimsby is leaning over her shoulder to say, "only we've arrived. And there's no way on God's earth me and the missus is sailing. Will you look at the way thon boat's bobbin' about!"

Celina follows the man's pointing finger to where, a few hundred yards out from the sea wall, a small ferry is bouncing up and down between walls of waves. It looks like a child's toy.

"It's the swell, see," the man explains. "It's a right bugger, if you'll excuse the French. Me and the missus'll shore up in a pension for the night. We don't mind. We like Orzola. It's quiet, and they do you a nice fish supper." He blinks at Celina, eyes watery behind thick lenses. "It's no' cod, like, the supper. We dinna know what it is, because it's in Spanish, but it tastes fine. You'd be welcome to join us? Wait till tomorrow?"

The bus driver turns to watch his passengers gather their belongings together. The German women, having hefted their tight little rucksacks onto their backs, are approaching, and Celina takes one last look at the photo before sliding it carefully back into its envelope. Then she stands and moves into the central aisle, blocking the women's way.

"Excuse me," she says. "Do you think it's dangerous to go on the ferry? It's just that, I really need to get to Graciosa today …"

"Oh no, it is not dangerous," one says, in very certain tones. "The sailors do not risk it if it is dangerous."

"Just very unpleasant," her friend puts in. "But only for the first ten minutes. Once you are round the point, it is fine." She laughs, not unsympathetically. "You might feel sick, but you will not die."

"We stay here in Orzola tonight," the first woman says. "Good luck, if you decide to go!" and they squeeze past her and, with cheery waves, are gone.

Celina looks at her case, which is sticking out of the luggage compartment behind the driver's seat and looking infinitely bigger than it did before, and then at the man from Grimsby. With a wink, he hauls it out for her. "In't 'alf 'eavy," he says. "Wot you got in it? Bodies?"

"Painting stuff." Celina tells him. "I'm hoping to paint."

The man from Grimsby gives a whistle. "It'll mibbe do you for ballast, then," he says, and then he and his wife turn into the wind and trundle off. "Mind and sit in the middle o' the boat," he calls back at her. "And we'll see you tomorrow, God willing!"

Celina struggles over to the sea wall, where the little boat is chugging laboriously into harbour. As it turns itself parallel with the wall, one of its two crew members unfurls a rope and, when the gap between boat and wall is narrow enough, leaps off and begins to wrap the rope round a capstan. The other sailor holds back the tiny knot of pale passengers, intent on disembarking as soon as possible.

Looking round for someone to help her, Celina sees another sailor sitting on the sea wall outside the ticket office. Like the other two, he wears a black salt-encrusted jumper and wide black trousers, and his navy-blue hat is moulded onto his dark curls as though neither could exist without the other. His face is brown and furrowed, like a pickled walnut, and he is gazing into the distance, chewing a matchstick.

"*Perdón, señor*," Celina says and, repeating the Spanish phrase she has been mentally practising, "is the wind too strong to permit us to sail today?"

The sailor shifts the matchstick from one side of his mouth to the other. Still gazing into the distance, he launches into a series of gruff, staccato sentences, the meaning of which completely eludes Celina but which, she assumes from the seaward sweep of his arms and the scathing shake of his head, probably translates into something like, 'If you think this wind is strong, lady, you don't know what a strong wind is.'

She is about to repeat her question when, in one swift, practised movement, the sailor lifts her case, carries it over to the quayside, and flings it unceremoniously onto the boat. Then he takes hold of her arm and leads her over to the ticket office where, with a few words to the man behind the desk and a short stab of his peg-like thumb, he leaves her to buy her ticket. That done, he waits as she pulls the billowing skirt of her dress into a tight bundle before marching her to the boat, where his colleague manhandles her aboard.

Remembering the advice of the man from Grimsby, Celina grips the side of the boat and claws her way along till she finds the most central seat. Overcome by exhaustion, anxiety, and a quite overwhelming wish to cry, she sits down to await her fate.

As she sits watching the other passengers – three in all – being hoisted aboard, Celina is reminded of a terrible childhood rollercoaster ride. They must have been about seven or eight at the time, she and Kalinda, and they had been strapped into the seat of a small carriage and hoisted up, backwards, to the summit to wait for the moment of release.

Kalinda, she remembers, had been wild with excitement. She hung over the side, scouring the sea of people below for whoever had brought them and, having spotting them, waved and whooped and shouted in delight. Meanwhile Celina, her candy-flossed tongue clinging dryly to the roof of her mouth, closed her eyes and prayed to Jesus, Friend of Little Children, to please, please not let her be sick. Terrified though she was of the descent to come, she then sat willing it to begin, because if only it would begin, it would end.

The rollercoaster was quite small, and the ride was neither very long nor hugely steep but still, it was heart-stoppingly dreadful. Furthermore Jesus, Friend of Little Children, failed to deliver, because as soon as she left the carriage, Celina threw up violently on the gravel path. In fairness, however, He did manage to prevent her from vomiting during the ride itself, which was evidence, albeit slight, of His divine mercy.

Celina's vomiting had fascinated Kalinda. She watched, wide-eyed, as her twin retched and spewed and wiped away the pink-speckled trails of sputum from her chin. And when, exhausted, Celina sank to the ground and sat in a ball of misery, she turned to their guardian for the day and asked, very loudly, 'Why does Celina have to do that?' and the guardian – and Celina can still hear her voice to this day – had replied loftily, 'Celina has to do that, dear, because Celina's stomach is not as strong as yours'.

Ever since that day, feelings of nausea bring back memories of the rollercoaster incident, which proved beyond doubt that her inferiority – hitherto confined to moral, intellectual and emotional areas – was also physical; and now, with her tongue as dry as it was then, but without the sticky childhood sweetness, she clings to the pole beside her seat and wills her hopeless stomach to stop churning, and the journey to start.

CHAPTER TWENTY ONE

Neither the cessation of churning in Celina's stomach, nor the start of the journey to Isla Graciosa, seem destined to happen very soon, for there is still an enormous array of cargo lined up on the quay.

For a while Celina watches the sailors hurl parcels, and boxes of fruit and vegetables, onto the boat. Then, as a crate of squawking chickens is lowered down, she closes her eyes and forces her mind away from the windswept harbour, and the sailors' cries, and the wild, wild sea, and instead she imagines herself, three days ago, in the Indian restaurant, with Mercedes. Although more cheerful than at their previous meeting, Mercedes had still been rather subdued.

'I don't know about moving back to the Hell-Hole,' she had said, "but I do have to go back and see Selestino's bedroom, now I know what happened. I can't involve the police again – I just couldn't stand more poking and prying – but I need to see for myself where that fireplace was, even though the thought makes me feel ill.'

She had given Celina a look so doleful that Celina had, finally, made the decision she had been toying with for the previous three days.

'I wish I could go with you,' she said, 'but you know I'm leaving for Graciosa tomorrow?' Then, ignoring Mercedes' cries of astonishment, she took a deep breath and let everything come out in a rush. 'It had to be this soon because Max has agreed to come and look after Raine and Luca, and I have to fit in with his schedule, but I was thinking - why don't you move in to my mother's studio? You won't be able to work on the Madonna, but perhaps there are other things you can do? Raine would be thrilled, and Luca wouldn't notice, and when I'm back I'll help you find somewhere permanent ..."

She sat back then to watch Mercedes' reaction, and think of a million reasons why she should say 'no', and why, obviously, it was better if she *did* say 'no', and was therefore quite shocked when Mercedes' face broke into a smile and she said, 'Oh honey, you have no idea how much this means to me. And I'm writing out the songs now, so it'll be bliss to have decent light. Thank you!'

Now, as the rope binding the boat to the quay is finally unravelled and, like a baby being born into a wide wild world, the little boat noses seawards, Celina grips the pole tight and imagines Mercedes, seated at Imogen's big table, hunched over yards and yards of manuscript, writing painfully slowly with pen and ink, like a latter-day monk.

And then, all in a rush, she remembers where she has seen the tail-biting snake. It was on a poster on Raine's bedroom wall, tearfully removed when he died. The details are vague, for Raine's bedroom is almost out of bounds, but she can just see it. Outlined in black, with red and yellow scales and reminiscent of a drawing from an ancient manuscript, it was printed on the front of the tee-shirt worn by Selestino Glass.

His name was on the poster too, in large golden letters above his head, and at the foot of the poster there was some other writing proclaiming, presumably, the title of whichever album was current at the time. No matter how Celina concentrates, however, the title remains hidden.

She may never have bothered to read what it was; or if she did, she has long forgotten.

The memory of those red and yellow scales draws her back to her brief last view of Mercedes' photograph, and the tiny carved scales she had suddenly noticed. There was something else, wasn't there, in the detail of that carving? Or did her eyes deceive her?

In the confines of Orzola's tiny harbour the swell is enormous now, and the boat yaws up and down so violently that forward movement seems impossible. Curious though she is to take another look at the photograph, the mere thought of dipping her head long enough to take it out of its envelope and scrutinise it makes her head swim. Instead, she looks over at her fellow-passengers to see how they are faring.

All three – a young couple and a tall, white-haired man – appear to be doing just fine. The young couple cling to one another and watch the waves with much the same delight at the adventure to come as eight-year-old Kalinda on the rollercoaster; and the man, standing proud and tall in a jaunty nautical striped tee-shirt and khaki shorts, stares calmly into the far distance like a carved figurehead.

His skin is mahogany brown and his mop of windswept white hair and short white beard accentuate the depth of its colour, and when he turns to face her she sees he has remarkably pale grey eyes. With a bright smile of encouragement, he gives her a thumbs-up, and when Celina tries, and fails, to return the smile, he carefully sidesteps his way across the deck and throws himself onto the seat beside her. Despite her anxiety, she notices the sharp peppery tang of his aftershave, and the neat trim of his beard.

"Hello," he calls over the crash of the waves. "You are English?" and he shuffles along the seat so that he is almost touching her. The boat has moved away from the harbour wall now and is making painfully slow progress past the great grey cliff-side. As it ascends and descends mountain after mountain of grey-green water, Celina's head swims giddily and she lets a cry of utter terror escape. As soon as it is out she glances at the man, hoping he will not take it as a cue to put an arm round her. She is relieved when he merely smiles again.

"My name is Wolf Hartmann," he tells her in a soft German voice, "and I cross El Rio all the time. You do not have to be afraid, you know. We will not capsize!" Taking hold of the metal pole by the side of the seat, he pulls himself up and points ahead to where a line of black jagged rocks is just visible through the foam. "Do you see the rocks?" he shouts down at her. "That is the Punta Fariones and, beyond it, the sea will be calm." He extends an arm towards Celina, who automatically pulls away, but all he does is motion for her to get up.

"It is better, I think, to stand," he says, the sparkle of pale grey eyes just visible through criss-crossed laughter-lines. "Imagine, perhaps, that you are on the back of a great white horse, galloping triumphantly over the waves. Imagine you are a brave knight in shining armour. Come on!"

He holds a brown arm out for her, and Celina pulls herself up by it, then hurriedly releases her hold and grasps the pole again. Eyes fixed on the black rocks, she concentrates on imagining her feet in silver stirrups and her hands gripping strands of white mane, as Wolf Hartmann's battle steed carries her over the crests of the waves. As she allows her body to embrace the movement of the boat, she becomes marginally less panic-stricken. Still horribly dizzy, she turns her attention to the land-mass alongside which they are sailing.

Despite the miasma of spray, the great grey-black wall

of rock which towers above her is mesmerising. The boat sails so close to it that there can surely be no sharp cliffs hidden under the surface, and she imagines that wall of rock extending down into the sea's unfathomable depths, like an iceberg whose tip is a fraction of its whole. The rock's surface is ridged and furrowed, eroded into vast grey arrowheads whose tips point skywards, but as the boat rides the waves Celina sees that in places the dark rock is scored into lighter, smoother channels. It looks as though small rivers have been stopped in their tracks and turned to stone.

"Do you see the scree slope?" Wolf points to the channels. "When the volcano was active, the lava flowed right down into the sea, and parts of it – the softer minerals – have been broken down over the centuries and now they are, how do you say?" – he raises the front of his cap, as though to rub the word out of his hair – "gravel."

Looking anew at the frozen moment of time before her, Celina superimposes flowing red ash onto its greyness and sees it as a freeze-frame of primeval chaos; a moment when the earth itself changed shape forever.

"I'm sorry," she tells Wolf, as her stomach gives a seismic heave and her mouth fills with sour liquid, "but I'm going to be sick." Feeling his hand lain gently on her back, she leans over the side and retches her own burning lava into the waves, which rise to swallow it.

"I'm sorry," she repeats, when she has sunk back down onto the seat to hug her misery. "I don't have a strong stomach, I'm afraid."

Wolf, sitting too, looks at her with concern. "Please," he says, "there is no need to apologise." He takes a breath as though to speak again, then pauses before asking awkwardly, "I do not wish to intrude, but do you have lodgings on the island? Somewhere you can rest when we arrive? I saw your suitcase …"

Celina pauses too before answering. He is close enough now for her to hear his breathing above the crash of the waves, and she is aware of his sharp peppery scent above the salt-smell. "I have a place arranged," she tells him. She tries her best to make her voice sound strong and decisive but there is, she knows, more than a telltale tremor in it. "I have to pick up keys somewhere," she adds. "For a house I own."

Her stomach gives another heave and she tries to steady her breathing. Despite the howling wind and the showers of sea spray she is boiling hot, and the thought of negotiating herself and her suitcase to the Calle de Buenavista where, apparently, a Señora Gomez will give her the keys to the Casa, is almost unbearable.

"I will help you, if you would like," Wolf says, as she knew he would. "For the past ten years, I have lived half the year on Graciosa. I know everyone!"

Not waiting for Celina's answer, he stands up again and points to a small black and white lighthouse, perched high on the nearest rock. "See?" he says. "We are rounding the Punta Fariones. Do you see the beacon? And can you feel how much calmer the sea is becoming?"

Shielding her eyes, Celina gazes ahead at the pair of serrated black rocks silhouetted against the sky and, sure enough, she feels the motion of the boat flatten out as it turns to sail past them. The second, most seaward, rock, from whose edge the slender lighthouse rises, is an almost spherical carbuncle. Its surface has been hewn into a giant face, that seems to guard the entrance into a bay bounded by high grey lava cliffs on one side, and the white sands of Isla Graciosa on the other.

Wolf gazes along the coastline, with its sprawling row of squat white houses nestling beneath the volcanoes. "Caleta de Sebo. The Bay of Grease," he says, laughing.

"So-called because of the whaling days, and perhaps not the prettiest of names, but it is my second home." He turns to her, suddenly solemn. "No matter how often I sail to Graciosa," he says, "the first sight of it always warms my heart."

Turning her attention away from the austere cliff-face on her left, Celina takes her first look at Caleta de Sebo and sees that it is bigger than she had imagined. Up till now, she has pictured it as a mere scattering of houses with perhaps a couple of streets, but now that the boat is nearing the harbour she realises that, actually, the Calle de Buenavista could take some finding, and her suitcase, with its enormous weight and tiny wheels, is going to be a nightmare to drag along the sand. To make matters worse, she now senses a certain urgency to find a toilet. Reaching into her bag, she finds the piece of paper on which she has written all the details of the Casa. She hands it to Wolf.

"I'd be very grateful for your help in collecting the keys," she says. "But, if you don't mind, I'd like to go to the house myself." A picture of the kitchen of the Casa de la Luna Cresciente, its big table loaded with food and wine and surrounded by those happy, laughing, people, flashes before her eyes. "I know it's silly," she adds, "but it's a sort of sentimental journey for me."

"Do not worry. I am a sentimental old fool too at times," Wolf assures her before gasping with embarrassment. "Oh no – please," he says, suddenly crestfallen, "I do not mean to say you are an old fool. Only I am an old fool. And – oh dear me – I do not even know your name ..." He bangs the side of his head in a comic gesture and, despite everything, Celina smiles.

"Celina," she says, extending her hand. "I should have introduced myself. Celina Wilde."

Wolf shakes her hand warmly. Then he reads the name

and address on the paper. "Señora Maria Gomez," he says, smiling in recognition. "That is our Maria del Mar, who runs the Pension Mariposa and, quite among ourselves, runs the whole of Caleta de Sebo too! The pension is not far from the harbour, but as for your Casa" – he scours the coastline and points towards a twin-topped volcano – "it sits a little apart from the village, in the lee of Montaña Pedro Barba. It will take a bit of time to get there with your case. Perhaps we should have some lunch first?"

A spasm of particularly urgent pain makes Celina clutch her stomach, and for a few moments she sits very still, with her head down, letting the cacophony of thuds and screaming voices, and the overwhelmingly fishy smell, drift over her. Then she allows Wolf to lead her down to the side of the boat, where she is borne aloft by two sailors and set down on the cobbled quay, to follow Wolf and her suitcase between shouting people, and crowing roosters, and crates and boxes and fish-laden wheelbarrows, till the cobbles give way to damp sand.

As they walk, the sand becomes progressively drier and lighter, and soon she is aware of wending her way between walls of white houses till at last, when she feels she really must collapse, they arrive at a dark blue door above which hang three rusty wrought-iron butterflies.

"Here we are," Wolf tells her gently. "Pension Mariposa." He points to a sun-bleached wooden bench, beside a row of scarred cacti by a whitewashed house wall. "Would you like to sit down while I talk to Maria? And then we must find some lunch and a drink for you."

Celina sinks gratefully down onto the bench and watches as Wolf knocks at the door, pushes it open and, calling, "Maria! *Hola!*" makes his way inside. She sits till the heat on her head is too much, then pads across the sand and slips gratefully into the cool darkness of Maria del Mar's house.

The hall is narrow and cluttered with small tables and cane chairs, and the tables are littered with plaster saints and madonnas. From behind one of the doors she can hear the duet of Wolf's soft baritone and Maria del Mar's rather grating soprano as, presumably, they discuss the English woman and her needs. Easing the next door open a crack she finds, to her intense relief, a toilet from whose ceiling hangs a large cage in which, on a perch, a miserable-looking cockatoo is pulling feathers out of its tail.

As she enters, the cockatoo raises its crest and stares at her. Then it stretches out one of its wings and makes a noise like someone breaking wind. The noise, interspersed with various burps and belches, continues until Celina, red-faced with embarrassment, re-emerges into a mercifully empty hall.

Feeling marginally better, but still not ready to face the sun again, she walks slowly back towards the door, looking at the array of gilt-framed Madonna-and-childs on the walls and wishing, for the hundredth time that day, that Mercedes was with her.

CHAPTER TWENTY TWO

When Wolf emerges from Pension Mariposa with a sombre Maria del Mar at his side and two keys dangling from his finger Celina realises that, despite her earlier reaction to his invitation to lunch, she is now ravenously hungry.

With a little bow, Wolf presents her with the keys and, thanking Maria, begins to haul the recalcitrant suitcase over the sand again. Celina smiles and mutters her own *Gracias* – which is greeted with an unsmiling *De nada* – then follows him.

As she watches him tug the suitcase along the sandy path, struggling now and then to right it when its wheels stick, it occurs to her that this casual encounter is now turning into a lunch date. Catching him up, she lays a proprietorial hand on the suitcase.

"I'm hugely grateful for all your help, Wolf" – she takes hold of the handgrip and tugs – "but I really can't take up any more of your time."

Wolf holds the case fast. "I have nothing at all planned for today," he says. "And your Casa is about half a mile away, you know." He nods his head in the direction of the wide expanse of sand that is, apparently, Graciosa's main thoroughfare.

Releasing her grip on the suitcase, Celina gazes into the distant, deserted village. The sun is hot on her head now, and she feels nauseous and empty at the same time.

"To be perfectly honest, Celina," Wolf is saying, "I am at a bit of a – how do you say? – loose end, at the moment. My partner has been away for several weeks, and I am just a little bit lonely. So, if you would allow me to help you settle into the island, you would be doing me a favour."

He turns his head swiftly away then, towards a narrow alleyway between two lines of buildings, at whose end a flash of sea glints. "I think we are both in need of shade, and lunch. And if it makes you feel better, we will 'go Dutch', yes?"

He turns back and grins at her. Then, not waiting for a reply, he pulls the suitcase towards the alleyway. Celina follows the sparkle of sea over his shoulder.

"Do you think Maria might let me use her phone? Or is there a phone box somewhere?"

Wolf's laugh answers both her questions. "There is a phone in the hardware store behind Pension Mariposa, but I would not waste my *pesetas* on it. And as for Maria, she has had too many bad experiences of people phoning long-distance and not paying the full amount."

He stops and points back the way they have come. "On the way to the Casa, we will pass the *supermercado*. It is closed today, of course, but you will be able to buy what you need tomorrow. Will you manage tonight?"

"I stayed in a hotel in Arrecife last night," Celina says. "So I was able to buy the essentials in the local shop, and a bottle of wine." Quite unexpectedly, tiny wingbeats of satisfaction flutter in the pit of her stomach as she realises she has done it, she has survived; she is here. "I'll be all right for tonight."

Steering the suitcase round a corner, Wolf stops at the foot of a flight of steps leading up to a restaurant. At the top of the steps is a balcony dotted with white tables shaded by blue parasols, above which hangs a sign with a blue parrot and the words *Loro Azul*. With much heaving and puffing, Wolf bumps the case up the steps, and as they near the top Celina takes hold of the wheels and together they manoeuvre it the rest of the way. Most of the tables are occupied, and as they make their way to a vacant one there is a flurry of hand-shaking and cheek-kissing as Wolf greets each of the customers in turn.

"It is quite a close-knit community," he explains when they are seated. "All the locals know one another of course, and there are regular visitors like me, who own property and come back year after year; and then there are hippies living in tents on the beach, and they tend to come and go. Most of them are here for the sun and the surfing, and some of them write poetry and songs, and all of them smoke dope, but on the whole they are pretty decent people."

He hands the menu to Celina and looks at her anxiously. "You do, occasionally, get a bad apple though, and Maria was worried that there might have been squatters in your house. It might be best, you know, if I were to see you safely in. Just to be on the safe side?"

Celina surveys the menu. Now that food is a reality she has lost the wish to eat, and the longing she had on the boat – to be alone in the Casa, with a shower and a bed – has returned with a vengeance. To add to her discomfort, she has a strong hunch that Wolf is a non-smoker and, though there is an ashtray on the table, she feels unable to light up.

"It's extremely kind of you, but I do really want to go

into the Casa on my own," she repeats. "I'll have a *tortilla* please, and a cup of peppermint tea."

Wolf waves at a young girl standing in the shadows, and when she has bounced over and kissed him lightly on both cheeks, he gives their order. As Wolf and the waitress chat in rapid and, for the most part incomprehensible, Spanish, Celina looks at the German carefully for the first time. He is probably in his early seventies, but his straight back and slim figure are youthfully attractive and, all in all, he is not bad-looking. Most importantly, though, he has a kind face, and the wrinkles etched around his grey eyes are testament to a lifetime of laughter. While wishing fervently she could do without Wolf Hartmann, she feels instinctively he is to be trusted.

"I'm hoping to find out about my father, actually," she decides to tell him, after the waitress, having brought a glass of wine and one of water, has gone to fetch the food. "Perhaps, when you have time, you could ask some of the older people if they know him? I'm afraid my Spanish isn't up to it."

"I would be delighted." Wolf raises his glass. "What do you know about him?"

"Very little. His name is Francisco Jesús Quesada and he and my mother, who was English, lived here, off and on, in the thirties. My mother was a painter, but as for my father, I really have no idea. He disappeared when my sister and I were about two, and hasn't been heard of since."

Wolf looks down to the almost-deserted harbour. "Everyone is having a *siesta* now," he says. "Later, though, when the sun is lower, the fishermen will come to dig for bait and there will be plenty of elderly men to ask. How old, approximately, would your father be?"

"I'm forty-nine" – Celina smiles at the memory of

Wolf's earlier embarrassment – "so my father, must be in his seventies. Mother was born in 1910, and I think Daddy was a bit younger. Seventy-five? Seventy-six, perhaps?"

She looks down at the empty harbour and imagines walking with Wolf in the evening sun, towards the old men with their spades, and listening to him talk to them. Many would, of course, shake their heads, but then perhaps one face would light up at the mention of her father's name, and there would be a volley of Spanish. Then Wolf would turn to her and say, 'Yes. He knows him. He still lives on Graciosa.' One of the men might even jump up, and point over to a boat, or a café, or a bowed figure painting at an easel by the harbour edge, and say, 'There he is! *Allí*! That's Francisco Jesús Quesada.'

It is possible, she thinks. Now that I am here, and I have the keys to the Casa in my bag, it is all possible. And for the most fleeting of moments, she sees her father, dark-skinned, white-haired, a little bowed but still bright-eyed, standing at the Casa door, waving her gently inside.

"Here we are. Food!" Wolf says as the waitress arrives with her *tortilla* and tea, and his own mound of fish and salted potatoes. Wishing her "*Guten appetit*!" he attacks his meal with gusto, occasionally watching as Celina shaves thin slivers off the solid *tortilla* slab and washes them down with sips of peppermint.

"So, what brought you to Graciosa?" she asks. She is desperately tired now, and there is a rocking motion inside her head, as though she were still at sea. The sun is high in the sky, its watery reflections painful to her eyes, and she knows she will have to rummage through her suitcase to find her hat before they begin the walk to the Casa. That will take an eternity, because it is right at the bottom of the case, carefully stuffed with underwear. The hat is – crazily – the red one, which is far too bright for this dull, dun-coloured place, and ludicrously warm too, and she remembers Raine's howls of ridicule as she watched her pack it, and her own insistence that it go with her. Draining her tea, she sits back in the parasol's shade and listens to Wolf.

"Like most tourists, I was originally drawn to Lanzarote by its sea and sun." He places his knife and fork neatly together on his empty plate. "In the sixties I came often – at first with my wife and daughter, and later alone – and I grew to love the simple beauty of the place. But sea and sun and desert landscapes you can get on any number of islands, and for me, the real pull to Lanzarote became César Manrique. Have you heard of him? The architect of Lanzarote?"

"The name sounds familiar. I feel I've read it somewhere – perhaps in a guide book. So, what did he do?"

"What did César do? Oh – where should I start?" Wolf rubs his beard. "César Manrique is a Canarian artist – a contemporary of Picasso – and when he was just seventeen, he left home to fight in the Spanish Civil War. It had a profound effect on him and, much later, he decided to make this island his life's work."

An unexpected gust of wind rips over the tables, ruffling the parasols and sending paper napkins and beer mats flying, and Celina sees that the clear blue of the sky has misted over, as though its Cerulean Blue had been overlaid with a light glaze of Titanium White. "The only thing I know about the Spanish Civil War," she confesses, "is Picasso's 'Guernica', and I don't really know the details of that either, except that it shows the brutality of war."

Wolf shrugs off her ignorance. "The Spanish Civil War was as brutal as any war, but it was more than that. It was a mad, sad war no one could win and it had little to do with Spain, or the real needs of the Spanish people."

He points down to the fishing boats, bobbing ever more furiously up and down on the breakers. "That sea," he says, pointing, "was the Spanish Civil War. The boats are the Spanish people, oppressed for centuries by Church and State, and the sea's pull – invisible yet brutally powerful – is the machinery of war.

"Make no mistake" – he looks back at Celina and his grey eyes have lost all their humour - "Spaniards killed fellow-Spaniards in their thousands, but the Civil War was always steered and powered by the Russians, and the Germans and Italians. The Russians bled the country of every last bar of gold, and in return gave it tanks that did not fire and bombs that blew up the men who threw them. And as for the dear Germans" – he smiles a wry smile – "they used the whole thing as a cynical practice-ground for the world war to come, while desperately trying to cajole and blackmail Franco into joining them in that war."

He takes several gulps of wine, then bangs his glass down on the table. "In that, fortunately, they failed, for how could Spain afford to fight another war with no gold, no grain, and no oil? There is an expression for that in German, and I think also in English, is there not? To 'cut your nose off …'" He laughs and appeals to Celina. "How does it go?"

"To 'cut off your nose to spite your face'," she tells him. "So, your César Manrique went off to fight when he was seventeen, which is just one year older than my daughter. He was really still a child."

"Manrique saw himself as the poet-soldier, the brave knight fighting for the fundamental values of his beloved Spain, and when the war ended, and his side won, what did he get for his pains?" Wolf waves over at the waitress, who scurries to his side to watch him with obvious amusement. "Nearly forty years under Generalisimo Franco" – he winks up at the girl, who winks back – "who sucked Spain's spirit till it was as dry as the bones of the slaughtered."

With a howl of frustration, Wolf runs his hands through his hair, ruffling it and smoothing it back down. Then, calm once more, he gives his empty glass to the girl, who runs off to refill it. Apologetically, he turns back to Celina.

"I am sorry," he says. "When I am angry I talk too much, and you are getting cold. All I really wanted to tell you was that Manrique has turned what could have been another ugly, commercialised tourist island into a work of art. Shall we go?"

Celina looks over at the suitcase, trying to summon up the energy required to go and open it and find something warm. "But you want another glass of wine …"

Wolf shakes his head and stands. "This wind is getting worse," he says. "We should get you to your Casa." He takes some notes out of his pocket, waves aside Celina's protests, and hands them to the waitress, who begins to count them. Then, at a signal from him, she pushes them all into her pocket and kisses him on both cheeks.

He leads the way down the steps, the suitcase overturning at each bump. "I can always have another glass of wine when I get home," he says as they walk back up to the main thoroughfare. "I live over there" – he points over, beyond the harbour wall, to a row of white houses that extends out beyond Caleta de Sabo – "just beyond the Playa Francesa. The house is called Canción del Viento – Song of the Wind – and its roof is domed and a bit higher than all the others. Just shorter than a Canarian palm, which is one of Manrique's rules for the buildings of Lanzarote! And it has an aluminium wind sculpture in its front garden, a copy of one of his designs, so you really cannot miss it."

He stops and waits while Celina opens the case and extracts a jumper, then fights with the wind to pull it over her head. Then they continue to walk, heads well down against the sandy gale. "The Canción also has a phone," Wolf shouts against the howl of the wind. "And you are more than welcome to use it whenever you need to."

Celina turns and thanks him and then, gritting her teeth and stolidly facing the ground, she struggles on. Looking ahead, even if it were possible, is pointless now, for the view of the village and the pathway ahead is fogged by whirling clouds of sand whipped up from the ground. She is tempted to ask Wolf how much longer they must walk, but the effort is too much and the reply, she is sure, would be disheartening.

Willing herself not to stop, not to faint, not to be sick, she hugs herself close. Soon, she will arrive at the Casa, and then she will sleep. And tomorrow she will wake up in her father's house, and the wind will have dropped, and the sun will shine, and she will walk along the Playa Francesa to the Canción del Viento, and phone Mercedes.

CHAPTER TWENTY THREE

The Casa de la Luna Cresciente sits on its own at the top of a slight rise, and even through the cloud of sand Celina can see her mother's passion for New Mexico in the unpainted sandstone of its walls and the soft, undulating lines of its roof.

At its centre point, the roof rises to form a small cupola housing a metal bell, and underneath is a porch flanked by two windows. The paintwork of the porch, the door, and the window-frames has faded to a very pale, dirty turquoise.

Shading his eyes, Wolf peers up to the top of the rise. "The house of an artist," he says, "but in need of a great deal of attention, I fear."

He releases his hold on Celina's suitcase and lets it rock itself upright. "You are sure you would not like me to wait and see that the key works? The lock might well be rusty, after all this time."

They both look up at the Casa's sun-bleached door. There is a raw plank of wood nailed across its centre, and smears of what might be black paint on its frame.

"Perhaps," Celina says, "you could just wait here till you see I'm inside? I'll wave to you from the window?" and when Wolf nods she holds out a formal hand. "Thank you," she says. "I honestly don't know what I would have done without you."

Wolf takes her solitary hand in both of his. "*Nichts zu danken*," he assures her and then adds, with mock solemnity, "Do not mention it. And remember – beyond the Playa Francesa, Canción del Viento, if there's anything you need. If you do not see it, César's wind sculpture will lead you to its door!"

Celina takes a firm hold on the suitcase handle and begins to drag it. Though the wind has abated a little, as she climbs she feels the sand under her feet become ever softer. Half-way to the top she stops and hauls herself round to see Wolf still watching her, and the sight of him standing so still, while the wind ruffles his hair and billows his shirt, makes her want to wave him to her. Telling herself not to be stupid, she straightens her back and forces her feet to carry her the rest of the way to the door. As she inserts the key, however, there is a little part of her that wishes it would not turn.

Up close, the Casa's front door is in bad repair, and the makeshift piece of unpainted wood is held loosely by several newish-looking nails. Below the wood is a very rusty lock. At first it seems impossible that the key could ever turn without the help of some oil, but as Celina cautiously eases it round she feels it engage and begin to move until, with a final dull click, the lock yields and the door creaks grudgingly open. There must be something piled behind the door, because the space it gives is just wide enough to allow her in if she turns sideways.

Leaving her case on the threshold, she squeezes into a narrow hallway similar in size to the one in Pension Mariposa. She leans against the wall, closes her eyes, and concentrates all her attention on the smells of the house.

And those smells could not be a more profound disappointment. How stupid she was to have imagined that the Casa de la Luna Cresciente would welcome her home with familial voices, and laughter, and the aroma of good wholesome Spanish cooking. And how idiotic she had been to picture her father there, waving her inside as though she were the Prodigal Daughter. Now, breathing in the sour stench of neglect and decay, she remembers the words Mercedes used to describe her dread of going back to the Hell-Hole. 'Part of me truly imagines Selestino will still be there' was what she had said, wasn't it? As though a place could hold the ghost of a loved one in its stones. As though their cells could still hang in its air.

Opening her eyes, she looks from one door to the next, but all her earlier excitement and anticipation has gone. If the Casa holds secrets, its entrance hall does not bode well for the kind of secrets these are.

All five doors that open off the hallway are thick with dark blistered varnish, and the tiled floor is all but hidden by sand. The corners are filled with debris – scrap paper, cigarette packets, crumpled beer cans, plastic bottles – and there is angry red graffiti on the walls. Telling herself to hurry up so that poor Wolf can be released from his blustery vigil, Celina pushes open the first door, and steps inside.

It is the sitting-room. To the left, underneath a bullfighting poster whose reds have long faded into pinks, there hangs an ancient wall-mounted radiator, and on either side of the radiator stands a wicker chair with red-striped cushions stuck firmly down by the imprints of grubby bottoms. Behind the farther chair there is an archway in which hangs a beaded curtain, its colours greyed and its beads heavy with filth and cobwebs.

Against the facing wall stands a cheap-looking wall-unit and to the right, below the window, a rectangular bamboo trough filled with terracotta flowerpots, their contents long turned to dust. Celina leans over the trough to check that Wolf has not abandoned her and when she sees that, of course, he has not, she waves.

For a while there is no returning movement and she wonders if Wolf can see her, but then he raises both arms and waves wildly back, with an exaggerated enthusiasm that almost makes her smile. She continues to watch him as he turns and, with a final throwaway raising of his arm, strides away.

Turning her back on the window she surveys the room, which has begun to rock gently to and fro. She takes a step towards one of the awful chairs, but the giddiness worsens and her head fills with a tingle of stars and, stretching her arm out behind her, she backs towards the window and leans against it. She tries to steady herself by taking long breaths, but the tingle worsens and darkness threatens, and now the dull pain in her stomach has become an urgent stabbing. It gives one awful spasm, and sends a foam of half-digested *tortilla* up into her gullet.

Praying she will not pass out, she runs out into the hall and fumbles her way to the end door which, in Pension Mariposa, led into the toilet. Hurling herself in, she throws up into the grimy wash-hand basin rather than the grimy toilet bowl. As she does, the realisation dawns that the likelihood of there being running water is remote. She tries each tap in turn, but neither yields a drop.

Desperate for something to remove the bitter taste from her mouth, she runs back out onto the windswept threshold, wrenches the door open, drags her case into the sitting room and throws it open. She takes out a fresh bottle of water and her toilet bag and, after she has drunk from the bottle, washes her face in the water that is left, using her tiny cake of Lily of the Valley soap. Then she pulls two dresses and a bath towel out of the case and heads for the room opposite.

It is, as she guessed, a bedroom, though it is difficult to make out its details because the window is obscured by folds of frayed sacking. She can, however, see an enormous bed, whose wrought-iron bedstead twists and curls into plant-like shapes. Even in the half-light she sees that the grey-striped mattress is covered in ominous brown marks.

As her eyes accustom to the gloom, she makes out a blackened area on the floor beside the bed, with a small pile of white ash at its centre. The blackened area is littered with shards of soot-caked glass, pieces of rubber tubing, hypodermic syringes, and empty beer cans,. Overwhelmed by the sense of an alien presence, she goes back to the house door and checks that it is locked. Then, the need for sleep erasing every other feeling, she rolls the bath-towel into a pillow and lays the two dresses over the soiled mattress. Biting back tears of disgust and disappointment, she climbs up onto the bed.

Burying her nose in the faint soap-scent of her towel, she imagines herself back in London, in Inge's room, breathing in its rosemary smell, then sinking down into the womb-like chair and hearing Inge gently ask, 'So – how was your trip?' As she speaks, Inge leans forward and pushes the box of tissues – pink today, in a box covered in pale pink roses – towards her.

Turning onto her stomach, Celina considers Inge's question carefully. How will she answer it? In just two weeks' time when, miraculously, that safe sweet-smelling room will be a reality, how will she describe all this to Inge?

'To begin with, it wasn't at all how I expected,' she watches herself say. 'But then that was my own stupid fault because I thought Caleta de Sebo would be a tiny village, and the Casa would be just yards from the sea, so that if it was dirty it would be a clean, wholesome dirt. It wasn't, though. It was the most disgusting, most threatening dirt imaginable, and I couldn't cope with it.'

A screech of seagulls, like the cackle of crones, high above the window threatens to draw her back to the present, but she presses her face harder into the towel and conjures up every last detail of Inge's face – the high cheekbones, the freckled skin, the little lines etched around the sensitive mouth, the understated nod of the head.

'And I must have known there would be no running water,' she hears herself continue, 'but I suppose I thought that didn't matter because the sea was on my doorstep. And of course I assumed the sun would always be shining, so that everything could be washed and sundried, and instead, when I arrived, it was wild and stormy. In fact, it was the most inhospitable place on earth, but I met someone – a man – on the ferry, and although at first I wasn't sure whether or not to trust him, I decided he was all right and he' – she imagines herself pausing then, looking over at Inge for reassurance or, perhaps, praise, and then concluding, more lightly – 'he was all right. He was nice, actually. Very nice …'

The seagulls' cackling has faded to an occasional guffaw, and at the same time the wind's howl has lessened. Gradually, as sleep beckons, the images in Celina's head begin to take on their own dreamlike life. Floating up and swimming through the air towards her, Inge pulls a bundle of tissues out from within her skirts and, with a whoop of joy, throws them upwards.

'Look, Celina!' she cries, pointing. 'Smell the roses!' and Celina watches the tissues split and divide into tiny pieces then float down slowly and gracefully to fill her lap with a scented pile of pale pink petals. Scooping them up in great soft handfuls, she presses them to her nose, and breathes in their fragrance ...

When she wakes, it takes her a few moments to remember where she is, but even when all her fragmented thoughts have slipped together again there is still something incongruous in the scene. Sitting up, she looks round the room and it is then, as she stares ahead at the wall, that she realises the wind has stopped, and all is silent.

She swings her legs off the high bed, eases herself upright and pads her way back into the sitting room. Parting the bead curtain, she steps under the archway into a kitchen, and shudders at the dry patter of tiny feet rippling away from her into the darkness, into their own filthy, hidden places.

Unable to move for fear of disturbing more insects, she looks round at the pots and pans skimmed with slime, the plates overgrown with mould, and the empty tins and milk cartons tossed into every corner. Suddenly decisive, she turns on her heels, marches back into the sitting room and takes a shoulder-bag out of her case. She throws in her toilet-bag, some clothes and, as an afterthought, the red hat and the bottle of wine, and goes out into the hall.

She is about to make her escape when the realisation that she no longer feels ill allows her curiosity to stir. Dumping the bags, she pushes open the door beside the sitting-room and takes a tentative look inside. The scene is equally depressing – grey mattresses on the floor, filth, hopelessness. She closes the door quickly and turns to the last room.

For a while she stands outside it, wondering if it is even worth the effort of looking in. Then, preparing herself for yet another squalid discovery, she pushes the door open, steps inside, and gazes around in amazement.

The room is larger, and much cleaner, than she expected. It has a big square window covered by shutters so cracked they let in enough light for her to make out, below its light covering of sand, a distinct flash of blue on the floor. Scraping the sand aside with her foot she sees that the floor is blotched and dotted with paint marks and, with a little cry, she throws herself down onto her knees and begins to wipe the sand aside.

Like a conservator searching for the true colours of an Old Master, she uncovers slowly, carefully, the bright Cerulean Blue, the subtle Naples Yellow, the bold French Ultramarine, the russet Indian Red of Imogen's palette; and when all the marks are uncovered she gazes down at them with a curious sense of homecoming. Then she stands up, throws open the shutters, and takes in the rest of the room.

To the left of the window stands a cheval mirror, its wooden frame carved into a design of twining leaves and its silvered surface angled towards the window. The surface reflects the last rays of afternoon sunshine, turning the whirling dust-motes to gold, and for a while Celina continues to stand very still in the middle of the room, staring at the perfectly square window. From far away a single church bell begins to chime and, hardly breathing because to breathe too hard would be to break the spell, she allows herself to feel the past fuse with the present.

For this, surely, was exactly how it was, all those years ago in the Casa de la Luna Cresciente: this pink late-afternoon light, this bell calling the faithful to Mass, this square window and the view of Montaña Pedro Barba it has always framed. This, for Imogen Wilde, was exactly what she wanted to paint, from every possible angle, and in every possible light.

Slamming the shutters to, Celina runs out, picks up her

bags and heads down the slope to a very different Caleta de Sebo. The sky is a clear deep blue now, broken only by bright white seagulls floating on the upcurrents. Cacti and aloe cast long dark shadows over the sand, and everything looks washed clean. If she and Wolf left footsteps in the sand's soft whiteness, they are gone.

At the foot of the slope she turns right and walks along the sand track. Up ahead, the road teems with people, all walking towards the tolling of the bell. Keeping a respectful distance, she walks alongside them.

Everyone who lives in the village, it seems, is on their way to Mass. Mostly, it is family groups: black-veiled mothers with babies in their arms and toddlers by the hand, and a gnarled grandmother, head cupped deeply inside a bell-shaped straw hat. Proud strutting fathers swagger beside their wives, and solitary village elders, seemingly oblivious to the chatter and laughter around, make their own slow progress towards the source of the bell. Slowing her pace, Celina falls in beside one elderly man and looks as closely as she dares at his leathery face and his silvered hair and his clouded, loose-set eyes.

How would it be, if this were Francisco Jesús Quesada, right beside her? What might she see of herself, mirrored in his face, that would set him apart from all the other old rheumy-eyed men? Would she, by some strange genetic memory, recognise him? And he her?

The pealing of the bell is loud now, and up ahead the line of people begins to curve. Celina quickens her pace and draws level with the little wooden church and, peering into its scented darkness sees, on the wall above the altar, a fishing boat in which stands a Madonna and Child. Above, canopied by a fishing-net, hangs a crucified Christ. For a moment she lingers, but the thought of Mercedes' reaction when she tells her what she has discovered in the Casa drives her away, down through the narrow streets and onto the shore.

Scouring the coastline, she searches for the domed roof and the Manrique wind-sculpture, but all she can make out is a curved line of houses, each separated from its neighbour by a little wall enclosing a neat cactus garden. The sky has turned to the indigo of evening and house lights glow, and she slips off her sandals and pads down to the firm sand by the sea where she can walk more briskly. Stepping into the sea, she walks on through the water till at last she sees, ahead, the twinkle of lights from a domed house standing on its own.

She breaks into a run, and when she finally stops to catch her breath she hears, very faintly, the sound of one long, plaintive note, and then another, and then a third. Trudging up over the shingle to the path, she follows the wind's song. Then she sees, silhouetted against the Prussian Blue sky, the outline of a great black metal fish on whose back sit the words 'Canción del Viente' in thick black letters.

The body of the fish is transected by seven wires, each a different length, and though the wind is no more than a light breeze now, still she hears its soft whisperings. Inside the lighted porch, a big straw-coloured dog raises its head, and then the blue door opens and Wolf appears. He is holding a wooden spoon and wearing a plastic apron which appears to give him tasselled breasts and a G-string, and when Celina sees him, and smells the aroma of good wholesome Spanish cooking that surrounds him, she laughs out loud at the relief of it all.

"I hope you don't mind," she says, handing him the wine, "but the Casa's impossible. I'll have to book into Pension Mariposa, but before I do I was wondering" – she follows the wooden spoon with which Wolf is pointing into a blue-tiled hallway – "if I could possibly have a shower and then use your phone?"

CHAPTER TWENTY FOUR

Early next morning Celina wakes in a bedroom whose white walls curve upwards into a ceiling studded with deep blue star-shaped windows. Her bed, in the centre of the room, stands on a floor tiled with blue-and-white interlocking stars, and the only pieces of furniture are a blue bentwood chair, a tiled bedside table, and a large washbowl made of opaque green glass.

It is the most perfect room she has ever seen, and she could almost believe she is a princess in a picture-book who, having fallen under a wicked spell, has been rescued by a noble knight and transported to Fairyland. For after the chaos of yesterday everything – no, *almost* everything – is surely as perfect as it could be, and for a while she luxuriates between the cool sheets, revelling in the room, and in the memories of last night.

The meal, with its tender meat, its salt-caked potatoes bathed in rich gravy, and its glass upon glass of red-velvet wine, was certainly perfection, as was the conversation that flowed well into the small hours. But as for the long-awaited phone call to Mercedes – it fell well short of perfection.

Swinging her legs over to stand on the cool tiles, she stretches up on tiptoe and raises her arms as high as they will go. She holds the taut posture, enjoying the unaccustomed feeling of nakedness – for a nightdress was not part of yesterday's packing plans – and runs her eyes up the slender brown arms and down the lithe brown body. Then she relaxes and lets herself bend at the waist till her hands trail on the floor.

Looking down between her breasts, she concentrates on maintaining the relaxation, before repeating the procedure twice more. Then she sits on the bed and casts her mind back once more to the less-than-perfect phone call.

Earlier yesterday evening, as she showered, the thought of telling Mercedes about Imogen's studio, and Imogen's paint marks, and Imogen's square window with its view of Pedro Barba, had sent shivers of anticipation up and down her spine, and certainly, when she had told her, Mercedes had reacted with exuberant delight. But as Celina described her perilous journey, and the sandstorm, and the condition of the Casa, the conversation began to turn into something of an interrogation.

'You're staying with a *man*?' Mercedes had screamed, and Celina, while assuring her it was just for one night, that it was really far too late to book into a pension, had felt herself grow more than a little angry at the singularly disapproving tone of Mercedes' voice.

Now, as she picks up her watch from the bedside table and checks the time, she revisits that anger. Why, after all, should she not stay with a man? Was she not old enough, and sensible enough, to judge who could, or could not, be trusted? And what gave Mercedes the right to disapprove anyway? and in such a loud voice that Raine heard, then echoed, the accusation?

Unhooking a towel from the back of the curved door,

she goes over to the glass wash-bowl, and as she looks down at its greenish opacity she pictures the two of them, as she pictured them last night, standing together in the hall in Highgate, raising eyebrows at one another, thick as thieves already. She turns both taps on, hard, takes the Lily of the Valley soap out of her toilet-bag, and rubs it into a lather. Pushing the whole irritating scenario to the back of her mind, she inhales the familiar perfume, then plunges her face deep into the scented water. It is like bathing in the Elixir of Life.

She slips on her dress, fishes her sandals out from under the bed and sets off down the marble stairway. It is 7 am and Wolf will not be up yet, but he has given her instructions on where everything is and she is anxious not to lose a minute, for today is the day the Casa is to be made habitable.

In the hallway, she notices gratefully the collection of cleaning items laid out by the door, before going to the kitchen where, as promised, her breakfast is on a tray, covered with a tea-towel. Flicking on the kettle, which has been filled in readiness, she unveils the breakfast tray and checks her watch again. At nine o' clock, Wolf has assured her, his *amigo* Paco will come to the Casa. He will connect the water, switch on the electricity, and fix the door. At eleven, another *amigo*, Marcelo, will arrive with his donkey-cart filled with essentials – mattresses, sheets, extra lighting for the studio. When these are off-loaded, the two *amigos* will fill the cart with the stuff Celina no longer wants, and then the massive cleaning operation will begin.

That accomplished, some 'feminine touches' (and last night Wolf had laughed delightedly as he used the words) will be added, and then the Casa will finally look like home. And while all this is happening, Wolf will be following up the leads to her father's identity he acquired, last night, by phone, from yet another *amigo*.

The coffee and croissants, and the honey, and the sunrise are delightful, but Celina does not linger over them. She washes her plate and mug, runs upstairs to clean her teeth and then, festooned with bags and cleaning equipment, slips the spare key for Cancion del Viento into her bag and steps out into the sunshine.

As briskly as her baggage will allow, she walks along the Playa Francesa, beside early-morning oystercatchers stabbing their way between barnacle-covered rocks, up through the village and past the church till, scrambling up the rise, she opens her own front door. Dumping the bags, she goes straight to her mother's studio, looks out of the window at the pink early-morning view of Pedro Barba, and casts her mind back to Highgate, to Imogen's series of volcano paintings.

They are, of course, very much a series, each view being painted from a slightly different viewpoint and, as the subtle variations in colour palette show, at a different time of day; but the four together form a whole that is so much more than the sum of its parts that to hang them separately would be unthinkable. She has never seen them as four separate pictures.

Now, in her mind's eye, Celina focuses all her attention on the first painting in the series; the one on the extreme left of the studio wall, which depicts the volcano head-on. Its viewpoint must have been just to the left of the window, and that is where she will set up her easel first. Impatient though she is to begin, however, as she looks around at the sand and dust and cobwebs in this, the cleanest room in the Casa, she knows it could well be tomorrow evening before she is ready to paint.

Running out into the hall and picking up the brush and bucket, she takes them into the smaller bedroom and sets them in a corner in readiness. She hauls out the filthy mattresses, trundling each in turn through the front door and hurling them as far away from the threshold as she can, and when the room is clear she brushes all its horrors into one heap in the centre of the floor to await Paco and Marcelo. She repeats the procedure in the other rooms, and by nine o' clock, when Paco arrives with a toolbox, a supply of black plastic bags, and a sparsely-toothed smile, every room has been emptied and swept.

Leaving Paco to wrestle with stopcocks and fuse-boxes, Celina walks down to the *supermercado* where, out of habit, the first thing she examines is the display of cigarettes. They are all Spanish brands she does not know and strangely, despite having abstained for what seems an eternity, she has no great need to light up. It also occurs to her that, having rid the Casa of so many awful odours, it would be a shame to pollute it again.

Moving away from temptation, she picks up the necessary foodstuffs and cleaning materials. She also chooses a bottle of wine, some candles, a box of incense cones and a small, very garish, plaster Madonna with a blue dress and a bright golden halo. Arms outstretched, the Madonna stands above a flat area designed to hold a tea-light or incense cone, and the prospect of sitting in the evening candlelight, breathing in sweet smoke, sends a ripple of pleasure through Celina as she proudly carries her purchases home.

At eleven on the dot Marcelo arrives with the donkey-cart, and he and Paco do their magic, and by noon the Casa is looking and smelling decidedly better. The toilet is usable, the kitchen hygienic, and in the living room the floor tiles are now a pale terracotta red. The cane chairs too have scrubbed up well, and will look quite reasonable when their cushions have dried in the sun, and when Paco and Marcelo and their ghastly load have disappeared down the slope, Celina sinks into one of the chairs, puts her feet on the other, and looks around with a feeling of profound satisfaction.

It will not be evening for at least four hours, and in the studio Imogen's paint marks glow as vibrantly as when they were spilt. The red hat hangs on the back of the door, and an easel and canvas is set up by the window, with palette, paints and brushes neatly laid out. Mercedes' photo is tacked to the wall by the window, and as Celina settles back in the chair and lets her thoughts drift back to the phone call again, it is as though her anger at Mercedes has been swept away with all the dirt, and been replaced with a rather pleasant feeling of curiosity.

For why, now she is calm enough to think about it, was Mercedes so concerned that she was spending a night with a man? Could it be because she was a tiny bit jealous? She closes her eyes and relives the last time she and Mercedes stood together, in the shadows of the Indian restaurant's cloakroom.

'Here are the spare house keys,' she had said, taking them out of her bag and pressing them into Mercedes' hand. 'I hope you'll enjoy the light, and that you'll be OK with Max, if you ever see him. And if Raine asks you if she can get a tattoo, on no account say 'yes'.'

Mercedes had said nothing as she took the keys, and for a while the two of them stood, tongue-tied, surrounded by the faint sound of sitar music and a woman's voice, singing a sweet sad song.

'I'll be just fine.' Mercedes had wrapped herself round Celina, had squeezed every ounce of her gratitude into her and Celina, feeling suddenly very small and not unpleasantly helpless, had let herself be enfolded once more in fragrant softness.

'You take care, honey,' Mercedes whispered into the crook of her neck, 'and don't worry about us. We'll be just fine.'

Then, as Celina moved closer, she stepped back and, holding her out at arms' length, looked straight into her eyes.

'God, you are so lucky to be going to the sun,' she said. 'For two pins, I'd come with you!' And, for one crazy, dizzy, moment, Celina had almost said, 'Then do. Come.'

CHAPTER TWENTY FIVE

Settling further back in the chair, Celina closes her eyes. Isla Graciosa is asleep, and she deserves a *siesta* too, but though she tells herself to relax, it is as though Wolf's Elixir of Life has given her limitless energy, and after a few minutes she gives up and goes back to the studio.

She flings the window wide, picks up her palette, and squeezes out a large mound of Cerulean Blue, followed by a small blob of French Ultramarine, and a gigantic turd of Mixing White. With one eye on the sky and one on the palette, she melds the colours together with a knife, till the Ultramarine has taken the edge off the Cerulean's too-heavenly sweetness. Then, with the widest flat brush, she applies the paint in bold sideways strokes.

Despite the open window, there is no movement in the air, and soon the smell of the paint fills the studio. Stepping back from the easel, Celina matches her afternoon sky with the one outside, and smiles at the accuracy of her colour.

It would have been silly to wait till evening simply because the first painting in Imogen's series is an evening view. She wants to paint now, and – come to think of it – this is exactly the sky she wants to paint. Not a pink-tinged evening sky like Imogen's, but a pale blue afternoon sky feathered with wispy cirrus clouds. For this is her painting, not her mother's, and she will paint it as she chooses.

She narrows her eyes and looks at the horizon, white and hazy, as though the sun has drawn the last vestiges of dew from the sand and kept them hanging there all day. Scooping up some white with a hard-bristled brush, she blends it into the blue of her horizon till it glows.

Then she chooses her colours for the volcano itself. There is Burnt Sienna which, mixed with plenty of white, will be its base colour, and Burnt Sienna's greyer cousin Raw Umber to form the deep clefts that run down from its summit. Its cinnabar stripes will be Indian Red, and its paler ones Naples Yellow, and these stripes will be painted with a fine brush to capture their calligraphic quality.

Filling a broad flat brush with the pale Burnt Sienna, Celina sketches in the shape of Pedro Barba. Looking more and more intently at the volcano, she moves different shades of brown around, juxtaposing light and dark till contours appear, then checking them with reality and changing them until they are just right. Dazzled by the blue of her sky, mesmerised by the sound of her paint-strokes, her nostrils filled with the rich heady smell of danger, she paints on and on till at last it seems as though, once more, time past has become time present.

For, if she casts her mind back to Highgate and scans along the row of paintings, was the third in Imogen's series not painted on such an afternoon? And if it was, did Imogen not see these just these lights and shades, hear just these sounds, breathe in just these smells?

And where was Francisco, on that bright sunny

afternoon? Had he swept aside the bright beaded curtain and gone into the little kitchen to make coffee? In a moment, would he push the studio door open just a crack, so that the coffee-aroma would be the only thing to disturb his wife's work?

Would Imogen, turning at that aroma, smile at her husband, and take the cup, and kiss him lightly on the cheek? Abandoning her brushes, would she allow herself to be led to the bedroom and into the big bed with its black curled bedposts? And would the perfect love she made with her husband result, in the fullness of time, in Kalinda and Celina: the Sun and the Moon?

Celina stops. She closes her eyes, then opens them again, and as she sees the shimmering shape flit across her painted sky she feels her stomach clench. There is a brightness in that sky of hers that does not belong, a luminosity that is not a quality of the paint but of the viewer. Looking away to the shadowed wall where the mirror stands, she checks what she already knows and yes – of course – the birds are flying over there too, searing across the carved wood, obliterating every shadow and every light with their wings, taking over as they always take over. Putting an end to everything worthwhile; ruining what she most wants to do.

Slamming the palette down, Celina throws herself onto the floor in the darkest corner of the room and, head on drawn-up knees, sits and seethes at the injustice of it all. Rivulets of sweat are running down her back and between her breasts and, suddenly unable to bear the dampness of her dress, she scrambles to her feet and pulls it over her head and off. Then she sinks back down into her miserable corner.

Before she closes her eyes again, though, she catches a glimpse of her reflection in the mirror's old glass. On a sudden impulse, she pulls herself up and walks over to face it. Then she takes off her pants, kicks them aside, and looks again.

Arms by her sides, she stands looking at her naked self – the highlighted cheekbones, the finely arched nose, the dark hair against the mellow skin. Then she fetches the hat from the back of the door, puts it on, and adjusts its angle.

Shyly, because she cannot remember ever examining her naked body in a mirror before, she looks at every detail of Celina Wilde. Taking her time, she lets her eyes drift downward, past the breasts that can still, after all those years, stand up for themselves, to the narrow waist and the broad, firm hips and the taut stomach with its two pale lines – one for Raine and the other, at right angles, for Luca – to the mound of hair between the long, slender legs.

The migraine's dazzle hovers over the dark triangle but, as Celina concentrates her gaze on it, and wonders if it was always so dramatically blue-black against the whiteness of the surrounding skin, it is as though the dazzle is forced aside. Willing herself to blank it out, to see beyond it, she continues to study the details of her own skin-tones, translating them into paint.

She imagines mixing the palest of flesh tones for the breasts, choosing the best brown for the areolas and mixing in, perhaps, a dash of red. Most important of all, she plans the Leaf Green shadows that will show the hard swell of the nipples, the soft curve of the belly, the overlapping muscles that hold the shoulders proud and strong. Then she pulls the mirror out from its corner and, taking the volcano painting off the easel, replaces it with a blank canvas.

She squeezes some Terre Verte onto her palette and mixes in a few drops of linseed oil till it moves more freely. Then she outlines the shape of her naked body with a fine sable rigger brush, and when she is satisfied her proportions are correct, she paints in the deepest shadows.

Using the Burnt Sienna on her palette, she begins to flesh herself out; and as she paints she feels the absolute rightness of what she is doing and – hot on the heels of that rightness – the absolute wrongness and futility of what she had intended to do before.

For it was folly to think of painting Pedro Barba as Imogen had done. It was futile to try to emulate or, more futile still, out-paint her mother. From now on, she will paint her own pictures, using her own subjects. And what is more – she adds a generous blob of Payne's Gray to the palette – she will not attempt naturalism. She will paint what will amount to an illustration of herself, with bold dark lines, and strong, clashing colours, and sharp, exaggerated shadows. She will forget Imogen's work. She will follow her own rules instead.

Carefully, with a firm, fine-edged brush, she runs a narrow line round one of her painted breasts. Then she takes a dry brush and blends the grey into the sandy brown interior, till the breast stands out pert and strong. She repeats the process with the other breast and then, very lightly and quickly, adds a hazy background of open window, sky and volcano. The shadows of the volcano, she sees, are lengthening.

The church bell chimes for evening mass, and she knows it is time she stopped. Tomorrow, when the face has dried, she will put in the all-important highlights, and then she will take Winsor Red and paint the hat. For now, however, she is so captivated by her own growing likeness, and so absorbed in her task, that despite the deepening shadows she cannot tear herself away.

So absorbed is she, in fact, that she does not hear the front door open, or the footfall on the hall floor, or even the slight creak of the studio door as it is eased gently open. All she notices, and turns towards, is the aroma that fills the studio, which is a mixture of sea and sun and sweat, with the tiniest hint of pepper.

CHAPTER TWENTY SIX

A series of thoughts runs through Celina's head during the short interval between her turning to see Wolf, and Wolf mumbling apologies and leaving the studio.

The first thought is that she should pull the hat off and clamp it over her pubic area, because Wolf's gaze is so strongly directed to its dark shadows that she could swear she feels its wiry curls eased apart and its innermost folds caressed, as though by a tiny tongue. This thought, however, is immediately dismissed as being too theatrical. Instead, she remains very still, watching him watching her.

The second thought, which emerges during these moments of still watchfulness, is that, although her dress is lying a few yards away and could easily be picked up, she actually has no wish to cover herself. For the feeling of being examined by Wolf's gentle eyes, in the studio's early evening glow, is quite remarkably pleasant.

And as the seconds tick away, and that remarkable pleasantness grows, it leads to the third and final thought which is that, were Wolf to walk towards her, and put his arms round her, and pull her to the floor, and make love to her on a sea of her mother's Cobalt Blue and Crimson Lake, she would willingly comply.

Wolf does not, however, walk towards her. Muttering 'Please forgive me, I should have knocked,' he backs out of the room, leaving her to pull on her pants and dress and switch on the lamp. When, after three firm knocks on the door, he reappears, she is standing demurely beside her easel, hat in hands. Her painted form, its head held high and its dark eyes staring proudly out, is the only hint that anything remotely intimate has happened between them.

"I am so sorry to have disturbed you. I should have knocked," Wolf repeats while Celina, talking over him, assures him that he has not disturbed her at all, that she is already finished for the day.

"I shouldn't have gone on so long anyway." She gathers up the brushes and inverts them into a jar of turpentine. "The light's almost gone."

Wolf puts the bag he is carrying onto the floor and, going over to the easel, examines the painting. "I like the boldness of your work." He grins at her. "You are quite a daring artist, I think!"

It is on the tip of Celina's tongue to protest, but she does not. "I'm an illustrator" – she draws her back straight – "and illustration, according to my dear departed mother, isn't worthy of being called 'true art'. But I've decided to stop listening to my mother."

She scrapes the remaining paint off her palette, dips the corner of a rag into the spirit and, with small, circular movements, clears the paint till the palette gleams. "As for being daring, I'm working on that. Do you know that today, for the first time, I've beaten the Schism. You remember I told you about it last night?"

Wolf smiles. "Wonderful! How?"

Celina stirs the brushes round and round, revelling in the turpentine's heady fumes. "The visual disturbance began as usual, but this time it was as though I could make myself look straight through it. Then, as I got more and more involved in my painting, it must have faded because all of a sudden I realised it had gone." She shakes her head at the thought of it, and there is no answering ache. "There was no sickness afterward either," she says. "Nothing."

"You stared fear in the face, perhaps? Pushed the bad memory away."

"Perhaps," Celina says slowly, "I didn't let myself see the bad memory because I was so absorbed in my own work. Is that wine?"

Wolf picks up the bag and, with a flourish, withdraws a deep green bottle with a picture of an erupting volcano, in red and gold, on its label. "I have news for you," he says, holding the bottle high. "Do you have wine glasses?"

"News about my father? You've found Francisco?"

Wolf walks over to the wall, slides down to sit on the floor, and rests the bottle casually on one knee. Turning it round and round, he savours the moment before answering. "I think so. I think I have found your Paco." He looks up at her, his eyes sparkling with humour. "Why not go and get glasses and a bottle-opener? There is still a bit of sunset left to enjoy."

"Paco?"

"Wine glasses?" Wolf laughs. "Bottle-opener?"

With a little howl of frustration, Celina runs to the kitchen and fetches two sparkling glasses from a shelf and, after some searching, a bottle-opener. When she returns to the studio, Wolf is examining Mercedes' photo.

"Paco?" Celina sits down on the floor. "My father's not Paco?"

"Not Paco who cleared your house." Squatting beside

218

her, Wolf uncorks the wine and pours. "Most men called Francisco use the name Paco. It comes from the followers of St Francis of Assisi. They wrote his name as Pater Comunitatis – Father of the Community – and if you take the first syllable of each word, you get Paco."

"So where is he? Where's my Paco?" Celina laughs at the possessive pronoun. "Is he here, on Graciosa?"

Wolf shakes his head. "He is not on Graciosa, but I have spoken to someone who knew him in the past."

"And he really is alive?"

Wolf holds up a hand of caution. "I need to do a little more research, but I believe he is. Federico, an elderly man who lives in the village of Pedro Barba, a few miles along the coast, told me he remembers a couple of artists living here in the thirties. The woman was English and the man Spanish, and he was called Paco. Federico thinks he may have heard about Paco recently, in relation to an exhibition. If he is right, then he is still working."

"So my father is an artist? I always hoped he was."

"According to Federico, yes." Wolf's face clouds a little. "Federico told me something else, too, which you might find upsetting." He looks out of the window at the last red streaks of sun and Celina, dizzy with wine and elation, watches a cloud of night insects zig-zag in towards the light. When Wolf turns back to her, she feels her throat tighten.

"What?" She raises her voice as anxiety threatens to thin her words. "What else did Federico say?"

"You remember yesterday, at the Loro Azul, I spoke about the Civil War?"

There is a small thud followed by the whirr of wings as a moth flies into the lamp then buzzes and bounces its dusty way around the inside of the shade. Celina watches the trapped insect fly round and round, each circle taking it nearer to the bulb.

"I remember," she says. "So, was my father involved?"

The moth has come to rest on the outer rim of the lampshade. Wolf stands and, carefully cupping his hands over it, lifts it clear. In its little echo-chamber, it resumes its frantic fluttering as he carries it over to the window and releases it into the night.

"I believe so, yes." He pulls the window closed, and as she waits for him to sit back down beside her, she remembers Imogen's words.

'Francisco is alive, but he is dead. Quite dead.'

"Was he damaged by the war?"

Wolf holds the bottle up to the light then leans over and pours the little that is left into Celina's glass. "Federico was not specific, but yes. Something like that." He turns, looks out at the darkness. "Few people involved in a war are not damaged by it. And now" – swinging round, he offers her his arm – "we really should go. Your friend said she would call again this evening, did she not?"

"Oh, my goodness, I had completely forgotten." Taking Wolf's arm, Celina scrambles to her feet and stands for a moment. The room is spinning, and it occurs to her she has not eaten for hours.

"She was going to go to the Hell-Hole today, which would have been upsetting," she says, as, arm in arm, they walk out into the hall. Her head is alarmingly light, and Mercedes, and Mercedes' visit to the Hell-Hole, and the trauma that visit must surely have caused, all seem very far away. She squeezes Wolf's arm and leans in against him as, giddily, she lets him lead her down the slope. "When do you think you'll know more about Paco?"

"Federico is a reliable sort. When he finds out more, he will phone. I was looking at the photo on your wall," he adds as, reaching the firm main street, they begin to hurry. "It is the carved mantelpiece you spoke about, in your friend's gloomy old flat?"

"That's right. Above the fireplace where Selestino and Kat died. Why?"

"The little snake is called an 'oroboros'. Did you know? Did either of them have an interest in alchemy?"

Rather reluctantly, Celina considers Wolf's question. Despite the fresh air, her head still swims and the desire to be still, and close to Wolf, has grown. She wishes they could sit down together, right here on the low flat rocks, and watch the crescent moon hang, like a golden smile, in the sky.

"Kat's mother's book was set at the time of the Great Fire, which I imagine is the right kind of time ... but Mercie never mentioned alchemy. Why?"

"It is probably nothing," Wolf says, "but alchemists used the oroboros to signify the union of opposites. The end in the beginning, and the beginning in the end."

A soft breeze is blowing up from the sea, and Celina shivers at its chill. There is something eerily familiar in Wolf's words, and she pictures Raine's poster again. "I'm sure I've heard that phrase," she says. "Maybe it's in one of Selestino's songs."

She tugs Wolf's arm till he stops, then leans into his warmth. "The newspapers made a big thing about Selestino's song lyrics, you know." She turns so that their bodies almost touch. "One of the things they claimed was that they had references to suicide. But I don't think that's necessarily a 'suicidal' phrase, do you?" Her head is full of Wolf's bittersweet scent now, and the little tongue of desire she felt in the studio is back. The word 'wanton' springs suddenly to mind.

"On the contrary" – Wolf takes a small but very deliberate step forward, and now she can feel his body lean lightly against hers – "I think it sounds rather hopeful. One door closes, another opens ..." His words tail away and Celina, leaning harder against him, feels his answering hardness.

"Listen," he dips his head so that their cheeks touch. "Can you hear my Aeolian harp? Is it not beautiful, the song of the wind?" He smiles down at her, and she sees a longing in his grey eyes to match her own.

Inclining her head to one side so that she can see the lone light of Cancion del Viente over his shoulder, she places her lips on his. She runs the tip of her tongue along them, and savours the taste of sea-salt and wine.

CHAPTER TWENTY SEVEN

The kiss, when it comes, is so gentle and tentative it makes Celina shudder.

She has never been kissed in this way before, not even in the early throes of her romance with Max. For Max was never tentative. Max did everything as though he already knew the outcome he wanted, and when he kissed her his lips were set hard against hers, his tongue slowly but insistently coaxing them to open.

He never *just* kissed her, either. His lips and tongue would work away, but soon his hands had to be on the move, sliding down her back, squeezing her breasts, exploring the ways he could reach where he wanted to be. In sex as in life, Max thrusted towards a goal that could not come soon enough.

This kiss of Wolf's is purely a kiss. His fingers press her close, but his hands stay in place at the small of her back. All she feels is the surprising softness of his beard and the gentle caressing of his lips, yet that caressing makes all the secret corners of her body quiver with desire. In their own time, without the need for another's fingers, these secret places are preparing themselves.

She opens her eyes and sees that Wolf's are already open, but the moment they look at one another she senses the stiffening in his upper body, the moving away. Anxious at this feeling of withdrawal, she cups a hand round his neck and weaves her fingers through his hair, coaxing him back to her. But soft and yielding though her body is, she can feel his continue to pull away.

"Celina ..." He moves his head down onto her shoulder, and the soft rasp of his beard on her cheek makes her press her openness more urgently against him. In answer, he repeats her name, but this time it sounds like a moan and, in some indefinable way, she feels she has failed him. The space between them widens a fraction more, and though his head remains close his breath feels hard and cold. Releasing him, she searches his face in vain for the familiar smile. His eyes are wide and serious, and for the first time she remembers the conveniently-forgotten partner.

"I am sorry, Celina. I should not have ..." Wolf looks towards the sea, then back at her, and she is shocked to see tears in his eyes. "I mean, you are very beautiful, and I like you very much, but I can not."

He gives her a little tug towards the Cancion del Viente, but she does not move. The giddy wantonness is gone and her face burns with shame. Were it not for the phone call, she would turn and run back to the Casa. "I am so sorry," Wolf repeats. "Please come home with me, and let me explain."

"It was my fault," she says. "Taking my clothes off ... Getting drunk"

With a shake of the head, Wolf drops his hand and looks at his watch. "It was not at all your fault. But, Celina, it is almost eight. Your friend will phone. We need to hurry."

He presses his interlocked fingers hard down on the top of his scalp and rubs, hard and furious. Then he runs the hands over his forehead and down onto his face, like a small child in disgrace. Peeping out, he gives her an impish grin. "If you come back with me," he says coquettishly, "I will serve you the best wine in the house, and the best olives, and the best bread in the entire island. Just do not be offended, and do not think for one moment that you are to blame …"

Checking her watch, Celina sees the tiniest of gaps between the minute hand and the hour. When she looks up, Wolf is offering his arm.

"You really have to come," he says. "Your friend was going to the Hell-Hole, remember? She might be upset …"

 Arms linked, in a not-unfriendly silence, they hurry along the path together. As they near the Cancion de Viente, Wolf pulls loose and breaks into a run, and when Celina arrives in the blue-tiled hall she sees him in the living room, the phone to his ear.

"It is all right, Mercedes," he is saying. "She is here. Celina is here." Covering the mouthpiece, he winces theatrically at Mercedes' shrieks which, even at this distance, Celina can plainly hear.

"Your friend," Wolf whispers needlessly. "Wine?"

Celina clamps the phone to her ear, and nods. Throwing herself onto the settee, she kicks off her sandals and swings her legs up and over its arm. As she hears Mercedes' breathless voice saying, 'Is that you, honey? Are you OK?' she sees, on the little mosaic-topped table beside her feet, a photograph that makes what has just happened painfully clear.

"I'm fine," she says. "How are you? Have you moved everything in?"

"Oh sure, honey. Raine's been an absolute sweetie and

helped me. But you would not believe the day I've had."
There is a silence, followed by the sound of swallowing.
"I mean, honestly, it has been one bloody drama after the
other, starting with bloody fucking Dawn and ending with
bloody fucking Matt ..."

The thought of bloody fucking Matt obviously tips
Mercedes over the edge, and she begins to cough. Picking
up the photo, Celina examines its details.

How could she not have noticed before? And why on
earth, when she was so open and honest about *her* life,
did Wolf not say?

"I don't know where to begin," Mercedes is saying.
"My mind's blown to hell and back." She gives a long
and painful wheeze. "Shit, honey, I'm going to have to
get the inhaler ..."

Celina replaces the photograph and watches Wolf tiptoe
in with a dish of *tapas*, a huge loaf of golden bread, and
two large goblets. He sets the *tapas* and one of the goblets
on the table beside the photograph. "His name is Angel,"
he whispers. "We have been together for fifteen years. I
thought you knew. I thought it was obvious ..."

Celina tears off a handful of white bread, skewers a
stuffed olive, and thinks back to last night. *Should* she
have known? Was the strategically-placed photograph
meant to be the clue? Or – the more likely explanation –
did Wolf try to tell her, and was she too delightfully
engrossed in telling him all about Max, and her mother,
and her art, and the Schism, to realise?

He is sitting in the chair opposite, trying to eat while his
dog nudges him insistently with its nose, and Celina has a
sudden urge to go over and hug him. Mercedes, however,
is speaking again.

"I hope you don't mind me asking, honey," she says,
"but who exactly is this Wolf guy? I mean, he sounds
nice, but Raine and I were just wondering if you're ...

romantically involved?"

Celina, mentally tweaking the already unlikely picture of Raine as an 'absolute sweetie' into the even more unlikely one of Raine showing the remotest concern about her mother's sexual wellbeing, smiles over at Wolf.

"Wolf is just a friend," she tells Mercedes firmly. "And he *is* nice. So, what's wrong?"

There is a sound like wind on the line. "I'm just so longing to see you," Mercedes says, and now there is a worrying edge of misery to her voice.

"What is it, Mercie? Dawn's not done something silly?"

The settee dips as, keeping a respectful distance, Wolf lowers himself down beside her and leans back into the cushions. For just a moment she wonders whether he might let his head fall onto her shoulder.

"Not exactly," Mercedes says. "But get this, honey – she knew about the old fireplace all along! She knew it had the snake and the date carved on it, and she never told me. The snake's called an 'oro-bor-os', by the way." She says the word carefully, in bits.

She takes a long preparatory breath then, during which Celina takes several mouthfuls of the richest, most mellow, red wine she has ever tasted.

"Apparently her book's about an alchemist's daughter in the seventeenth century," Mercedes goes on, "who was trying to make a magical golden oroboros. When Kat found that carving in Selestino's bedroom, it proved to her that the alchemist's laboratory had been right there, in the Hell-Hole."

"So there *is* a connection with alchemy! Wolf thought perhaps there was." Celina laughs. "So the fireplace started speaking to Dawn, as well as the stones?"

Mercedes makes a noise that could be a laugh or a sob. "I reckon Dawn was the one who wanted to light fires in that fireplace. I reckon she wanted to make her story come true, in some crazy way, so she encouraged Kat to do it. Then, of course, it all got out of hand and now, finally, she's beginning to realise what she's done."

Celina skewers another olive. She is suddenly ravenous. With difficulty, she concentrates on Dawn's plight. "It's *her* fault Kat and Selestino died, you mean? It was nothing to do with your faulty wiring?"

Mercedes makes an explosive sound. "According to Dawn, it's still my fucking fault!" she yells. "It's always going to be my fucking fault!"

"But how? How can any of it be your fault, Mercie?"

"Because now she's saying Selestino drugged the two of them up, so they were too high, or too drunk, to escape from the fire they started. Christ, honey, you should have heard her! She was talking complete nonsense, like she was literally raving mad ..."

She stops to wheeze, and Celina gives Wolf a pained glance. "What sort of nonsense?" she asks.

Mercedes takes a long, laboured breath. "All sorts of things. About them taking drugs, mainly, and all that ... oh, and the bucket. She kept going on about the bucket. In the end I had to call a nurse, and they sedated her. And after that I went to the Hell-Hole, and you can imagine how good *that* was ..."

Finally running out of steam, Mercedes sighs a long, deep sigh and then, before Celina can decide what comment could possibly be sympathetic enough to cover the day's multiple disasters, ends with, "So you know what, honey? I've decided to take a complete break. I'm going to come out and join you! What do you think?"

There is a silence, in which Celina tries to work out exactly what she does think, before Mercedes gives her an arrival date – Friday – and an arrival time and flight number.

"Raine agrees it's the best thing for me to do,"

Mercedes adds, as though that absolutely clinches it. "Can you believe it, honey? I'm going to see the Casa de la Luna Cresciente for myself! And I'm going to see *you*!"

CHAPTER TWENTY EIGHT

"How long have you known Mercedes?"

Hours have passed, and Wolf's salted fish and *patatas bravas* are long eaten and his coffee long drunk. His telephone answering machine has also been listened to, and Federico's message more or less translated. He has definite news of Paco. He needs to talk, *cara a cara*. Face to face.

Celina is sprawled on the settee, while Wolf lies on the floor, his dog's contented head on his stomach. She looks down at Wolf, and the dog, lying among the mess of breadcrumbs and olive stones and wine glasses. "About as long as I've known you," she says, and laughs at the wonder of it all. "Why?"

"She seems to rely very heavily on you, that is all. As though she has known you for a long time."

Celina ponders his words. From time to time throughout the evening, as she and Wolf talked about Mercedes and her story, she has found herself wondering just how she feels her imminent arrival. The news should fill her with excitement and pleasurable anticipation, but at the moment she is not at all sure that it does.

"The death of her son must be terribly difficult for her," Wolf goes on. "And to have him blamed for the death of another ..." He sits up. "Do you think he did give Kat drugs? And had sex with her?"

"I don't think he had sex with her, no. From everything Mercie tells me, Kat was like a little sister to Selestino. And all rock singers use drugs, surely?" Celina hauls herself off the settee and searches for her sandals. She is suddenly weary. "To be honest, I think this Dawn's psychotic, and I wonder how long she may have been delusional. She's desperate to push the blame away from herself and onto Mercedes and Selestino, but would *you* encourage your fifteen-year old daughter to spend time with a rock star in his late twenties? I'm sure I wouldn't."

She eases a sandal out from under the dog and slips it on.

"Is Dawn Mercie's lover?"

Celina stops, one foot poised above the second sandal. Heat rushes up into her face. "I've never thought about it," she says. "What makes you think she might be?"

With a series of grunts and groans, Wolf gets to his feet. "Would you like me to make you cocoa?" he asks, and Celina follows him through to the kitchen and watches him pour milk into a pan.

"The reason I ask is that Mercie sounds like a very feisty woman," Wolf says as he spoons cocoa powder into a mug. "Which makes me wonder why she allows herself to be so hurt by someone who is obviously mentally ill." He smiles at Celina. "Your Mercie strikes me as a woman who prefers to control than to be controlled, so why does she not distance herself from Dawn? Why go on torturing herself, if she is not in love with her?"

He pours the hot milk onto the cocoa powder and stirs, and Celina watches the froth gather in swirls round the spoon. It has never occurred to her that Mercedes and Dawn might be lovers, but then, her track record in such matters is hardly exemplary. Neither has it occurred to her that Mercedes prefers to control rather than be controlled. Taking the cocoa, she changes the subject. "Where's Angel?"

"Angel is touring in the States. He is a cellist. I miss him very much, which does *not* explain my disgraceful behaviour tonight." Wolf smiles the sheepish smile. "I am very relieved we can still be friends, Celina. For a little while, I thought I had – how do you say? – 'blown it'!"

Celina takes a sip of cocoa. "Actually, you know what? I'm not ready for a relationship with anyone yet. I'm just getting used to being free." She heads towards the door. "Was Angel the man you left your wife for?"

Wolf laughs at the directness of her question. "I left Beatrix for Josip, a gigantic double-bassist from Croatia. And I left Josip when I discovered that I, and the double bass, were not the only things regularly held between his marvellous thighs."

He holds the door open for her. "Angel was the angel who rescued me," he says, "and he continues to rescue me every day we are together. One of these days, I will take you up to the crater of Montaña del Mojon, where we had our first kiss." They walk out into the hall. "When did you say Mercie arrives?"

"Friday. At 10.15."

"Friday? Then I can give you a lift to meet her. Some friends arrive from Austria on Friday afternoon, to play a concert." He nods over at two cardboard boxes stacked by the door. "Feminine touches, by the way. I will come with you in the morning and help you carry them."

Celina shakes her head. "Thanks, but I can take one in

the morning, and collect the other when I come back in the evening for Mercie's phone call. Tomorrow I want to concentrate on painting. I've only three days before Mercie arrives."

"Then I will go after breakfast to Pedro Barba village and see what Federico has discovered," Wolf says. "He sounded quite excited. As excited as Federico ever gets, anyway!"

Celina looks at Wolf's laughing eyes. "Are we allowed a goodnight kiss?" she says, and waits as Wolf pecks her on both cheeks, then very gently on the lips. Carefully, she climbs the spiral staircase to the magical little room, drinks her cocoa, and sleeps soundly till morning.

It is dark when she wakes, and even with her eyes shut she senses it is still very early; but as soon as she looks up into the shadows spiralling above her head, the waves of excitement are so strong she cannot stay in bed a moment longer.

Throwing off the sheet, she swings her legs off the bed and lets them absorb the coolness of the marble floor. Then she dresses, and goes downstairs where she eats and drinks standing at the table. Hoisting one of Wolf's boxes under her arm, she slips out into the morning mist.

The air is moist and smells of sea, and as she opens the gate she looks into the distance, where harbour lights wink through the dawn. To her right, the Famara Cliffs are gaunt and grey on a steadily brightening background. The only noise, apart from the sea's constant thrum, is her footsteps and the steady clink of Wolf's treasures. Now and then, a seabird gives a dry call.

The harbour is deserted, and as she passes in front of the Loro Azul all the little streetlights go out one by one and suddenly it seems lighter than before, as though day has begun. Looking beyond the masts of the sailing boats towards the volcanic crags, she sees the pink beginnings of a glow in the sky. Anxious, suddenly, to reach the Casa before sunrise, she quickens her pace, and when she arrives she goes immediately to the studio, and stands at the easel, looking at her portrait.

There is barely enough light to see, but the picture's bold lines, and the stark interplay of its dark and light, please her, and for a while she walks this way and that, noticing details she will later accentuate and flaws she will erase.

Taking the red hat from its hook on the door, she turns it this way and that, and imagines the proud angle at which, when the light is sufficient, she will place it on the portrait's head. Its scarlet will stand out well in front of the dull browns of the Pedro Barba volcano, and there will be no doubt in the viewer's mind that the scarlet is symbolic of fire and molten lava. And, if she can capture the smouldering look in her eyes with which, yesterday, she so captivated Wolf, that same fire and molten lava will be mirrored in the passion of her own painted face.

It is still too dark to paint, so she watches from the window as the first colours appear, and the shadows of the small prickly bushes lengthen. Then she runs to the front door, where a bright golden edge has appeared along the topmost crags, quickly spreading upwards to send broad shafts of light, like chalky fingers, across the dark rock.

This first moment of daybreak is magical, and for a while Celina stands in the porch, her back against the wall, watching. Then something – a shadow perhaps – makes her look down at the wall to her left, where a raised rectangular area seems smoother than the surrounding sandstone. When she rubs it, a tile appears, with the words *Ntra. Sra. Del Carmen* and *Stella Maris* printed at the top

The tile shows a Madonna in golden robes, with the

Baby Jesus, in pink, in her arms. The holy pair are standing in front of a backdrop of wild, wild sea and grey, threatening sky in which seagulls wheel. Below the seagulls, a boat leans perilously to one side while, some distance away, a tiny rowing boat, laden with passengers, makes for the shore.

The colours of the tile, protected by who-knows-how-many years of sand, are as bright as the day Imogen and Francisco set it in place; and as the sun continues to burnish the Madonna's gold, Celina runs back through to the back of the Casa.

Awestruck, she watches the sunrise transform the desert landscape around Pedro Barba. Awestruck, because this, surely, must have been Imogen's magic moment too, this sudden bringing-to-life of the landscape by the sun's rays. She must have longed to capture on her canvas the daily moment when perspective is reborn.

Celina continues to look out over the vastness of the plain, with its sandy hillocks topped by hostile-looking thorn bushes and, here and there, an unexpectedly vivid patch of green.

How far away, she wonders, is Pedro Barba? From here, it looks at least an hour's walk, but it is hard to judge distances in the almost uniform flatness. The only way to know for sure is to walk to the foot of the volcano. Throwing some apples and a bottle of water into her bag, she collects the hat from the studio. She locks the Casa and, keeping her eyes firmly fixed on the volcano, begins to walk.

The sun is warm on her back now and, mindful that it would be foolish to be out on the plain when it is at its height, she walks as briskly as she can towards her goal. She tries to make her path as straight as a die, but increasingly the clusters of thorn bushes force her to deviate from her chosen way. Despite its powdery coating the ground is firm, and when she stops and looks back at the Casa it is already very small and insignificant.

Drawing her dress around her, she squats on the sand, takes the water bottle out of her bag, and drinks. The red hat is heavy on her head, so she takes it off and hangs it on the top of a thorn bush, then stretches her legs out into the sun. For the first time, she examines closely the ground beneath her feet. The sand is almost white, but there are scatterings of small sun-bleached snails' shells accentuating the whiteness. She scoops some up, rolls them round her palm.

Did Imogen bring snail shells back to the Casa from her desert walks? Did she and Paco sit together, in the rose-pink evenings, decorating the rims of their cactus pots? Gathering up handfuls, Celina pours them into her bag. Then she puts on her hat and walks on.

The Pedro Barba volcano is close enough now for her to be able to see the details of its surface, the cracks and fissures in the outer grey that reveal the sandy-yellow layer below and, here and there, the odd patch of deep red. As she strides even more purposefully onwards, she mentally lays out another palette of colour.

Her footsteps have a rhythm now, attuned as she is to the varying textures of the sand. Instinctively, she avoids the pale, soft patches and keeps to the darker, firm areas, till a shallow little gully stops her in her tracks. From the crispness of its sides and the feather-like indentations in the firm sand around it, she sees it is a dry river-bed.

Sitting down, she lets her ears accustom to the silence, and gradually begins to hear the twitterings of birds, the raspings of crickets, the soft buzzings of flies. On either side, she sees low grey-green shrubs whose succulent branches end in yellowish bud-like swellings and, mesmerised by this small oasis in the desert, she continues to sit and look around at it all.

The sun is becoming uncomfortably hot, but when she checks her watch it is only a few minutes after nine. The walk, which from the Casa had looked so eternally long, has not been more than a mile or so. Standing up, she scans around and sees that her views of the coast, and the Casa, have completely disappeared and with them the sense of connection to something which could have served as a retreat. All her points of reference having gone, all familiarity vanished, she is like a castaway in this sea of undulating scrubland. Her only landmark, still far away but towering above her now, is Montaña Pedro Barba itself.

With no view of the distance walked to act as a comparison, it is impossible to calculate how far she still has to go, and for a while she stands, wondering how long it will be before she is at the foot of the volcano. Then, as she pulls herself up onto firmer ground and begins to walk again, she sees a tiny dot of white, almost directly in front of her, bright against the lowest foothills.

Cursing her lack of binoculars, she peers at the dot. It could, perhaps, be a plastic bag blowing in the wind, or a seabird perched low on the rocks, but the more she looks, the brighter and more solid it appears. As she continues to gaze at it, she realises that it must be someone walking, and the realisation that she is not alone on the desert plain makes her feel suddenly vulnerable.

She tells herself not to be stupid, that the chances of the distant figure having any malicious intent towards her, or indeed of having noticed her at all, are remote. Nevertheless, she takes off the red hat and pushes it into her bag and, standing as still as she can, continues to watch the figure's progress. From the determined way it strides out, it looks like a man, and again she reassures herself with the thought that, had he spotted her, and had any designs on her, he would surely have altered his path and be heading straight down the plain towards her.

Forcing herself to remain calm, she continues to watch the figure and for a while, as it moves across the volcano's base, she begins to relax. From time to time she even loses sight of it, like a star which, when watched, disappears into the blackness of the night; but when she blinks and looks again she sees it is still there. Calmly, she stands and waits for the man's path to pass her by.

Without the hat, however, her head is unhealthily hot, so she crouches down under a cluster of small shrubs. When her eyes have accommodated to the closeness of everything, she begins to take in the details of the microcosm of desert life around her.

A few inches away a snail, its moist body hidden deep within the yellow-and-brown whorls of its shell, hangs on a branch under a roof of criss-crossed spider webs. Beyond it, its carapace blending perfectly with the blue-green shadows, crouches a grasshopper whose singing has been silenced by her presence. Breathing as quietly as she can, she shifts her position, and as she does, the grasshopper turns and, poised as though on a spring, observes her through big black comic-book eyes.

Beneath her arms and hands thin black beetles slither in and out of the sand like tiny fish, and all around her small shiny things hop so fast she cannot make them out. Soon her eyelids grow heavy and she knows, from the strange, dreamlike thoughts that flit into her mind and out again, that she could easily fall asleep. Blinking herself awake, she looks up at the sky, where small mounds of cumulus clouds drift imperceptibly by, their top edges sharp and brightly sunlit and their lower edges trailing in loose, curl-like shapes.

The cloud strands remind her of Mercedes' hair, and she imagines painting her as, naked and free as a bird, she drifts her way down through the hazy mass of blue and white. Then, one by one, a host of other images she might paint appear before her inner eye.

Giant beetles with glistening horns that clamber among other-worldly trees. Dry river-beds in which stealthy snakes slither below the glowing wings of dreamlike birds. Skies whose blues shimmer above bright red and amber volcanoes ...it is as though her imagination has been suddenly freed, and now there are no limits to its possibilities. The rules of perspective and shading she knows so well are ready to be broken, and a new, exciting reality created. Suddenly nothing is more important than starting to paint in this bold new way, and she has only three days of solitude left in which to do it.

Cautiously, like a soldier in a trench, she kneels up and looks to her left, but the man has changed direction now and is almost directly level with her, so close that she can make out a black cap and some sort of turquoise scarf round his neck. And as she realises that his progress is now quite definitely directed towards her, she feels a small stab of fear.

Gathering up her bag, she breaks into a run till the sand catches her feet and makes her stumble. The ground is gradually falling away beneath her, and ahead is a series of sandy mounds. When she skirts these, she will surely see the Casa again and then she will, somehow, be safe. But when she passes the mounds there is still no Casa and, the river-bed having petered out, the sun is the only indication of what direction to take. She could, she realises, be walking at quite the wrong angle, past the Casa and towards the coastal path to the village of Pedro Barba.

The thought of Pedro Barba reminds her of Wolf, and she checks her watch. It is 10.15, and if Wolf had breakfast at eight and walked along the coastal path to Federico's house, he could have reached it before ten and be leaving round about now. She hurries on, hoping to see his familiar figure.

She pulls the hat out of her bag and puts it back on and, as she does, risks a quick look behind her. Some small part of her must still have clung to the hope that the whole thing was coincidence, and that the man was not really following her at all because, as she sees he is rapidly gaining on her, her stomach lurches sickeningly. To break into a run at this stage would only show her fear and – since the man is almost certainly an innocent walker like herself – make her look and feel extremely silly. She turns and waits till he catches her up.

He is, perhaps, two or three hundred yards from her now, and from time to time he shouts something at her which she cannot understand. Taking a few steps towards him, Celina prepares herself to smile. She lifts one hand and shades her eyes, and as she does she sees that the man too is smiling, and that he is not a mad rapist after all, but Wolf Hartmann.

"*Buenos días, chica!*" Grinning from ear to ear, Wolf draws level with her, and now she sees that he is waving a piece of paper triumphantly in his hand. "You walk so fast." He doubles up to catch his breath. "Did you not hear me calling you? I thought you would never stop."

Flopping down onto the sand, he gives her the paper. Then he unclips a metal flask from the little nylon backpack he is wearing, drinks deeply from it, and watches as Celina opens out the paper and reads. The words *Galeria Cuatro Gatos*, and *Arte de la Guerra Civil Española*, written with a pencil in careful capitals, dance before her eyes.

"Paco has a picture in this exhibition," Wolf explains, wiping water from his beard. "It is an exhibition of art inspired by the Spanish Civil War" – he takes another gulp from his bottle – "and it opens next week, in

Arrecife. Normally, at this time of the year, he would be in Madrid, but he has stayed on in Arrecife to see his picture hung. Can you believe it?"

Shading his eyes, he looks eagerly up at her. "What is wrong, Celina?" he asks. "Are you not pleased I have found your Paco at last?"

Celina re-reads the capitals. Then she looks down at Wolf. "Of course I'm pleased," she tells him. "But you just scared me witless, stalking me like that!"

"Stalking you?" Wolf scrambles to his feet. "What on earth do you mean? I was on my way to the Casa to see you and then – lo and behold! – I spotted your hat. Then you disappeared, so I went on walking, looking for you."

He scrambles to his feet and, putting his arms round her waist, pulls her to him. "I am sorry I frightened you," he says, rubbing her back gently. "Of course, now I see how threatened you must have felt, out here all on your own. There is nowhere to hide in a desert, is there?"

Celina pulls herself away and allows herself a smile. "How come you're here anyway? Surely you can't have been to see Federico?"

"Federico came to see me! Just as I finished my breakfast, he arrived at my door. He had decided to spend the morning digging for bait, and thought he would save me a journey. Then I thought I would walk across the plain and cut down to the Casa in time for coffee. So what do you think, Celina? Your Paco is exhibiting in Arrecife next week! What could be better?"

Celina slips the note into her bag. "It's wonderful," she says, and now, as the reality sinks in, she feels a tiny buzz of excitement. She turns towards the sun. "Let's go!" she says, walking ahead. "I need a coffee!"

Wolf pads along beside her, indicating now and then the direction they should take with boyish pushes. "So, did you enjoy your first volcano sunrise?"

Celina squints out from under her hat at the sun which, now a misty mass of yellow light, sits high above them in the sky. "I imagined my mother striding out towards her volcano, planning the painting she'd do when she got back to her studio." She smiles at Wolf. "Just like I've been doing. I've had so many ideas!"

Wolf quickens his pace to keep up with her. "Isn't it strange," he says, "that you came to Graciosa to find your father, and now you have also found your mother?"

Taking Celina's hand, he breaks into a run, and as the two of them reach the summit of the next sandy rise they see the Casa, on its backdrop of sparkling sea.

CHAPTER TWENTY NINE

At eight o'clock on the dot that evening, as Wolf and Celina are sipping their pre-prandial sherries, the phone rings. Celina picks it up, and hears not Mercie's, but Raine's, voice.

"Mummy?" Her voice, far away and tentative, makes Celina's heart sink.

"What's wrong?" she says.

"Nothing. Nothing at all. Everything's fine," Raine replies so quickly Celina's panic doubles. "We were late home, and Mercie's still in the shower. She asked me to ring you in case you worried."

In the pause that follows, Celina wonders which phone Raine is using because, for some reason, she wants to be able to picture her in the hall, or the bedroom, or the studio. The feeling that, in her absence, all kinds of rules might be being broken, disquiets her.

"How are you?" she asks and then, instead of 'How are you getting on with Daddy?' or 'How are you getting on with Mercie?' – which is what she actually wants to know – "How's school?"

Raine answers both questions with a non-committal grunt.

"I'm on study leave today and tomorrow, actually," she adds. "Are you OK?"

"I'm fine," Celina assures her. "I didn't know you had study leave. Did you tell me?"

A silence follows, during which Celina wracks her brain. Is it possible that, in the days before she left for Lanzarote, Raine gave her some kind of hand-out detailing the arrangements for study leave? And did she entirely forget the contents of that hand-out, which should, of course, have been passed on to Max, or Mercedes, or both? Or is it possible – which is equally likely – that Raine is making the whole thing up?

She is wondering whether there is any point in pursuing the matter, when Raine asks, "Have you found Abuelo?"

"I think so. His name's Paco, and he's an artist, and he's got a picture in an exhibition in Arrecife next week. We're going to meet him, I hope. Isn't that exciting?"

The response is immediate, and deeply suspicious. "Is 'we' you and the 'Wolf' man?"

"Wolf is going to take me," Celina responds brightly. "And I imagine Mercie will come too. We'll probably go next week, all three of us."

She tries to hear if Raine's breathing is louder or quicker than normal. "It would have been lovely if you and Luca could have come too," she says, and suddenly, quite unexpectedly, her eyes fill with tears and she prays that Raine will say something – anything – to give her some sort of clue to how she is feeling. "Would you have liked to be here to meet him too?"

Raine makes a sound Celina cannot place. "Would you?" she repeats, wishing she could tilt Raine's beautiful chin up, and look straight into Raine's beautiful eyes.

Raine repeats the same sound, which turns out to be a

muffled 'Uh-huh', and Celina presses the phone close to her ear and listens for signs of Mercedes' approach.

"Raine ..." she begins, and then she stops because now tears are rolling down her cheeks. "You know the poster of Selestino you used to have in your bedroom? The big one, above your bed?"

There is another 'Uh-huh'.

"What did it say at the bottom?"

"'My End is my Beginning'," Raine replies promptly. "His last album. Why?"

Celina takes another breath in. "Oh ... nothing," she says. "I just wondered. Perhaps you'd show it to Mercie?" Then, quickly, she asks, "What have you been studying in your study leave?"

There is a long sniff from the other end of the line. "I've been doing a lot of Spanish, actually. And Mercie's been helping me. She's really good at Spanish."

She places, Celina notices, the very slightest of emphases on the word 'she', but Celina is careful not to rise to it.

"I'm sure she is," she says. "I'm sure she's miles better than me," but she can sense now that Raine is bristling for a fight. Sure enough, there is anger in her voice as she cuts in.

"Yes, actually, she is. She's really good. And she said there was Spanish writing on the back of Abuela's paintings, so we took them off the wall, and there was, and I translated it and Mercie said I have an excellent command of the language.

"Here she is," she finishes brusquely as, with another series of muffled noises, the phone is passed over and Mercedes' voice cuts in.

"What's up, honey? Is everything OK?"

"Everything's fine. How are you? How are you and Raine?"

There is a guffaw from Mercedes' end of the line and Celina, sensing Raine's continuing presence in the hall, sees the wink Mercedes gives her and the shy, pleased smile with which Raine returns it. "Getting on like a house on fire!" Mercedes says. "She's on study leave, so I showed her round *Imago* this morning and taught her a bunch of Art History, and this afternoon we've been doing Spanish. She's really good. Did you know?"

Celina swallows back the picture of Raine and Mercedes at the feet of the Madonna, and wonders vaguely why Raine chose not to mention the *Imago* visit. "I believe," she says primly, "she has an excellent command of the language ..."

"I hope you don't mind," Mercedes breaks in, "but I got her to help me take your mom's paintings down to see the Spanish on the back. I remembered you told me there was writing on them, and I thought it might have something to do with your dad's disappearance. I also thought it would be a good exercise for Raine. Pretty neat, huh?"

"Pretty neat indeed. So, what does it say?"

"Some kind of poem, we reckon. Or maybe a verse of a song. It's called *Cara al Sol* and each painting has one line. Raine thought maybe that was why your mom put them there, to make sure the paintings were always hung in the right order. Anyway, does *Cara al Sol* mean anything to you?"

"'Face to the sun'," Celina translates. "No, I can't say it means anything at all ..."

"Not to worry, honey. I made Raine write it all out – the Spanish first, and then the translation – and I'll bring it with me when I come. It sounds like a man leaving his lover to fight in a war, and saying he might not return. Anyway – I got my air tickets, and I am beyond excited! How about your dad? Did you find out anything?"

"He's called Paco, and he's an artist! I'd always hoped

perhaps he was, but to know is just wonderful."

There is a crescendo of *Oh-my-gawd*s from Mercedes, and Celina listens hard, wondering whether Raine really is still there, and whether she is, in her own way, as excited as Mercedes.

"And what's even more remarkable is, he's got a picture in an exhibition that opens in Arrecife next week!" She reaches into her bag for Federico's note. "It's called *Arte de la Guerra Civil Española*."

As she reads, it occurs to her that it is really only now, in talking to Mercedes and Raine, that she feels the reality of the situation. "Can you believe I'm actually going to meet my father?" she repeats. "Can you?"

A flash of blue moves by the window and she sees that Wolf is bending down to pick up something. Straightening up, he hurls it against the wall, and as it bounces off with a dull thud the dog appears, skidding in a cloud of sand and gravel.

"Art of the Spanish Civil War," Mercedes is saying. "Was your dad involved, do you think?"

Barking hysterically, the dog runs for its ball, and as Wolf prepares to throw it again he catches Celina's eye. "I'd better go, Mercie," she says. "Wolf eats around now."

There is a little pause, and this time Celina hears Raine calling from some distant part of the house.

"I promised Raine and Luca we'd go to McDonalds tonight," Mercedes says. "I know, I know, it's awful," she adds when Celina makes no response. "Max was very disapproving and refused to come and honestly, honey, I did try to talk them into something else but that's what they want, and they're missing you like crazy and actually" – her voice drops to a whisper – "I'd rather Max didn't come anyway. He's *so* not my type ..."

"Are they?" Celina squeezes the phone, tight.

"Are they what?"

"Missing me?"

"Christ, honey," Mercedes shrieks, "do you need to ask? Of course they are! So, let's talk again tomorrow night, OK?"

"Wait a minute!" Celina screams, as a rustling sound at Mercedes' end signals her intention to hang up. For some reason, Senga the Tattooist and her terrible tray have suddenly popped into her mind.

"I just wanted to check you haven't let Raine get a tattoo? You haven't, have you? I mean, I know she's going to wheedle at you ..."

But Mercedes does not answer and, with a cheery *Hasta la vista*, is gone.

CHAPTER THIRTY

"Would you have liked your son and daughter to be with you when you met your father?"

It is early on Friday morning, and Celina and Wolf are on their way along an almost-deserted coastal road to Arrecife, in the car they picked up in Orzola.

Today's crossing from Graciosa with Wolf could not have been more different from their first wild voyage across El Rio. Sailing out of Caleta harbour on a calm blue sea, they had sat together, watching the white foam lap the sides of the boat as the pale brown coastline slipped silkily by. And as, rounding the Punta Fariones, Celina felt the swell of the open sea, she grinned across at Wolf and, without needing to be told, stood up to mount the waves.

The car, a blue Morris Minor with a permanently rolled-down cloth roof, belongs to another member of Wolf's seemingly endless circle of *amigos*, and emits an engine noise so deafening it effectively precludes conversation. For the first part of the journey, Celina has been happy to look out at the sea, holding tight to the ribbons of the straw hat with which she has finally replaced the red one.

The straw hat, bought in Graciosa's *supermercado*, is of the deep-rimmed style worn by the women of the island, and encloses the head like a great bell, keeping the sun off every inch of the face and neck. When she wears it, Celina feel like a blinkered plough-horse, private and secure in her own shady space.

As Wolf slows down to ask the question, her attention is drawn away from the waves and over to the other side of the road, to a group of reddish-grey rocks, eroded into bizarre, human-like shapes. The group is so unexpected, and so different from the flat scrubland all around that she points across to it and asks Wolf to stop. With an ominous knocking sound, the Morris comes to a halt and Wolf switches off the engine.

"Aren't they remarkable?" Celina says. "They remind me of Max Ernst's decalcomania work. You know? The paintings of rocks that look like surreal figures?"

Wolf heaves the handbrake into position. "Would you like to get out? We have plenty of time. If you like" – he leans over to the back seat – "I can take a photo of them for you?"

Together they get out of the car and cross to the prickly verge. Cautiously, Wolf picks his way over rocks and between cactus bushes and photographs the group of rocks from several different angles.

"You would like to paint these rocks?" he shouts as they drive off again.

"Perhaps. Perhaps I want to paint fantasy pictures – pictures that tell magical stories, based on the natural scenery but changing it by exaggerating its light and shadows, and introducing other-worldly elements. I could have dragons coming out of the craters of volcanoes, or gigantic insects and spiders under enormous cactus plants!'"

She is about to add, 'And naked women floating through clouds,' but replaces it with, "I need time to experiment."

"Time to find your style."

"Exactly. You know, these past three days have been amazing. I've had the whole day to look, and paint, and think, and simply be." Closing her eyes, she recalls dreamily her days of solitude.

The first thing she had done was to finish the self-portrait. Then she had carried the still-gleaming canvas into the living-room and hung it on the wall, in place of the bullfighting poster. Stepping back to the door, she imagined the moment when Mercedes would come in and see it.

It would, surely, be the first thing she would notice, and for a while Celina stood looking at it, trying to see it as Mercedes would, and to imagine her reaction. Could she fail to be impressed by the dramatic shading, the brave use of colour? More to the point, could she fail to see the passion in the dark eyes that smouldered from the shade of the red hat? For this portrait – and Celina's spine had tingled at the thought – was one that could seduce its viewers.

With the portrait finished, the remaining mornings were spent wandering across flat, sunny rocks, peering into rock pools and sketching their tiny occupants, or capturing the play of shadow and light on the sea, or the outline of cliffs against sky. In the afternoons, when the sun was too hot, the best of the sketches were cut out and stuck round the walls of the sitting-room, and when the sun dipped there was more painting – of volcanoes this time – in its rosy glow.

When evening fell, and the church bells began to chime, candles and the Madonna's incense cone were lit and then Celina sat, with a glass of wine, looking around at her handiwork, glowing with sun and pride and utter happiness.

"I'm thinking of keeping the Casa," she says, "and spending part of the year on Graciosa."

Wolf flashes a delighted smile at her. "Buying your sister out? What a fabulous idea!"

"I was so at peace this week, you know. I didn't think so much as look, and feel. And in looking and feeling, I seemed to understand the form of things in some sort of fundamental way. Everything – the cliffs, the waves, even the dusty old cacti – seemed to glow with their own light. It was like being drunk, or on drugs. Not that I've ever taken drugs, but that's how I imagine the heightened sensations they give. Am I making sense?"

"Perhaps it is what they call 'inspiration'?"

"Perhaps, but I've been inspired before. This was more. This was like altered perception. I was completely in the moment, and my senses were so intense I could reduce things to their most important shapes. It's a lot to do with understanding light and shade, and how shadows make form, and where the most important light is ... Do I sound pretentious?"

"You sound happier than I have ever heard you sound." Wolf lays his right arm lightly across her shoulders and steers the car single-handedly. "*Would* you" – he slows down and turns to look at her – "have liked your son and daughter to be there when you met your father?"

Celina looks out over the bay, at the plumes of white spray rising like smoke from the crests of indigo waves, and this time she gives Wolf's question her full attention.

"I've thought about it often, and I'm not at all sure that I would."

"May I ask why not?"

Celina takes off her sunhat. "I'm hugely excited to think that I'm going to meet him at last but …"

"But?"

"But I have certain worries too. You know I told you how strange my mother always was about my father?"

"I remember," Wolf nods. "The 'alive-but dead' thing."

Two cars pass them, and Wolf increases speed. "I suppose it could simply be the words of a bitter woman who has fallen out of love, but it could also imply a great change in a person, such that their personality is no longer as it was …"

"I keep wondering about the Spanish Civil War," Celina raises her voice above the engine's roar. "I mean, Paco must have been involved, if he has a painting in the Arte de la Guerra Civil Española, and Mercie told me something the other day that made me think he might have been a soldier."

"What did she say?"

"In my mother's studio, there are four paintings of the Pedro Barba volcano, which have always hung in a certain order. A couple of days ago she and Raine took them down and translated what was written on the back, and it sounded like a war song. Raine thought perhaps Imogen wrote it on the backs so that the pictures would always be hung in the right order."

"That seems needlessly complicated. Would it not have been simpler to give each painting a number?"

"My mother was a needlessly complicated woman. It's the sort of pretentious, arty-farty thing she might well have done."

Wolf glances at her. "Can you remember what the song was?"

"*Cara al Sol*. Face to the sun."

She looks expectantly at Wolf, but Wolf is gravely

silent. Then, just loudly enough to be heard above the engine, he begins to sing.

"Cara al Sol con la camisa nueva
Que tu bordaste en rojo ayer
Me hallara la muerte si me lleva
Y no te vuelvo a ver ...

"It is a hymn," he says, grimly watching the road ahead, where a queue of cars has built up. "Look at the traffic," he goes on, and Celina notices his sudden, forced, gaiety as he waves brightly ahead at the blocked road. "I hope we will not be too late for a coffee! Are you thirsty? Did you remember to bring water?"

"What kind of hymn?"

Wolf pushes down his foot and the Morris lurches forward. "Seriously," he yells, "you need to drink all the time in this heat. Otherwise you will get a headache."

"Is it a hymn from the Spanish Civil War?" Celina insists and this time, when Wolf turns to face her, his face is older.

"Yes," he says. "It is a hymn from the Spanish Civil War. Now will you please drink some water, and give me some?"

Celina opens her bag and takes out two bottles. "Federico said it was usually just the woman who stayed in the Casa. That the man was often away." She hands Wolf a bottle. "That surely must mean that Paco was a soldier, away at the war."

She drinks, and watches Wolf drink too. When he has finished he hands her the bottle in silence, and as they gather speed she makes out, in the far distance, a conglomeration of buildings against a backdrop of pale red volcanoes.

"Do you suppose," she tries again, "he came back from

the war maimed, or scarred out of recognition, or shell-shocked? Could he be mentally unhinged? Mad, even?"

But Wolf does not respond. Pressing his foot down hard, he accelerates towards Arrecife.

CHAPTER THIRTY ONE

"Mercedes' plane arrives at ten?" Wolf asks. "Or is it 10.30?"

They have reached the outskirts of Arrecife now, and are crawling along in a steady stream of traffic, the noise of which drowns out the Morris' din. The sun is well on the way to being uncomfortably hot, and the air is thick with exhaust fumes. Celina wishes the roof were not permanently rolled-up.

She looks at her watch. "10.15. We still have nearly an hour. Will there be time for a coffee?"

"I think so. And if you like, when you have met Mercedes, I can take you both into town? I have a dental appointment before I meet Rosa and Bille. Is that all right?"

"That's fine. Perhaps you can take us to a good restaurant?"

"I will take you to the Guernika. It serves good *tapas* and there is an art store opposite which you will like. Perhaps we can meet back there later for a meal? It would be nice for you to meet Rosa and Bille."

"Rosa plays cello, and Bille violin?" Celina says, and Wolf nods. "Now I have to concentrate on finding the car park," he says. "Are you excited at seeing your friend?"

Celina considers his question. Although her stomach flutters, the answer is not the straightforward 'yes' it would have been a week ago. "I'm looking forward to showing Mercie the island, and the Casa," she says slowly. "But I'm hoping there's not too much *Angst*." She darts a look at Wolf. "I'm hoping she'll want to draw and paint …"

"… and not talk about Dawn and Selestino all the time?"

He steers the Morris down a ramp into the dark coolness of the car park, and for a moment they sit, accustoming their eyes to the gloom.

"Why did you say 'Dawn and Selestino'?"

Wolf gives a frown. "Because I am guessing you do not want to spend all your time trying to solve a puzzle which may not have an answer."

"But why 'Dawn and Selestino'?"

Wolf laughs. "No reason. Dawn and Kat, then." He opens the door and climbs out. "Let's get that coffee. I know a quick way to the café!"

He leads the way up into the airport complex and, leaving Celina at a table, goes to fetch two froth-topped coffees. As they drink, he indicates the Arrivals board. "Her flight has landed," he says. "Perhaps you should go."

Celina picks up her bag and her coffee. She stands, looking down at Wolf. It feels suddenly like the end of the comfortable, easy twosome. Pulling her back straight, she walks off to join the little crowd gathered behind the barrier. Then she fixes her eyes on the dark space opposite that is soon to be filled by Mercedes Grey, and tells herself she does not – repeat, not – need a cigarette.

Soon the first arrivals begin to round the corner and make their way down the entrance ramp. Most pull small cases behind them and all look rather bewildered, as though four hours of enforced isolation in a miniature No-Man's Land has constricted their pupils and dulled their senses and now, in the light of normality, they cannot quite take everything in.

For the most part they are tourists, with no excited friends or relatives waiting to meet them. Now and then, however, a surge of people rushes past Celina and, in a shower of hugs and kisses, pulls someone from the crowd and leads them away. Mercedes, however, is nowhere to be seen, and as the hordes thin out to a trickle and the trickle peters out entirely Celina begins to wonder whether she could possibly have missed the plane or even – and here she wonders if she feels bitterly disappointed or monumentally relieved – decided at the last moment not to come after all.

Sipping the last tepid dregs of coffee, she mentally compiles a list of possible reasons for Mercedes' non-appearance. As she sifts through her imagination for suitably melodramatic scenarios (Raine falling ill; Luca committing a crime of such enormity that it requires two adults to sort it out; Mercedes being overcome by asthma; Max – surely not? – falling ill) a heat-wave rises from somewhere round about her knees and, escalating more rapidly than usual, erupts around her waist in a torrent of perspiration. She looks down in dismay at her red dress, but the dampness has mostly been absorbed by the fabric. Taking a tissue out of her bag, she dabs her brow and, still watching the corner wall, backs away from the Arrivals area.

The heat is all in her head now, leaving the rest of her ice-cold and in need of another, hotter, coffee, but she is not quite ready to give up and re-join Wolf. Sitting down on the first of a row of vacant plastic chairs, she takes out a packet of *supermercado* cigarettes and lights up.

Perhaps it is just as well that Mercedes has not come. Perhaps it is better, safer, for the next stage in their relationship – if there is to be a next stage – to happen in

London. Perhaps another week alone is what she really wants. Another peaceful week, finding her father and finding her style …

A shadow on the edge of her vision makes her look over towards the clear white corner where, earlier, all those passengers' shadows had been cast, and she sees that, once again, shadows are hovering there. She jumps up, walks forward and sees, marching briskly round the corner, three smartly-uniformed figures – one man and two women. The figures continue to march into the airport concourse, heading straight for her, and for a terrible moment she sees them as police officers, come to tell her about Mercedes' airborne asthma attack and subsequent removal to the city's hospital. Then she sees they are, in fact, cabin crew.

Aware, suddenly, of how long Wolf has waited, Celina finishes her cigarette and begins to walk back to the café. She has not gone far when she hears a voice behind her, calling her name and, turning, sees Mercedes running towards her. The green stripe in her hair has been replaced by a shocking-pink one, and she is wearing a scarlet-and-green striped kaftan and hauling an enormous case which appears to have a mind of its own. Tied to the case is a huge multicoloured sombrero, and as she gets closer, Celina sees that the case has lost a wheel.

"Oh honey," Mercedes cries as, abandoning the wounded case, she runs over and flings her arms round her, "you have no idea what an awful time I've had." She squeezes closer, howls her misery into the nape of Celina's neck and then, releasing her, plants a kiss on her lips and repeats, "You really have no idea!"

One on either side of the suitcase, they make their halting way to the café, where Wolf stands to greet them. At the sight of Wolf's outstretched hand, Mercedes drops the case again and runs over to pump it warmly. Beside

Mercedes' scarlet-and-green vastness, Wolf looks small and rather vulnerable.

"You must be Mercedes," he says, laughing as he extricates himself from Mercedes' grasp. He kneels to examine the suitcase.

"Mercie. Call me Mercie." Mercedes takes off her backpack, flings it onto the table and then, collapsing into the chair and wheezing painfully, rummages around for her inhaler. She takes three deep puffs and looks pleadingly at Celina. "I have never in my life," she says between gasps, "needed a coffee like I need a coffee now. That bloody thing" – she takes a metal wheel out of her backpack and hands it to Wolf– "got tangled up in somebody's pushchair. Could you get me one, honey? Large and black!"

Celina looks down at Wolf. "Another coffee?" He pushes the sombrero to one side and nods. "It might help," she observes, "if you untied the hat."

"Shall I get you a cake too?" she asks Mercedes.

Immediately Mercedes' face lights up. "Do they do *chocolate con churros*?" She closes her eyes. "I would kill for *chocolate con churros* right now ..."

"You like *chocolate con churros*?" Wolf looks up from the case. "I must introduce you to my partner then. Angel has been known to eat four platefuls in an evening." He stands and peers over at the cake advertisements hanging above the restaurant counter. "It is an embarrassment," he adds, "to go for *chocolate con churros* with Angel. He always ends up with a chocolate-streaked chin!"

He seems on the point of expanding on the implications of Angel's chocolate-flavoured chin, but decides to go back to fixing Mercedes' case instead. Catching Celina's eye, Mercedes winks, pulls her lower lip into a pout, and mouths 'Shame'.

"If there's no *churros*," Celina says, smiling back, "I'll

just choose you something nice."

When she returns to the table with her loaded tray, Mercedes is in full flight. "You have no idea," she is telling Wolf, "how ghastly these women were. Thanks, honey ..." She takes her coffee and a plateful of *magdalenas* from Celina. "These women next to me on the plane," she explains as Celina sits down, "drank vodka shots all the way from Heathrow to Arrecife. They had dozens of the things, all different flavours, and they drank their way through the whole frigging fruit basket. And the more they drank, the more they talked. Oh sweet Jesus, could those guys talk."

She raises her eyebrows at Celina, then looks at Wolf and her as though seeing them for the first time.

"Oh-my-gawd," she says, "can you believe I'm actually in Lanzarote? And it's hot? London's freezing, and the studio heating's packed in, so the top of my ladder's like an iceberg!" She turns to Wolf. "Has Celina told you about my Madonna?"

"She has told me a little, and I think I can imagine its visual impact," Wolf says politely. "In particular, I like very much the idea of a cabinet of curiosities. In German, you know, we call them *Wunderkammern*. A friend of Rosa's, in Vienna, she makes them. But they are very anarchic *Wunderkammern* ..."

"I'd like Celina to help me make the cabinet of curiosities." Mercedes beams over at Celina. "Would you, honey? Paint a little miniature background for each of Selestino's treasures?"

"I'd love to," Celina says, and is about ask more when Wolf looks at his watch again.

"I am so sorry, Celina, but my appointment is soon. We really need to – how do you say? – put on our skates." He takes Mercedes' case and leads them out of the airport building. Trailing a little way behind, Celina watches them talk and laugh together. When they arrive at the car, Mercedes stands by the passenger door and Wolf, pushing the seat forward, motions to her to get inside while he trundles her case round to the boot.

Mercedes looks in at the tiny space. Then she turns to Celina. "Would you mind terribly squeezing in, honey? You're so much slimmer …."

Squashed in the back seat, Celina tells herself to keep calm; that Mercedes has had a long journey, that it is only polite to give her the better seat. But as they drive out into the sunshine and head along the main road to Arrecife, the annoyance that has been niggling all morning expands with the heat. She feels like a sea snail, beached in the sun, that has retreated deep into its shell and formed a hard husk over the entrance to protect its soft, moist parts.

As they drive to Arrecife, Wolf and Mercedes revel in a conversation made private by the Morris' engine noise. Every now and then, one or other throws back their head in delighted laughter, and Celina reflects that *this* is more than likely the source of her inner rage. She was never good at threesomes. In a threesome, she is always the odd one out.

There is something else, too, that is causing her anger. If she is honest, Celina did not expect Wolf to like Mercedes. She thought he would find her too domineering, too voluble. Judging from the continued laughter, however, this is not the case.

Now, as she cranes to hear what Wolf is telling Mercedes about the anarchic nature of Rosa's friend's *Wunderkammern,* Celina reruns two of Wolf's observations about Mercedes. They are observations which shocked her when he made them and, judging from her discomfort now, continue to bother her.

His first observation was that Dawn could be Mercedes' lover, and that, Celina decides, needs urgent clarification. The second - his seemingly casual remark about 'Dawn and Selestino.' – is more complicated. She will have to play that one by ear …

The Morris swerves and draws in to the side of the sea-lined main street. Wolf turns and grins at her. He points over towards a church spire. "You see the church?" he says. "That is the Iglesia de San Gines, in the Plaza de las Palmas. *Guernika* is just a few yards from it, and anyone will direct you."

Celina waits as, with some difficulty, Mercedes heaves herself out of the car. She leans back in to kiss Wolf on both cheeks, then holds the door wide for Celina to clamber out onto the pavement. As the Morris roars away, she turns to her with a beaming smile.

"Oh honey," she says. "Wolf is such a sweetie! Now, let's grab ourselves some Spanish *vino*!" and she hoists her backpack onto her shoulder and strides off in the direction of the church.

CHAPTER THIRTY TWO

Guernika is in one of the cobbled streets that meander down from the Plaza de las Palmas and Celina and Mercedes have, by mutual consent, taken a table in its shadiest corner.

A big brass ceiling fan purrs, and guitar music plays softly in the distance. Soon the table is spread with a selection of *tapas*, with a carafe of red wine at its centre.

"*Salut,* honey. Great to see you again!" Mercedes gulps half her wine and watches while Celina take two small, tentative sips. She leans forward. "Are you all right, honey? You've been helluva quiet ..."

Celina forces a smile. "I'm fine," she says. "Just a bit tired." She pauses. "It's great to see you too."

Mercedes, looking unconvinced, spears something that looks like a pickled walnut. "So," she says as she chews, "you've found your father? Gawd, that is awesome."

Celina nods. "I'm getting nervous about it though, because of what my mother said, you know?" She looks down at Mercedes' capacious backpack. "I don't suppose you have the thing she wrote on the backs of the paintings in there, do you?"

"I have *everything* in there, honey." Mercedes hauls the bag up and takes out a folded piece of paper, which she slides over to Celina. At the sight of Raine's careful handwriting, with its flamboyant little loops and its 'i'-dots in the form of circles, a lump forms in Celina's throat. Smoothing the paper out, she reads the Spanish version aloud:

Cara al sol con la camisa nueva
Que tu bordaste en rojo ayer
Me hallara la muerte si me lleva
Y no te vuelvo a ver

"Great accent," Mercedes says. "Very sexy. Now read the translation."

"Facing the sun," Celina reads, "in my new shirt
"That you embroidered in red yesterday
"That is how death will find me if it takes me
"And I will not see you again."

Keeping her hand on the paper, she leans back in her seat and continues to look at her daughter's handwriting.

"Wolf told me it's a battle hymn," she says. "But why did my mother write it across the back of her paintings?"

"I have a theory," Merecdes says. "But I don't know if you'll like it."

She gives Celina another look of concern and Celina, remembering Wolf's observations, silently raises one eyebrow. She has, she reflects, a theory too. And Mercedes may not like it either …

"I was thinking that, if your father was a soldier in the Civil War, maybe this was your mom's way of keeping him in her thoughts when he was away fighting. Which means that, at that time, your mom was very much in love with your father. But it's only a theory."

Celina looks up sharply. "Why did you say you didn't know if I'd like it?"

Mercedes shrugs. "It's just that, up till now, everything you've said about your mom has been kinda negative ..."

"And your theory proves she was capable of loving and being loved?" She can hear the anger edging her voice, and makes a deliberate effort to soften it. "Actually, you know, in the past few days, I've come to the same conclusion, which makes me wonder even more what went so badly wrong. I used to blame myself, but now I just don't know."

Mercedes taps her hand, very gently, several times. She smiles across the table at her. "Maybe when you meet your father, you can ask him?"

It is such a tender action, and her smiled words are so gentle, that Celina feels her shell-husk melt a little. Despite the swimming sensation in her head, she takes another sip of wine. Then she sits up straight in her chair.

"May I ask you a very personal question?"

Mercedes frowns. "Of course," she says. "Fire away."

Celina rubs a finger round the rim of her glass. Her heart is beating wildly now, and the familiar heat is rising up into her cheeks. "Are you and Dawn lovers?"

Tentatively, she looks up to see Mercedes' reaction, but Mercedes is calmly probing about in the *tapas* dish, as casually as though she has just been asked which type of olive she prefers.

"No," she says. "We're not, but I guess I can see why you might have thought so." She looks up, as though suddenly realising the significance of the question. "Oh my god, honey, why didn't you ask me sooner? You must have been one helluva confused!"

Abandoning the *tapas*, she takes both Celina's hands in

hers and squeezes them warmly.

"You do know that Dawn's very young? Much younger than me?" She gives Celina a wink. "I don't really go for younger women ..."

Celina sits very still. Inside, it feels as though everything is trembling, and she thinks of Inge's fragrant sanctuary, and how she trembled there at the thought of words unspoken.

"I met Dawn about five years ago, when she came to an art class I was running," Mercedes is explaining. "She was going through a bad patch, breaking up with her husband, and I suppose I was a kind of mother figure. I stepped into that role, anyway. And I've stayed in it ever since."

Celina takes a breath in. "How old was Selestino when you and Dawn met?"

"He'd be twenty. Why?"

She stares across the table at Celina, and suddenly the ceiling fan, and the guitar music, are louder than before. "What are you suggesting?" she says. And then, "You're not suggesting Selestino and Dawn were lovers?"

Celina pauses. "If it was true," she says, "and if it was made public, it would pretty well prove that Selestino's friendship with Kat was just that – a friendship. But perhaps it isn't true ..?" She sees a flicker of recognition in Mercedes' face.

"Dawn did like Selestino, always," Mercedes says slowly. "She loved talking to him, and he was always much better than me at listening to her when she was going on about the book ..."

She looks up at the tiny golden cherubs painted on the ceiling. "And there was that day at the Monument, that I'd forgotten till I saw the photographs." She looks back at Celina. "I felt completely cut out, that day, you know. As though the three of them knew something I didn't ..."

Celina takes the oroboros photo out of her bag and lays it on top of Raine's writing.

"Do you see this?" She points to the tiny scales. "You would need a magnifying glass to be sure, but in certain lights I think I see traces of red and yellow paint. And in the poster of Selestino's last album, he's wearing a tee-shirt with a red and yellow oroboros on the front. Did Raine show you?"

Mercedes nods. "She did. And she tried to wheedle an oroboros tattoo out of me too. So" – she sweeps the result of the wheedling aside – "are you suggesting Selestino gave Dawn the idea for her book? Or was it the other way round? They discovered the fireplace, and dreamt up the story of the alchemist's daughter together?"

"I don't know. Either way, it suggests a closeness, doesn't it?"

Mercedes sighs. "I'd love to think it was true, because it would sure clear Selestino's name. But, you know honey, I can't imagine Dawn in love with my son. I can't imagine her in love with anyone, actually, except herself."

There is a silence, and then all of a sudden Mercedes slams her hands down on the table. "You know what?" she says. "I'm sick to death of secrets. I'm sick to death of questions with no answers. I'm sick to death of this whole business with Dawn" – she gives a throaty laugh – "and I bet you are too." The table heaves as she stands up. "I'm going to the *servicios*," she announces. "How about you order another bottle?"

Left alone, Celina beckons to the waiter and orders the wine. Then, sipping water, she looks back at Raine's Spanish translation. As she re-reads the words she sees her mother kneeling on the paint-flecked floor of her island studio, the four paintings face-down before her and a 4B pencil in her hand, writing across the rough backs of their canvases. What was *her* secret? she wonders. What was the reality behind Imogen Wilde?

She looks up to see Mercedes flopping back down. To her relief, she looks completely calm. "I've brought a whole stack of painting stuff with me," she says. "I'm hoping you and I can paint volcanoes together …?" And she gives Celina a look so smouldering it would do any volcano justice, then pours herself a glass of the new wine.

They have just clicked their glasses when the restaurant's glass door darkens and a man and two women come in. They stand for a moment on the threshold, surveying the tables, and then the man waves over in their direction.

"Celina!" Wolf cries. "You are still here!" He has a brochure in his hand, and when he holds it up she makes out, above a brightly-coloured illustration, the word *ARTE* in bold red capitals.

"This is Rosa." Wolf ushers the taller of the two women to their table. She has fine, golden-red hair that frames her pale, freckled face in tiny wisps, and although she holds herself very straight, there is not the slightest sense of tension in her body.

While the other woman, Bille, goes to find a table further down the restaurant, Rosa extends her hand towards Celina and shakes it warmly. Then she leans past her to greet Mercedes, and Celina catches the earthy, sharp freshness of her scent. It is like exotic wood or pine-needles, and when she turns to wave back at Bille, Celina wonders at the fluidity of her movements. She is like a dancer, rather than a musician.

"We have made a discovery," Rosa says, glancing at Wolf.

"We went for a little walk," Wolf takes up, "and, quite by chance, we found the Galeria Cuatro Gatas. They were in the process of setting up the exhibition, but when we told them about your father they were happy for us to come in."

"And there, on the wall, was your father's painting," Rosa continues, "so we spoke to the gallery owner and he said that, if you like, we can pay a quick visit before you leave for Orzola."

"Would you like to do that?" Wolf adds.

Celina nods eagerly. "Would that be all right, Mercie?"

"Sure, honey," Mercedes says, though Celina notices she stifles a yawn.

"Or would you prefer to wait here?" she says. "I don't mind, if you'd rather have a rest."

To her surprise Mercedes seems quite put out by the offer. "I can sleep in the car," she assures her, and she looks over at the table Bille has found. "If you guys are going to eat," she tells Rosa, "we'll join you." And, gathering up her things, she takes Rosa's arm and steers her towards the table.

CHAPTER THIRTY THREE

When they have all sat down, Celina looks at Wolf's brochure. Under the bold red *Arte de la Guerra Civil Española* is a picture, in stark red and black, and when Celina focuses her attention on it she is, for a moment or two, quite unable to gather her thoughts.

"But it's dreadful," she whispers. "Utterly dreadful."

"It is a propaganda poster," Wolf whispers back. "It is intended to shock."

He joins her in her examination of the poster, and she is grateful for his warmth beside her.

"This poster is designed to highlight the work of the *Socorro Rojo*." He points out the red letters at the bottom left of the poster. "The 'Red Aid' was set up by the P.O.U.M." – he indicates the black letters on the right – "which stands for the *Partido Obrero de Unificacion Marxista*, or Workers' Party of Marxist Unification."

"The Communists?"

Wolf hesitates. "The Marxists."

Celina looks back at the poster. Its lines are quick and free, as though it was hastily made in response to a burning need.

"Is it solely an exhibition of propaganda posters?"

"There are paintings too," Wolf says, "on the subject of the war, but" – he puts a hand on her arm and presses his concern down into her – "your father's contribution is a poster. I am glad we found the gallery this afternoon," he adds, "because it is best for you to be forewarned."

Celina turns back to the Socorro Rojo poster. The word *Criminales!* is printed across the top, and its centrepiece is a woman, painted in coarse black brushstrokes. In her big hands she holds the limp body of a child, blood dripping from its chest. The woman's face is in profile and the visible eye, closed in anguish, is depicted in a single line. Her eyebrows, following that same sorrowful line, mirror the silent scream that will always echo out of that drawing. The woman's scream of '*Criminales!*'

Putting the brochure down, Celina sits back in her chair. In the distance, she can smell food and hear the rise and fall of voices and, every now and then, Mercedes' laugh, but the poster occupies all her thoughts.

"Is my father's poster as shocking as this one?" she whispers to Wolf.

"The content is not so harrowing, no." His voice is deliberately reassuring, but it frightens Celina.

"What is the content?"

"It is more political. More of a rallying-cry. A recruitment poster."

"For the P.O.U.M?"

She listens to Wolf's silence. "No," he says. "Another party." Then he scrapes the last of his food off his plate and stands. "You and I will go," he says. "Just us. It will be better that way."

Celina looks over at Mercedes. She has pressed herself close to Rosa now, and is talking brightly to her as she eats, her hands gesticulating wildly. Going round to her chair, Celina leans between them.

"Wolf and I are going to the gallery." She presses a cheek against Mercedes'. "We won't be long," and together she and Wolf walk out into the evening sun.

"It is not far," Wolf says, pointing to the next corner. "Are you all right?" When she nods, he says nothing more, but leads her in silence along the cobbled lane and round the corner into an even narrower *calle*.

The *calle* is in shadow, and Celina is grateful for the cool air, fragrant with a hint of the sea. She is also grateful for Wolf's continued silence, as they stop outside a bright red door with, above, a sign painted with four gauntly misshapen black cats stretching themselves along the top of the letters *Galerie Cuatro Gatas*.

The stone staircase leading up to the gallery is narrow, a criss-cross of thick green-tinted window panes on each landing barely illuminating the next flight. This gloomy, unprepossessing staircase reminds Celina of the one at *Imago*, although here there no broken window panes, nor any evidence of dirt or litter. Walking more and more slowly, she and Wolf climb up four storeys and at last arrive at another bright red door on which is painted the gallery name, with the same four cavorting cats. The door is slightly open.

Celina waits while Wolf recovers his breath. "Do you hear music?" She moves closer to the door and listens. Faintly, she hears the strains of a song and, pushing the door wider open, steps inside.

There is a strong smell of new paint in the gallery, and abandoned paintbrushes and paint tins sit among crumpled piles of dirty sheeting and empty beer bottles. Two walls have already been hung, and there are pictures leaning against the other two, but whoever is hanging them has disappeared. Celina wends her way round the various obstacles into the centre of the big room and stands, without looking at anything in particular, listening.

Even here inside the gallery, the music is soft enough not to intrude, but the more she listens to its insistent rhythm and the clipped, marshal tones of massed male voices, the more she feels it is not the kind of music that should be played like this – softly, in the background. The Spanish words are impossible for her to understand but it is, quite definitely, a marching-song, a clarion call, and there is something in the fervour with which it is sung that both inspires and unnerves her. She looks round the artworks one by one and Wolf, joining her, waits patiently as she scours the walls for her father's picture.

As expected, these artworks are for the most part propaganda posters with clear bold print and depictions of strength and might. Some are done in sombre browns and military olives, but many are painted in strident colours that march out of the wall like the soldiers they depict. The sense of movement and resolve in the painted images is accentuated by the marching music, and once more Celina strains to make out the words the men are singing. Concentrating her attention on the nearest poster, she imagines those men, rifles on their shoulders, eyes fixed firmly forward, all in step to one great communal heartbeat. All ready to die for the same grim cause.

"Which one is Paco's?" she asks at last, and in answer Wolf leads her across to a painting whose vivid reds and blacks against a blue cloudless sky are so striking that Celina cannot believe it was not the first she noticed.

"This is your Paco's poster," Wolf tells her. "See?" and he points to the signature in the right-hand corner. Simply-written, in capitals, the little red 'Paco' is hardly noticeable. Bending, Celina stares at its delicate yet firm brushstrokes. Then she backs away, and lets the whole painting sink in.

Like the poster reproduced on the gallery brochure, her father's also features a woman, but no wail of grief issues from this woman's mouth. In contrast, Paco's woman stands tall and proud, her profile strong and brown against the sky, and her eyes wide open despite the glare of the sun in her face. In her left hand she holds two dead cockerels, their heads lolling over her big muscular fist as their blood drips down onto the skirts of her grey dress, and in her right hand she holds a large black and red flag.

A yellow sun illuminates her face and above the flag, following the lines of its furls, is written, in red, *CARA AL SOL*.

Celina stares at the words and as she mouths them she hears their echo coming, clear as day, from the singing, marching men.

"*Cara al sol*," she repeats, "*con la camisa nueva*. 'Facing the sun in my new shirt'." She looks at Wolf. "It's the battle-hymn my mother wrote across the back of her volcano paintings. And that's what those soldiers are singing …"

There is a sound of clattering and a distant door slamming and then two men, carrying a narrow wooden table, emerge from a small door at the side of the gallery. "It is all right," Wolf assures her. "I met these men earlier. I will explain we will not stay long," and he walks across the room and begins to talk to the men.

Celina steps closer to her father's poster and focuses all her attention on the woman's flag. It is red, with a central black panel on which some sort of military design is painted, also in red. On a sudden impulse, she crouches down to kneel on the floor. She looks up at the red painted shape, as a small child would look, and when Wolf returns she is still kneeling, looking.

"That's it," she says, scrambling to her feet. "That's the image my mother was painting when I disturbed her.

Exactly that, I remember now. In my memory I always saw sharp things, violent things" – her words jumble over one another – "and I thought, I presumed, they were knives, but they're not, they're arrows. And there was a kind of red mass in the middle which I thought was a pool of blood, but it's a bridge. It's a bundle of arrows in front of a bridge, isn't it?"

She hears Wolf draw in breath. "Not a bridge," he tells her. "A yoke. The image on the flag is the yoke and arrows – the flag of the Falangists. And that song you hear is *Cara al Sol*, the Falangist hymn."

She feels herself sway, as though the balance of her body has shifted. "My father was a Falangist?" she says. "A Fascist?" She shakes her head in disbelief. "Surely not? Surely he couldn't have been?"

Over by the door the two men are hovering, waiting to be gone. "Please, Celina" – Wolf takes her hand and leads her towards the door – "do not judge your father by your own time and your own standards. He lived in a very different time and place, and I am sure he felt it was his duty to go and fight for the liberty of Spain."

"But to fight on the Fascist side" – Celina shakes her head in disbelief – "was like being a Nazi ..." She stops, face flushing. "I'm sorry," she says, "but I can't help but be shocked."

Wolf smiles at the two men as they hold the door open for them, and wishes them *Buenos noches*. "Do not worry," he tells Celina as they begin their descent. "We Germans are not proud of what we were, but we must constantly take comfort in the knowledge that we acted in good faith. We did not know the intent of our leader, or the atrocities to come." He stops on the first landing and, leaning his elbow on the window-frame, waits till the two men pass. Then he puts a hand on Celina's shoulder.

"I want to tell you what happened to César Manrique,

when he returned from the war." He pauses, glances sideways, then back at Celina. "He too fought on the Falangist side, and when he came back to Lanzarote the first thing he did, so they say, was to go up onto the roof of his parents' house, take off his uniform, pour petrol over it, and burn it. From that day on he refused to speak about the war. He immersed himself in his art."

Celina turns to the window and focuses on the darkening sky. Its greyness is streaked with thin lines of cloud whose undersides reflect the light of the setting sun, like a shoal of red-bellied fishes. From below, she can hear the men calling to them, and she sees Wolf is standing at the head of the stairs. Reluctantly, she pulls herself away from the window and follows him down, her footsteps as heavy as his.

"César Manrique was nothing more than a child when he went off to fight," Wolf says as they negotiate the dark stairway together. "He had been raised in a simple Catholic faith, and when he heard stories of red hordes burning down Spanish churches, and smashing their icons, and pissing on their altars, of course he wanted to fight. To him, there was no choice."

They reach the last flight, illuminated by a thin yellow light from the open door. With another apologetic, *Buenos noches*, Wolf lets the men see them out into the *calle*, then hurries Celina along the cobbles.

"It is later than I thought," Wolf tells her as they reach the door of *Guernika* and Wolf begins to push it open. "We should not miss the last ferry!" Celina, however, pulls him away, and he lets the door close again.

"Perhaps," he says, "when Paco came home, he too burned his Falangist uniform? Perhaps he too was ashamed of what he had been forced to do?"

He tries to smile at her but she refuses to meet his eye, and only when he puts a hand under her chin and eases it up does she connect with his smile and feel, despite herself, a small sense of calm. Looking over his shoulder she can see, through the glass door, Mercedes and Rosa sitting close together, their faces candlelit, talking together while Bille, the bystander, watches.

"I need to ask you what I asked you before," Celina says. "Do you think my father was scarred beyond recognition by the war? Is that why my mother said he was 'alive but dead'?"

"I think perhaps everyone is scarred beyond recognition by war, Celina. But most of us" – Wolf pushes open the door and the scent of candle-smoke and wine and garlic drifts out to season the night air – "still manage to be lovable."

CHAPTER THIRTY FOUR

"I had such a strange dream last night," Celina tells Mercedes. "About the Hell-Hole."

It is the next morning and, having breakfasted late, they are at the Playa Francesa. Mercedes, in her sombrero and white kaftan, is sitting on a flat rock with her feet in a rock-pool, and Celina has hers in a smaller pool on the next level down. Opposite, across the narrow strip of sea, the Famara Cliffs rise up, misty with heat. From the harbour comes the soft steady clink of moorings and the slow flap of sails.

There has been a certain reticence between the two women since they arrived on Graciosa. Last night, as the Morris roared along to catch the last ferry, it had been too noisy for thought, let alone conversation, and the ferry crossing, in chilly semi-darkness, had been something of a disappointment. Then, on the ride to the Casa on Marcelo's donkey cart, it was as though both were too engrossed in their own thoughts to appreciate the romance of the moonlight and the thrum of hooves on sand. And when Celina unlocked the Casa's door and led

Mercedes proudly in, there had been a similar sense of anticlimax.

"Oh-my-gawd, I'm dying for a pee," Mercedes had announced as she stepped over the threshold and Celina, too tired even to remember all the things she had imagined Mercedes saying when she first entered the Casa (of which 'Oh-my-gawd, I'm dying for a pee' was not one), had pointed wearily to the bathroom door and headed for the kitchen to open a bottle of wine.

When, finally, Mercedes found her way back, to be greeted by a dozen flickering candles, and the plaster Madonna loaded with incense, her reaction was singularly muted.

"Gawd, this is heavenly, honey," she had managed to say. "And that is bloody amazing" she had added, looking up at Celina's self-portrait. Then she sank into one of the chairs, took the glass of wine Celina handed her, and turned all her attention to the blister on her left foot. She did not, to Celina's particular disappointment, even comment on the plaster Madonna.

They had both settled back in the chairs with their glasses and then Celina, remembering, had run back into the kitchen for crisps and olives and *magdalenas*, but despite her best efforts, the atmosphere had continued to be strained. As they sat in silence Celina tried to work out what had once again gone wrong.

Was Mercedes upset because she had gone to the gallery with Wolf? It was on the tip of her tongue to simply ask her if that was the reason, but she had been unable to find a way to ask that would not exacerbate the situation. For the truth of the matter was that she had not wanted Mercedes to be there. In this stressful situation, she had wanted to be alone with calm, dependable Wolf.

And in any case, had Mercedes not been happily engrossed in talking to Rosa? Rather too happily engrossed, in fact, for the two of them had seemed oblivious to everyone as they talked and laughed together. Was that the real reason she, Celina, had agreed so readily to go alone with Wolf? Was she a little jealous?

Or perhaps, it was the other way round. Perhaps Mercedes had noticed the spell Rosa had instantly cast on Celina? And it occurred again to Celina that, close though she felt to Mercedes, they had only known one another for the shortest of times.

"I'm sorry to be such lousy company," Mercedes had said at last and, pushing herself out of the chair, moved heavily towards the door. She let herself be shown into the guest room, and had collapsed onto the bed and fallen fast asleep. Returning to the living-room, Celina refilled her glass, reloaded the Madonna, and smoked five cigarettes, one after the other.

"About the Hell-Hole? Really?" Holding her sombrero against the sea breeze, Mercedes peers down into the rock pool and wiggles her toes. "But you've never been there."

"Try not to move your feet." Celina watches the host of tiny shrimps scuttle back into the shadows for cover. "I somehow knew it was Kat's bedroom, with the fireplace in it," she continues, "but the walls were painted with things from a René Magritte painting – men in bowler hats falling out of blue skies, and boots with toes, and a tuba in flames – and I was watching myself standing there, and thinking 'This is Mercie's Hell-Hole, but it's not nearly as bad as she said it was.'

"I've been thinking a lot about Magritte, actually," she adds, "and wondering if that's the way I might like to paint. I love how he distorts everyday objects and gives them a new meaning ..."

She looks over at Mercedes for confirmation, but she is bending over the rock pool, staring down at the area round her foot where the little flotilla of shrimps has congregated around her blister. With their whiskery antennae, they are subjecting it to careful examination, and every now and then one of them takes the tiniest of nibbles, before reversing into the safety of the shadows.

"You're sure I won't catch something from them?" Mercedes says.

"Salt water's Nature's antiseptic," Celina says breezily. "And the fireplace didn't have a carving on it. It was covered in big roses. And on the mantelpiece there was a candle, and plate of *magdalenas* and a knife."

"Crazy," Mercedes says, still eyeing the shrimps doubtfully. "Was I there?"

Celina pauses. "There was a presence behind me, and I had the sense that it was you. But then I turned, and it was my mother."

Mercedes withdraws her feet from the water. "How old was your mother in the dream?"

"It's interesting you should ask. She was young, and she was smiling at me. A rather sympathetic smile."

Mercedes looks at her in surprise. "I've never heard you talk about your mother like that before."

"Like what?"

"Like you liked her."

Gazing down into the water, Celina concentrates hard on that part of the dream when, turning to face the shadowy presence behind her, she had seen it change from Mercedes to Imogen.

"She looked the way my mother looks in a recurrent dream I've had since I was a child," she says slowly. "She was wearing a cornflower blue dress with scarlet poppies. But she wasn't angry with me, like she is in the dream. She was looking at the paintings on the walls, and she was approving of them."

"So *you* had done the Magritte images and the big roses?"

Celina nods. "I remember thinking at the time that they were so crazy and surreal, that my mother should hate them. But she didn't. And there was something else that was different. Up till now, in the recurrent dream, my mother's been tall, but in this dream she was smaller than me, and somehow delicate. Can you imagine? Imogen Wilde, *delicate*!"

Celina watches Mercedes take out a drawing-block and crayon box. "I meant to ask," she says, remembering, "how you felt when you went back to the Hell-Hole. I imagine it was difficult?"

Mercedes holds up a piece of blue chalk and examines it. "Bloody difficult," she says. "And in the end there was nothing more to see. Just the great big burnt-out patch on the wall and floor."

"No sign of the plywood covering?"

"Nothing. But then, the police were very thorough. They'd have found it if it had been there."

Narrowing her eyes, she looks hard at the sea, before sweeping the crayon across the paper in a series of broad, light strokes. "I reckon the only thing the police were interested in was the bucket."

"The bucket?"

"There was a metal bucket beside the burnt-out bodies." Mercedes keeps her eyes firmly on the horizon as she speaks. "It was the only thing on that side of the room that wasn't reduced to ashes."

"So what happened to it?"

Mercedes shrugs. "They took it away. And if they found out anything from it, I never heard. It wasn't mine," she adds. "Mine was plastic."

She turns her attention back to her sea drawing, and Celina watches as, lightly and effortlessly, she allows the whiteness of the rough paper to shine through and create sparkles in the blue water. With a sharp grey crayon, she draws the crisp outline of the Famara Cliffs.

"Maybe when we get back home," Mercedes says, "I'll confront Dawn. Ask her outright about her and Selestino. And ask her about the oroboros too – if it was painted when they found it. It would be just like Dawn to want it stripped, you know. She always needs everything to be authentic."

She turns the crayon on its side and rubs its colour hard onto the paper, pausing now and then to blend it in with her fingertip. Moving a little closer, Celina too takes out her drawing-pad and opens it.

"Do you think you should?" she says. "Confront Dawn?"

"Why not?"

Celina begins to draw in short, tentative lines. "If Dawn really was Selestino's lover, she's hardly going to admit it now. And if she did admit it, you'd surely want to make it public to clear Selestino of the paedophile charges. Wouldn't you ..?"

Mercedes sits in silence for a while. "I would," she says. "But if I did, the press would rip Dawn to shreds. So, really, I couldn't."

"So maybe ignorance is better?"

"And maybe, for Dawn, madness is." Mercedes turns her page over and smiles at Celina.

"Know what? As soon as I get home, I'm going to put all this behind me. I'm going to finish the Madonna, find a new studio, mount the *Songs of Selestino* exhibition, and get myself a therapist. In that order."

She peers down into the deep crater of Celina's sunhat. "Would you be my partner in the exhibition?" she says. "Set up the cabinet of curiosities? You said you might ..."

"When you say 'be my partner'," Celina says slowly, "what exactly do you mean?"

Mercedes smirks. "In the business sense, of course. We could put on joint exhibitions, call ourselves 'Grey and Wilde', take London by storm. What do you think, honey? Wouldn't it be a blast?"

Celina looks out across the bay. The sun has disappeared behind a cloud, but her face is hot. Undoing the ribbon of her sunhat, she sets it on the rock beside her. When she really thinks about it, there are several reasons why a partnership with Mercedes could be anything but a 'blast', but for a while she keeps her own council.

"I need to get the thing with my father over," she says. "Then I'll be able to think about the future." She smiles at Mercedes and, for a fleeting moment, everything seems possible. "But don't you think 'Wilde and Grey' sounds better?"

Laughing, Mercedes plants a kiss on both Celina's cheeks. "Way better! And tonight, we'll drink to it! Are you still worried about meeting him?"

Celina nods. "I'm scared of how he'll be."

"You know you won't be alone when you meet him," Celina smells chalk as Mercedes strokes the side of her cheek with the back of her hand. "I mean, Wolf and I will be there too, to support you."

Celina closes her eyes tight and concentrates on the feel of Mercedes' hand on her cheek. When she stops stroking, she wills her to start again.

"I've to meet him in Arrecife, in the Hotel Lancelot, the big hotel on the sea front where I spent my first night." She pauses. "I'm very grateful for your support, you and Wolf, but I've always imagined I'd meet my father alone …"

"Christ, honey, I didn't mean we'd be there for the actual meeting! But we'll be there, in Arrecife, with you, won't we?"

"Would you be very upset if I went to Arrecife on my

own?" she says. Pressing herself against Mercedes' side, she rests her chin on her shoulder. "Would you?"

Mercedes waits a few more moments before replying. "I'd cope," she says. "And I understand." Then she dips her head and gazes very long and hard at Celina's lips. "And would *you* be very upset if I kissed you?"

Placing one hand on the back of Celina's neck, she draws her face close and encloses her lips in sweet, moist, softness.

CHAPTER THIRTY FIVE

The sea, on Celina's lone crossing to Orzola, is definitely choppier than the one she made with Wolf, and even in the calm waters of the bay she feels the insistent drag of the current.

Standing at the back of the boat with her suitcase held tightly between her legs, she gives a final wave to Wolf, then looks upwards to the skyline of Isla Graciosa. Its pale beaches and pinkish-grey volcanoes are so deeply-etched on her mind that it is incredible to think that, only a matter of days ago, all she knew about it came from a grainy photo and a map. Now, she has taken so many parts of Graciosa to herself, and each of these parts has its name and its story.

First, perched at the very end of the coastline, is the Montaña Amarillo – the Yellow Mountain – which is the view Wolf sees every day from his balcony. A little way to its right, and slightly higher, is the Montaña del Mojon – the 'landmark' – with the deep crater where Wolf and Angel had their first kiss. Beside it, and most familiar of all with its painterly curves, is her own Pedro Barba which, today, Mercedes plans to paint.

Holding herself steady by the boat's rail, Celina picks out the Casa, with its newly-painted turquoise woodwork. For a moment, she imagines she sees the shape of Mercedes' sombrero, but it is surely a trick of the light, for it is only eight o' clock and Mercedes will be sound asleep. Still Celina stares at her house until she can see it no longer. Then, turning towards the Playa Francesa, she tries to pick out the rocks upon which she and Mercedes had their first – and, in the event, last – kiss.

It had, she reflects, been one of those rare moments when life stands still, like a boat caught between two conflicting currents. For the sweetness of Mercedes' lips had swept away all her misgivings, and for that one snatch of time she allowed herself to revel at the touch of her hands, big but infinitely gentle. Laying her head on the swell of Mercedes' breasts, she breathed in her scent and caressed the soft down of her cheeks. But though her body longed to spread itself out, as the big hands moved onto her own breasts and she felt her nipples rise to their touch, she pulled away.

'I can't, Mercie,' she said. 'Not now. Not yet.' And she had taken hold of one sleeve of the white kaftan and tugged it, willing Mercedes to understand. 'I *so* value your friendship, but these days I keep making mistakes, and I don't want to make one with you. I can't make one with you ...'

'You do still want to work with me, though?' Mercedes had said and then, with an exaggerated pout, had added, 'You do ... *like* me?' She had winked then – and it was a wink so full of innuendo that Celina had to forcibly stop herself from falling straight back into her arms.

'Yes,' she had said, with a prim smile, 'I want to work with you. And I like you very much indeed.' Then, hand in hand, they had walked back to the Casa in peaceful silence.

'By the way' – Celina stopped at the foot of the rise – 'you never told me. *Did* you take Raine to get a tattoo?'

Mercedes' silence spoke volumes. 'Just a tiny one. An oroboros, on the back of her shoulder.' She grinned. 'Incredibly tasteful, and virtually painless.' And then, 'You're not too angry, are you?'

Celina shook her head. 'Did you say 'virtually painless'?'

Mercedes nodded. 'Why?' With an almighty guffaw she flung her arm round Celina's shoulders. 'You wouldn't?' she said, squeezing hard. '*Would* you?'

Celina pulled herself out of the embrace. Smiling, she returned Mercedes' wink.'I will if you will,' she said.

The boat is rounding the point now, heading for the wilder waters of El Rio, and before it begins to rock and rear in earnest, Celina squeezes her suitcase tightly between her knees to stop any movement from harming what lies inside.

For there are precious things in the suitcase, and as she packed them she had felt like an adventurer in a story-book, arming herself with a magic sword, or an enchanted shield. Now, as the boat begins its slow gallop towards Orzola, she pictures again her weapons of protection, and feels calm despite the raging waters.

No matter what this journey reveals, and no matter how Francisco Jesús Quesada has changed, there is no doubt that she is on the point of knowing the truth of his story; and after every frightening story, however grim and unpalatable the secrets it reveals, there comes a point when the last page is reached and the book is closed and its horrors somehow assimilated.

And if – or when – that happens with Paco's story, she knows that the contents of her suitcase will protect her own identity, fragile though it still is. For despite the fact that her search for a style is far from over, the things she has packed are solid proof that she is an artist and – for better or worse – she is also the 'Wilde' of 'Wilde and Grey'.

She has packed two things. One is a notebook containing the first sketches for the cabinet of curiosities, with the oroboros photograph safely inside its pages. The other, swathed in layer upon layer of Wolf's bubble-wrap, is her self-portrait. Whether she will have the opportunity, or indeed the wish, to show it to her father she does not know, but last night, as she packed, she decided to take it, and now she is glad she has given herself the possibility.

It was very late last night when Mercedes, with some effort of will on both their parts, had gone to bed in the guest room and Celina finally got around to packing, and it was as she was laying the swathed portrait to rest that she remembered something from her childhood that had lain dormant till then.

Quite suddenly, this packing of artworks for a parent to see transported her back to the last days of a school year, and she saw Kalinda and herself, with their big leather cases, waiting to be driven home.

Unlike Kalinda's neat and tidy assemblage of clothes and towels and science books, her case had always been filled with the year's drawings and paintings, and when they were home, and Imogen finally found time to pay them some attention, it was these that Celina showed her.

Pulling them out one by one from beneath the mass of socks and blouses and gym shorts, she held each up in turn and, ignoring Kalinda's sighs, searched her mother's face for the smile that would indicate approval.

The memory had come to her so suddenly, and so vividly, that for a moment she had felt small again, her suitcase huge. She had stopped packing then and, looking over at the big bed, had concentrated on bringing every detail of the memory to mind.

Had Imogen's lips ever betrayed the occasional smile of approval as the pictures were shown? Had her stern features ever softened, and had she ever deigned to give her young daughter a word of encouragement?

A week ago, had she talked to Mercedes or Wolf or Inge about it, she would almost certainly have said 'no'; that her mother had never done anything but criticise and belittle her work. But last night, in her mother and father's bedroom, the memory of a very different Imogen wormed its way up.

It was an Imogen who, triggered by one or other of Celina's artistic offerings, had run to her studio and presented Celina with a sheet of thick white paper, a bundle of broad-nibbed pens, and a bottle of black China Ink.

It is the ink Celina remembers best - the soft, tarry smell of it and the utter depth of its blackness as, taking Celina's hand in hers, Imogen guided the nib across the paper's luxurious surface. The line that emerged, shiny at first then dulling as it seeped into the paper's fibres, had sent shivers of delight down Celina's young spine.

'See how you can turn the nib,' Imogen had told her as she altered the pen's angle, 'so that your line is not always the same width. See how alive the line is then? So much better than the dead lines one gets from those awful pens they give children nowadays.'

She had released her hold then, and watched as Celina drew the blackest of black lines, and when the line dwindled to grey, had tipped the bottle of ink towards her and told her to take some more. She had left Celina then, to find for herself those bold lines of hers which would, one day, illustrate the finest children's stories.

So strong were the details of the memory – the texture of the paper, the gold of the nib, the smell of the ink –

that Celina could not believe it had never surfaced before. And now, as the sea calms and the boat slows, it occurs to her that this good memory has been weighed down by a lifetime of bad ones. Perhaps, given time and opportunity, more good memories will surface.

Soon the boat sails into Orzola harbour and, climbing gratefully into the waiting bus, Celina gives way to the heaviness in her eyes and sleeps her way to Arrecife.

Delivered by taxi to the Hotel Lancelot, she bumps the case up its marble steps and through its glass doors. She collects her room keys from the reception desk and takes the lift up to her room, and as she opens the curtains and steps out onto her balcony to gaze at the wide sea it dawns on her that this, finally, is it. The preparations, and the journey, are over. The time for the meeting is nigh.

The arrangement is that her father will be in the reception area at 2.30, and it is just after one, so there is plenty of time for lunch. But her stomach flutters with tiny wings, and eating is the last thing she wants to do. Lifting the case onto the bed, she takes out the modest pile of clothes to uncover the swathes of bubble-wrap beneath. She unwraps the self-portrait and props it up at the head of the bed. Then she hangs up the dress and smoothes out its creases.

The dress she has chosen to wear to meet her father is the red one, and she chose it last night because its colour reminded her of Paco's bright Falangist flag, borne aloft by the woman with the two dead cockerels. Now, however, in this discretely dove-grey room, it suddenly seems too bright and obvious. Standing in front of the mirror, she examines the pale green one she is wearing, wondering if she could simply shower and put it back on.

Leaving the final decision till later, she slips the dress off and hangs it up. In the bathroom, she fills the big bath, squeezes the entire contents of the liquid soap sachet into the steaming water, whisks it till it froths and, sinking under the bubbles, concentrates on calming herself down.

For the first few moments, the stillness and scented soap bubbles are blissful, but very soon the anxieties begin to seep out into that stillness, and she remembers the look of concern on Wolf's face as, this morning, they said their goodbyes at Caleta harbour.

"You are quite sure you want to go alone?" he had asked again.

"Thanks, but I'm fine," Celina had insisted. Then she had leaned over and taken his arm. "He *can* speak English? I won't have to rely on my Spanish?"

Wolf had smiled and assured her he had asked Federico, and Federico had put his mind at rest; but nevertheless there was something in Wolf's face that made Celina lean further over the dark gap between them to ask another question. It was a question she had often thought, but never dared ask.

"Did Federico ask the gallery people how my father was, physically?"

The final hooter had sounded then, and the sailors began to pull on the ropes and shout at the stragglers on the pier. Straightening up so that Celina's hold on him was broken, Wolf looked into the distance, towards the bay.

"Did he?" she repeated, and knew from Wolf's expression that he had.

"I did not really understand what Federico said," Wolf called down at her, "so I decided not to tell you, in case I had it wrong. It was a strange expression, which I did not know. A colloquialism ..."

"What colloquialism?" Celina screamed across the widening gap at him. "What did Federico say?"

"I think it would translate as" – Wolf had shaken his head, as though forcing the words out against their will –

"'he is not the man he was'. But I could be wrong."

His words, mixed with the sailors' calls and the roar and churn of the engines, had faded until at last Celina could only lip-read. "Do not worry," she saw him tell her. "It will be all right ..."

She had turned away then, had made her way back to her case and, all journey long, had kept his words at bay; but now, in her bath of bubbles, they scream at her. Hauling herself out of the water, she dries herself on one of the big soft towels, puts on the green dress, and takes a beer from the mini-bar.

Lying on the bed, she drinks the beer, and as it mellows her thoughts she opens her notebook at her first sketches for the cabinet of curiosities. She pictures herself, in some new studio somewhere, painting tiny backgrounds inside the Madonna's belly, while Mercedes winds the strip of Selestino's songs around the huge pink-painted body.

Jumping off the bed, she checks herself in the mirror, steps out into the hall and takes the lift down to the reception area. She sits in the first of the black leather armchairs, and watches the big glass door.

The reception area is deserted. Staring straight ahead at the empty marble space beyond the glass, Celina holds her bag tightly against her stomach and concentrates on breathing.

A squeal of brakes from outside makes her sit bolt upright and, a moment later, a young couple run up the hotel steps and into the foyer. They look at the hotel tariff and then, giggling together, run back out. Relieved, Celina leans back in the chair and looks at the clock on the wall opposite. It is 2.35. Perhaps he will not come.

Then, slowly, a darkly-clothed figure makes its way towards the door. Celina watches it push its way in, then relaxes back in her chair again as an elderly woman, her grey hair drawn back into a tight bun, strides stiffly but decisively into the hotel lobby. Leaning both her hands on a silver cane, the woman stands in the centre of the hall, her dark eyes sweeping, crow-like, over the empty chairs before alighting on Celina.

The eyes are so dark, and their gaze so bright and penetrating, that Celina feels intensely uncomfortable. Avoiding the eyes, she focuses instead on the hands gripping the cane, with their crimson-painted nails, and their long, fine fingers, and their big silver rings. Then she sees one hand lifted off the cane, and extended towards her.

Without knowing why, she rises out of her chair and takes the extended hand in hers. And only then, when she is holding the woman's hand, does she dare to look directly into the bright, dark, familiar eyes.

"Celina?" the woman says, and when Celina nods, she continues, "*Soy Francisca, tu padre.*"

Withdrawing her hand, she leans hard on the cane, draws her back straight and, in crisp, well-rehearsed English, repeats, "I am Francisca, your father."

CHAPTER THIRTY SIX

"May I?"

Raising one carefully-manicured eyebrow, Francisca Jesús Quesada points her cane at the chair beside the one Celina has just vacated, and Celina, unable to find a voice, makes do with another nod. She waits as Francisca eases herself stiffly down, arranges her skirts, and lodges the cane firmly between her legs, before sitting down beside her.

"Was it dreadful of me to give you such a shock, Celina?" She turns round in her chair and holds her right palm inches from the side of Celina's head, as though not quite daring to touch her.

Still unable to find any words, Celina lowers her lids to escape the intensity of Francisca's gaze, then leans her head into the curve of her palm. Warmed by her father's time-worn skin, she darts an upwards look and sees a melting in Francisca's expression, a softening of the dark eyes.

"I know it was very naughty of me not to tell you of

my" – Francisca gives a little smile – "change in circumstances. But you see, when they told me you were here, looking for me, it was like the most wonderful dream. And then I became afraid that if you knew what had become of me you would be appalled, or frightened, and perhaps would not want to see me. Which would have been heartbreaking."

As she speaks, she places her left hand on the other side of Celina's head and cradles it tenderly, and Celina lets her eyes drop to the slight swell of her father's breasts, and the fitted waistline of the black dress, and the bright red lining that has spilled from the black cape.

"I wouldn't have been appalled," she says, "but I suppose I might have been a bit nervous." She darts a look back up into her father's eyes and then away again. "I would still have come though," she adds, and as she does she feels a sudden desire to laugh. "What I mean is" – she lets some of the trapped laughter bubble out – "this isn't half as bad as all the other things I was imagining. Nothing like as bad!"

"What on earth were you imagining, child?"

Francisca lets go of Celina's face and Celina, looking at her properly for the first time, sees the fine, straight nose, and the high cheekbones, and the shrewd dark eyes, and is reminded both of her own reflection, and of her mother's beloved Georgia O'Keeffe. She shrugs and shakes her head. "It doesn't matter," she says.

Putting a finger under Celina's chin, Francisca tips up her head, "When you were a child, Celina, what did they tell you about me?"

"They didn't tell me anything. I only knew you had gone and, somehow, I also knew you wouldn't ever come back. I thought perhaps you had died and then, very recently, I discovered you were still alive." She takes a deep breath in, and smiles. "And then I thought," she says carefully, "that you had been injured in the Civil War."

At the mention of the word 'war', Francisca's body tenses and a small 'pah!' explodes from the corner of her mouth.

"The Civil War? Me? Oh no, child, I did not go to war, and it was as well that I did not, for I would have fought on the wrong side." She tries to smile, but Celina sees her eyes are filmed with tears.

"The Falangist side?"

Francisca gives another, louder, '*pah*!' "Of course, the Falangist side. The Nationalist side." She pulls her face into an expression of utter contempt. "It is hard, now, for people to understand how it was, in those days. Everything was in ruins, you know, and then out of the chaos rose José Antonio Prima de Rivera, like a knight in shining armour, and he was the voice of sanity, the voice of order. I never, for one moment, doubted he was right."

She breaks off and Celina, touching her hand gently, wishes she could make herself call her by name. "I think," she says, "I understand."

"I was desperate to uphold the old Spanish values, you see, and I believed all the *paparruchadas* - the claptrap - the Falangists spoke. Even when they shot Lorca, you know, I told myself it was just because he was a queer."

She gives a wry smile. "Listen to me!" she laughs. "'Just because he was a queer.' What nonsense I talk, and to be talking politics at all with my daughter when I should be talking about so much more important things …"

Leaning over towards Celina, she takes hold of both her hands. Gently, she examines each in turn. They are identical in colour and form to her own. Even the nail varnish is the same shade of red.

"Your mother is still alive?" she says.

"She died last year." They are close now, and Celina

298

can smell the coconut scent of Francisca's hair, and the faint lavender of her skin. As she breaks the news, she sees her father's face wince with pain, and the tears gather in the loose red channels below the eyes. Taking Francisca in her arms, she feels a man's sinewy strength return her embrace. Then, quite out of the blue, she too is crying, with a grief so raw she might just this minute have heard the news of Imogen's death herself. Resting her head on her father's shoulders, she allows the tears to flow and, for the first time, is comforted in her loss.

"Imogen could never bear this side of me," her father whispers. "She suspected it, of that I am sure, but it was only after the war, when we were back in London and you and Kalinda were little, that she saw it for herself. And then, when it stared her in the face and she could no longer deny it, we both knew it was the end."

Pulling herself straight, she gives Celina a long look. "Your mother was a great colourist," she says, "but at heart she was a woman of blacks and whites. And in those days, you know, this kind of thing was not spoken about. It was hard for people to understand. Impossible for them to understand."

She gives Celina a tiny shake, as though driving the point home. "I had to choose between being the woman I knew I was, and being your father; and I had to choose the former. I had to desert you, in order to be Francisca." She gives Celina another shake. "Can you forgive me, child?"

There is a rush of air, like a hot dry wind, rushing in Celina's ears. "Of course," she says. "And I can't tell you how glad I am to have found you."

Behind them, there is the sound of the lift door swishing open. A young woman in hotel uniform makes her way to the reception desk. "There's a restaurant here," Celina says, "if you would like?" but Francisca plants her cane on the marble tiles and pulls herself to her feet.

"This place is too bourgeois. We will go to my studio, and I will make you a coffee!" and she begins to head towards the door. When she realises Celina is not following her, she swings round. "You are an artist?" she asks sharply. "You paint?"

"I'm an illustrator. I've illustrated lots of children's books, and I'm actually quite well-known in Britain, but now I want to paint, seriously. I brought my first painting with me, to show you," she says. "It's in my room. Could we?"

She leads Francisca to the lift, and when they are in the bedroom she watches as she examines the self-portrait.

"It reminds me of a Hopper," she says. "I saw a Hopper exhibition in the sixties, in New York."

Bending close, she examines the brushstrokes, and Celina watches her amber pendant bounce on and off the canvas. There is a thick silver layer sandwiched between the two slices of amber, and as the pendant swings towards her she sees, momentarily, a flash of curved glass. Leaning over the bed, she picks up her notebook.

"You paint well." Francisca says at last, and it sounds more like a matter of fact than a compliment. "In fact, you paint rather like I do. We paint little dramas, you and I."

"Like your poster, in the Arte de la Guerra Civil Española. The woman with the Falangist flag and the two cockerels …"

"*La mujer que no teme la luz,*" Francisca murmurs. "When you come to my studio, you will see I paint her over and over again."

"And the two cockerels? What do they mean?" Celina asks, and she slips the fireplace photograph out from the pages of the notebook and holds it to her chest.

"It is from a poem of Lorca's," Francisca explains. "*La*

mujer que no teme la luz; la mujer que mata dos gallos en un segundo. 'The woman who is not afraid of the light; the woman who kills two cockerels in one second'.

"After Imogen threw me out and I returned to Spain, this woman became my vision of strength and womanhood. I painted her, and her dead cockerels, many, many times. It was as though" – she turns and smiles sadly at Celina – "if I painted her, I could become her. What is the photograph?"

"It's a woodcarving, on an old mantelpiece." Celina points to the amber pendant. "Is that a magnifying glass?"

Francisca pushes the side of the pendant, and a circle of convex glass pops out. She begins to pull the pendant over her head, but Celina stops her.

"I'd love to use it," she says, "but I wonder – could we go to your studio first. Is it far?"

"It is far." Francisca turns brusquely towards the door and pulls it open. "But we will take a taxi."

Pushing the photograph back into the notebook, and slipping the notebook into her bag, Celina joins her.

"What should I call you?" she asks as they wait at the door for the taxi to arrive. "'Daddy' sounds odd, and 'Francisca' is rather formal."

Leaning both hands on her cane, Francisca makes a thoughtful little humming sound. "I still sign my paintings 'Paco'. So, if you like, that is what you may call me." She turns and grins. "Is that in order?"

"Yes," Celina says, as Francisca hails a taxi. "'Paco' is perfect.

CHAPTER THIRTY SEVEN

The steep cobbled maze of lanes that leads to Paco's studio seems to go on forever, and Celina notices that every time the taxi bumps over a particularly high stone she grits her teeth and winces with pain.

"Are you all right?" she asks.

"I have arthritis in my left hip." Paco smiles grimly. "It could be worse, but it is a great nuisance, particularly here in Lanzarote. When I am in Madrid, everything is so much closer" – she closes her eyes at a series of particularly vicious jolts – "and smoother."

They continue to climb until the taxi comes to a halt at a wide road junction where the ground flattens out, and Paco points ahead to a sandy open area bordered by dusty palm trees. Beyond the sandy area, and matching it in colour, stands a line of tall, sun-bleached buildings.

"That is where I live and work when I am here. I am fortunate to have found a ground floor atelier." Paco bends forward and tell the driver where to park.

"So, you work most of the time in Madrid?" Celina asks when she and Paco are standing together outside a big wooden door. Paco unlocks the door and shows Celina into a dark hall that smells of damp sacking.

"My real work, so to speak, is in Madrid." She leads Celina into the darkness and unlocks another, smaller door. "I design posters, you know, and that makes me money to live. But my real art" – she pushes the door wide and motions to Celina to step into a small, dimly-lit passageway – "is here."

She leads Celina to the end of the passageway, where there is a third door. She clicks a switch and, as the lights come on, Celina sees that this is a passageway like no other, and she is transported back to her dream of the Hell-Hole, transformed by art.

The wonder begins at the studio door. It is white, and on it is painted, in red cursive letters, the word 'Paco'; but the signature does not end with the final 'o'. From the top of the letter comes a flourish of loops that sweep upwards to join the tail of a brightly-feathered bird. Joyfully exuberant, this bird flies on to join the others that soar on kaleidoscope wings across the walls, to the main entrance.

Celina stands, gazing at the cacophony of colour. "They look as though they flew right out of your soul and onto the walls!"

She turns to smile her appreciation at Paco, but Paco is already inside the studio, taking off her cape. Beckoning impatiently to her to come in, she takes a step back and, leaning forwards on her cane, orders her to '*Mira!*'

Obediently, Celina looks around her father's studio, at the prints and canvases that occupy every last inch of wall space. Dizzily, she turns from painting to painting, unable to focus till at last, smiling at her confusion, Paco comes to her aid.

"It does have its own crazy kind of logic." She steers Celina round to the wall opposite, which is hung with prints. "Let me first show you the work I most admire," she says. She points to the portrait of a woman whose face is exploding into a myriad of spheres that go on to orbit around her head and shoulders.

Underneath, in black on a deep grey foreground, is a signature as short and to the point as Paco's own. Celina reads the word 'Dali', and immediately she is back in Highgate, on that night when she too felt she was disintegrating, with only the silent images of Mrs Thatcher and the wide-eyed man with the waxed moustache for company.

"This is *Galatea of the Spheres*," Paco tells her. "Is it not magnificent, how Dali unites the artistry of the Renaissance with the findings of quantum physics? And of course, at its heart, as in so much of his work" – she waves her hand round in a gesture expansive enough to include the whole wall – "is his Muse; his beloved Gala."

She moves Celina on to the next print, in which the Virgin Mary is seated, with the baby Jesus on her knee, in front of an altar on which is laid an array of shells and fishes. Behind the mother and child, on a broad grey beach, winged angels reach out their arms as though beckoning.

"Here she is again, as the *Virgen del Mar*, the Madonna of the Sea." She waits till Celina has had time to examine the print, before guiding her away from the Dali wall to the line of paintings on their left.

"In this series" – she smiles coyly at Celina – "I have tried, in my own way, to emulate my Dali. Do you see?" She jabs a finger at the nearest painting, in which a beautiful dark-haired young woman lies naked in a boat while, behind her, two mounds of rock rise out of a deep blue sea.

The rocks echo the curves of the woman's recumbent body, as though flesh and blood had been transformed into stone. By the side of the smaller rock there stands a little black-and-white lighthouse.

"My mother," Celina whispers. "On Isla Graciosa." She moves on to the next painting, in which Imogen lies naked on a beach that surely must be the Playa Francesa. In the sea beside her, a rock formation imitates, in sandy-brown stone, every contour of her body.

Silently, Celina walks up and down in front of the paintings, lost in admiration. Then, out of the corner of her eye, she notices several flashes of red, and moves to stand in front of three very different, yet very familiar, depictions of Imogen.

In the first two, she holds the Falangist flag aloft in her right hand, and the two dead cockerels in her left. In the third, she stands on the doorstep of a sand-coloured house with an undulating roof and a turquoise door. She is wearing a cornflower-blue dress, patterned with scarlet poppies, and one hand rests tenderly on her belly.

Paco's footsteps are so light Celina is surprised to turn and see she is beside her. "Our Casa de la Luna Cresciente," she says, following Celina's gaze. "Imogen's adobe folly. It is still standing? I could never bring myself to go back ..."

Celina nods. "It's standing, and it's wonderful. Perhaps one day we'll go together?"

With the hint of an answering nod, Paco smiles. "When I first saw you this afternoon," she says, "you reminded me so much of your mother, that for one crazy moment I thought she had come back to me. And in a way, she has."

Then she becomes suddenly business-like. "What about Kalinda?" she asks brusquely. "Is Kalinda an artist too? And have you both married? And are there grandchildren?"

"Kalinda is a maths teacher," Celina says. "And yes, we

both married, but Kalinda, as usual, was more successful than me." She stops smiling, but Paco gives her an impatient little shake that urges her to continue. "I have two children," she says, "called Raine and Luca, and they are going to love your paintings."

She looks along the 'Imogen' wall again, and pictures Raine and Luca standing beside her, looking too. "Raine is quite artistic," she continues, "and Luca" – the name catches in her throat – "is yet to find himself."

Linking arms, Paco guides Celina to the third wall, where a series of posters shout out the horrors of AIDS, and rape, and Female Genital Mutilation. "This is what I do in my nice clean studio in Madrid, where my brushes and oils are swapped for pens and black China ink."

She comes to a halt at the corner, where the largest 'Imogen' painting of all hangs. "And what about Kalinda? Would Kalinda love my paintings?"

Celina looks up at a naked Imogen, standing in a rock pool with water dripping down from her hair to lodge, like tiny seed-pearls, in the dark nest of her pubic hair. With one hand she pulls away the surface of the water, as though it were the finest gauze, to reveal a host of Vermilion shrimps, Magenta sea-anemones, and Cobalt Blue fish.

"I'm not sure what kind of art Kalinda likes," she says, as she imagines this painting hanging on Kalinda's magnolia wall, above Kalinda's off-white calf-leather three-piece suite. "We were always very different from one another, you know."

Giving the floor a sharp 'rap' with her cane, Paco laughs a triumphant little laugh. "I knew it!" she says in delight. "I knew it from the moment I held you both. I said to Imogen, 'This one is the quiet one, and she must be called Celina, the moon; and this one is much more confident, and so it is she who should be named after the sun. In the end, however" – she arches her eyebrows at Celina, in mock disapproval - "it was my quiet little moon-twin, was it not, who burst into the forbidden studio and – how do you say? – *desbarató los planes* …?"

Suddenly grave, she holds Celina with the same eyes as, all those years ago, looked down in horror from the easel; and in the silence between them Celina feels a great calmness descend, as the circle of time closes, like a snake biting its tail.

"I think you might mean 'upset the applecart'," she says, taking Paco by the hands. "It was my fault, wasn't it? Mother came to the studio to fetch me, and saw you in her dress, and then everything ended."

"My life as a man ended." Paco gives a little sigh. "But surely, you do not really remember that day, Celina? You were so small. You cannot recall the terrible drama you caused?"

She looks deep into Celina's eyes and Celina shakes her head. "I was too young, Paco," she says. "I can't really remember."

A look of relief floods Paco's face and then, as though standing to attention, she clicks her heels and pulls the amber magnifying glass over her head.

"And now" – she hands the glass to Celina – "that is enough of the past. You have something you want to examine more closely, have you not?"

As Celina opens the magnifying glass, Paco suddenly turns on her heels and walks away as rapidly as her arthritic knee will allow. "What an atrocious father I am!" she calls over her shoulder. "I promised you coffee hours ago!"

Laughing, Celina follows Paco into the narrow, windowless little room, but as soon as she crosses its threshold, a pungent, oily smell catches in her nostrils and she backs away again into the studio. At a safe distance she stands, watching Paco fill a kettle at the sink at the far end of what is evidently a store-room, its shelves piled high with paint tins and canvases.

As she puts the kettle on a small primus stove, Celina peers into the little room, trying to spot the source of the smell. It reminds her a little of turpentine, but it is heavier and has a fishy under-smell that makes her feel more and more uneasy.

"Let us leave this to boil, and move away from the monstrous smell," Paco says and gestures towards two bentwood chairs at the other end of the room. Sitting down, Celina watches Paco march back into the store-room, pick up a metal bucket, and shake its contents out. A pile of dirty cloths tumbles onto the floor, and the fishy smell immediately grows in intensity. Turning her back on the store-room, Paco rejoins Celina, and Celina holds the oroboros photograph for her to see.

"It's an old mantelpiece," she explains, "with an alchemical image carved into it." She hands the photograph to Paco, who points a scarlet-nailed finger at the oroboros.

"This is the little tail-eating serpent, is it not?" she says. "The one who constantly renews itself?"

Celina nods. "The oroboros," she says.

Paco raises her eyebrows. "Is that what you call it? I did not know. I only know its meaning - 'the end in the beginning, the beginning in the end'. In alchemy, there are no opposites, you know. Above is in below, hot in cold, hard in soft" – she winks at Celina – "female in male. So, what are we to examine?"

Celina opens the magnifying-glass's amber cover and slides the lens out. Holding the photograph still, she moves the glass in and out until the oroboros carving is clear.

"Here," she says at last, and she hands the magnifying-glass to Paco. "Do you see slivers of red and yellow?"

Paco takes a quick look and nods. "It has been stripped of its colour," she says. "But not very well."

The smell from the store room has reached them with a vengeance now, and Celina's head begins to pound. Handing the magnifying-glass back to Paco, she gets up.

"Would you mind terribly if we finished our coffee outside? The smell of turpentine gives me a headache." Together they walk to the door.

"The oroboros was a favourite symbol of my friend's son," Celina explains, as they go out into the passageway. "He and his friend died in a strange fire that seemed to come from that fireplace, and it was assumed it was a double suicide. My friend has never accepted that."

"Suicide by fire!" Paco laughs explosively. "Just like my Dali who, they say, tried to kill himself by setting his bed alight. But it did not work. Fire is a very poor method of committing suicide!"

She lays a hand on Celina's arm. "Shall we go and eat?" she asks, and she goes to the coat-stand and, matador-like, sweeps her off and over her shoulders.

"That smell, by the way," she says as they walk through the tunnel of flying birds to the big front door, "is not turpentine. It is linseed oil which, as you may know, has the most peculiar chemical property of *combustión espontánea* ..."

"Spontaneous combustion?" Celina translates. "How do you mean?"

"If you leave rags soaked in linseed oil in a bucket, as my cretin of an assistant did, and the temperature rises, they can ignite *espontáneamente*! And if you had not come today, Celina, I should have gone to Madrid, and my entire studio could have been destroyed. I wonder" – she winks at Celina – "whether my insurance would have accepted it as an Act of God?"

She pulls open the door, and a shaft of bright sunlight sears through the passageway, lighting up the birds' colours in all their splendour.

"What was your assistant using linseed oil for?"

"To bring back the lustre to some stripped wood. Why do you ask?"

Celina looks along the wall at the flock of flying birds. She pictures Dawn, caged in by her own madness, wracked by guilt, raving about her book, and her daughter, and that bucket of hers, and she wonders whether, when she returns to Graciosa, she will tell Mercedes about the properties of linseed oil.

She probably will. No one, after all, can be blamed for an Act of God …

"After lunch," Paco continues, "we might go to the Iglesia de San Gines and light a candle to Our Lady?" She smiles a beatific smile at Celina. "To thank her for returning you to me, and also for averting the *conflagración*?"

Celina searches Paco's twinkling eyes for traces of irony, but finds none. "I'd like that," she says, and she follows her out into the sun.

EPILOGUE

When Celina walks into Inge's consulting-room, three things have changed.

Firstly, Inge is wearing a dark grey satin dress, and her hair is drawn back into a knot to reveal a pair of simple diamond earrings. When she walks towards Celina to take her jacket, her black leather shoes click smartly on the floor.

Secondly, the rosemary scent has gone, and instead the air has a hint of pine to it; and thirdly, in place of the sea picture, there hangs one of a sun-dappled forest path.

The first two changes are perfectly in order, and in fact Celina already knows the reason for the first, but the third – the sentimentally-rendered watercolour – she finds instantly, and quite remarkably, offensive.

She stops at the first marshmallow chair. "May I sit on the other side today?" she asks, and she walks round the table and props her briefcase against one of its legs. She is wearing a dress of pale cream wool, and when Inge has settled herself opposite it is odd to see her, the sombrely-dressed one, in the patients' chair.

"I am sorry this has to be a short appointment." Inge

311

repeats her earlier phone call. "A colleague died suddenly, and the funeral ..." she finishes the sentence with a sad smile.

"It was good of you to see me at all," Celina assures her. "I'm very grateful."

"So," Inge looks Celina up and down, "you had a successful trip? You found your father?"

"I found my father, and I also found the explanation of the Schism. But that wasn't all. In a way, I found my mother too and, perhaps, the reason for that awful fear I felt at her death."

Inge raises her eyebrows, and Celina continues.

"I mean, there were probably all sorts of reasons, but I think the main one was the realisation that, with my mother dead, I had no more chances to repair things between us. On Graciosa, I somehow did."

"Your father told you things about your mother that you had not known?" Inge says. "He painted her in a new light?"

Celina pauses. "The Casa itself painted a new picture of her. But yes, my father did too. My father, by the way" – the little laughter-bubble tickles at the back of her throat and she watches Inge's expression with interest – "is living as a woman. I'm not sure how far down the line of transitioning she is but, to be honest, it's not important for me to know. Man or woman, Paco is first and foremost my father."

Inge receives the information with the most discreet of gasps. "That was what the Schism memory was," Celina goes on. "It was my father I saw at the easel, not my mother, and now that I know the real story, it's as though what's always held me back has gone. I really can move forward."

As she speaks she looks over at her dove grey jacket, and the bright red hat, hanging on the door, waiting for her. There is a narrow edge of sun filtering through the low window, casting shadowy fingers on the wall.

"I had all sorts of love affairs when I was in Lanzarote, too," she says, and this time Inge allows herself a delighted laugh. "It was as if the passion I've been holding in all these years erupted, and I simply had to express it."

"And - if I may ask - did you?"

Celina feels herself blush like a schoolgirl. "I didn't go too far, because I don't want to involve another person till I'm surer about what I really want. In the end, I expressed passion through my painting instead, and that's what I intend to keep doing for a while." Noticing Inge's frown, she adds, "I will go too far though, one day!"

She moves forward in her chair. "I still have the most frighteningly dark moments, though."

"But these frighteningly dark moments are only thoughts, Celina," Inge says quietly. "You can, as it were, put spaces between them. You are not powerless."

"No, I am no longer powerless. I'd like to keep seeing you, though."

Inge smiles. "Of course. And what about your work?"

Celina looks down at her briefcase and pictures the final sketches for Mercedes' cabinet of curiosities.

"I'm collaborating with Mercie on an exhibition at the moment." She hears the swell of pride in her voice, and feels the flush of joy. "We've just found a new studio, which we're calling *Wilde and Grey*. This afternoon, we move in a ten-foot high, bright pink, Madonna. Don't ask …"

Inge smiles. "So you found your style?"

"Perhaps. Surrealism, I think will be my style. For now, anyway."

"And you like working with someone else?"

Celina pauses. "Up to a point. But not just with Mercie.

With all sorts of people." She looks over at the jacket again. "Vienna, too, attracts me ..."

As though seeing the longing in Celina's eyes, Inge stands. "I will see you in a week's time then? And today there is no charge."

Outside in the sunshine, Celina checks her watch. She should, she knows, hurry to the studio, but the consultation has been so short, surely Mercedes will not expect her yet. Slowly, she turns and walks down the leafy street, looking idly in at the fashionable shop windows.

In the window of a particularly exclusive shop, a straw panama catches her eye. It has a dark blue satin band with white spots, and it is exorbitantly expensive. But who knows where she could be this summer? And how elegant she will need to look?

Taking off the red hat, she walks in.

Acknowledgements

I would like to thank Marcelo Domingez and Richard Mulhearn for their help with the Spanish I needed for my research, and Luz Caceres Paton for correcting the Spanish in the book.

Federico Guadalupe Guadalupe, of the Hotel Lancelot, Arrecife, gave me historical details about Graciosa, and Paloma Quesada Perez guided initial research in Arrecife. Eileen Silcocks, with whom I discovered Lanzarote, helped recall details of the island. Julia Donaldson and Nicola Morgan encouraged and empathised during difficult times.

Jacqueline FitzGibbon, Susan Harris, Moira Kinniburgh and Catherine Pellegrino were my editors, and their help was invaluable.

I would also like to thank Mikki Aronoff, in Albequerque, and Professor Emmy Warlick, of the University of Denver. Mikki showed me the magic of the New Mexican desert, and was an inspiration throughout the writing of the book. Emmy opened my eyes to the 'faraway' New Mexican landscapes of Georgia O'Keeffe.

Diana Finn, in Lochwinnoch, took enormous care to make the author photograph just what I wanted, and Vivien Adam, also in Lochwinnoch, made my promotional video. My two friends, Moira Kinniburgh and Helen Mulhearn, were a constant source of comfort!

And finally, my partner Adam McLean advised me on Alchemy and Surrealism. He also sorted out a multitude of technical difficulties, and kept me more or less sane.

Printed in Great Britain
by Amazon